A
CUT
FOR
A
CUT

A
CUT
FOR
A
CUT

CAROL WYER

THOMAS & MERCER

Text copyright © 2021 by Carol Wyer
All rights reserved.

No part of this book may be reproduced, or stored in a retrieval system, or transmitted in any form or by any means, electronic, mechanical, photocopying, recording, or otherwise, without express written permission of the publisher.

Published by Thomas & Mercer, Seattle

www.apub.com

Amazon, the Amazon logo, and Thomas & Mercer are trademarks of Amazon.com, Inc., or its affiliates.

ISBN-13: 9781542020930
ISBN-10: 154202093X

Cover design by Dominic Forbes

Printed in the United States of America

A
CUT
FOR
A
CUT

PROLOGUE

It's mid-August and only one streetlight is working in this area of Stoke-on-Trent. Kate is crazy to even consider being in this part of town, let alone at one in the morning, but those were the terms agreed: time, venue and a thousand pounds in cash. She sinks further into her car seat, eyes darting from the wing mirror to the rear-view mirror and back to the empty doorway, searching for any sign of life, or trouble. If Farai thinks for one second that she's disobeyed him or brought support, he'll not show up.

'Kate, you're too tense,' Chris's voice cautions. 'You need to loosen up and gain control of the situation. You know the drill in circumstances like this and you have what he wants – money. This guy will answer your questions if you act your usual, confident self. At the moment, you're behaving like a rookie.'

She rubs her hands dry. Chris has a point. She isn't usually this nervous, but so much is riding on this meeting. 'I just want him to give me something. Anything.'

'You can't force this to happen. If he has any information, you'll get it. Come on, Kate. Treat it like any other police operation.'

'But it isn't like the others! This is about you!'

She catches a movement and stops talking to herself. A tall man in a black parka appears; his skull-like face, framed by a furry hood, turns in her direction. She opens the car door and steps out onto the crumbling pavement, with the envelope containing the money firmly grasped in her hand.

The closer she gets to him, the calmer she becomes. He looks ill. His face is lined and his skin is stretched paper-thin. Individual whiskers protrude from his chin, tiny curls of grey wire.

'DI Young.' His voice is deep and rich, filled with an energy that doesn't seem present in his body. 'Show me your phone.' She passes it to him. It's switched off as requested. He checks it and returns it to her open hand. 'Open your blouse.'

'I'm not wearing a wire.'

'Prove it.'

She jams her phone and envelope into her coat pocket, unbuttons her shirt and holds it wide open, exposing her exercise bra. 'Satisfied?'

'Now hand over the money.'

She does up her buttons and shakes her head. 'No. Not until you've told me everything you know about what happened at the Maddox Club in January.'

He hesitates, takes in her fierce look and puts his hands in his pockets. 'Okay, but you didn't hear this from me. Are we clear on that?'

She nods.

'That night, I sent one of my boys and two girls to a regular client – the club manager, Durand. He rang me in the early hours, told me not to expect my boy back . . . that he'd met with "an unfortunate accident". He also told me the club was terminating my contract with immediate effect.' Kate already knows about Farai's arrangement to supply sex workers to the Maddox Club. This is not fresh news and her fingers tighten around the wedge of notes inside the envelope, unwilling to hand over such a large amount for such meagre information.

Farai stares into the distance, nostrils flared. Then a laugh, like the sound of distant thunder, rumbles, and he says, 'I told Durand I'd require "com-pen-say-tion" for the sudden termination and for the loss of my boy – fifty grand. He agreed to my request on the understanding it was a one-off payment. The guest who'd booked my boy would pay up and Durand would arrange delivery of the funds.' A rhythmic pulsing has begun in Kate's ears brought about by a sudden increase in her heartbeat. This was something they hadn't uncovered during the official investigation.

Farai continues, 'A week later, we met at a pub in town. Durand had already ordered me a whisky – a double, and one for himself. I should've guessed he was up to something. He was sweaty and edgy. He kept turning around every few minutes, like he was worried somebody would show up and blow his brains out. I didn't pay enough attention. I figured he was shit-scared that I'd already squealed to the cops, that they knew about the boy and they'd show up any minute. Turned out I was way off target. I don't know what he slipped in my drink but I started talking and didn't stop. He asked questions and I couldn't shut the fuck up. I told him all sorts of shit I shouldn't have, about my business and then boom! He undid his shirt. Fucker was wearing a wire. He told me to keep quiet about losing my boy or I'd go down for supplying underage kids to the club and once I was banged up in jail, I'd be meeting my maker sooner than I intended.'

'He threatened to have you killed in prison?'

'Uh-huh.'

He pats his pocket, pulls out a packet of cigarettes and flips one between his lips. He searches again for a lighter, flicking it several times before it sparks. 'You want to know the truth? The truth is my boy was killed and the scumbag who murdered him, well, he had mighty powerful friends.' He waves his cigarette in her direction as he speaks. 'One of them was a copper, and together with

3

Durand, they set me up good and proper, so I wouldn't speak out about what really happened. And they refused to pay me a penny. Nothing! Bastards like them, with money and influence, they get away with anything . . . including murder.'

'We know the boy was underage, but what about the two girls you also sent to the club that night. How old were they?' In an off-the-record conversation with Kate, Superintendent John Dickson had confessed to having sex with one of them on the night in question, although he'd insisted the girl was an adult. Farai eyes her cautiously.

'You sure you won't drag me into this?'

'I can't force you to stand in a witness box and swear on the Bible, but if you tell me, I'll find a way to use it without you taking any fall. For now, it won't go any further than us. How old were the girls you sent to the club that night in January?'

He sucks on his cigarette, the end briefly glowing orange-red.

'They were fourteen.'

'Both of them?'

'Yes. The request was specifically for girls and none over the age of fourteen.' It's as she suspected. Dickson had slept with a minor.

'I need their names.'

'I can't tell you.'

'Then I can't give you this money.' She holds his stare until he gives a low laugh.

'Okay, DI Young. Their names are Rosa and Stanka.'

'And do these girls have second names?'

'I'm sure they do, but I only know their first names.'

'Do you know the names of the guests they slept with?'

'No idea. If the girls knew, they didn't tell me.'

'Can I speak to Rosa and Stanka?'

'No. They're no longer in Stoke. I thought it wise to move my operation.'

'Where to?'

'It doesn't matter where.'

'Who was the policeman involved in setting you up?'

'Before I tell you that, I want my money. I'm not getting stitched up again.'

She passes him the stuffed envelope. The full amount is there in twenty-pound notes and he seems happy enough to accept her honesty without checking. 'Count it, if you want.'

'I trust you.'

'You don't know me. Count it.'

He shoves it in his pocket. 'I know it's all there. You wouldn't cross me. I like you, DI Kate Young. You've got balls and a look in your eyes that tells me you aren't afraid of anything or anyone.'

'Tell me, Farai. Who convinced Durand to wear a wire and set you up?'

'Bloke called Dickson.'

'John Dickson?'

'I only know his surname.'

'Are you certain?'

'Yeah. Durand let slip his name when I threatened him afterwards. Said if anything happened to him or his family, or if I even turned up again, Dickson would have me banged up so quickly I wouldn't have time to kiss my arse goodbye.'

'And has Dickson contacted you?'

He seems to consider her question as he blows smoke into the night air. 'I heard he was looking for me and my girls, but by then I'd disappeared, and I intend on staying disappeared. I made an exception for you. You got justice for my boy, and that fucker Dickson needs bringing down. You're the person to do that.'

This information is certainly enough to charge Dickson with having sex with a minor, but she wants more. Dickson had been good friends with the man who'd killed the young male prostitute, the same man who'd hired a gunman to murder her husband, Chris. As far as she's concerned, Dickson is guilty of more than sleeping with an underage sex worker and she is going to keep digging until she has every scrap of evidence possible to send him down for a long time. She has one last question. 'Did Durand ever mention anything about hiring a hitman?' It was a long shot and, judging by his expression, a pointless one.

'Not to me. But you know as well as I do, when a person is in danger and cornered, they'll do anything to survive, no matter who they are.' He sucks briefly on the cigarette, letting the smoke encircle his words. 'Now, we're done. You know everything I know. Don't contact me again. This was a one-off.' He doesn't wait for a response, as he slips past her into the darkness.

Back in her car she undoes her blouse again and rummages in the sports bra for the tiny black device she'd secreted there. As large as a paperclip, measuring only 0.7 inches by 1.8 inches by 0.24 inches, it promises a pickup audio range of up to forty feet. She turns it off then says, 'Let's hope it caught his every word.'

'It ought to have. You tested it enough times in various bras,' she replies in her dead husband Chris's voice. 'Let's get it back home and find out.'

CHAPTER ONE

Cracks of thunder rumbled in the distance. Soft rain began to patter and, in the warm glow of the overhead lamp, formed dark golden circles like coins on the slabs. Laura slipped the key into the metal postbox, where it landed with a clatter, and set off on the path that ran one hundred metres down a slope, towards the main road. She followed it by instinct rather than vision, guided only by the dim light thrown over the car park at the foot of the descent.

She'd left the class later than intended, detained by two of the regulars who'd questioned her about the virtues of Bikram hot yoga, and then gone on to talk at length about their recent trip to India. Ordinarily, the hour-long class would have been over by eight and she'd now be at home, Charcoal, her Persian cat, curled on her lap and a cold glass of wine in her hand.

The sky ripped apart with a flash that whitewashed the entire area with its brilliance. The storm was fast approaching. With any luck, she'd make it back to her cottage before it began raining more heavily.

It had been seven months since Laura had moved from Stafford, a busy town of around nine hundred thousand residents, to Abbots Bromley, a village approximately fourteen miles away, with a population of less than two thousand. The sudden and unexpected break-up of her relationship had sent her already fragile mental health spiralling, making the move essential. When faced with the emotional fallout, Laura had reacted in the only way she knew how, and fled from the person who'd crushed her love with cruel words and unwarranted iciness. The green fields surrounding Abbots Bromley, the quaint cottages that lined the streets and the gentler pace of life had all assisted her recovery and although she still had some way to go, she was making progress at last.

The twice-weekly exercise class was proving more beneficial than any of the therapy sessions she'd been attending. Her doctor had advised her to take up yoga a couple of years ago, to help relieve the stress that swamped her on a daily basis. She'd never imagined she'd pass on her knowledge to others. When the regular instructor had been called away to care for her sick mother in Bakewell, Laura had willingly stepped in, initially for a couple of weeks, which had since turned into six. She hadn't minded.

A sound like a gargantuan tractor rumbled across the heavens and she drew her cardigan more tightly over her loose top. She'd almost reached the car park and only had to cross the road and scurry along the pavement towards the cottages at the far end of the village to be safely out of the weather. Hers was a mid-terrace, one-bedroomed, renovated property. It had once belonged to the private school, part of Abbots Bromley's history since the 1800s, until it had been requisitioned for housing.

It never ceased to surprise her how peaceful the village was. It was cut off, not only from the nearby towns, but from modern-day life. The hub of the community was the village hall where every activity or event, from art classes to theatrical performances, took place. Here, people knew their neighbours, and would gather in the pub, butcher's or local store to gossip. Laura hadn't progressed to that stage yet. She wasn't ready to share anything about herself with her neighbours, well meaning or otherwise. What she treasured above everything else was the anonymity she had here. In Abbots

Bromley, she was only known as the temporary yoga teacher, her past completely erased. And she wanted to keep it that way.

A thunderclap reverberated throughout her entire body, rooting her to a moss-covered slab and a primitive instinct accelerated her heartbeat. Storms didn't usually unnerve her and she struggled to comprehend why she felt so uneasy this time. There were only a few cars in the restaurant car park and nobody in sight. Ten metres separated her from the road and the lane home. She hoisted her bag onto her shoulder, preparing to make a dash for it.

The arm came out of nowhere. Muscular and powerful, it smashed against her neck, rendering all thought and action impossible, and within seconds, she slipped to the ground.

◆ ◆ ◆

DI Kate Young drained her glass and studied the label on the Cloudy Bay Sauvignon bottle. It had cost her stepsister a fortune, well over the usual five pounds Kate was prepared to splash out on a bottle of wine. But there was no denying it had been delicious. Although she had no idea what guava was supposed to taste like, she'd appreciated the fruity flavours and subtle hint of herbs. Trust Tilly to choose a wine that was 13 per cent proof alcohol and insist on opening the second bottle.

Kate placed the bottle on the carpet and then stretched and yawned. It was the most relaxed she'd felt in a long while. The alcohol had helped dull the anxiety she'd been experiencing over seeing Tilly again. It had been decades since they'd parted, a lifetime since Tilly had headed to Australia, arm in arm with Jordan, Kate's ex-fiancé. Years of estrangement and hatred. Too much wasted time. Too many harboured grievances. But now she was here in Kate's home, together with her five-year-old son, Daniel, the spitting image of his mother, with glossy brown hair, eyes like shining conkers and a smile that had pierced Kate's heart.

The wine had played its part, making Kate feel more mellow and relaxed, and with Daniel fast asleep, she and Tilly had been catching up. It was gone midnight but sleep was still some way off. Kate was unwound, not tired. She glanced at the photograph of her deceased husband, the man who had advised her to rekindle her relationship with Tilly. He'd convinced her to let bygones be bygones, reminded her that nothing was more important than family and, able at last to let go of the hurt, she'd allowed Tilly back into her life. Chris had been her crutch. With him by her side, she'd managed to banish the past and all the hurt. He'd saved her from herself, yet he was gone, taken from her, and Tilly was back.

Chris had been killed in January and she had her own way of handling the loss – revenge. She was convinced her boss, Superintendent Dickson, had also played a part in Chris's death and for that he would pay. Chris, ever the journalist, had left behind a handwritten journal and a file on his computer, both suggesting Dickson was corrupt.

The journal stated Dickson was involved in a paedophile ring that Chris had been investigating. The trail had led him to a gentlemen's club where underage sex workers had been offered to club members. That discovery had cost Chris his life. He'd stumbled across more than he realised when he interviewed one of the club members, a man responsible for the death of one of the young prostitutes and who, soon afterwards, hired a hitman to silence Chris.

Dickson had not only been friends with the murderer, but had stayed overnight in the room next door to him on the night the boy had died. Although Dickson claimed to have no knowledge of what had transpired, Kate didn't believe him.

The file on Chris's computer listed the names of police officers believed to be corrupt. Dickson's name was among many she knew, including her mentor and boss, DCI William Chase. William had been her father's friend and partner long before she had begun working under him. After her father had passed away, he'd stepped in and become a father figure, mentoring her as she made her way up the ranks. Whether DCI Chase was corrupt or not, Kate was concentrating her efforts on finding out the truth about Dickson. She had a hunch he'd been involved in hiring the hitman, whether by suggestion, or actually assisting his friend in tracking down a man on the dark web. For that reason alone, Dickson had become her primary focus. She owed it to Chris.

In truth, she didn't need anyone else – not even Tilly – because she still had Chris. At least, a manufactured version of her deceased husband, created out of need and despair: a version that existed only in her mind. It was insane. Any psychiatrist would advise her to let go of such an unhealthy practice. But, as aware as she was of what she was doing, she was not going to stop pretending. Behaving as she did might not be normal, yet it worked for her. She was perfectly satisfied with things as they were – her and Chris, working together to bring Dickson to justice.

'Jeez, is that the time already?' Tilly's local accent had vanished during her years abroad. She'd embraced everything her new home had to offer, including the Australian drawl.

'It's okay.'

She sprang to her feet. 'No, no. I ought to let you get some sleep.'

'Really, it's fine. I don't sleep much these days.'

A frown tugged at Tilly's perfectly arched eyebrows. 'Yeah, I can't even begin to imagine how hard it's been for you.' She picked up the silver-framed photograph on the table beside her chair. Something in Kate wanted to snap at her stepsister, make her put back the picture, but she bit her lip. Tilly wasn't doing anything wrong. Kate was simply accustomed to not having guests or visitors. Her self-imposed isolation had made her super-protective of her personal effects, especially those that reminded her strongly of Chris. It had been a spur-of-the-moment decision to allow Tilly and Daniel to stay overnight rather than travel back to their rented accommodation in Stafford where they'd been living for the last five days.

'I wish I'd met Chris. He sounded great, Kate. A good man.'

'He was.' She didn't want to talk about her husband. Tilly had stolen Kate's first love, Jordan, but she would never have taken Chris. He might have convinced Kate to rekindle her relationship with her stepsister, but had circumstances been different, and he'd still been alive, she would have kept the contact to a minimum, perhaps via telephone or Skype. But with Chris gone, there was no possibility of history repeating itself.

Although he was dead, Kate felt closer to him than when he'd been alive. She would frequently picture him by her side and hold conversations with him.

'Stay calm, Kate, she'll shut the fuck up in a minute.' His imagined whispering made her smile. Tilly misinterpreted it for a fond memory and replaced the photo with a small sigh.

'So, what have you got planned for us tomorrow?' She corrected herself with a giggle. 'I mean *today*.'

'I thought we'd take Daniel to Drayton Manor Theme Park. I'm sure we can find plenty there to entertain both him and us.'

'They've got a wine tent then, have they?' Tilly gave another snigger, dragging Kate back through time, to a past in which they'd shared a bedroom and established common ground. Kate had hated her father for finding love again, almost as much as Tilly had despised her mother, Ellen, for marrying Kate's father. The resentful girls had sought solace and companionship in each other.

'Probably not wise to glug wine immediately before going on some of the scarier rides.'

'Nah, it's a bloody *good* idea. It might make me brave enough to face getting on them and stop me from screaming my head off, or wetting my knickers.' She didn't mean it. Not much fazed Tilly. Not these days. She ran a women's shelter in Sydney and had come across all sorts of horror and misery. Kate admired her for standing up for those who'd gone through hell. She was aiming for light-hearted and Kate rewarded her with a small smile. Tilly slumped onto another chair, the one Chris had always sat in, and in spite of herself, Kate winced at the action. Tilly's face turned serious. 'Listen, I've said it before but I want to say it face to face. For what it's worth, I'm truly sorry about how things turned out. I don't only mean about Chris. I mean about me . . . Jordan . . . you . . . everything.'

'It's water under the bridge.'

'All the same, I had to say it.' She lifted dark, damp eyes and, for a second, Kate believed the freshly formed tears were for her until Tilly spoke again. 'I can't believe they both died within weeks of each other.' The sadness was for her mother, Ellen. Following her divorce from Kate's father, Ellen had joined Tilly and Jordan in Australia, where she had died in a freak motorbike accident only a month after Kate's father had passed away in the UK.

'Spooky, eh?'

'Mum thought the world of Jordan. She'd have been devastated about us splitting up. Funnily enough, it was soon after she'd gone. I realised he'd been playing me for a fool.'

Kate said nothing. Tilly had already spoken at length about the break-up. Jordan had been seeing another woman behind her back. The ensuing argument had resulted in an irate Tilly grabbing her son, along with a few personal items, before heading to a hotel and booking a flight to the UK, to the only person she could count on as a friend – Kate.

Tilly dabbed at her eyes with a tissue then said, 'What goes around comes around.' Kate didn't see it the same way. Now, looking back, Kate realised her stepsister probably hadn't intended to steal Jordan from her. She'd been attracted to his inner strength, his composure and kindness, and he, in turn, to her fragility. Kate, his fiancée at the time, had been independent and assured, whereas Tilly had triggered a 'knight-in-shining-armour' response. In retrospect, they had made a better match than she and Jordan. Tilly might have run off with Jordan, but it didn't necessarily follow that she deserved to be unhappy, nor did little Daniel, who would now not see his father. She was about to say so when Tilly spoke.

'I took Daniel to the old place in Uttoxeter yesterday.'

'You didn't tell me that.'

'It looked the same, apart from a fresh lick of paint and some fixed baskets on the window ledges.' Tilly was referring to their home. The eighteenth-century, two-storey house in Balance Street had been in dire need of renovation, but it was close to the police station where her father had worked. With tired décor and out-of-date fittings, it had still exuded a grandeur. Kate remembered being charmed by the fanlight over the front door and the columns on either side, making her feel as if she were entering a temple.

Tilly was still talking. 'The town's changed quite a bit and that new retail park – wow! Daniel loved the CineBowl.' The CineBowl was a large entertainment centre with an ice rink, an eight-lane tenpin bowling alley and a cinema. Back when Kate and Tilly had lived in Uttoxeter, the only entertainment had been a few shops, a small cinema and Bramshall Park, where both girls had spent most of their free time.

'I've not been to Uttoxeter for ages,' said Kate. Although she'd inherited the family house, she'd sold it and used the proceeds to pay off the mortgage on her own home, one she would never leave because Chris still lived there, in spirit if not in body.

Tilly chewed at her bottom lip before saying, 'I couldn't face going to the park.'

Bramshall Park held horrific memories for Tilly, who'd been attacked and raped there when she was only fourteen. That event, along with a deep admiration for her father, had led to Kate joining the police so she might be able to help others like Tilly find justice.

She continued, 'I'm worried that I'll never be able to go back there.'

'It wasn't your fault, what happened.'

'Maybe I was dressed too—'

'You were a schoolgirl. You dressed the same way as almost every girl that age did. You weren't to blame.' Kate's voice rose. After the ordeal, Tilly had shut herself off from her numerous friends and gradually faded away, eaten up by a mixture of fear and self-loathing. It had almost been her undoing.

Unbeknown to her mother and Kate's father, she had been in a far worse state than either suspected and had it not been for Kate, who'd come home earlier than expected, Tilly would have taken her own life. Kate brushed aside the memory of the pills lined up on her dressing table. Tilly had only swallowed three or four before Kate burst in and caught her in the act. She'd rushed her to the bathroom, forced her to be sick and then disposed of the remaining pills. She'd cradled her stepsister while she sobbed and then promised never to mention the episode to either parent. It had remained their secret to this day.

Kate let a brief silence rest between them then said gently, 'We never really talked openly about what happened in Bramshall Park. I mean, I knew what happened, but we never discussed it, stepsister to stepsister, did we?'

'I couldn't open up to anyone. I couldn't tell my mum, you or, later, even Jordan. I struggled terribly until he suggested I attended a meeting for rape victims in Sydney. After listening to other women talk about their experiences, I finally opened up. I told them things I didn't tell you, or even the police at the time.'

Kate's eyes opened wide. 'You kept information from the police?'

'I was a kid – an utterly terrified kid. Talking about it at the time only made me relive the whole horrible experience, minute by minute, second by second. It was an endless series of questions from police officers, officials, doctors, nurses, counsellors . . . I became so muddled. I wanted everyone to stop asking questions and leave me alone.

'They were never going to find the bastard who raped me, were they? And if they had, what would have happened next? Humiliating court appearances, my name in the newspapers, every-one knowing . . . knowing I was raped and judging me, saying I probably deserved it.'

'No! They wouldn't have—'

'You don't know that! I believed I deserved it, so why wouldn't they? Anyway, I couldn't face any of it. It was easier to give them the minimum amount of information and go home.'

There was little sense in pointing out that Tilly could have helped find the person who attacked her and possibly saved oth-ers from suffering the same fate. It was clear from her expression that she already knew the consequences of her inaction, and it was another piece of shame she carried around with her. 'What did you leave out of your statement? Did you see his face?'

'No. He wore a balaclava. I couldn't give them a description. I omitted some details about the actual rape, the really embarrassing stuff.' Her lips trembled. 'He was rough. He jumped me and forced me to the ground, face first, and pinned me down. He hissed that I was a "filthy, disgusting bitch" and other vile, offensive things the whole time he was raping me. And he called me by my name.'

'He knew your name? Did you recognise his voice?'

'No. The balaclava muffled it and he spoke so low and menacingly, like a growl, I couldn't make it out. I was so scared, Kate. I was desperate for it to be over. I wasn't even sure he'd let me live afterwards. I thought he was going to kill me.'

'Don't go back to Uttoxeter. Don't punish yourself,' said Kate.

Tilly shrugged. 'Visiting the place where it happened might help me put it all behind me, once and for all. Recently, the nightmares have become worse, probably because of the stress over Jordan.'

Kate was about to offer more placatory advice, but Tilly shook herself and offered a small smile. 'Maybe, once I'm more settled in, I'll be able to return to the exact spot where it happened; after all, I've visited Uttoxeter now. It's a step in the right direction.'

'Possibly so. But you don't have to force yourself to visit the site or remind yourself of what occurred.'

'I do if I want to start a new life here.'

A burst of warmth flooded Kate's veins as she acknowledged it would be lovely to have her stepsister and nephew around. The plan was for Tilly to stay for a few weeks to find her feet then, if Daniel seemed okay with everything, they'd go back to tie up her affairs in Australia before returning for good.

'I'm doing what I can to get settled. I've even got in touch on Facebook with a few of my old schoolfriends from back then.' She reeled off a few names Kate remembered. 'And a couple of weeks ago, I got a friend request from Ryan Holder. Do you remember him?'

The name rang a bell, although his face evaded her. She shook her head.

'He was a few years above us in school. In terms of looks, he wasn't really my usual type, but I hoped by going out with him, one of his better-looking mates would notice me.' She grimaced. 'It worked and I dropped him like the proverbial hot coal. Anyhow, he's forgiven me for dumping him. Said he deserved it because he was such a nerd.'

'Is he married?'

'No. But I'm not interested in him in that way. He isn't interested either. We've been having a bit of a giggle about stuff and the people back then. I forgot that he was such easy company. It's been nice to have other memories to think about rather than what happened that day in Bramshall Park.' Her face clouded over momentarily, then she gave a small shake of her head as if to shake off the thoughts. 'Enough of this maudlin crap. No more dragging up the past. We should be concentrating on the future and deciding what to do with it. It's great to have you back in my life, Kate. I've missed you.'

'I've missed you too, Tilly.'

Kate rose from her chair and made for the oak cabinet where she kept the whisky – a collection amassed over the time she and Chris had been together. It had been his favourite tipple and he'd taught her how to appreciate a fine whisky to the point where she now enjoyed them as much as he had. 'Fancy a nightcap?'

'Why not?'

She reached for a single malt, not one of the more expensive bottles Chris had purchased during one of his overseas assignments. There were some things she wasn't willing to share with Tilly. She dragged out two crystal tumblers. 'Tell me about the kangaroos. I read somewhere that there are two red kangaroos for every person living in Australia.'

Tilly chuckled. 'Wouldn't surprise me. There was a large mob of them on the golf course last week.'

'Playing golf? What was their handicap?'

'The fact they can't walk backwards.'

Kate poured the drinks and chinked her glass against Tilly's.

'To new beginnings,' said Tilly.

'To new beginnings.'

CHAPTER TWO

A thousand seagulls screeched in Kate's head as she wrestled from a dreamless sleep to discover it was almost 10 a.m. Her mobile was trilling at full volume. She snatched it from the bedside cabinet. One whisky had turned to two, then three, and now her tongue, a swollen piece of felt in her parched mouth, could barely move.

As it was, she didn't have to say a great deal. DCI William Chase did all the talking. 'Morning, Kate. I know you're not on duty, but you're needed urgently. The body of a young woman has been uncovered in an industrial bin outside Variations restaurant in Abbots Bromley, and we think this is definitely one for your team.'

Kate tried swallowing and managed a croaky 'Any ID?'

'Nothing on her.'

'Okay. On my way.'

She cast off the duvet and stood up, catching sight of herself in the mirror. She didn't look too bad for somebody who'd drunk more in one night than in the entire month beforehand. However, she still didn't trust herself to drive. There was bound to be too much alcohol in her system. She rang twenty-three-year-old Emma Donaldson, one of two detective sergeants in her small team, who, judging by the grunts in the background, was at her brother Greg's martial arts academy. Emma, the only girl in a family of seven, spent most of her free time training in Taekwondo.

'Guv.'

'We've been called in.'

Emma didn't question her superior. She'd understood something serious had occurred.

'Would you mind picking me up?' asked Kate.

'No probs. I'll be fifteen minutes.'

'That's fine. See you then.'

Kate would fill her in during the drive to Abbots Bromley. She could do with a quick pick-me-up shower but she had two more people to call, the first, DS Morgan Meredith, who'd given up a promising athletic career to join the police force and who was already making a good impression on his superiors. A year older than Emma, he complemented Emma's skills and, as far as Kate was concerned, was one of only a handful of officers she could trust. The last person she had to notify was their newest recruit, twenty-seven-year-old DC Jamie Webster, who'd transferred from Newcastle-upon-Tyne to Stoke with his pregnant wife, Chloe, and eighteen-month-old son, Zach, to be closer to his wife's family. He was extremely keen, even willing to take on any amount of overtime in an attempt to procure promotion and the increase in salary it would bring to help support his ever-growing family.

It irked Kate to be in charge of such a small team. She'd wanted to return to her former duties, leading the twelve-man unit she'd been in charge of before an incident on a train in March, where she'd mistaken a civilian for a gunman and almost attacked him, had forced her to take time off. On her return, she'd been confined to working with Emma and Morgan and although she'd proven her worth, DCI William Chase and Superintendent John Dickson had not allowed her to pick up where she'd left off. Jamie was a compromise: an extra individual brought in to help assist the team in their investigations, although neither his good humour nor skills were enough to appease Kate.

Once she'd contacted everyone in the unit, she headed to the bathroom where, seeing her clothes cast haphazardly on the stool, her mind jumped to Chris's office. The key was in her back pocket. She couldn't risk anyone stumbling upon the information she'd been assembling there. She'd locked the office before Tilly had arrived, and was glad she'd taken the precaution, especially as she now had to leave both her stepsister and Daniel alone in the house. Besides, it was Chris's room and she didn't want anyone other than her to enter it.

'I'd take it with you, if I were you. You remember how nosey she used to be? Going through your belongings, borrowing your make-up or clothes without permission?' said Chris.

'How do you know? You never met Tilly.'

'I know all your thoughts, memories, everything, Kate. I'm inside your head. I know everything you know. You and me – we are bound together for eternity. Whatever you think I think and vice versa. It's what you wanted, remember? You need me.'

'Not now, Chris. This isn't helpful.' She shouldn't allow this indulgence, this pretence he was with her, even though it provided the crutch she required to get through the days. She fished out the key from her jeans and placed it on the shelf to take with her. On this occasion, she didn't require make-believe advice. There was no way she wanted Tilly snooping about the office.

Showered and dressed, she knocked back two painkillers with a bottle of cold water. There was no time for breakfast or even a cup of coffee. She'd grab something to eat later. For now, the pills would have to work their magic.

'Hi.' A pink-eyed Tilly, wearing Kate's dressing gown, stood in the kitchen doorway. 'I thought I heard you up and about.'

'Sorry. I tried not to disturb you. I was going to leave you a note. I've been called to work unexpectedly.'

'Crap. I suppose that means the day trip is off.' Tilly wandered in, dropped onto a bar stool and yawned, hand stretched wide over her mouth.

'I'm afraid so. You can stay here, catch up on some sleep, and we'll sort something out later. Maybe go to the cinema or a meal—'

'You don't need to entertain us, Kate. We'll be fine. We've got somewhere to stay and loads of stuff to do, old friends to visit, sights to see. As soon as Daniel gets up, we'll head back to Stafford. Give me a ring when you get off work and we'll sort out something.'

'You sure?'

'Of course. Last night's stay was unplanned. It's probably best for both of us if we take this slowly. There's still a lot of catching up to do. Call me. We'll arrange a trip to the theme park another day. There'll be other opportunities.'

'Yeah, there will be. Okay. When you leave, pull the front door to until you hear a loud click. It'll lock automatically. I'll ring you as soon as I can. We could meet up in town if you prefer, maybe grab lunch together.'

'Whatever you fancy.' Tilly hung her head then drew a breath. 'I meant what I said about Jordan. If I could turn back the clock . . .'

'Let it go. You've apologised enough.'

'Jordan and me . . . well . . . no . . . you're right. Forget it. I don't even know what I'm trying to say. I can see you're over him. You and Chris seemed to be . . . perfect.'

'Yeah. We were pretty solid.' A car horn sounded. Emma had arrived to collect her, in the nick of time. 'I have to dash. I'll call you later.'

'Sure.'

'Give Daniel a hug for me. I promise him and you a trip to Drayton Manor before too long.' She faltered for a moment. She'd have given anything to have had a child with Chris, a little boy resembling him; someone she could have loved and who would have reminded her daily of her husband. Daniel was adorable; a happy, carefree child who'd accepted her as if he'd known her all his life. She shrugged off the thoughts, picked up her holdall containing the gear she'd need for the day and made for the front door.

'Got the office key?' whispered Chris.

'Yes. Now buzz off.'

◆　◆　◆

Character cottages with dusty-rose, primrose-yellow and duck-blue doors and adorned with colourful floral wreaths lined the main road, hung with bunting in preparation for the imminent Abbots Bromley Horn Dance. The folk dance dated back to the Middle Ages and was due to be performed on Wakes Monday, in two days' time. The original horns were actually reindeer antlers and carbon-dated to be about a thousand years old. They were collected early in the morning from St Nicholas' Church by dancers called deer-men, dressed in Tudor-style costumes, before being paraded around the village, surrounding farms and pubs, where the dancers would perform, several times throughout the day, before returning the horns that same evening. The event attracted visitors from around the globe and makeshift tents had been erected on a small green in front of the Goats Head pub, a sixteenth-century black-and-white timbered inn, reputedly where the highwayman Dick Turpin spent a night after stealing his horse, Black Bess, from a Rugeley horse fair.

'And here we are again,' said Emma. 'I can't believe a small place like this could be such a crime hotspot.'

'To be fair, the last murder actually took place a couple of miles away, but I take your point.'

In May, Kate had led the murder investigation that had begun in Admaston, one side of Blithfield Reservoir, and ended the other side, in Abbots Bromley itself. Rounding the bend and unable to pass the emergency vehicles blocking the narrow road, they drew up behind a Forensics van, left their car and walked up the street, where they came to a halt on a footpath marked with a signpost to the village hall. It bordered a grass verge separating the path from a restaurant, Variations, and an expanse of tarmac, cordoned off with blue-and-white crime scene tape that fluttered in a gentle breeze, like the festive bunting strung above the road. White-suited forensic staff were already in situ, combing the area for clues.

Kate held up the pass hanging from her lanyard and gave their names to the officer in charge of the crime scene log. 'DI Kate Young and DS Donaldson.' She picked up a pair of shoe protectors from a box and slipped them on, and, looking across at the nearest van, spied Ervin Saunders, Head of Forensics, in the process of suiting up. He smiled.

'Morning, both. I would say *good* morning, but it clearly isn't, certainly not for the unfortunate victim.' Slightly eccentric in dress and manner, he was wearing tweed plus fours with long khaki socks and brogues. On anyone else they would look ridiculous but on Ervin, with his aristocratic features and devil-may-care attitude, they seemed perfectly normal attire. He shrugged the paper suit over a cream shirt and waistcoat, then reached for some overshoes.

'I guess you haven't had a chance to look at the victim yet?' she asked.

He balanced on one foot. 'You guessed right. I was in a meeting and only arrived a few minutes ago.'

A fresh-faced officer with strawberry-blond hair approached Kate. 'Ma'am. The head chef at Variations restaurant has given a statement, but I wondered if your officers wanted to speak to him. He discovered the body.'

'Yes, ask him to stay put. We'll talk to him once we've seen the victim.'

The officer walked back towards the white-rendered building with a multi-paned window overlooking the car park.

'We need to find out who ate there last night,' she said to Emma, who agreed.

'Apparently the food's very good,' said Ervin, lifting the hood to cover his thick hair. His eyes twinkled. 'Although, I expect they might knock off a Michelin star for the dead body in the waste bins. Ready to take a look at her, then?'

Kate's mouth curled slightly. Humour, even dark, was always welcome in this profession. She emulated Ervin's movements and ducked under the cordon, aware of Emma doing the same, and made for the photographer standing at the far side of the car park, in front of woodland and two industrial-sized grey bins. The trees were so tightly packed together Kate couldn't see beyond the first few trunks. Unless the killer had been pencil-thin, they were unlikely to have approached from that direction.

Emma spoke up. 'Morgan's arrived.'

He nodded a greeting. 'What have we got so far?'

Kate shrugged. 'Not sure yet other than it's a female victim—' She was cut off by the photographer.

'I'm finished if you want to take a look.'

She edged forward with Ervin, her nose wrinkling at the sour stench. On top of the heaped rubbish lay the body of a half-naked woman, her pale legs bruised and blood-streaked. Of slight build, she didn't take up a great deal of space. Her eyes were shut, her lips apart and one elegant hand covered half of her porcelain features, while her chestnut hair flowed over the black bags heaped below her, like a broken mermaid on sea-sprayed black boulders.

'Can we get her out of there?' Kate asked.

'Yes, I can arrange that.' Ervin organised his team, who lifted the frail body onto a tarpaulin already placed on the ground. While she was being laid out, he peered inside the bin. 'There's a foam exercise mat in here.'

'It could well belong to the victim,' said Emma.

Ervin pulled out a pair of black yoga pants with a stretch waistband and tie cuffs, a Nike Swoosh logo on the front. 'And these. They look like they'd fit her.'

He reached back into the bin and extracted a pair of stretchy, form-fitting shoes with a green leaf pattern, pale pink edging, matching toe guard and a green elastic strap. 'I'm no expert of women's fashion, but I'd say these are special flex shoes for exercise such as Pilates or yoga.'

Emma cast an eye over the small FitKicks label attached to the heel and agreed. 'Looks like she'd been attending a yoga or Pilates class before she was attacked.'

'Do they hold exercise classes at the village hall?' asked Kate.

'I believe so,' said Morgan.

'Check it out, will you?' Kate's attention was drawn to the lean figure crossing the tarmac with long strides, a pathologist's case in his hand. Harvey Fuller, in his late forties, could be mistaken for an older man with his old-fashioned wire-rimmed glasses, white hair and neatly trimmed silver beard. Only clear cobalt-blue eyes under heavy, black brows betrayed the fact he was younger than first impressions suggested, and his athletic build, concealed beneath baggy suits, indicated he was a man in excellent physical shape.

'Morning, all. Not the best start to the day, is it?' He planted his case on the ground and began donning gloves to examine the deceased. 'I thought you were supposed to be off duty.'

'Apparently, we're invaluable,' said Morgan. 'They needed their best crime-busting unit on this one.'

The corners of Harvey's eyes crinkled. 'Right, let's take a look at her.' He crouched by the girl. His movements were practised and deft, first lifting the victim's eyelids to examine bloodshot eyes. 'She has petechiae in both eyes and the light bruising around the lips is possibly a result of her attacker holding a hand tightly over her mouth to silence her.' He felt the girl's throat and pointed out the purplish markings either side. 'These abrasions suggest the attacker inflicted significant force on the neck structures and vessels, probably in an attempt to throttle her, but this abrasion on the left-hand side, under the jaw, appears to have been caused by a sharp strike or blow.'

He contemplated the circular mark approximately two centimetres in diameter. 'I've seen marks similar to this before. The last time was on a young man involved in a street fight with another who was practised in martial arts. I think your victim suffered a direct strike to the vagus nerve.'

Emma's eyebrows lifted. 'A vagus strike? You think our killer might be trained in martial arts?'

Kate broke in with 'Hang on a second. You're losing me here. What's a vagus strike?'

Emma explained. 'It's a self-defence technique that's very hard to master. You don't need to exert a great deal of force to stun somebody, but you do need to get the angle of attack spot on. Get it wrong and you can kill a person.'

'That's right. The vagus nerve is the longest of the cranial nerves that leads to major organs including the heart, lungs and intestines and regulates heartbeat and breathing,' said Harvey. 'Penetrative force to the exact spot where it runs down the side of the neck can result in loss of consciousness for a few seconds, or, if it's powerful enough, death.'

'You think she died because of a blow to her neck?' asked Kate.

'I'll know more when I open her up.' He continued checking the body, turning over the victim's hands. 'There's more bruising on the wrists, no doubt where she was held forcefully in position . . . and there's light grazing to her palms and . . .' he checked her legs before speaking again, 'to her knees and shins, where there are also traces of dirt or soil and some slight green staining.'

'From grass?' asked Kate.

'That would be my guess. And look here.' He pointed to marks on her inner thighs. 'It's automatic for a rape victim to try and keep their legs firmly pressed together.' A memory burst before Kate's eyes, of Tilly's tear-stained face as she tugged a sweater over her thin frame, dragging it down as far as she could over black-and-blue contusions in almost identical places on her thighs. She blinked it away.

Harvey began the process of checking for lividity; next he would establish body core temperature and maybe deduce an approximate time of death. Morgan was already throwing out theories.

'She was attacked and raped. She grappled with him and the attacker threw a punch or a blow to her neck, unintentionally killing her.'

'That's one theory, or maybe the reverse happened and the attacker deliberately disabled her with a vagus strike, so he could rape her and then killed her . . . or killed her and then raped her,' said Emma.

Kate nodded her agreement. 'Whatever the order of events, I think we need to be aware that the killer might be trained in martial arts. How would you inflict such a blow, Emma?'

'You strike with the middle knuckle.'

'Then can we assume the size of the abrasion on her neck is roughly the same size as the killer's middle knuckle?' said Kate.

'The proximal knuckle,' said Harvey. 'And yes, it's likely that bruising was caused by it.'

Kate nodded thoughtfully. 'Thanks.'

'And then, there's this,' said Harvey.

Morgan let out a low whistle.

'What the—?' Emma's words faded into the background as Kate stared at the sight in front of her. Harvey had lifted the woman's stained top to reveal deep, blood-filled scratches under her right shoulder that spelled out one word – *MINE*.

Harvey leant in closer, shook his head. 'I can't tell what was used to carve the letters but it was thin-bladed and, judging by the coagulation, he did it while she was alive.'

Morgan lifted his head to the sky with a mumbled 'Fucking sick freak.'

'Possession,' said Kate. 'He wanted her to know he *owned* her.'

Emma unclenched her fist slowly. 'I'll head up to the hall and see what classes were on and if anyone knows our victim.'

'Good idea. Morgan, would you talk to the chef? See if he has anything to add to his statement.' Kate turned her attention to Harvey, studying dark-purple discoloration between the victim's shoulder blades and across her back and hips.

Harvey reached for the rectal thermometer in his case and caught Kate's eye. 'The level of rigor mortis suggests the attack happened last night and lividity marks are commensurate with the body having rested against bin bags in situ for several hours.'

Kate looked away as he checked the body's core temperature. His voice reached her thoughts, which had strayed back momentarily to her stepsister.

This girl reminded her of a younger Tilly, petite, almost frail, with nut-brown eyes and silky, deep-brunette hair.

Harvey checked his thermometer with an 'Uh-huh'.

After approximately thirty minutes to an hour, a body enters the second stage in death, an *algor mortis* or *death chill* phase, where every hour thereafter, the body temperature drops approximately 1.5 degrees Celsius until it reaches an ambient temperature. Harvey would subtract the rectal temperature from the normal body temperature and then divide the difference between the two by 1.5 to gain an approximate time of death.

Having made his calculations, Harvey spoke again. 'She most likely died between eight and ten last night.'

Ervin reappeared, only his eyes and forehead visible, eyebrows drawing together deeply as he spotted the message on the victim's back. 'What the hell?'

'I know. It's not been scrawled angrily or in a hurry. Look how neatly it's been carved,' said Kate.

'And all the letters appear to be the same size and height. The killer is very controlled.'

'My thoughts exactly.'

'We've found signs of a scuffle up the bank. There are drops of blood.'

'And we believe the victim has grass stains on her legs,' said Kate.

'Then I think we've pinpointed exactly where the rape took place. You want to check it out?'

'Thanks, Harvey,' she said, before following Ervin over the grass to where several markers had been set out, next to small rust-coloured stains, blood, possibly from the wound in the victim's back. Ervin pointed out shredded blades and exposed earth where heels and fingers had scrabbled for leverage, or to escape the attacker. Ervin fell silent.

'You okay?' she asked.

'Oh, me? Yes. Sorry, I was miles away . . . in the zone. Not a great place to be.'

She understood. Ervin would have been envisaging the possible scenarios as if he'd been present, witnessing them. She too could imagine the woman's anguished cries of terror as she was forced onto the grassy bank, raped and then mutilated, only metres away from safety and the restaurant, yet unable to attract any attention.

A person willing to carry out all of this and then kill their victim so close to a car park, road and restaurant was either extremely self-assured or was so desperate, or fixated, on their actions, they threw caution to the wind. Would someone who took time to carve a message into the victim's flesh and who was disciplined in martial arts and capable of inflicting specific damage to the vagus nerve be the latter? It seemed unlikely to Kate. To her mind, the attacker had calculated he wouldn't be disturbed, and had possibly been stalking the victim for some time in order to establish the prime location and moment to act.

She examined the squashed and torn grass blades, imagined the brute force on the back of the woman's neck required to hold her in position while she was raped. Maybe the victim had been unconscious for a great deal of the attack, only coming to towards the end of her ordeal, when she attempted to break free and flee. She wore no jewellery. Could the killer have removed such items? She headed back towards the bins, Ervin by her side.

'Harvey, any signs she wore a wedding ring?'

He shook his head. 'Nothing to suggest one was forcibly removed. The skin isn't slightly shinier or smoother on her ring finger, nor are there any tan lines or callouses that might be present. However, if she'd only had a ring for a while, none of those would be visible.'

'Okay. Thanks. Nothing else to help us identify her?' She looked at Ervin.

'Not so far, but we're checking every bin bag. No house keys, no phone and no ID yet. Killer might have taken them.'

'Then we'd better hope somebody at the village hall knew who she was. I'm going to join Emma. Let me know if you find anything at all.'

She rang Jamie's mobile as she made her way up the path.

'Sorry, guv. I'm only just leaving Stoke. I had to drop Zach off at his nanna's then I got held up in traffic.'

'Then it's probably best if you turn around and head to base to wait for instructions. We have a female victim who was attacked, raped and probably strangled last night. We haven't identified her yet, but we might hit lucky, so hang fire there. I'll need you to check out a few names for us.'

'Sure thing. Sorry. I wasn't expecting to get called in—'

'It's okay. I understand. We were called in last-minute. I'll ring as soon as I have something for you.' She shoved the phone back in her pocket. Jamie was a decent enough officer although he might have to sort out his work/life balance, like they all did, if he wanted to make promotion as he hoped.

◆ ◆ ◆

The path, wide enough for a small vehicle, wound past a children's play area to another small car park, empty of vehicles. A one-time chapel, the village hall was a red-brick, single-storey building, with a sloped, tiled roof and, above the aged door, the words *Abbots Bromley Parish Hall* written in a half-moon around a circular stone sign of the Staffordshire knot. A number of posters adorned the glass-covered notice board next to the wide entrance, advertising events and classes. Kate pushed open the door and called out Emma's name. She followed the response to a room with high windows that looked out onto a blue sky. Stacks of chairs were piled against the wall apart from one, on which sat a man in his late sixties, bald scalp, head in his hands. Emma was crouched beside him.

'This is Peter Grantham, the caretaker. Peter, this is DI Young, who is heading the investigation.'

The man, beetle-browed and ravaged by time, looked up. Misery elongated his features. He lowered his trembling hands.

'Morning, sir. Can we get you anything? A drink of water—?'

'No. Thank you. I'm fine.'

Emma got to her feet and approached Kate. She lowered her voice. 'Mr Grantham told me Laura Dean taught a yoga class last night. It was due to finish around eight o'clock. The description he gave matches that of the victim.'

Kate glanced in the man's direction. He'd overheard. Rheumy eyes locked onto hers. His voice faltered. 'Laura's been killed, hasn't she? If I'd locked up the hall as usual, I'd have accompanied her down the path and halfway down the road, but my little dog hasn't been very well recently and I was worried about her, especially as there was a storm brewing. She gets unnerved during storms, you see? Goes into a right frenzy, so I asked Laura if she'd lock up after the class and post the keys in the box. She didn't mind in the least, so I left her to it. I came in about an hour ago to prepare the other room for a music event later today. I'd no idea she'd been hurt.'

Kate was firm. 'We can't jump to conclusions, sir.'

He lifted his arms in a helpless gesture. 'I've lived in Abbots Bromley all my life. It's a normal village. Nothing like this has ever happened here before. This is . . . this is dreadful.' He pinched his nose, shaking his head to halt any further displays of emotion.

'Where does Laura live?' asked Kate.

'In one of the cottages opposite the old school. The one with a blue door – Bluebell Cottage.'

'And where do you live?'

He opened his mouth but no sound emerged. He shook his head instead.

'Mr Grantham's house is on the far side of the field behind the hall, which he crossed to get here and is why he didn't see the police vehicles on the main road. That's correct, isn't it, sir?' said Emma.

Peter nodded. 'I can see the hall from my bedroom window.'

Kate asked, 'Did you notice anything odd or anybody acting strangely last night when you left?'

'No. I didn't see a soul and after I got in, I turned on the telly and I didn't peer across until it was time for bed. The lights were off then.'

'How long have you been the caretaker here?'

'Since I retired from the brewery. About five years.'

'And what do your duties entail?' asked Kate.

'Well, we don't leave the hall unlocked unless there's a class or event on, so it's my job to open up, put out chairs if they're needed, tidy up afterwards and then lock the hall up again. I also keep an eye on the place, come across now and again to deter any vandals or local kids from hanging around.'

'Have you had much trouble from vandals?'

'Only once, when some lads came in from another village and caused some bother. That'd be about a year ago.'

'And you open up and lock up after the yoga class on Fridays?'

'That's right. I come over ten minutes or so before the class begins, then return once it's finished. Cassie's the instructor, but she had to go to Bakewell to look after her poorly mum. Laura's been standing in for her the last few weeks, running both of her classes: Tuesday mornings, eleven until twelve, and Friday evenings, seven 'til eight. On Fridays, I normally walk down the road with Laura and stop off for a pint at the pub.'

'What do you do while the class is on?'

'I'm usually at home or at one of my friends' houses in the village, and pop back around lock-up time. I don't go far.'

'But last night, you were worried about your dog, so you stayed at home?'

'That's correct. On account of the storm. Betsy hates the thunder. Scares her witless.'

'Was the storm still in progress around the time the class finished?'

'Yes. It had been rumbling for a good hour by then. We had a few nasty thunderclaps and quite a bit of lightning, but little to no rain. By about half eight, it was moving away.'

'I see. Well, if you think of anything else that might help us with our enquiries, would you contact us, please?' Kate looked at Emma, who reached for a business card and held it out. Peter took it with a shaking hand.

'I hope you find who—' He stopped and shook his head.

'We'll do everything we can.' Kate led the way out of the building where she paused to take in the surroundings.

'Where's Peter's house?' she asked Emma.

'Over there.' Emma stepped towards a gate at the end of the path and pointed out the dwelling in the distance. The upstairs window was visible and overlooked the hall. From it, Peter would be able to see if the lights were on at the hall. 'I've got the names of a couple of women who attended the class.'

'Good. We'll need to find out who else was there last night. If the body is Laura's, then we need an address for her next of kin.' Kate was off again, this time in the opposite direction, phone clasped to her ear.

'Jamie,' she said. 'You in the office?'

'In and awaiting instructions.'

'Can you pull up information on Laura Dean? She lives in Bluebell Cottage, on the main street in Abbots Bromley, opposite the old school.'

'On it.'

She ended the call and drew to a halt at the sight of Morgan, crossing the car park at speed. He drew up in front of her and Emma.

35

'The chef has spotted the victim using the path to the village hall on several occasions. He doesn't know her name but is sure she takes the yoga class every Tuesday morning and Friday evening.'

'Then it *is* most likely to be Laura Dean,' said Emma.

'It certainly looks that way.' Kate lowered her head, stared at the tarmac for a moment. 'Morgan, will you interview a couple of women who were at the class last night?' Emma tore out the page with the names and addresses from her notebook and passed it over to Morgan. 'Emma, come with me. I want to check out Laura's house. See if anyone else is living there.'

She was on the move yet again, long strides down the road, in the direction of the old school and a house with a blue door, Emma trotting to keep pace. Kate's face was set stern. The body hadn't been formally identified, and under normal circumstances she would wait until it was, but in a small village like this, where news and gossip would spread quickly, time was of the essence. The next twenty-four hours, while people's memories were freshest, would be vital, and Kate was counting on this tight-knit community to provide valuable clues.

It took only five minutes to reach the terraced cottages. Laura's was the middle one, bang opposite the school entrance. Kate rattled the door knocker, half-hidden by a blue floral wreath, and stood back, staring up at bedroom windows. There was no sign of movement.

'I don't think she's in,' said a voice. 'Normally, I can hear her music through the walls but there's not a sound this morning.'

Kate lifted her ID card. 'DI Young, and this is DS Donaldson. I'm sorry, what's your name?'

'Shalini Towcester.'

'Shalini, when did you last see Laura?'

'Last night. I bumped into her up the road. She was on her way to a yoga class.' The woman, in her mid-forties, cradled a white dog in her arms. 'Why are you trying to contact Laura?' In spite of her casual tone, she couldn't disguise the curiosity in her voice. Kate deflected her question.

'Did you speak to her?'

'We had a couple of words about the Horn Dance festival. I'm on the committee for it this year and asked if she was attending the church service on the big day. She said it wasn't her "thing".'

'How long have you lived here?'

'Twenty years, though not always in this house. I used to live at the other end of the village then, after my divorce, I moved here. I didn't want to leave Abbots Bromley and all my friends.'

'Are you very friendly with Laura?'

She let out a half-laugh. 'Laura? No. I hardly know her. After she first moved in, I did the neighbourly thing, invited her around for coffee only to be rebuffed. I got the impression she didn't want to become pally with anyone. I was surprised when she agreed to take over the yoga class.'

'Do you ever go to the classes?'

'No, I'm a member at YOLO's gym on the way to Lichfield. I prefer cardio activity.'

'Does anyone else live here?'

'Only her.'

'Thank you. Tell me, Shalini, after you saw Laura last night, what did you do?'

'Came home, watched television.'

'Did you walk your dog?'

'Ye-es.'

'What time would that have been?'

'Seven thirty.'

'Where did you walk?'

'Down Radmore Lane towards the cricket field, and back home.' The voice had grown wary.

'You didn't head towards the village hall?'

Shalini's eyes narrowed. 'No.'

'Thank you, Shalini. You've been most helpful. Another officer will be along in due course to take a statement from you.'

Shalini opened her mouth, obviously thought better of asking any questions, and closed it again. She nodded dumbly instead. Kate spun on her heel and paced back up the road, Emma by her side. 'It won't be long before people start putting two and two together and speculate who the victim is. We need to notify her next of kin before that happens.'

Kate was aware of curious faces at windows, observing their movements as she and Emma retraced their steps to the car park. Was it possible for somebody to attack a woman and flee unnoticed in a place where little seemed to escape the residents? Surely somebody here would have spotted suspicious activity and be able to assist them.

CHAPTER THREE

An alarm rattle went up as a startled blackbird, disturbed by the white-suits, scuttled from under the bushes and flew away with noisy screams. Kate ignored the racket, her attention on the crime scene. Several numbered markers had been placed in positions around the car park, along the path and on the grassy bank, one close to the scuff marks.

Kate shut her eyes momentarily, trying to picture Laura walking down the path towards the main road. She might have been surprised by her attacker as she left the hall. Or somebody who had accompanied the young woman down the path might have then turned on her.

'I don't suppose you've found anything to shed light on what happened, have you, Ervin?'

She knew it was a big ask, especially as the team hadn't been on site for very long. In an area like this, frequented by the public, retrieving evidence relevant to the case was a tall order. Ervin handed a clear polythene evidence bag to a fellow officer, who dropped it into a container. He turned his attention to the question.

'Sweet wrappers, cigarette ends, a butterfly back from an earring, a key ring, top from a drinks can.' Ervin reeled off more items. Kate lifted her hand to halt his spiel.

'I was hoping the killer had been careless and left a big clue. Like they do on television dramas.'

'Ah, if only! Real-time forensics would be too dull for most people to watch.'

'As would real-time policework.'

'True.' He gave a half-hearted smile, his eyes scouring the car park as he spoke. 'I suspect you're going to have your work cut out here. There doesn't appear to be any CCTV overlooking the car park or, for that matter, anywhere along the main road. I guess they're not used to high crime rates around here.'

Kate would double-check. Sometimes, people had home security on their properties. Harvey was in the process of packing up his medical case, a sign he was ready for the body to be removed. She remained close to the wall. There was no further need for her to trample over the scene and risk any cross-contamination of evidence. Harvey picked his way towards her.

'Aggressive force used. There's no evidence of semen but she was certainly violated. I'll send the medics in to collect her and get back to you as soon as I can.'

'Thanks, Harvey.'

Emma, who'd been talking to a uniformed officer, signalled for Kate to join her. The news wasn't hopeful.

'Plain clothes have canvassed the immediate area and it appears nobody saw a thing. Thanks to the weather, those people whose sitting rooms overlook the road had their blinds or curtains drawn. Looks like our killer chose the perfect night to attack his victim.'

'Damn! We're going to be reliant on those who attended the yoga class and anyone at the restaurant,' said Kate.

'And anyone who is currently out at work and is still to be questioned.'

'How many of those are there?'

Emma gave a half-hearted shrug. 'Only six houses along this stretch of the main road. We've extended the area and officers are now canvassing everyone who lives beyond the green to the far end of the village.'

'And I bet those people will also have had their curtains closed.' No sooner had Kate finished her sentence than her phone rang. Jamie sounded animated.

'Guv, we have a formal ID. It *is* Laura Dean.'

'How come we have that so quickly?'

'Ervin sent across the victim's prints. We have a match.'

'She has form?'

'In February this year, she was caught shoplifting and given a penalty notice for disorder. I've grabbed some basic info on her which I'll email you. The next of kin is her father, Richard Dean. I'm sending details across to you now.'

'Good work.'

'He lives in Sutton Coldfield.'

'I'll head over there to break the bad news to him. Can you arrange for a FLO to visit him?' The Family Liaison Officer would be an experienced officer, trained to support bereaved families and able to provide a two-way flow of information between the family and the investigative team.

'Yes, guv.'

'And find out as much as you can about her: social media, friends, work, everything.'

Jamie was true to his word. The photo and details arrived in her inbox within seconds. There was no mistake as to the identity of the woman in the industrial bin.

Emma took one look at the picture and nodded in agreement. 'Definitely Laura.'

'Okay. I think we're done here. Time to break the bad news to her father.'

She set off again, this time towards the car. The sun sparkled off clean windows and the whole village exuded a friendly, comfortable air about it. It was a most unlikely location for such a terrible act to have taken place. Overhead bunting fluttered in a gentle breeze, and tiny flowers in terracotta pots bounced their fragile heads in unison. Could the attacker be a resident – a monster who lived hidden among the locals?

The word *MINE* cut into Laura's flesh was significant. It suggested desire or possession. The perpetrator could be somebody who'd been rebuffed by Laura, an ex-lover, or somebody consumed by jealousy, who wanted Laura for themselves. Until they learned more about Laura, they wouldn't know where to begin.

No sooner had she fastened her seatbelt than Morgan rang. She put him on speakerphone.

'The women at the class don't recall seeing anyone milling around outside, but they have given me the names of everyone else who attended, so I'll speak to them.'

'What could they tell you about Laura?' asked Kate.

'Nothing other than she moved to the village in late February, was really into yoga and lived alone.'

'Nothing else? I find that hard to believe! Don't villagers usually make it their business to find out everything about new people who move in? I'd have thought they'd have quizzed her on every aspect of her life.'

'According to them, since the redevelopment of the school and the surrounding area, there's been a sharp increase in families and singletons, like Laura, relocating from nearby big towns. I was under the impression those people are still regarded as outsiders and the locals haven't been interested in integrating with them.'

'Yet they attended a class run by one?'

'It seems if Laura hadn't volunteered to take the classes, they'd have fallen by the wayside until the instructor came back and . . .

Laura didn't charge anyone to attend. She said she wasn't officially qualified to take it, so she couldn't accept payment. She took them because she enjoyed yoga.'

'That's odd,' mumbled Emma. 'Who'd be willing to hold a class twice a week and not get paid for their efforts?'

Kate agreed. 'Did they know anything at all about her?'

'Only that she'd spent some time in India. Hence her love and knowledge of yoga. They said she was a very good instructor.'

'I'll wait on Jamie then to find out more about her.'

'I'll crack on with the other class members and then speak to those diners who ate at the restaurant last night.'

'Cheers. We're going to talk to her father.'

'Catch you later.'

After she ended the call, Kate stared out of the window. 'Seems odd to me.'

'What does?'

'A single young woman moving to a sleepy village and not wanting to get involved with anybody other than fellow yoga enthusiasts.'

'Maybe she didn't want anybody to find out about her shoplifting episode. When did she get caught?'

'February the first.'

'And she moved late February. I suppose that could have been the catalyst.' Emma overtook a small Kia, driven by an elderly man. A poodle stared out from the passenger seat, tongue out, like an errant child. They'd left the village behind and were motoring past fields of shorn wheat. Kate's phone vibrated with an incoming message. Expecting it to be from Jamie, she hesitated when she saw Tilly's name. This case would keep her from spending as much time with her stepsister as she'd like. She wasn't keen on the idea of Tilly having to settle back in the area alone, without the moral support she clearly required.

Thanks again for letting us stay overnight.

Ring me when you get a chance.

Daniel sends his love.

Tilly X

She messaged back a quick reply and added a couple of kisses. *Damn!* This wasn't how it was supposed to be. She needed time to become reacquainted with Tilly and help her find more permanent accommodation and, of course, there was also Daniel. Kate already felt a huge fondness for her nephew. She'd been looking forward to seeing more of him and fulfilling her duties as an aunt. The truth was, Tilly had returned at an opportune time. With Chris gone, there was a yawning chasm in Kate's life, waiting to be filled.

Chris's voice whispered in her ear. 'And me? Where do I fit in? Or am I no longer important?' She wanted to reply that of course he was important. She still intended to pursue her investigations to prove Dickson had been partly responsible for her husband's death, but she had to spend time with Tilly and now she had to prioritise further, with the investigation demanding her fullest attention. Minutes were lost to thought until they joined the queue of traffic, inching forward onto a roundabout, and her phone buzzed again. This time it was Jamie.

'I've got a quick update for you. Until February the third, Laura Dean was a legal secretary for Tomkins Solicitors in Stafford. Geoffrey Tomkins, who's the senior partner there, told me she was very quiet, unassuming and efficient. He has no idea why she left, but I'm sure it's no coincidence she did so two days after being picked up for shoplifting. According to her employment records, she hasn't worked since.'

'What about her finances? How's she managed to get by for seven months without a job?'

'I've put in a request for those details and another to her mobile provider. I've gained access to her Facebook account, but everything before February the third – photographs and information – has been deleted.'

'What sort of things did she post?'

'Mostly positive affirmation quotes, the sort you read about loving yourself and being grateful for little things. There are a handful of photos of her with some people who I assume are friends and I'm in the process of trying to identify and get details about them.'

'Good job. Keep us informed.' She ended the call.

'I've got Facebook and Insta friends,' said Emma, 'who also post inspirational quotes. In real life, they're some of the most depressed people I know. Maybe Laura was too.'

'Could have been the case. You got many friends on social media?'

'Yeah. Quite a few, but they're mostly from college days, or people I know from the gym and the Taekwondo circuit, or my brother's mates. I can't be bothered to hang out on the other platforms although I usually keep my Insta up to date. You?'

'I let it lapse after . . . Chris died.' News of Chris's death had been in all the newspapers and even on the national news. She'd become an unwilling celebrity overnight, one who couldn't come to terms with his loss, and one who was in such serious denial, she'd abandoned all forms of social media and not returned to it since.

She could almost feel Chris's hand on her knee, giving it a gentle squeeze and a whispered, 'You don't need anyone, Kate. There's you and me and we're doing fine.'

Her lips twitched involuntarily in response and she spotted the look that flittered across Emma's face. It was clear she still had doubts about Kate's sanity. She gave a smile. 'I'll probably pick it back up. My stepsister's over from Australia with my five-year-old nephew. I promised I'd take them out and about. Might post some photos from our day trips to let people know I'm back in the land of the living.'

It did the job. The shadow on Emma's face vanished. 'I didn't know you had a stepsister.'

'We lost touch when she moved abroad. She returned a week ago. She's probably going to settle back here permanently. We've been playing catch-up. She stayed over at my place last night.'

'That's good . . . Really good.' Emma's head bounced lightly.

Kate aimed for another smile and was rewarded with one in return.

Although the Royal Town of Sutton Coldfield covered a vast area, Richard Dean lived in Four Oaks, a residential area on the northern edge, bordering Sutton Park, away from the hustle and bustle of the town. Turning off the main drag, they found themselves in Ethelred Close where thick-trunked trees and green foliage helped create an impression of privacy. It was an illusion sustained in the private car park, surrounded by glossy-leaved bushes, where they emerged from the car to the sound of cooing doves overhead.

'Which building does he live in?' asked Emma.

Autumn invariably brought the unwelcome bite of frosty mornings, but also offered an array of breathtaking hues. Kate drank in the tall acers with deep burgundy and startling red foliage, nestling next to the russet-brown of beech trees and slender, pale-yellow-leaved rowans, all creating a theatrical backdrop for several red-brick, flat-roofed buildings. She dragged her attention back to the question. 'Bottom floor. Far side.' They crossed to a pathway that wound the length of the dwellings, where damp grass clippings, recently thrown out onto the gravel, stuck to their shoes. The sudden rattling of a train sent wings clapping in applause as several doves rose in unison and scattered across the sky.

The door to Richard's flat, like all the others, was painted white to match the window frames, except he'd added a slate sign with the message, 'Doorbell broken . . . Yell *ding dong* really loudly'. In spite of it, she rang the bell and the man with the sense of humour opened the door. Kate immediately saw the likeness. Laura had inherited several facial features along with his thick, chestnut-brown hair. He was of slight build, stooped and tall at over six foot, a pair of glasses perched on an aquiline nose.

'Richard Dean?'

'That's me.'

'I'm DI Kate—'

'I know who you are. I watch the news.' He tightened his grip on the doorframe, his fingers long and pale, like an artist's or a musician's. Laura's fingers had been long and lean too.

Kate lifted her ID and continued. 'This is DS Sullivan. Could we come in, please?'

His voice dropped to little more than a gasp. 'What's this about?'

'Sir, it would be better if we could talk inside.'

He shuffled backwards and they found themselves inside an orderly front room. The main centrepiece was a grand, quilted Chesterfield sofa, on which lay a copy of *The Daily Telegraph* folded open at a half-completed crossword puzzle. A mug of wishy-washy liquid had been left in an empty space on a shelf, next to a row of novels, all with white spines and the name of the author written in large blood-red font: Richard M. Dean. Laura's father was an author.

'Would you mind sitting down, Mr Dean?' Kate said.

He obeyed without question, his Adam's apple lifting and dropping.

'I have some very bad news I must tell you. We believe your daughter, Laura, was attacked late last night, and I'm very sorry to inform you she is dead.'

'No!' His fist flew to his mouth and he tapped it against his lips, beating back sharp intakes of breath. His eyes turned glassy and his voice thickened. 'No. Not Laura.'

'Sir, we're sure it is your daughter, although we would still like you to formally identify her.'

His fist unfurled and he rubbed his palm over his face and chin. 'Is there a chance it isn't her?'

'I'm afraid not.'

He looked away. 'When? When do I need to see her?' he said, his voice cracking.

'A Family Liaison Officer is on their way and will go through everything with you. They'll help explain what you'll be required to do.'

She was met with a slow, accepting nod. A tear breached his eyelashes to slide down his face. 'Attacked?'

'I'm afraid so.'

'How did she die?'

'We haven't had it confirmed yet, but we believe she was strangled.' Kate felt the weight of his regard. 'We also believe she was raped.'

His chin trembled with emotion and although his lips parted, no sound other than a low moan escaped.

'Is there anyone we can ring or fetch for you?'

'No. Steve will be home very shortly.' He covered his mouth again and made several attempts to control his breathing. Finally, he spoke. 'Have you any idea who—?'

'Not yet, so we really would appreciate any help you can give us.'

He rubbed tears from his cheeks and tried to speak again. 'I doubt I'll be much use to you. You see, several years ago, Laura and I . . . we had a difference of opinion over my choice of partner. She hardly ever visits . . . visited. I wish with all my heart I could tell you more. We used to be close, particularly after Megan, my wife, passed away, but that bond was broken a long time ago.' He swiped at more tears with the back of his hand. 'Laura struggled with the fact I had found love again and felt abandoned, even though nothing could be further from the truth. Steve and I both wanted her to be part of our lives.'

'Did you ever visit her?'

'No. She didn't want us to. She'd come here now and again. You see, my relationship with Steve was a bone of contention between us. It wasn't that she was homophobic, merely – well, to be blunt – jealous. After her mother died, we became dependent on each other and then Steve came on the scene, and it was too much for her to handle.'

Kate understood. She'd experienced similar emotions when her father had started going out with Ellen, emotions that had intensified on discovering Ellen and Tilly were going to move in with them. The difference had been that she'd tried to keep her relationship with her father on track. In the end, when Ellen had walked out, she'd been glad she hadn't abandoned him.

'Recently, we'd started to make a little progress and I firmly believed she'd come around in time . . . yet now, here we are . . . out of time.' His words caught in his throat.

'Mr Dean, what was Laura like?'

A crooked smile appeared. 'Quiet. Timid even. We nicknamed her "Mouse" when she was younger. She changed a great deal around the time Megan fell ill. She was a teenager at the time. We had several rows over her appearance, attitude, schoolwork – all the usual things. I'm not sure if she was any worse than others her age, but it was certainly a very testing time. She used to shut herself away in her room for hours on end. Megan was worried that Laura was becoming too reclusive and tried to coax her out of it, to no avail, of course. After Megan passed away, she became worse. Never went out with friends and spent every free moment looking after the house and me. It was as if she was trying to take Megan's place. I took her to task over it and explained she had to find her own feet and get out and about. She confessed she didn't find it easy to make friends and felt more comfortable at home. I let it drop and we settled into a routine and then, when I thought the time was right, I told her about Steve. It turned out it wasn't the right time at all.'

'She took the news badly?' said Kate.

He nodded. 'She went wild, screaming, lashing out with her fists, yelling that I'd never loved Megan. It was horrible. She wouldn't listen to a word I had to say and, a week later, she took off, found a place to rent and started her own life. I hadn't intended it to happen that way.' He stared into the distance. His nostrils quivered and he sniffed again. 'And that's pretty much all I can tell you about Laura. Dreadful, isn't it? I can tell you lots about her as a teenager, or as a child, but as an adult . . . well, I can't tell you much at all, because the truth is . . . I knew very little about my own daughter.'

'Did you know she'd moved to Abbots Bromley?'

'Not until a chance meeting with her boss, or should I say, ex-boss, Geoffrey Tomkins, at a sporting function in May this year. Geoffrey mentioned she'd not only handed in her notice unexpectedly in February, but moved away, leaving no forwarding address. As soon as I heard, I rang her to ask why she'd packed up and gone. Her response saddened me. Contrary to the nursery rhyme, words – or hurtful comments, I suppose – really did hurt her. Affected her so deeply, she said she wasn't sure she'd ever love again.'

'What sort of comments?'

'I don't know the exact details, only that Laura had taken them to heart. My efforts to mollify her fell on stony ground. As I said a moment or two ago, she was desperately sensitive. She gave me sufficient cause for concern that I dropped in on her at her new house. We had a pleasant conversation about the village and she told me she was going to adopt a cat. She wouldn't discuss her ex with me or what had happened between them. She said it hurt too much to even think about it, let alone talk about it.'

'What about money? How did she intend to manage without an income?'

'After Laura was born, Megan and I set up a trust fund for her. If I had a good year, I'd feed any excess royalties from my books into it. As soon as Megan found out she was terminally ill, she arranged for half of her life insurance money to be put into the trust on her death. The amount she received per annum covered her mortgage, utility bills, reasonable household expenses and a little extra to live on. She could have survived on that money alone for decades without working.' His words ebbed.

'When did you first learn about Laura's relationship?'

'I guessed rather than knew for certain. There were tell-tale signs: she'd changed her appearance, and attitude – she was more confident and definitely happier.' He closed his eyes for a moment. 'She had a glow about her.'

'And that was when?'

'Summertime.'

'But you never asked her outright about it?'

'No. She obviously didn't want to tell me about the chap and it wasn't until early December, when she visited me on my birthday, that I figured it had come to an end. The glow had vanished.'

'Didn't you see her in between times?'

'No, she was always too busy.'

'What about text messages or telephone calls?'

'I don't do texting and Laura wasn't into lengthy heart-to-heart telephone conversations. Truth was, we didn't have a great deal to tell each other.' He dropped his head. 'At the time, I noticed she'd lost weight but I put her appearance down to over-exercise and work.' His eyes grew moist and he hung his head. 'What a dreadful father I turned out to be.'

Although the man seemed genuinely remorseful, Kate couldn't understand why he'd kept his distance from his only daughter, especially given she'd already lost her mother. Her own father would never have behaved that way and although Ellen and Tilly had come into their lives, she'd always shared a special closeness with him. Were these tears for the loss of a daughter, or tears of regret for the man who couldn't turn back the clock and make amends?

The front door handle rattled and a tubby man stepped into the flat. The plastic carrier bags dropped onto the carpet with soft thuds and he yanked off his beanie hat to reveal ginger hair, the same colour as his full beard. His eyes flicked to Kate and Emma, then to his partner.

'Richard? What's going on?'

'It's Laura. She's been . . . murdered.'

'Oh my Lord! No!'

He hurtled towards his boyfriend, dropped onto the settee and put solid arms around him. Richard sobbed into his shoulder.

'How well did you know Laura, sir?' Kate asked, even though she could already guess the response.

'Hardly at all. She hated the fact her father had moved on and found love again, so she invariably visited when I was out at work. But this . . . this is dreadful news.'

Kate placed a business card on the coffee table. 'Another police officer will be with you very shortly. My personal number is on the card should you wish to talk to me at any time during the investigation. Again, I'd like to say how very sorry I am to bring you such bad news.'

◆ ◆ ◆

Emma snapped her seatbelt into place with a firm click. 'It sounds to me as if Laura had some sort of breakdown after her relationship ended. I can't imagine why else she'd jack in a decent job, race off to live in a backwater place like Abbots Bromley, and not even tell her father where she'd gone. And it would help account for her sudden shoplifting episode.'

'She might have shoplifted before and not been caught. However, I agree with you. It sounds as if she was struggling with everything, and going to Abbots Bromley meant she could start afresh. It would help if we could speak to her ex.' Branches, stirred by a sudden gust of wind, caused leaves, like golden confetti, to tumble against the windscreen. 'I know she didn't exactly see eye to eye with her dad, but why all the secrecy and denial? She could simply have revealed she was seeing somebody without going into too many details.'

Kate's mobile vibrated again. A quick glance at the message sent her nerves tingling when she realised who it was from.

Dad wants to talk to you, urgently.

Sierra.

Sierra Monroe's father, Cooper, was in jail for concealing the body of the teenaged sex worker murdered at the gentlemen's club that Chris had been investigating. If Cooper wanted to see her, it could only be because he had something important to tell her. Throughout questioning, the ex-SAS serviceman had claimed he'd told them everything; however, Kate had seen something in his face and was convinced he was in possession of information he couldn't or wouldn't share. The fact he now wanted to speak to her urgently suggested she'd been right and, at last, he was going to spill. He might even provide the breakthrough she'd been hoping for – something on Dickson, who had been staying at the club on the night of the murder. *Yes!* Emma glanced in her direction but she shoved the phone in her pocket and maintained a poker face. Cooper was unconnected to their current investigation and her priority had to be this case. For the moment, he'd have to wait.

CHAPTER FOUR

He drops a lit match onto the petrol-soaked objects and, watching the flames lick around Laura's personal possessions, he pops open the can of beer.

Like father, like son.

The familiar memory surfaces to mingle with the flames and he is transported in time . . .

He stands in the corridor, eye to the keyhole where he has a clear sight of the scene unfolding behind his half-sister's bedroom door. He doesn't shift from the crouched position for fear of alerting his father to his presence, even though his father is distracted. His half-sister, her face almost hidden by her shining chestnut hair, tugs at the bottom of her long T-shirt.

'What do you say to me?'

'Sorry.'

'Sorry, what?'

'Sorry, Daddy.'

'Louder!'

'Sorry, Daddy.'

Her eyes, the colour of dark cocoa powder, melt with tears, but his father slaps her cheek and her hand rushes to the patch, releasing her grip on her clothing, which rises up to reveal naked flesh. He can't see what happens next but suddenly his father pushes her face into the bed and drops his trousers.

His heart hammers with a mixture of excitement and terror. His father's face contorts from an angry sneer into a mask of ecstasy. Each thrust is accompanied by a low, angry grunt until his mouth drops open wide and he lifts his head to the ceiling, giving a mighty roar of exultation. The boy knows what will happen next. He's seen the same performance time and time again. His half-sister is only thirteen, but she will keep her mouth shut if she knows what's good for her.

His father puts a large hand around her throat and squeezes slightly. Her eyes stare wildly at him. 'You know what will happen if you say a word.'

'Yes, Daddy.'

'Good girl. You belong to me. Remember that – you're mine!'

He slips away silently. One day, he will be as powerful as his father.

◆ ◆ ◆

The childhood memory fades and he sips his beer while bright flames engulf Laura's wallet and other contents from her bag, including her mobile phone. Once the ashes have cooled, he'll bury them in the garden. He left nothing at the car park to identify her and although he knows the police will eventually find out who she is, he bought himself some time.

It's only been a few hours since he attacked Laura, yet try as he might, he can't savour the usual gratification when recalling the event or the terrified look on his victims' faces. With her delicate features, beautiful eyes and slim body, she'd almost been the perfect embodiment of his first love. Then she'd broken the spell by spitting at him instead of letting him play out his fantasy of wrapping his hands around her throat, and he'd lost control. Instead of releasing her with words and memories to haunt her for the rest of her life, he'd expunged her life force.

It was an unfortunate accident. Some say watching the life drain from another human being is the most powerful feeling imaginable, but it hadn't been for him. He'd felt disgusted, not by what had happened, but with Laura. He'd kicked at her floppy limbs and cursed her. She was useless to him. By dying, she had ruined the enactment. She was supposed to be the perfect stand-in for his first love, the one he truly wanted, and now he'll have to move on to another replacement. Although, if he plays his cards right, he might not have to keep finding substitutes, because he will be able to woo his first love back to him and this time, she won't get away.

CHAPTER FIVE

Kate clomped into the workspace she shared with her team: a pathetically inadequate room with desks jammed in so close together, it required contortionist abilities to pass between them. She'd requested a larger space, only to be informed the budget wouldn't extend to relocating her unit. Her original office had been more spacious and modern. She had her suspicions that keeping her boxed up in such inferior quarters was part of Superintendent Dickson's efforts to wear her down and push her to request a transfer, or even resign from the force. Although Kate couldn't prove anything yet, she suspected Dickson was trying to wear her down before she could uncover information to link him to the death of the sex worker, or to Chris's death. He was playing a game of cat and mouse with her, ensuring she was aware he was in control. Not only had he kept her shut away, he'd not allowed her to resume command of her old unit; however, being Kate, she was determined to rise above it and not let him see it was getting to her. She could work anywhere. Space wasn't important. What mattered most were the members of her team, and hers were level-headed, dedicated officers. She would let Dickson continue to believe he held all the cards. If she didn't keep up the pretence, her own life could well be in danger.

In one corner, an untidy stack of files on a cabinet towered behind Jamie's close-shaven head, threatening to topple onto him. Oblivious to the chaos, he lifted a home-made egg sandwich from a plastic container, eyes pinned to a Facebook page on the computer screen. A strip light, the sole source of light in the room, hummed constantly above him. Kate pulled her chair across, stood on it and tapped the end of the light until the noise abated.

'Thanks, guv. I hit it earlier but it started up again. Bloody thing needs replacing,' said Jamie.

'I'll ask maintenance again to sort it. How far have you got?'

'I managed to collect details on several of her Facebook friends, those she had the most contact with. She seems to have been closest to a paediatric nurse at Stoke Hospital, name of Alicia McCarty.' He held up a sticky note. 'And I have something else interesting here. It's a private conversation between Alicia and Laura in which Alicia mentions a bloke called Kevin. He might be the reason Laura deleted her old posts.'

Kate shimmied past Emma to Jamie's desk and crouched down to read the message.

Alicia: Good to have you back on FB, babe. You feeling better?

Laura: Yeah, it was about time I pulled myself together again.

Alicia: I see you blocked Kevin.

Laura: I didn't want him screwing up my life again.

Alicia: Stupid bastard. You should have blocked him when he first started leaving those bloody hearts under every picture.

Laura: I know.

Alicia: He was always a tosser, even when we were at school.

Laura: I felt sorry for him.

Alicia: I know, babe. You're far too nice. You fancy meeting at Enzo's later for a drink to celebrate you being back on social media?

Laura: What time?

Alicia: Six.

Laura: See you then.

Jamie waited until she'd finished before continuing with 'I checked school records and uncovered a Kevin Shire who was in the same year as Laura and Alicia. It must be him they're talking about, and . . . he lives only five miles away from Abbots Bromley, in another village: Hamstall Ridware.'

'Then I want an address and contact details for this man as well.'

Jamie turned his attention to the task, pausing only to wipe egg from the desk with his thumb.

Kate headed back to her corner, once again, skirting around Emma, her mobile locked in position between ear and neck as she talked quietly and typed simultaneously. Kate's team was experienced. She had no qualms they wouldn't follow procedure and work efficiently. The next few hours would be critical for gathering information if they wanted to apprehend the attacker quickly and, judging by the serious faces in the office, everyone wanted that result. Kate eased into the corridor to ring Alicia. The voice at the other end was light and melodic.

'Hello, Alicia McCarty.'

'Alicia, this is DI Kate Young from Stoke-on-Trent station. I'm afraid I have some bad news concerning one of your friends, Laura Dean.'

'What's happened to her? Is she okay?'

'I'm very sorry to tell you she was found dead this morning.'

There was a sharp intake of breath, a half-sob. 'How? How did she die?'

'We believe she was attacked on her way home from a yoga class. I really need to talk to you, Alicia. You might be able to help me find out who did this to her.'

'This . . . can't be happening.' The groan was low and soft, filled with sorrow. Kate overheard concerned voices. A muffled voice replaced Alicia's. Kate strained to hear what was happening, deduced the person was taking charge. There was more shuffling, the sound of possible scraping of chair legs across a tiled floor, mumbled thanks and Alicia was back on the line.

'DI Young, are you still there?'

'I'm here. Are you okay?'

'Sorry, I came over dizzy and had to sit down. Somebody's going to take me home.'

'Where is home?'

Kate recognised the road, only a short drive from the hospital. 'Would it be all right if I meet you there?' she asked.

'Yes.' Alicia sounded vague, distant as the shock set in. This woman might be able to give them some answers and Kate couldn't hold off.

'I'll be there in twenty minutes.'

◆ ◆ ◆

Alicia was a tall, lean brunette, with a heart-shaped face and eyes that radiated warmth. She sat at her kitchen table, clenching a glass of water, and blinked back tears.

'I still can't believe it,' she said.

'Do you feel up to talking about Laura?' asked Kate.

Alicia nodded.

'What can you tell me about her?'

'She was a gentle, kind person. I've known her for a long time. We've been best friends since school. Whenever I was on a downer, she'd let me rant or get drunk with me and when I was on a high, she'd laugh with me. She was a really good friend.'

'Did you see her often?'

'Even with my shifts, we always managed to meet up at least one night or lunchtime a week. And we chatted online most days.'

'Facebook?'

'Not so much on there. Mostly WhatsApp.' She put down the glass of water and turned her attention to a thin leather bracelet, fiddling with it as she spoke. 'What about her cat? Will somebody look after Charcoal?'

'We haven't been inside her house yet. Do you know if anyone had a spare set of keys to get in?'

She shook her head. 'Laura was protective of her personal space. Nobody has a key, not even me.'

'We'll arrange for somebody to get in and collect the cat.'

'She only got him a month ago. From the animal rescue centre in Ashbourne. Maybe they'd take him back.' Her voice trailed off.

'Don't worry about Charcoal. We'll sort him out.'

Alicia gave a small nod.

'Do you know her father?'

'Yes, but I haven't seen him in years, not since her mum died.'

'That must have been tough for them both.' Visions of a younger Kate swam before her eyes. If it hadn't been for her father, she'd have drowned in sorrow.

'It was. Especially as they fell out soon after her mum died. Laura was in a bad way and struggling to come to terms with what had happened. She got it into her head that he was to blame for Megan getting cancer. At the time, I thought she was being over-dramatic and didn't know how to help her, but now I understand why. She was simply going through one of the stages of grief.'

Kate was familiar with the five stages: denial, anger, bargaining, depression and acceptance. In the wake of her parents' deaths she'd faced them all.

'Laura couldn't accept Megan had just been an unfortunate victim to cancer and she hunted for a reason as to why she'd become ill. She settled on the fact there'd been a lot of tension and arguments in the weeks prior to Megan's diagnosis. Her parents had been having marital difficulties and Laura was sure the stress of it all had brought on the cancer. She became really angry with her dad and was going to leave home, but she had nowhere to go, and eventually they patched things up. For a while, they got on well, better even than they had when Megan was alive, that was until she found out he'd been secretly seeing Steve. She walked out and stayed with me, until she could rent a place of her own. Things were never right after that. She rarely visited him.'

'I suppose she felt let down.'

'She felt duped. It might have been okay if her dad had just told her the truth instead of hiding it from her. Apparently, he and Steve had been in a relationship for some time before Laura found out. Laura was hurt and betrayed. That was the thing with Laura, she loved you with all her heart, but if you let her down, she couldn't cope. She'd run off.'

Like Tilly, thought Kate. Many years ago, her stepsister had run away from her problems and now was doing the same thing by running from her husband.

'Steve was the reason she kept contact with her dad to a minimum. Every time she saw his boyfriend, she was reminded that her dad had found love again, and forgotten all about Megan. It really ate into her.'

'And you were at school together?'

'That's right. Same class.'

'What can you tell me about Kevin Shire?'

'Kevin!'

'I understand from a conversation she had with you on Facebook, she'd been having difficulties with him.'

'You read our conversation?' Her eyes screwed up. 'Is that even legal?'

'It is when we're investigating a murder. We have to look at every scrap of evidence available.'

'I . . . suppose so. It seems a bit . . . Never mind. Kevin always had the hots for Laura at school and asked her out a few times. Laura wasn't interested in the slightest – not in him or anyone. She didn't want any relationship that would end up like her mum and dad's, so she steered clear of them all. In the end, he gave up pestering her and we lost contact with Kevin until eight months ago, when we bumped into him at a school reunion. He was different . . . gentle, polite and seemed pleased to see us. He wasn't up to mingling much, so he stuck with us all night. After a few drinks, we friended each other on Facebook. It didn't seem like a big deal.' She caressed the bracelet, fingers searching for the clasp, as she began to twirl it slowly around her narrow wrist.

'At first, he only left the odd comment on her posts, then he started liking every photo Laura put up. We joked about it, saying she could have put up any old crap and he'd have liked it. Then he changed all the "likes" to "loves" and left little hearts under every photo, even those going back years. I told Laura he was beginning to act weirdly and that he might still have a crush on her. She wouldn't have any of it, said the guy was lonely and unhappy, and she didn't want to hurt his feelings by blocking him or telling him to stop. It wasn't until he began sending private messages – poems and love song links – that she started to get creeped out. Then he FaceTimed her and asked her out. She told him she was seeing somebody else and he apologised, said he'd misread the signs but even so, he kept leaving those stupid love heart emojis and kisses under every picture of her.'

'Why didn't she block him at that point?'

'I honestly don't know. She insisted he was harmless and he'd get bored.'

'Did he?'

Alicia shook her head. 'He began waiting outside the solicitors' offices for her to finish work. He'd invite her for a friendly drink or meal and she'd brush him off, only for him to reappear a few days later. The day he appeared with a massive bunch of red roses, she threatened him with the police and he burst into tears! She caved in and they went to a café to talk it through. She thought they'd reached an understanding, and accepted she'd be there for him as a friend.'

'But Kevin didn't see it the same way?'

'He persisted in leaving emoji hearts on all her posts and then Laura's boyfriend got the wrong end of the stick, thought she was two-timing him with Kevin, and split up with her. She was absolutely wrecked. She came off social media altogether, wouldn't eat, wouldn't speak to anyone, not even me. Then she started taking medication for depression and did some stupid shit. You probably know about the shoplifting incident in February.'

'Yes.'

'She was going through a really crappy time. Her head was all over the place and she didn't even know why she stole the clothes from Primark. Getting into trouble with the police made matters worse. She chucked in her job, moved out of her flat in Stafford and headed for a spot where she could be more anonymous, where nobody knew about the shoplifting, her relationship, nothing.'

'To Abbots Bromley?'

'Yeah. She thought she could live there in relative obscurity.'

'It's quite near to where Kevin lives.'

'He lives in Stafford, doesn't he?'

'He lives in Hamstall Ridware, which is only five miles away from Abbots Bromley.'

'Shit! I didn't know that. He definitely told us at the reunion party that he lived in Stafford.'

Kate nodded. 'Did Laura reinstate her Facebook page after she moved?'

'Yes, but she deleted everything from it before then and started afresh.'

'Having first blocked Kevin?'

'Yes.'

'You said her boyfriend split up with her because of Kevin. What do you know about this man?'

'Nothing.'

'Nothing at all?'

'No.'

'Surely she must have let slip a first name or shown you a photograph of him?'

Alicia lifted damp eyes. 'You had to know Laura to understand her. She wasn't like my other friends. She was a very private person.'

'Even with you?'

'She'd have told me eventually, but after he dumped her, she wouldn't talk about him at all.'

It was a similar explanation to the one Laura's father had given. For some odd reason, Laura had kept her boyfriend's identity a secret. 'No first name?'

'No.' Alicia blew her nose. Kate searched for any indication the woman was holding back information and saw nothing other than desolation at the loss of a dear friend.

'Are you sure there's nothing you can tell us about this man? Maybe where he lived, or worked, or what make of car he drove?'

'I wish I could help you, but I can't. She didn't tell me a single thing about him.'

'Did you ask her why she wouldn't tell you?'

'No, and that's why we remained friends for such a long time. We understood each other.'

Alicia rotated the bracelet rhythmically around her wrist as she spoke, each sentence accompanied by pulling and twisting, until Kate thought it would break apart. Tears trickled down her already-flushed cheeks. Kate eased off with the questions, instead thanking the young woman for her time and ensuring she'd be okay alone until her housemate turned up.

◆ ◆ ◆

Ervin had excelled himself and arranged for two officers, as well as a locksmith, to meet Kate at Laura's house. It didn't take many minutes before the front door opened onto a wooden staircase and

Kate found herself walking into a simple, light and bright room. The soles of her shoes squeaked across the pale wooden floorboards and she halted in front of a tan, two-seater settee, filled with plump cushions and a throw in muted colours. Above it, the words *love your journey* were written on the cream wall in a large cursive, gold font. The room was calming and Kate wondered if this had been Laura's spiritual space, a thought compounded by the white, ornate shrine, containing a collection of crystals, ornaments and a golden Buddha.

Kate directed the officers to search for laptops, mobile devices, anything that could help them to learn more about the victim. 'Oh,' she added, 'and look out for a cat!'

The living room surprised Kate. A shining houseplant seemed to beckon to her, and she couldn't resist caressing one of the strangely comforting rubber-textured leaves. It was one of five plants, all flourishing in white containers that occupied some of the floor space. She peered through the slats of snow-white wooden shutters and watched a tractor rumble past. There was no sound or vibration from it in this room. She pulled away, caught a glimpse of herself in a white-framed mirror as she traversed into another room, also small and minimalist, with large prints of gentle waves covering the walls and four pale blue wishbone chairs around a matching circular table. A copy of *Spirit & Destiny* magazine lay open on the table and, next to it, an empty china mug bearing a design of a hummingbird.

The last room on the ground floor was a galley kitchen, uncluttered apart from a litter tray and a grey cat tree containing five platforms, hanging balls, an integrated basket and a cushion at the highest point. She opened drawers, checked cupboards, but there was no mobile phone. She approached the back door, glanced at the empty food bowl and the name on it – Charcoal. The rectangular window at eye-height gave her a glimpse into a garden much smaller than her own, with only room enough for a bench and another cat house, a truly magnificent structure with two sets of ladders leading to separate sleeping areas, a dangling play rope, several platforms and hammocks. It was clear Laura had adored her feline companion. At the top of it, some two hundred centimetres from the ground, was a curled-up ball of dark grey fur.

She returned to the sitting room, and headed upstairs. 'I've found the cat,' she called.

'I'll collect it when we finish,' came the reply from behind an open door. Kate followed the voice, and peered into a generously proportioned bedroom with a separate dressing area, filled with white louvred door wardrobes, where an officer was conducting a search of the contents.

Struck by the room's luminosity, she entered. It was longer than it was wide: a king-sized bed in the middle of the room and, in front of a wide window, a cream wicker chair with white cushions. Kate drifted towards a bookcase, picked up the photograph of a woman posing with an open book in her hand. Pale-faced and hollow-cheeked, she was still hauntingly beautiful. She guessed it to be Megan. Laura's mother. She replaced it next to another healthy plant and caught sight of her own pasty complexion in a stand-alone mirror; white tealights were carefully balanced on its base. She tucked in her blouse and moved through the archway separating the sleeping accommodation from the dressing space. The open wardrobes revealed pairs of what Kate would call sensible shoes, flat-heeled and comfortable, all polished and lined in pairs on racks. The clothes were assembled according to colour – white to the left and black to the right. Laura favoured neutral colours punctuated by a few items in pink. The officer was on his knees, rifling through labelled boxes. The block capital letters denoted their contents: tax returns, bills, house documents, bank statements, photographs. Laura's world had been one of order.

'No electronic devices?' she asked the officer.

'Nothing.'

The killer must have taken her phone. 'She had internet access, didn't she?'

He glanced up. 'Sure, but she doesn't seem to have used anything to connect to it other than a Bluetooth speaker over there on the bedside locker.'

The other officer appeared and dangled a set of car keys. 'Keys to a Smart car.'

A quick phone call would ascertain the vehicle's registration, although Kate was sure she'd spotted a silver and white Smart car parked nearby. She took the key, headed for the furthest window in the bedroom and aimed it at the car in the street. The rear lights flashed on and off. Locking it again, she stepped around the male officer, reached for the box of photographs and opened the lid. There were only a handful of pictures, mostly of Laura as a child with two adults. One was the woman in the picture, and she recognised Richard Dean's solemn face as the other. There were a few snaps of Laura in India. The date on the back indicated they were taken in 2018. She pulled out one – an iconic image of the Taj Mahal, with Laura seated on the very bench where Princess Diana had posed in 1992, in a now famous shot, capturing her disintegrating marriage. She looked at Laura's half-smile and pale face, searching for a clue as to who she really was, but saw only loneliness. Her phone rang and Emma's name flashed up.

'We've got Kevin Shire here for interview.'

'I'm on my way. Don't start for twenty minutes. I should be back soon after that.'

She replaced the photos and handed over the car key. 'I have to go.' The locksmith would ensure the place was left securely. 'Oh, the cat is in the garden, on top of a cat tree house. Make sure you take it with you.'

Back at the station, she raced upstairs to the room adjacent to the one where Emma and Jamie were questioning Laura's old schoolfriend, Kevin. She settled in front of the monitor to watch.

With an acne-riddled complexion and eyes so pale they almost looked white, Kevin sat slack-jawed as Emma asked him about his movements the evening before. He picked at the skin around his thumb, already inflamed. His voice was light, barely audible.

'I don't understand,' he said.

'You don't understand the question?' asked Emma.

'I understand the question. You're asking me where I was last night. What I don't understand is why you're asking me. Why me?' He looked from Emma to Jamie, confusion pulling at his features, elongating them as if his face was melting away.

'I've already explained we're looking into Laura Dean's death. We know you were friends with her and we're talking to everyone who knew her.'

'Did she die last night?'

'Kevin, I'm asking you for help.'

'I don't get it. What happened to her?'

'For the moment, we're treating her death as suspicious and are waiting for the results of a post-mortem, which will give us some answers.' Emma delivered the line with practised ease. In the room, invisible to them, Kate nodded approvingly. It was wise not to give out too much information, especially at this stage of an investigation. 'And we're talking to as many people as possible who knew her.'

He turned pleading eyes onto Jamie. '*You* don't think I hurt her, do you?'

'Kevin, please answer my question.' Emma's voice carried gravitas and had the desired effect.

'I would never harm a hair on her head. Laura was lovely.'

'You liked her?'

'A lot. She was kind and helped me through a difficult time.'

'You were in the same class, weren't you?'

'That's right.'

'What was your relationship with Laura back then?'

'Relationship? There wasn't any *relationship*.'

'Were you friends then?'

'Not especially.'

'Did you like her?'

'I'm not sure what you're trying to suggest. I guess so. She was pretty but I was a . . . I wasn't the most attractive boy in the class and girls didn't notice me.' He gave a reptilian blink. Kate's gaze sharpened as she studied his body language; there was no defensive posturing, no fiddling, no squirming at the questions. He was either telling the truth or masterful at disguising his reactions.

'When did you last see Laura?'

He cocked his head to one side and appeared to ponder the question. 'Ages ago. Last November or maybe early December. I can't be sure.'

'Tell me what happened the last time you saw her.'

'We argued.' The answer was filled with sadness and accompanied by a small sigh. Kate couldn't decide if it was genuine or not. There was something about this man that screamed distrustful to her.

'What did you argue about?'

'It was stupid, really. Laura got it into her head I was being too, what was the word she used, "clingy"? I didn't see it that way.'

'And what made her interpret your actions otherwise?'

He gave a loose shrug. 'Honestly? I really don't know. She said I was too active on her Facebook page, liking all her posts and leaving comments. I wasn't any more active than a lot of her other close friends. It's not like I wrote anything threatening. Quite the opposite in fact.'

'Did she explain why she was bothered by your actions?'

'No, only that she wanted me to stop messaging her, commenting on her posts and she didn't want to see me any more. We'd been popping out now and again for a coffee and a chat after work. It had given us both a chance to talk things through. She still missed her mum. Her dad shacked up with a bloke, you know? She couldn't stand his new partner.' He blinked again. The once. Kate focused on his face. There were no involuntary twitches that accompanied emotion, no furrowing of brows, no sign of anything. 'I never fully understood why she put a stop to our meet-ups but I respected her wishes and backed off.' Kate shook her head. The man was lying. She hoped Emma was picking up on the same signals.

'And what happened next?'

This time he stared at the ceiling before replying. 'I liked a selfie she posted. It was dumb of me but some people had already liked it and I stupidly thought it would boost her confidence if she saw how popular the post was.'

'Why would that help her?' asked Emma.

'Laura didn't understand how pretty she really was. She always put herself down, made out she was uninteresting. She wasn't able to accept a compliment. She was the same at school.'

'And what happened next?'

'She got majorly pissed at me and messaged me some bullshit about how I'd ruined her life. I answered but by then, she'd already disabled her account. I didn't understand what she was so het up about, but I figured it would blow over. After a couple of weeks, when she hadn't come back on Facebook, I stopped by Tomkins Solicitors to see if she was okay. She wouldn't see me. Apparently, she was too tied up with work, so I tried her friend, Alicia, but she'd blocked me on Facebook too. I gave up then. Laura clearly didn't want anything to do with me. I haven't seen her since.'

'Were you aware she'd moved to Abbots Bromley in late February this year?'

His eyes opened wide, mouth too in an over-exaggerated display of surprise. Kate honed in on every minor movement. You could tell a lot by people's reactions and what they didn't say, as much as what they actually said. 'How did I not know that? I sometimes drink in the Goats Head.' He'd offered the information without hesitation. Kate had come across suspects before who'd voluntarily given away information in an attempt to appear helpful and innocent. Kate was confident Emma would see through any act. She was playing it cool, picking up on his response and using it as direction for her next question.

'Really? When did you last drink in there?' She maintained an almost casual tone, nodding encouragement.

'Last night.'

'You were in Abbots Bromley last night?'

'Uh-huh.'

'What time would this have been?'

'I got there about seven and stayed for a couple of hours.'

'Is there anybody who can vouch for your movements?'

'Hang on a minute, why would they need to do that?'

'I'd prefer it if you answered the question.'

'Was she killed in Abbots Bromley? That's it, isn't it? She was murdered in the village and you think I did it. Well, I didn't. I was in the pub all night.'

'And who can vouch for that?'

'Erm. Well, I didn't see anyone there I know. Maybe the barman would remember me. I sat on my own.'

'You were in the pub for two hours, on your own?'

Kevin merely shrugged a response. 'I often drink on my own. That isn't a crime, is it?' He looked at Jamie, moistened his lips.

'Mate, I didn't kill her.'

'I'm not your mate. My name is DC Webster.'

Kevin pouted for a moment. 'Sorry, *DC Webster*.'

'Tell me, Kevin, do you work out at all?' asked Emma.

'Work out?'

'At a gym? A club?'

'I don't have a membership anywhere.'

'Are you saying you don't work out?'

'I sometimes work out at home, and go running now and again.'

'What about martial arts?'

'I did Judo when I was a kid. Why?'

Emma ignored his question. 'What level did you reach?'

'Shodan.'

'You must have been keen. How many years did you practise?'

'Six. Then I gave it up. Why are you asking me about Judo?'

Again, Emma did not answer his question. 'We're going to need a list of names of the people who were at the pub with you and anyone else who you think saw you there,' said Emma.

'I don't know the names of any of the guys who were drinking there!'

'But you go there sometimes to drink.'

'Exactly. *Sometimes.* I go there when I don't want to be with loads of people I know. I go to several different pubs in the area. Break things up a bit.' He waved his hands in front of his face, his voice faltering. 'You can't possibly think I'd hurt Laura.'

'You need to help us out here, Kevin. Surely, you can remember who else was in the pub. Maybe you spoke to somebody, a greeting, a quick word in the gents—'

'No. I only spoke to the barman when I ordered. I went to a spot in the corner out of the way and played a game on my phone, enjoyed a quiet drink, then went home.'

'You drove home?'

'Yes.'

'After how many pints?'

'A couple. Then I went on to soft drinks after that, on account of the fact I intended to drive home.' He gave her a hard stare.

'We shall have to confirm that.'

He didn't reply.

'Okay, Kevin. We need to eliminate you from our enquiries and to do that we not only require a confirmation of your alibi, but a DNA sample.'

'Really?'

'It's standard procedure. DC Webster will administer that in a moment. It doesn't take long.'

'Maybe you should also do one on the two lads I saw hanging about near the green when I was outside smoking. They looked like troublemakers.'

'What makes you say that?'

'The way they were acting. They were sharing a bottle which I'm pretty certain contained alcohol and were shouting obscenities for no good reason. I stubbed out my fag and moved off before they clocked me.'

'Can you describe them?'

'About sixteen or so. One was tall with dark hair. To be honest, I kept my head down. I didn't want to wind them up and give them a reason to come across and start on me.'

'What time would this have been?'

'About eight.' His statement was followed by yet another blink. 'I wasn't into Laura. I liked her, that's all. I wasn't ready for another relationship. I'd had a serious one for a while and I still haven't really got over it.'

'Who with?'

'Doesn't matter. She's dead.'

'I'm sorry to hear that. What happened?'

'Leukaemia. Holly died earlier this year.'

Kate felt this was an add-on, an unnecessary piece of information to try and steer them away from him. Emma obviously felt the same way.

'You must have been very upset.'

'Yes. I still have trouble talking about it.'

'I can imagine. You must really miss Holly . . . What was her surname?' she asked pleasantly.

He hesitated for only a brief second. 'Whitmore, but I don't want to discuss it. I thought you should know that I only thought of Laura as a friend.'

Emma gave him a sympathetic smile and went through the remainder of her questions, but they yielded nothing. Even after the interview ended, Kate continued to observe Kevin. There were grounds to doubt his honesty. Firstly, for a man who'd claimed to like Laura a lot, he'd shown little emotion at the news of her death. His reactions had seemed almost rehearsed. He'd also volunteered information about his whereabouts and about spotting two teenagers, before being asked for it, and come up with a story about a dead girlfriend at the eleventh hour, presumably to deflect interest from him. And he had practised a martial art to a decent level. She checked on her phone and discovered shodan, or first dan, as it was also called, was the lowest level of black belt rank in Japanese martial arts. With practice, Kevin would be able to pull off a vagus strike. Jamie swabbed him for DNA and, when he was finished, handed the man a business card. Kevin stood up and pocketed it and, as he did so, he deliberately looked up, staring directly into the camera lens, before giving one last blink and moving away.

CHAPTER SIX

He's only been going out with her for two weeks and already he is head over heels in love. He has to pinch himself to make sure it's true, that he is going out with the girl he's fancied since he first set eyes on her. She is his first and only proper girlfriend: funny, pretty and very sexy. He pats his pocket and the concert tickets rustle. He's spent all his savings on them and they'll be worth every penny to see the look on her face when he hands them to her. She's been dead keen to see the band.

The school canteen is brimming with kids and he can't see her at first. He clears a path through younger pupils carrying lunch trays, who block his view, and finally spots her at the far end of the canteen, sitting at a table with his best mate. His heart soars. She is so hot!

He reaches them at last and drops down beside her and reaches for one of her hands. She pulls it away immediately.

'What's up?' he asks.

'Nothing. I thought we'd called it a day.'

'What? When?' He can hardly catch his breath.

'When I told you I wanted some space. Yesterday in the library.'

'I didn't think you meant—'

She gives him a pitying look which makes it worse.

'Can we talk about this?'

'We did. Yesterday.'

'That wasn't talking!' Catching sight of the sly glances and grins, he stops himself. He's making a total dick of himself in front of his mate. 'Well, it's your loss,' he says, trying to save face.

'Whatever,' she replies and waves him away with a waft of her hand.

He stands up, walks away humiliated, the tickets in his pocket rustling and mocking him as he pushes past the other kids and races outside.

That anger still burns in him today. Because of her, he's never been able to form any meaningful relationships with women, and has been forced to deal with the rejection and hurt in his own way, with others who remind him of his first love.

He rests his head against the chairback, eyes unfocused, recalling the memory of his first love, the girl who'd started all of this. He wants to feel her silken hair against his face and touch her lily-white skin, and carve his message into her flesh with his blade – a message that will prove to her how passionate he feels about her. The thought of gripping her throat with his hands and squeezing excites him further still and he has to draw deep, shuddering breaths to calm down his racing heart. When he is finally in control, he logs onto Facebook. They've been messaging each other regularly and now he feels like upping the ante.

It had been a long day and, gathered in the office, the team caught up on what they'd discovered so far. Morgan had been going through notes taken while interviewing all the members of Laura's yoga class, his voice raised to drown out the angry wasp-like noise emanating from the strip light.

Kate scowled. 'Can somebody whack that sodding thing? It's driving me mad.'

Jamie yanked his chair into position, leapt onto it and gave the base of the light a quick thump with the edge of a balled fist. The noise ceased.

'None of the women at the class saw anything unusual?' Kate said.

'Nope. Not a thing.' Morgan's notebook dropped onto the desk with a slap and he joined it, sitting with hands on wide thighs as he listened to Kate, who directed her next question at Jamie.

'Where are we with CCTV?'

'None in the village or surrounding areas, guv.'

'Not even in the pubs?'

'Only in the Goats Head, and the only surveillance camera there covers the till area.'

Kate kept her eyes on Jamie. 'What about the statements from diners at the restaurant? Anything useful?'

'The curtains were closed so nobody saw anything unusual.'

'And the guys working in the kitchen didn't notice anything out of the ordinary at all, no one hanging about outside, no teenagers, not even the ladies leaving the yoga class?' asked Kate.

'Not a thing. There's one small window facing the car park. Only somebody working at the bench under it could have spotted anything.'

'But Variations wasn't exactly brimming with hungry diners! The staff must have taken some time off and popped outside, or even taken rubbish outside to the bins.'

'Apparently, it was so quiet the manager took the decision to send three of them home at eight, leaving only himself, one chef and one waiter on duty. They didn't have any breaks, finished their shift at ten and all left at the same time.'

'Then I guess we'll have to take their word for it, for now.'

The restaurant staff, who'd already given voluntary DNA samples, had alibis for their whereabouts between eight and nine o'clock and, for the moment, weren't under any suspicion.

'This isn't looking good. Come on, guys. It's a small village. Surely someone caught sight of unusual activity? Where are we on those teenagers Kevin claimed to have spotted?'

Emma looked up from her notes. 'I haven't got any leads or names, although another witness, who lives on the main street opposite the Goats Head pub, confirmed there were a couple of boys hanging about the village. Her description of them was as vague as Kevin's.'

'Did she spot Kevin smoking outside the pub?'

'I'm afraid not. She only noticed the lads, loitering near the bus shelter. She spotted the bottle too. Thought it might have been vodka.'

'Keep asking. How far are we with Kevin?'

'Still gathering information, guv,' said Jamie.

Morgan cocked his head. 'If Kevin was obsessed with Laura and she rejected him, once at school and again last year, it would help explain the word *MINE* cut into her.'

'I agree, but facts lead us to the answers, not speculation, so stick at it, everyone.'

Morgan gave a grunt and slid from the desk onto his seat and fired up his laptop.

Kate dragged out a banana from her desk drawer, peeled back the pitted skin and took a bite, her attention drawn to the photo of Laura on the whiteboard.

It was unlikely to have been a spur-of-the-moment attack. Abbots Bromley wasn't heavily populated and, in comparison to a city centre, where there were constant movements of traffic and people, it was quiet. Several scenarios sprang to mind: Laura's assailant knew she was instructing the class and had lain in wait for her;

81

he was waiting for any lone female to leave the yoga class, and Laura happened to be the one he chanced on; or he had his sights on somebody else and, unable to isolate and attack her, he'd chosen Laura as a last-minute substitute. The possibilities swam about in her mind like overlarge fish in a bowl.

She chewed and at the same time stared hard at the picture of the young woman as if it held the answer. In a small way, Laura reminded her of Tilly when she was younger. They were both doll-like, slender, almost fragile, and then there were the eyes. Both had dark brown eyes.

A memory floated to the surface: Tilly crying into her shoulder and Kate stroking her thick dark hair. Even though she'd been able to help in some small way, she'd never been able to put an end to the nightmares or the guilt that had eaten into Tilly. No justice was ever served for Tilly. Now, Kate had a duty to help her come to terms, once and for all, with what had transpired, so she could return to Staffordshire, close to Kate, who would make sure she never experienced any such horror again.

She dragged her gaze from Laura's face and made a silent vow that they would find whoever had murdered her.

'And me, Kate? Don't forget about me.'

Kate closed her eyes briefly. *I won't.* She couldn't forget him, yet in the last few hours, she'd barely given Chris a thought.

Shit! Cooper. She checked the time. Six. There wasn't time to arrange to see Cooper tonight. The visit would have to wait until tomorrow. She messaged Tilly, telling her she was still at the office and asking how her day had been. The reply came back immediately:

No probs, sis.

We're fine.

Had a fun day.

Daniel's got a new video game. We're playing it now.

Speak soon.

XX

She'd added three hearts.

'Kate.' Emma's voice was loud in the small room. 'I think we need to get hold of Kevin again. He made up that stuff about having a girlfriend who died.'

'She doesn't exist?'

'Holly Whitmore *did* die of leukaemia.' Emma craned her neck around to speak to Kate. 'However, according to her social media account, which is still active and run by this bloke, she was dating somebody called Floyd Evanshaw, not Kevin Shire.'

Morgan was on his feet in a flash, crashing past cabinets, knocking files onto the floor. 'Let me see.' Kate adjusted her screen so pictures of a pretty girl wearing dungarees came into view. A young man with a hipster beard had an arm draped over her bare olive-skinned shoulder.

Morgan shook his head. 'The lying shitweasel.'

'Read it out, Emma,' said Kate.

'"It's been a year since you left us but the light you left behind still shines in my heart. I miss you with every breath I make. Sending you love until we meet again, my angel." It was written only a few days ago.'

Kate's heart thudded solidly. 'Have you checked to see if Kevin was one of her friends?'

'Not had a chance yet.'

'Okay. Try now.'

Emma typed his name into the relevant box and checked the results. 'No Kevin here.'

Morgan crouched beside her, the seams of his trousers straining. 'Check out Floyd's page.'

Holly's page was replaced by her boyfriend's, and a header of the pair of them, together with a woolly dog on a sandy beach. 'I'll try Kevin's name again.'

There was no sound from anyone as Emma's fingers caressed the keyboard. 'And there he is! Kevin *is* one of Floyd's friends. He knew all about Floyd and Holly.'

Kate, who'd been holding on to the banana skin the entire time, placed it in the bin and rubbed her palms together. 'Okay, check this out with their parents and see if Holly knew or even went out with Kevin, before you haul his arse here. That man has some explaining to do. Good job, Emma.'

Morgan headed back to his desk, stopping to scoop up the files and replace them.

'I've got another possible lead,' said Jamie. 'I've been following up on those people we couldn't canvass this morning, and spoke to a bloke who lives three doors down from Variations restaurant. Last night, at about eight, he heard a commotion, opened his curtains to see what it was, and saw two lads running down the road on the opposite side of the street. He's given me a description of one of them. I'll head back to Abbots Bromley and bang on a few doors and see if anyone recognises the boy.' He picked up his jacket. 'Anyone want any grub? I'll stop off at Benito's on the way back and get a takeaway selection for us.'

Even though Benito's décor was stuck in the eighties, its tapas were the best in the area. The team had an open tab system running with the proprietor, which they settled at the end of each month.

'Defo,' Morgan replied. 'Make sure you get plenty of those steak and chorizo meatballs and don't scoff them all before I get back.'

'Wouldn't dare. Guv, anything you fancy?'

'Happy with whatever you choose.'

'Me too.' Emma stuck her thumb up in thanks as Jamie pulled on his jacket then disappeared.

Kate headed to the washroom. If they could prove Kevin was their perpetrator, it would be an excellent result. It would enable her to have a day or two off and take Tilly and Daniel out as anticipated. She lowered her head and washed her hands. It had become habit to envisage Chris by her side during such small routines and she spoke quietly.

'It's looking promising, Chris. Kevin has some serious explaining to do.'

She looked up at the mirror to continue the conversation in his voice, only to discover he wasn't there. She was overcome with a sudden emptiness. Where was he? She hadn't seen him since . . .

That's when it hit her. She'd been so busy thinking about this case, and about Tilly, that Chris had faded away. If she kept this up, she'd never be able to reconnect with him and she'd lose him completely. How could she rectify this? The answer was simple – contact the man who wanted to talk to her, Cooper.

She was about to ring the prison to arrange to see him, when voices outside reminded her that somebody could come in and overhear her monologuing. At present, she was unsure who else, other than her team, she could trust. Walls had ears. If Dickson had been, as she suspected, involved in hiring the hitman to do away with Chris, he wouldn't have any compunction in meting out the same punishment to Kate. She exited into the car park where only ten vehicles, including Dickson's BMW, were parked, and sprinted lightly to her own car from which she rang HM Thamesbury Prison to arrange a visit for the following morning.

Once she'd ended the call, she stared out towards the anonymous brick building, its windows in darkness, apart from two or three. Was it her imagination or did a sliver of light escape from the blinds in Dickson's office? Was he watching her? She didn't dare speak aloud to the man who lived only in her imagination. The light disappeared and Chris's voice seemed loud in her ear.

'I expect Cooper wants to discuss what happened at the Maddox Club. Something he's withheld until this moment. He's had plenty of time to think things over and wants to come clean. Maybe he hopes whatever he tells you will get him an early release.'

Kate nodded. She was sure Cooper had withheld a vital piece of evidence regarding that case, one that would implicate Dickson. He'd known more about the murder that had taken place there than he'd let on, and she'd bet her life Dickson had also been involved in arranging Chris's murder. 'I'll nail him, Chris. If it takes me the rest of my life, I'll make Dickson pay.'

She clambered back out of her car into the icy cold, and raced for the door, hoping she didn't bump into him on the staircase. On the off-chance she did, she had a story prepared about talking to an informant. Dickson was not going to catch her out.

CHAPTER SEVEN

Heather Gault was one of several CIOs, or Civilian Investigation Officers, who worked in Trentham House. She wasn't a police officer or a detective, but she assisted them and generally it was a job she enjoyed. In recent weeks, she'd discovered not every police officer was as dedicated as she imagined, some even crooked. She'd been hoping for a phone call that would give her the information she needed to point the finger at one of them. However, it appeared her source had not yet built up sufficient courage to come forward as requested. Heather would try contacting her again later. However, having come to the end of a long shift, she was now eager to clock off and head out for the evening.

She held her hands under the dryer and waited until the digital display had reached zero before removing them. It was better, she argued, than wiping them on her trousers as she'd had to do many times after discovering the dispenser had run out of paper towels. The countdown ended, the whirring ceased and she moved to the sink, rooted in her bag for a tube of hand cream, which she rubbed gently into her skin. She sniffed at her armpits and screwed up her face at the sour aroma. Further hunting in her bag yielded a mini deodorant spray, which she shoved down her blouse and, lifting her arm, squirted liberally until the whole washroom smelt of roses.

She rummaged again, this time pulling out a lipstick, which she rolled over her full lips. She gave a light coral pout at her reflection. She'd do. It was only drinks and nibbles in company, not a full-on date. The door to the ladies opened and Deepa Singh's smiling face appeared. Heather wondered what kept her colleague perpetually happy and wished she had a tiny portion of whatever it was that kept Deepa enthused.

'I'll see you tomorrow afternoon.'

'Absolutely. Five on the dot. I'll be there.'

Deepa was holding a baby shower and Heather had bought *the* most beautifully soft baby-blue blanket and a darling stuffed rabbit.

'See you then.' Deepa blew a kiss and disappeared. Heather unclipped the barrette holding her heavy, chestnut hair in place and let it fall naturally to frame her face. She dabbed light powder onto her eyelids to help set off her best feature: irises the colour of dark chocolate and often described as 'come-to-bed' eyes. Satisfied she looked good enough, she tossed everything back into the bag, hoping he'd be pleased with her last-minute decision to drop by.

Trentham House foyer was still brightly lit and although a coat was hanging on the back of the chair, indicating somebody was still around, there was nobody on reception. She was probably one of, if not the last to leave. She and Deepa had put in a full day to get on top of the backlog and clear the decks for Monday morning.

The door closed behind her and she trotted down the steps to the driveway that served as a car park for visitors. Staff had to use the municipal car park, only a hundred metres down the road. She shouldered her bag and checked her phone. There were still no messages from her source. She hoped the girl hadn't changed her mind. With her head lowered she was unaware of movement in the bushes or the figure disentangling itself from the shadows until she glanced up. And by then, it was too late.

CHAPTER EIGHT

Kevin Shire folded into his seat, and stared wide-eyed at Kate.

'I don't understand. Why have you brought me to the station?'

'We need to ask you a few more questions.'

'Shouldn't there be a solicitor or somebody here with me?'

'This is a voluntary interview. You're assisting us with our enquiries but if you'd prefer to have a solicitor, we can arrange it for you.'

'*Assisting with enquiries*. You're not charging me?'

'Why would we do that?'

The pink tongue flicked out, brushed lightly over his lips. The eyes didn't blink. 'I . . . I might be in trouble.'

'Do you want to explain what you mean?' Kate mirrored his stillness with her own.

'You know, don't you?'

'Know what, Kevin?'

'About Holly. You've checked out my story, haven't you?'

Morgan took over, opening his folder and extracted a piece of paper. 'This is a statement made by Mr Floyd Evanshaw. I'd like to read it to you.'

Kevin lowered his head and picked at the dried blood around his thumbnail while Morgan continued. '"Holly and I met in October 2018, at a mutual friend's party. We hit it off and went exclusive a few weeks later. She moved in with me March 2019. She was my world. Ask any of our friends and they'll tell you we were soulmates. In December that same year, she began to feel run-down and was tired all of the time. She thought it was work-related or a dose of seasonal flu. We didn't realise how serious it was until she started noticing she was bruising herself frequently and was feeling increasingly lousy, so we went to the doctor's. They discovered she had acute myeloid leukaemia. Weeks after the diagnosis, we lost her. I still can't believe she's gone."' Morgan looked up from the statement. 'Mr Evanshaw told me you and he were friends, and you were also at the same party in Stoke-on-Trent. He felt guilty, because you'd been chatting to Holly until he cut in and took her off for a dance. He apologised to you later and you "laughed it off". Holly was never your girlfriend.' Morgan returned the paper to the folder and shut it. Kevin didn't look up.

Kate let the silence hang. A droplet of fresh blood seeped from Kevin's nail. 'Why did you tell us that Holly was your girlfriend?'

Silence.

'You're not helping yourself here.'

Kevin stopped pulling at his thumb.

'We could caution you and hold you in a cell for wasting our time. You don't want us to do that, do you?'

He shook his head, his greasy hair glistening in the light.

'Then put us straight.'

He stuttered, 'I . . . I . . .' Then, 'Isn't it obvious?'

'I'd like to hear it from you.'

'I thought you suspected me of killing Laura. I panicked.'

'If you didn't kill her, you only had to tell the truth.'

Kevin released a snort. 'Yeah, right.' He lifted his head at last, fastened the eerie, grey-white eyes on Kate. 'I only wanted her to like me.'

'Tell me what happened on Facebook,' said Kate.

'You know what happened. She got annoyed about me liking her posts.'

'Did you know she was seeing somebody at the time?'

He nodded.

'Did she tell you who she was going out with?'

'No, only that she was in love and she and I could never be more than friends.'

'And that hurt you?' said Kate.

His voice changed timbre. 'Yes, it hurt. I didn't know about a boyfriend. There was nothing on Facebook about any relationship. She bloody well led me on and let me believe I had a chance with her.'

'How so?'

'By the way she looked at me and how she spoke. It felt . . . intimate. I could sense we had a thing going on. She rubbished me when I tried to make her see that too.'

Morgan rested his arms on the table, leaning closer towards Kevin. 'And that pissed you off big time, didn't it? You didn't like being given the runaround. Did it make you angry?'

Kate let him continue. The intimidation was deliberate to discombobulate the man.

'I . . . No . . . Yes . . . I *didn't* kill her.'

'I bet you wanted to though. First, she's all nice to you and then, when you get up the courage and invite her out, she gives you the brush-off. And then, she tells you to sling your hook. I'd be pretty annoyed if anyone did that to me.' The words tumbled from Morgan's lips without any pauses, a *rat-a-tat-tat*. Kevin blinked three times in a row.

'No. I did exactly as she asked.'

Morgan growled. 'You didn't. You kept liking her posts, even stuck up stupid heart emojis under some of them. What sort of message does that send out, eh? You knew exactly what you were doing. You *wanted* her boyfriend to suspect she was cheating on him. And you weren't surprised when that's what happened. I'll wager you were really fucking pleased with yourself.'

'No!'

Morgan didn't stop. 'I guess the surprise was, she was furious with you. You'd expected her to fall into your arms, weeping and wailing. Instead, she cut herself off Facebook and from you. Not what you expected, eh? What did she say to you, Kevin?'

'Nothing.'

'What did she *say* to you?' Morgan's voice was loud in the small room.

Kevin's lips began to tremble. 'That she wouldn't go out with me even if I was the last man on the planet.'

'Ah! I bet you hated her for that!'

'No! I didn't hate her. I hated myself!' His eyes glistened with tears. 'I hated . . . *myself.*'

Morgan sat back, allowing Kate to take over.

'Did you try to apologise to her, Kevin?' she asked.

'No. I let it go. I gave up. Laura was somebody I'd put on a pedestal. I'd got it into my head she was perfect. Then after she'd let rip at me and told me what a douchebag I was, I saw she wasn't. There was a side to her I'd never seen before – one I didn't like. She sent me a message, a long, hateful message and then shut down her Facebook account so I couldn't reply to it. To be honest, I didn't want to reply. She wouldn't have listened to anything I had to say. I didn't know she'd moved to Abbots Bromley and if I had known, I'd have steered well clear of the place.' He dropped his head into his hands. Kate watched as his shoulders shook with quiet sobs, then terminated the interview. If Kevin was responsible, they'd have to find evidence to prove it because they certainly weren't going to get a confession from him.

◆ ◆ ◆

Kate dunked the crispy chicken into the tiny pot of sriracha hot sauce and bit into it, without appreciating or even tasting any of the flavour. The others seemed to be tucking in with more enthusiasm, especially Morgan, who sat back in his chair, popping meatballs into his mouth like they were popcorn.

Jamie slugged from a can of Red Bull, his free hand working the keyboard. Kate marvelled at his speed and proficiency. She'd been in the job a long time, yet she couldn't type or 'screen surf' as well as any of her team. They'd got a lead on one of the youths spotted in Abbots Bromley at the time of Laura's death and were name-checking on the general database.

Emma sat on the edge of her desk, watching him out of the corner of her eye while stabbing at calamari in a cardboard tray. She paused, piece in mid-air. 'That's him. Davey Watkins.' She scooted forward on her desk, eyes narrowing. 'He's been in trouble before.'

'What for?' asked Morgan.

'Sexting. Three years ago. He was thirteen at the time. It was classed as Outcome 21,' said Jamie, scribbling onto a yellow sticky note.

Outcome 21 allowed police to list a crime as having happened but no formal criminal justice action was taken.

'Here you go, Emma, his contact details. He's not from the village.'

Emma took the note. 'Milton Farm, Dunstall. Where's that?'

A map materialised on Jamie's screen and he pointed out the appropriate place, almost nine miles from the village. 'He'd need transport to get to Abbots Bromley.'

Kate nodded. 'Talk to him. Find out why he went there rather than any of the surrounding villages, or even to Burton-on-Trent, which is closer to where he lives.'

Emma got to her feet and jangled her keys. 'Beats me. You coming, Morgan?'

Morgan scrunched up his box and dropped it in the bin. 'Right behind you.'

'Emma, are you done with your tapas?' Jamie shot her a pleading look.

'Help yourself.'

Morgan swooped on the box first, grabbing the largest piece of calamari, before waving it triumphantly under Jamie's nose with a 'Too slow, mate', before racing off after Emma.

It was past ten o'clock and they had nothing new to go on. Kate dismissed Jamie and soaked up the silence he left in his wake. She attached one paperclip to another and idly wondered who Laura's mysterious boyfriend might have been and why she'd kept his identity secret, even from her closest friend. She added a third and fourth clip to the chain and dangled it over her desk. If only the puzzle pieces of this investigation would clip together so easily. She had no intention of leaving the office until she'd heard from Emma and Morgan. If they had reason to believe Davey was responsible for, or had borne witness to, the attack on Laura, she'd be here when they brought him in for questioning.

'Don't put off Cooper,' whispered Chris.

'I fully intend to see him tomorrow, as planned.'

His words stung. She wouldn't set Chris aside. If what Cooper had to tell her related to Chris's death, she would follow it up and yet, at the same time, she knew she couldn't abandon Laura to focus on Chris. Both demanded her attention.

She shut her eyes and thought about the man who she still loved with every atom of her being. With a sinking sensation in the pit of her stomach she realised she could no longer picture the intense green of his irises. She hunted for memories that might rekindle the exact shade and found her mind muddying the pictures. Cold fingers clawed at her heart. Her recollections of Chris were fading. Alicia had mentioned the five stages of grief and Kate knew that unless she kept the anger over his death burning, she would pass through each stage and reach the final one – acceptance. Her desire to uncover the truth behind his death fuelled her and kept memories of him burning brightly. If she didn't continue looking into Dickson, or the other corrupt officers Chris had been investigating, precious, clear memories would be replaced by fragmented, vague ones. She would forget the strength of his love or the essence of his being and he would be gone forever.

A new image replaced Chris's face, one that was much clearer – Laura's. And along with it came a fresh thought. What if Tilly had not escaped her attacker and had met a similar horrific fate? The paperclips fell quietly and she bent over her keyboard. She had to find Laura's killer. To reach the answer, Kate needed to find out more about the woman.

CHAPTER NINE

Kate leant back against her seat, suppressing a yawn. The latest suspects, the two youths who'd been hanging around Abbots Bromley, had stuck to their stories. Neither of them had spotted Laura and didn't recall seeing Kevin outside the pub. Although it had been necessary to interview them, it had cost the investigation precious time.

Morgan tossed the file onto his desk. 'Flipping heck. What a waste of time. I don't know about you but I'm knackered.'

'I feel fine,' Emma replied. 'You could do with cutting out the crap food and exercising more.'

'We can't all be ninja experts like you,' he replied with a grin.

'Very funny.'

'Actually, Emma,' said Kate. 'I wanted to talk to you about martial arts. It can wait until later today, after you've had some sleep.'

'No, it's fine. Like I said, I'm not tired.'

'I'll leave you both to it then.' Morgan shrugged on his coat and made for the door.

Emma sat on the side of her desk. 'What do you want to know?'

'Anything you can tell me about the vagus strike.'

'Okay. Well, it's a self-defence technique: one that's quite easy to learn and execute. However, it has to be performed with a certain amount of force and, of course, precision. Get it wrong and it will kill a person. Whoever attacked Laura would have known that and I'm guessing they implemented the manoeuvre purely to render her unconscious.'

'How much of an expert would you need to be to perform this sort of manoeuvre?'

'You don't actually need a great deal of physical strength or peak physical fitness to execute one; however, like any self-defence training, you need to practise it regularly. It's always performed against a dummy, not a living person, for obvious reasons, and is never used as an offensive technique. It should only be used in the direst of situations, when the chips are down and you're fighting for your life. So again, I'm going out on a limb when I suggest the killer is confident in employing the technique, or doesn't care if he gets it wrong.'

'You reckon Kevin might be able to perform it?'

She pulled a face. 'He was only young when he took up Judo and he wouldn't have come across it during classes back then. Still, if he still practises at home, he might be able to pull it off. It takes skill though.'

Kate folded her arms and see-sawed between their perpetrator being Kevin or somebody else altogether, and decided to keep the options wide open. 'Then could we be looking for somebody who is trained to a high level of proficiency or is an instructor?'

'That's more likely.'

'Is it something you've tried?'

'No. I tend to focus on Taekwondo kicks and punches, although I do sometimes practise neck and body strikes. These sorts of nerve strikes are practised in other martial arts disciplines such as Jujitsu, Karate or Kenpo too.'

'Do you think you could look further into it for me? It's your area of expertise. Ask about and see if anyone has been seen practising it in local gyms. Maybe your brother would know of somebody.'

'Yeah. Sure.'

'I've also got a favour to ask.'

'Fire away.'

'You know my stepsister, Tilly, is staying in the UK?'

'Yes.'

'Could you spare a little time when you're next training to go through some basic self-defence moves with her? She's over here on her own and I'd feel more comfortable if I knew she could handle herself when she's out and about.'

'Of course. I train at Greg's gym every morning before work. If she wants to pop along, I'll happily show her a few. Give her my phone number so we can arrange to meet there.'

'Thanks, Emma. I really appreciate that.' Kate had already messaged Tilly earlier on and asked if she'd be willing to take a self-defence class and received a positive answer. It might help give Tilly back some self-confidence. And, if she was going to be living the life of a single woman for a while, Kate would feel happier if Tilly could defend herself, should the situation arise.

Emma quickly packed up and departed, leaving Kate alone with her thoughts. So far, she'd not discovered anything new to help her track down Laura's killer. Tomorrow, she'd check with Forensics and see if anything had been retrieved from her house which might cast a clue as to the identity of the man responsible.

The clock hands moved closer towards half past one and she decided to go home for a few hours' sleep. It was one thing to throw yourself into an investigation and another to burn out too quickly.

'And you need to be on your game when you speak to Cooper later this morning,' said Chris.

'I'll be—' She checked herself. She ought not to keep talking aloud to her imagined dead husband. It was bordering on madness. She reached for the door handle and halted. Be that as it may, believing he was with her helped her, more than she cared to admit. 'I'll be perfectly fine,' she murmured.

CHAPTER TEN

The cheating, prick-teasing bitch! She'd been all over him, made him believe they were an item – boyfriend and girlfriend – and then dumped him. He'd treated her nicely, respectfully, and yet it hadn't been good enough. He should have treated her like his father treated his own half-sister. It's been over a year since she ditched him and he still hasn't got over it. The hurt is still as raw. Unbeknown to her, he's trailed her on several occasions, each time waiting for an opportunity to play out the scene he's fantasised over for months. There's nobody about in the park and his pulse quickens at the prospect of what is to come. This time, he'll be in charge. She won't be able to control him or his emotions. She will be completely in his power. A voice in his head whispers, she's mine *and he slips a knitted balaclava over his face and hugs the shadows of the trees.*

She doesn't hear his quickening footsteps or sense his presence until he is upon her and knocks her over with a body blow. She's so slight, she instantly tumbles to the ground and before she can recover, he has dragged her out of sight. He unleashes the demons, curses her, forces her down. She complies and when it's over he's buzzing. She's his at last. He leans forward to tell her and without warning, she lashes out, her nails gouging his hand, causing blood to instantly seep from the wound. He makes no sound of alarm, covers it with his other hand before she realises the extent of the injury and hisses that she should go and not look back, or he'll kill her. She leaves, a sobbing broken mess.

His hand has four deep scratches. They'll heal in time. For now, he ought to keep them hidden. He studies them and smiles. Somehow, they make the whole experience feel even more real. He licks the wounds created by her nails, trying to taste any residue of her that might be in his blood, while imaginary trumpets sound victoriously in his head. He owns her! He ought to celebrate in some way, do something to ensure he always remembers this wonderful moment. A tattoo maybe? He ponders the possibility and as blood bubbles and begins to crust on his wounds, he considers the possibility of getting an inked drawing of a black heart to represent the bitch who broke his own heart, along with a single drop of blood to remind him that, in the end, he broke her.

The memories fade and he pummels the punchbag, causing it to swing with such velocity it's in danger of knocking him out. He grunts with the effort before finally standing back and sucking in air. His face burns hot with the effort and rivulets of sweat sting his eyes, causing him to blink repeatedly, but he feels good – invincible. The workout has helped him come to terms with the disappointment that his victims aren't providing him with the gratification they should. Even when he is in the zone, forcing them into submission while recalling every detail of what it had felt like to overcome his first love, he's been finding it increasingly difficult to accept these women are embodiments of her, chosen specifically to allow him to relive those precious moments. During this frenzied workout, he's accepted what he'd already begun to suspect – he wants her, again. He wipes his forehead with his arm, nods at the guy who's been watching him work out.

'Got some anger there, mate,' says the man.

'Yeah, not so much now.'

'Worked it out of your system, eh?'

'You could say that,' he replies, grinning in a friendly fashion. If the bloke really knew who he was imagining when he smashed his fist

into the bag, he wouldn't be so quick to chat. That's the good thing about working out at this gym. Nobody pays you much attention. Everyone here is heavily into training, so it isn't unusual to see someone hammering fists against a bag or opponent, or even kicking it, or for somebody to spend a long time in the corner of the room with a dummy, practising vagus strikes.

'Catch you later,' he says. 'Have a good workout.'

◆　◆　◆

Kate drank in the cool air, inhaling deeply to dispel any residual mugginess from a deep and dreamless sleep. After only three hours' sleep, she was limbering up for the run that would set her up for the day.

This morning, she'd chosen to make the journey to Blithfield Reservoir to exercise, not because it was right next to the village where Laura had died, but because it would only be a short drive afterwards to Thamesbury Prison for her meeting with Cooper at eight o'clock.

There was another important reason she liked to come here to run. Every time she crossed the causeway and parked up, she felt oddly at peace, because here, her connection with Chris seemed to grow stronger. He would come more into focus as she pounded around the ancient woodlands, keenly aware of his presence, almost as if he was matching her stride for stride, as he had done when he was alive. She needed to refresh the connection, especially as the ability to conjure up a clear picture of her husband, his mannerisms and even the exact timbre of his voice was in danger of waning.

There were rumours about submerged homes and lives lost during the creation of the reservoir, none of which Kate believed given there was no documented evidence to prove that was the case, yet on cooler mornings when pockets of wispy clouds hung above the water, she would become aware of arms, barely visible to the naked eye, beckoning her closer to the water's edge. On those days, the reservoir was wild, remote and full of mystery. If she strained her ears, she'd hear more than an occasional nasal honk from wild-fowl, sounds like muffled calls for help. Today, there were none and the water was glassy. A grey heron rose lazily from the reeds and began a graceful lolling, long legs trailing, its identical twin mirrored below. She released the tension from between her shoulders with a shake, glanced across the water, reflecting pale blue skies and flames of orange, crimson and gold from the changing foliage surrounding it, then powered away from the water's front, towards the trees and tranquillity.

Kate thundered through the damp woods, navigating roots that curled and twisted their way through the mounds of soggy leaves on the path, her breath coming in rasps as she took the slope at speed. From here, she would reach the wild flower meadow and head back towards the lake to complete the second phase of this lengthy circuit.

'Recording aside, what you really could do with is a signed statement from Farai and a full confession from Cooper Monroe,' said Chris, reminding her of the conversation she'd recorded only a fortnight earlier, when she'd been singularly focused on uncovering the level of corruption surrounding Dickson and determining if he was central to the decision to have Chris murdered.

The quality of the recording had been good and the conversation between her and Farai clear. It had since been downloaded to a USB stick already containing the file of corrupt officers that Chris had left on his computer. She still had to think of a place to safely store it.

'Fat chance of a statement, and the recording won't stand up in court. There's not enough proof it was Farai speaking. Let's hope

Cooper can dish more dirt on Dickson. If he can, I'm going to make damn sure Dickson gets what he deserves.'

Cooper had driven the sex workers to the Maddox Club back in January, on the night the boy was killed. He'd been paid to bury the body and keep schtum before being asked to beat up Chris, who'd been investigating the club. Cooper had refused to harm the journalist but in doing so, set off the chain of events that resulted in the hire of a hitman from the dark web, who'd gunned down Kate's husband, along with other innocent passengers, on a train.

Birds scattered from treetops, wings beating as fast as her heart. Dickson had kept back vital information from the investigative team at the time. He'd helped cover up a boy's death, threatened Farai, who would have been a valuable witness, and protected the man responsible for the boy's death. Because of his actions, there was no doubt in Kate's mind that Dickson had also helped the same man hire the hitman or, at the very least, known he was going to pay somebody to silence her husband.

Her feet slip-slapped over the grass and she turned her concentration once more to her breathing. She had to maintain her stamina for the final push, through the forest and back along the road to her car. She'd dry off with a towel in the car and give herself a spray with deodorant before she headed to the prison. She doubted Cooper would be too bothered by the smell of perspiration. He'd been a member of the SAS and had fought cheek by jowl with others in life-threatening situations where no one would worry first about personal hygiene.

Her phone vibrated against the top of her arm where it had been secured and, coming to a halt, she used the Bluetooth connection to speak aloud.

'DI Young.'

'DI Young, this is Callum Fullerton, the governor at Thamesbury Prison. You were due to meet Cooper Monroe at eight this morning.'

'That's right.'

'I'm afraid that will no longer be possible. Mr Monroe was found dead in the showers, earlier this morning. It appears he took his own life.'

'No, that's impossible. He was going to speak to me about something important.'

'I'm sorry.'

'Are you sure he took his own life and wasn't attacked?'

'There's no doubt. He slashed his own throat. By the time he was discovered, he'd already lost a great deal of blood. I'm afraid he died on the way to the infirmary.'

'Have you spoken to his daughter?'

'Yes, directly before I contacted you. I'm sorry to give you bad news. I hope this doesn't directly impact your investigation.'

'I don't know what he had to tell me, so I can't tell if it was significant or not. Sir, did he seem to have any enemies or struggle while he was with you?'

'No. He was a model prisoner. Would probably have got out on parole at the earliest opportunity. Great shame. It seems the last few days he'd been quieter than usual, not himself. The chaplain confirmed he'd recently spoken with regret about his past demeanours. I guess he suddenly decided it was too much for him.'

Kate didn't imagine that was the case. Cooper had been one of an elite special forces unit and faced far worse situations than life in prison. On top of that, he adored his daughter, Sierra. He wouldn't have killed himself. Something in the governor's tone suggested she ought not to voice such opinions, so she thanked him for his time.

'Shit! Now what?'

'I don't know.' Chris's voice echoed the horror in her own. 'We won't ever know what he had to say.'

She froze, her thoughts colliding. Farai had been warned he wouldn't come out of prison alive. Could it be possible? 'What if somebody found out about our meeting today and decided it was too risky to let Cooper talk to me? What if Dickson had him killed to prevent him from speaking to me?'

'That's a lot of what ifs, Kate. Yet, I can't imagine he'd ask to see you, then top himself the morning he was due to tell you something important.'

Kate kicked at a stone, sending it spinning in the air and landing with a soft plop against a tree. 'Shit! I really needed to question him. This screws up everything.'

A grey squirrel raced onto the pathway, came to a swift halt when it spied Kate standing motionless and scurried away as she released a low groan that grew in intensity until it became an angry scream that roared through the trees.

CHAPTER ELEVEN

He pauses in front of the floor-length mirror in the corner of his garage to admire his muscular, gleaming torso. He flexes powerful fingers still aching from the recent exertion with the hand grip strengthener, then grins and springs forward, right arm extended towards his neck, ready to deliver a knuckle punch to his reflection, halting before he strikes the glass. He steps back again and permits himself another smile. He is a dangerous killing machine. A wolf in sheep's clothing. Who could imagine he wields such power in his fists?

He's performed the vagus strike manoeuvre so often he can do it with his eyes closed. It's imperative to inflict damage to the nerve itself rather than to the muscles that protect it. The only way he can cause the greatest damage to the nerve fibres is by penetrative force and so he must drive in from the front where the soft tissues lie. It takes skill and practice. Too hard and he'll kill. Too soft and his victim might escape. He's only got it wrong once before and that body has never been uncovered.

The crashing symbols and violin introduction to Morrissey's 'At Last I Am Born' ring out. It's a good thing he set the alarm on his mobile to warn him it's time to get ready for work, where he'll blend in with the others to become an ordinary bloke. Nobody there has a clue of what he is capable of. Ordinary men don't wield the power he does. He is an avenger, a demigod.

He allows himself a moment of satisfaction and the opportunity to relive the previous evening when he'd shown that bitch who was in charge, truly in charge. For a while, he'd been transported back in time to his first conquest as he tugged on her luscious hair, which fell like thick chocolate waves, and stared into her innocent brown eyes. Oh, yes. It had rekindled that delicious moment when he'd thrust his first love to her knees and made her surrender to him.

Without warning the euphoria evaporates, exactly as it did on Friday in Abbots Bromley. Usually, a re-enactment of that very first attack would sustain him for weeks, but ever since she came back into his life, each one has only lasted a few hours. So far, he has been unable to find out where she lives and determine a routine that would allow him to track her down and plan an attack. The frustration is eating at him. He wants her so badly he is unable to fully enjoy his array of stand-ins. The urge to find her and have her again is ruining everything.

He picks up a towel and wipes his face then stares again in the mirror, disappointed by what he now sees. This new power ought to be displayed across his features, yet it has already drained away, leaving an ordinary man, and so his mood shifts, to be replaced by bitter disappointment.

He's more formidable than his father ever was and still he feels unfulfilled. He wipes his face one last time and sets his jaw. In those few moments, with Morrissey singing in the background, a decision has been made. He's destined to repeat the act to relive the euphoria he craves and keep practising for that special someone – his first love.

He will strike again.

Tomorrow.

◆ ◆ ◆

With her plans to speak to Cooper scuppered, Kate jogged back to where she'd parked. The news of his death had come as a severe blow and, try as she might, she couldn't shake the idea that Cooper had been deliberately silenced. If so, it begged the question why. No matter how many other alternatives she considered – angered cellmates, other people with vendettas – the fact he'd died the very morning of their meeting rang alarm bells. The only other person who knew he wished to speak to her was his daughter, Sierra. She might have let it slip to the wrong person, or somebody on the inside had found out and warned concerned parties about Cooper's intention to meet with Kate. *Dickson?*

There'd be no chance of her persuading the prison authorities to look into his death. That much had been clear from the governor's stand-offish nature over the phone. There might not even be an autopsy or an investigation into the actual cause of death. Not unless she could persuade Sierra to request one. An image of a dewy-eyed Kate, head held high, walking behind her father's coffin, stuck in her mind's eye and for a moment, she thought of the pain Sierra would be experiencing. Her mission would have to wait. Sierra needed time to digest the horrible news.

She flung herself into the driving seat and glared ahead. Balling her fists, she thumped the steering wheel. A flock of geese lifted off as if disturbed by the noise, amidst noisy honking and synchronised flapping. The cacophony of noise grew ever louder, filling the whole sky as increased numbers joined them and grouped into a perfect V-formation to continue their lengthy, southbound journey. The sight distracted her and she silently wished them all a safe flight.

Chris had once told her that geese looked after their own during migration. 'They never leave a man down,' he'd said. If one was struggling during flight or so sick or weary it had to land, two others would flank it and either fly alongside or land with the ailing bird, to ensure its safety and, if it were to perish, the remaining pair would take off together, looking out for each other. Chris had been her own personal travelling companion, somebody who'd never leave her to fend for herself. She didn't need to speak out loud to know he was with her still, as he always would be. Blowing out her cheeks and straightening up, she turned on the engine. It was time to return to the station, via her house for a quick shower. She'd check up on the team and see if there was any new information regarding Laura Dean and talk to Sierra later in the day.

She edged out onto the causeway. The geese were already in the distance, their distinct flight pattern still visible. DCI William Chase rang before she'd reached the halfway point.

'Morning, Kate.'

Until she'd discovered Chris's file, she'd have trusted William with her life. Since that day, an invisible barrier had been erected and their old, easy friendship was strained. She knew she was to blame. She'd kept William at arm's length, refusing any invitations to supper or for drinks at his house, and avoiding him so he wouldn't notice the change in her attitude, or guess she had suspicions about him. Luckily, the last couple of months, he'd become heavily occupied at work and she'd had even less contact than usual with him. She kept her voice level, tone pleasant.

'Morning, William. Everything okay?'

'Hi, Kate. I'm afraid not. I've been informed a woman's body has been uncovered in an industrial bin, at the public car park on Newbury Avenue. Looks like another violent rape attack. I'd like you to check out the scene.'

'Do we know who the woman is?'

'Not yet.'

Kate was familiar with the road and area. She'd been there on a few occasions to visit Trentham House where several Civilian Investigation Officers, trained in the techniques of criminal prosecution, worked alongside police officers to assist on numerous low-level cases. 'I'll be there in fifteen to twenty minutes.'

'Turn on the blue lights. I want you there as soon as possible.'

Emma and Morgan were waiting by their squad car, already in protective clothing. Kate joined them and pulled out a white suit, slipping it over her running gear.

'What have we got?' she asked.

'Bad news. The victim's been identified,' said Emma. 'It's Heather Gault.'

'Oh, shit . . . *shit!*' Heather was bright, dedicated and easy to get on with. Kate had worked with her on several operations in her time and had nothing but respect for the CIO.

'Her car's in the car park. She must have been at work yesterday. I'll double-check and see what time she left,' said Morgan.

'If this is linked to Laura's death, we'll have to up our game. She's one of our own. We're going to have everyone at Trentham House on our backs.'

Emma mumbled, 'Uh-huh. Exactly what we need right now. Extra pressure.'

'It's all part of the job. We can handle it.' Kate snapped on a pair of plastic gloves. 'Who found her?'

'A couple hunting for somewhere to dump a busted sofa, spotted the container and tried their luck here.'

'Not really their lucky day. Must have been a bit of a shock. At least they had the decency to ring the police and admit what they were doing. Got their names and address?'

'Yeah, we'll talk to them later,' said Emma.

'Why was the skip here in the first place?' Kate asked.

'There's some renovation work going on at the building overlooking the car park. There isn't a front drive so the container got placed as close to it as possible.'

'Were the workmen here yesterday?'

'Don't know but we'll look into it.'

'Good. Okay. Let's go.'

Kate struggled to see beyond Heather's swollen face and remember how she'd looked before this senseless attack: flawless skin, neat nose, wide, brown eyes and perfect, bow-shaped lips, now invisible behind a mask of dried blood. Kate searched for signs to remind her of who Heather had been but could not associate this broken body, in a torn blouse, with the woman who prided herself as much on her appearance as her talent. Her eyes rested on manicured lilac nails and the silver bracelet she always wore. Her hands were delicate, unblemished and small, like a young girl's. Like Laura, thirty-one-year-old Heather was of slight build and, with her youthful looks, could have easily passed for a woman in her early-to-mid-twenties. The odds this was the work of the same attacker were beginning to stack up.

Ervin let out a noisy sigh. 'Oh, can you believe this? Heather of all people! This shouldn't have happened.'

Kate glanced up, took in the heavily creased forehead. Ervin was gregarious and, if he took a liking to you, adopted you as a friend for life. She wondered how close he had been to Heather. She didn't need to ask. He cleared his throat then said, 'I didn't have a lot of dealings with her, but I liked her. And, not long ago, she sent me a bottle of my favourite brandy as a thank you. Very thoughtful of her.'

'Yes,' said Kate, remembering the neatly written card Heather had sent her after Chris's death, expressing sorrow and offering her condolences. 'She was what I'd call a genuine person and very driven. I enjoyed working with her. I'm sure many others felt the same way. Shit, Ervin. She was always so groomed. What a horrible, undignified ending to her life, half-naked like this, discarded among rubbish. This is definitely the same MO, isn't it?' Kate asked.

'Sadly so. He's left his calling card. Give me a hand, Morgan,' said Ervin. Together they turned the body over slightly to reveal the bloodstain on the back of her blouse, under her right shoulder, and Ervin lifted the material sufficiently for Kate to see the letters, etched into her skin and smeared with blood – *MINE.*

Morgan sucked in a sharp breath. 'The sick, twisted bastard. Poor Heather. She didn't deserve this.'

'How could he leave her in this state? Look at her face!' Emma turned away, her hand over her mouth.

'You okay?' asked Kate.

'Give me a minute.'

Kate gave the nod for Ervin to lay Heather down again. She couldn't imagine what terror Heather had experienced. One thing was certain, she would have fought for her life and, in so doing, undoubtedly prolonged the suffering. She had an urge to cover her up, so her colleagues couldn't see her nakedness. 'Did he throw her clothes in the skip, like he did Laura's?'

'No. And once again, it looks like there's no handbag or phone.'

Morgan got to his feet and put a hand on Emma's arm. She turned back with a nod. Her eyes were glassy with unshed tears. She cleared her throat. 'Do you suppose this sicko took them as trophies?'

'At this stage, I'm ruling nothing out,' Kate replied.

Ervin pointed out the abrasions on her neck. 'The markings here are much like those we found on Laura.'

Kate dropped onto her haunches and examined the dark bruising. 'Emma, what do you make of this?'

Emma joined her and considered the circular bruise to the left-hand side of Heather's throat. 'Yes, probably caused by a vagus strike, although I'd like Harvey's opinion.'

'He should be here soon,' said Ervin. 'He was in the lab when I spoke to him and said he'd get here as soon as possible. So, she was most likely rendered unconscious and then attacked somewhere. The question is where? There are no obvious signs of a struggle having taken place here in this car park.'

'But surely she was jumped in this car park? Her vehicle's over there,' said Emma, pointing out a blue Audi TT.

'She obviously had a whack on the nose during the altercation and quite a nosebleed, yet there's no sign of blood droplets, not from that or from the letters carved into her. There'd be some stain-ing on the ground if the attack had happened here. I've extended the search between here and Trentham House.'

Kate wandered across to Heather's car, cupped her hands and peered through the driver's window. She couldn't spot a handbag or phone and the doors were locked. She turned at the sound of a voice. One of Ervin's team was calling him.

'Boss! We've found something outside the dentist's surgery.' Ervin set off along Newbury Avenue, pursued by Kate, Morgan and Emma. The tree-lined road of imposing Victorian houses had once been inhabited by wealthy individuals. Today, those same houses were occupied by businesses – a children's nursery, various medi-cal practices, financial consultants and an estate agency – but they came to a halt outside one embellished with an octagonal tower and covered with a steep roof: a dentist's surgery. The officer beckoned them towards a rectangular piece of lawn and a fountain, a grey stone basin inside which stood a large stone ball.

'We've found blood stains on this,' he said.

'Stay here,' said Ervin, crossing the grass and stooping to exam-ine the reddish-brown staining.

'I take it those patches of scuffed earth weren't caused by rabbits,' said Morgan. The lawn looked as if somebody had tried to rip out handfuls of grass. While an animal might have created the mess, Kate was sure the damage occurred when Heather had tried to escape her attacker. She followed the gouges towards the fountain. Ervin met her eyes.

'It looks like she might have either fallen or been pushed against this fountain base and hit her face here.'

Kate imagined the woman, struggling to free herself from her assailant, reaching out, clawing at grass. Had she broken free only to slip on dewy grass and collide with the basin?

Another voice interrupted her musings. 'Boss, we've found some clothing.'

The speaker held thick-leaved branches aside to reveal a black court shoe, lying on its side next to a pair of lace knickers.

Emma let out a soft 'Oh, shit.'

Morgan gave her a sad smile. 'We can't do any more than our job, Emma. We have to treat her the same as any other victim.'

'But she wasn't any other victim. She was one of our own. She was one of our colleagues,' she repeated.

Morgan squeezed her shoulder. 'We'll catch him, Emma.'

Kate made no comment. The fact she hadn't known Heather that well was by the by. She felt as strongly as her team about tracking down the perpetrator.

Ervin called out, 'Sorry, Kate. We need to get on. I'll be in touch as soon as we have anything for you.'

'Thanks, Ervin. Let me know if you find her mobile and bag. She'll have had them on her.' The trio traipsed back to their vehicles.

Morgan yanked off the blue overshoes. 'Why did he leave her clothing under a bush? Why not dump it in the container, along with her body, or leave it and her here?'

Kate already had a theory. 'He wanted to dump her body. Just like he dumped Laura's. It's his way of showing us he had no respect for these women. As for the clothes, I don't know. I guess he didn't care about them.'

'Fucker,' said Emma, under her breath.

'He might have been in a hurry, or concerned somebody would spot him if he returned to collect the clothing,' said Morgan.

'True,' said Kate. 'I think we can assume he took her phone and handbag. Just as he kept Laura's house keys and mobile.'

'Yeah. Bastard was trying to make it harder for us by removing anything that might identify the victims.' Morgan gave a nod in the direction of the car park. 'Heads up! DCI Chase is here.'

William, dressed in official uniform, spotted Kate and walked towards her. His face wore the expression of a seasoned detective who had seen the worst and yet was still harrowed by the cruelty in the world. For the briefest of moments, Kate felt a familiar sense of affection for the man who'd supported her throughout her career, a man who would soon be taking retirement and would spend his days with his cats and his bees. The sensation evaporated as quickly as it had surfaced.

'Heather Gault. Who'd have believed it? This is a very sad day indeed. Kate, are we dealing with the same person who attacked and killed Laura?'

'Yes. There's no doubt.'

His eyes burrowed into hers but try as she might, she couldn't find any of the usual warmth in their depths. She assumed he was extremely upset about Heather as it was unlikely he'd got wind of her private investigation into Chris's death. However, she didn't need to conjure up Chris's voice to remind her that *somebody* had known about it. And that somebody had made sure Cooper couldn't talk to her.

William gave a curt nod. 'That's all I needed to hear. Find whoever did this.'

◆ ◆ ◆

Kate attached the photograph of Heather, looking wistful, in a soft, pale pink jumper that complemented her skin tone, to the whiteboard. It was important to remember these victims were people who'd had families, ambitions, loves and hopes. Not only had Laura and Heather lost their lives, but they'd also suffered a terrifying ordeal prior to being murdered. If there'd been any doubt that Laura's death had been the result of accidental force, finding Heather had proven otherwise. Kate was certain their attacker had intended killing them. She would have spoken to Heather's parents but they lived on Guernsey, and officers on the island had been dispatched to give them the bad news. It was up to Kate and her team to track down the perpetrator and bring them to justice.

Faced with endless lists of friends, family and colleagues who needed contacting, everyone was working to full capacity. Keyboards clicked, voices filled the room reminiscent of a telemarketing bureau, as each of them pulled their weight. Kate requested the technical team sift through footage of CCTV cameras in the vicinity of Newbury Avenue, in the hope they might throw up something, although at the moment, everything they did seemed to be little more than shooting in the dark. Phone call after phone call was terminated with a quiet sigh and stabbing of buttons as yet another was made. Heather's death had increased the urgency of the investigation.

Emma put down her phone, scribbled something on a notepad and shook her head at Kate. 'Heather was working with Deepa Singh all day yesterday, and she doesn't recall seeing anybody outside when she left at around six.'

'Was she parked in the car park too?'

'No. Her husband collected her. He didn't spot anyone either.'

Jamie stopped typing and spoke loudly. 'What I don't get is how the attacker would know Heather was going to be the last to leave. What if Deepa was the intended victim?'

Kate scratched thoughtfully at an eyebrow. Had the assailant intended on attacking Deepa and been put off by the arrival of her husband? She considered the possibility of somebody observing Trentham House all day, waiting for either woman to emerge. It didn't add up. Especially when she looked at the victims. It was difficult to ignore the similarities between them and she couldn't shake off the feeling their attacker had deliberately selected them.

'I can't explain it either,' she replied. 'At the moment, I'm working on a hunch that the killer is a calculating bastard and knew Heather was at Trentham House and, also, what time she'd be clocking off.'

'But how would he know?' Jamie sounded like a persistent toddler.

Kate didn't explain she always trusted her instinct. 'He knew his victims' habits. He might even have been known to both women.' Another thought struck her – the victims' phones. She stabbed her notebook with a pencil and said in a commanding voice, 'Have we heard back from either woman's mobile provider yet?'

Morgan answered. 'Nothing yet.'

'Nothing! Why haven't you pushed them harder? Don't they know we're dealing with a double murder investigation?'

Jamie held up both hands. 'My bad. That was my job, but I got involved in other stuff and didn't chase them up.'

'Get hold of them now. Tell them it's imperative we have that information today. The answer might lie in their phone logs or text messages.'

'Will do.'

'I don't need to remind you how crucial this has become and not only because Heather was one of our own. Two deaths in two days. If I'm honest, I'm concerned he'll rape and kill again, very soon.'

Jamie spoke again. 'I've been trying to establish connections between both women, and there's one that stands out – they both worked in Stafford. Not only did they work in the same town, but Laura was at Tomkins Solicitors, which is only three streets away from Newbury Avenue. They might have known each other, drunk at the same coffee houses, visited the same shops . . . I don't know. I'm only chucking it out there as a possibility. I've looked at their social media accounts and can't see any common connections there, but they could have bumped into each other.'

Kate folded her arms and considered his theory. There was another possibility, especially given the assailant was most likely a follower of martial arts. 'Was Heather a member of any gyms or did she attend regular exercise classes? If so, check to see if Laura was a member at any point too.'

'Good call, guv,' said Jamie, noting it down.

Emma heaved a sigh. 'I can't get my head around her being killed this way. I liked her a lot. Remember when she worked on that big fraud case? She was so attentive during meetings, like a kid at school, eager to learn.'

'Yeah. I remember that. She was really energetic, like a mini tornado, whirling around the office. If you asked her to do something, she was off, getting the information before you'd finished your sentence. Nice woman. Great officer. Hey! What about cases she was working on? Maybe she ran into Laura that way,' Morgan offered.

Emma opened her mouth then shut it again with a shake of her head.

'Go on,' Kate urged.

'I was going to suggest she might have been looking into claims that Kevin was stalking Laura, but then realised Laura didn't report him.'

'Take a look at her open cases,' said Kate. 'We can't leave any stone unturned. I think we're dealing with somebody who was familiar with these women's routines or had been stalking them. This man studies their habits, and waits for an opportunity to strike. I think that tells us we're dealing with somebody known to both these women. As for Kevin, see if there's anything to connect him to Heather. We haven't discounted him as a possible suspect.'

'What about Laura's ex-boyfriend?' said Emma. 'We haven't identified him. He might have known both victims.'

'I don't see how that would work,' said Jamie, screwing up his face. 'He was going out with Laura, then dumped her cos he was jealous over some stupid Facebook posts and then, a few months later, attacked her. Nah.'

Kate was going to agree but Morgan leant across his desk, pointing a pen at Jamie. 'Hang on a sec. The guy could be unstable. If he was so freaking jealous over a bloke liking Laura's Facebook posts that he dumped her, he could also be unstable enough to attack her. And what about the message he cut into her – *MINE*. The guy's possessive. You can't dismiss the suggestion.'

Kate gave a half-nod. 'Okay, but what about Heather? He'd have to know her too.'

'Maybe he did,' offered Emma. 'If Laura was dating somebody from work, it would explain why she wouldn't tell anyone who the man was, and also why she chucked in her job soon after the relationship ended. Heather might have had contact with that same person.'

Jamie swatted her words away with a dismissive 'Nah. That's guesswork.'

Emma scowled at him. 'It's called discussing theories.'

'Whatever you call it, it isn't proper policing.' Jamie swung back to his computer screen.

They were disturbed by a knock at the door. One of the forensic officers who had accompanied Kate to Laura's house was holding up an evidence bag.

'Sorry to disturb you, ma'am. We've just found this hidden between the folds of a book at the property we searched. We weren't sure if it was significant or not.'

Kate took the bag and studied the contents: a small photograph of Laura, another woman and two men, all wearing rainbow-striped party hats and pulling faces for the camera. She passed the picture around.

'It's been taken in one of those party photo booths you can hire,' said Jamie. 'We wanted to hire one for my mum's sixtieth party but it cost a fortune. Well out of our price bracket.'

'What book did you find this in?' Kate asked the officer.

'A book of Shakespeare's sonnets, bookmarking the poem *Shall I compare thee to a summer's day?*'

'Okay. Thanks for this. It might well be useful.'

Once the officer had left, Jamie piped up. 'You think the boyfriend gave her the book, guv?'

'I was thinking along those lines, yes. And, if one of the men in this photo was her boyfriend. It would help if we could identify them.'

Emma tapped at her keyboard. 'I'm going to test out my theory and check her work colleagues.'

From where Kate sat, she could see the Tomkins Solicitors' website and various profiles of the employees. Jamie scooted into position behind Emma, who clicked the mouse over and over again, pausing at a photo of the senior partner, Geoffrey Tomkins.

'You honestly think Laura would date any of these fossils?' said Jamie.

'Don't be so ageist,' snapped Emma.

'Oh, for fuck's sake. I'm only making a perfectly reasonable point.'

'Stop!' Kate's voice was loud.

Jamie caught sight of the photo displayed on the screen. 'Fuck me!'

The picture was of a dark-haired, strong-jawed man in his late thirties. Emma read out the caption below: 'Christian Laurent, Head of Matrimonial Finance and Collaborative Law Department.'

Kate got to her feet to take a closer look. It was definitely the man in the photo booth picture. Emma continued through the profiles of the other partners, but there were no images of either the woman in the photo or the other man. 'There's only one way to find out if they were dating and that's to ask him. Jamie, find out everything you can about him, and Morgan, talk to Heather's colleagues. See if she had any dealings with Tomkins Solicitors or, more specifically, Christian.' She turned around at the sound of her name being spoken. William was at the door.

'The super wants a quick word,' he said.

'Sure.'

William vanished from sight and Kate checked her watch. It was a few minutes after midday. She steeled herself for the meeting. It would never do to show John Dickson any emotion. Given he could get a progress update from William, there had to be an alternative reason for wanting to speak to her face to face. As she bounded up the staircase, Chris's voice was loud in her ear. 'Be careful of what you give away.'

'Oh, I shall. I'll be very cautious indeed.'

CHAPTER TWELVE

A motionless silhouette, framed in light from the window, Superintendent John Dickson did not turn immediately to face her. It was probably part of his game to destabilise her, make her feel inferior or, in some way, at fault. She wouldn't buckle. He'd have to try harder than this. Kate remained with her legs planted, back straight, head lifted, waiting for him to acknowledge her presence. When he finally turned around, she was surprised to see anxiety etched across his features. His voice was gentle.

'Thank you for coming in. Please sit down.'

She took the proffered seat. This wasn't what she expected. She couldn't guess what he was up to.

He joined her, relaxed into his large chair, one leg over the other, hands draped over the leather armrests. 'We haven't chatted in quite a while, have we?'

'No, sir.'

'That's been my fault. There've been many pressing matters to deal with. Actually, I've been meaning to have a talk with you for some time.'

His soft smile didn't fool her, and hairs on the back of her neck rose like hackles. His insincerity was evident, exposed by a coldness in his eyes. She played along.

'I understand.'

'How have you been coping?'

She wasn't fazed by the odd question. He was either feigning politeness or trying to unnerve her by reminding her of what had happened when she'd suffered a major setback and breakdown in March. Since her comeback in May, she'd been doing her job well and he knew it. Her success rate spoke for itself. 'Fine, thank you, sir. No problems.'

'Now, Kate, you don't need to put on a brave face for me. It's only been four months since you uncovered the truth about Chris's death. You've been through hell this year and—'

She couldn't contain herself. 'As you know, sir, I was signed off by the psychiatrist and doctor, who both deemed me fit enough for duties. With respect, I don't see what the issue is here.'

An edge crept into his voice. 'There is no issue. I was merely ensuring you feel up to continuing with this case, especially as it has now turned into a double homicide.'

Again, she played along. 'I appreciate your concern for my well-being; however, I see no reason for me to step away from the investigation. I'm most definitely up to the challenge and fully focused on bringing the perpetrator to justice.'

'That's good to hear. In that case, I'd like to discuss the latest, tragic development.' He gave a sad shake of his head to compound his words. 'It goes without saying that this investigation is likely to attract a great deal of interest from both the public and top brass, who want it to run without a hitch. Heather was a valued CIO and her death has affected us all.'

'Yes, sir.'

The crawling sensation across her neck didn't let up. He was hesitating, pretending to tiptoe in a pre-planned direction. The tiny cough, an apparent clearing of his throat, gave it away. It was the precursor to a punchline.

'I'll be frank with you, Kate. I still have some doubts about you. I worry you are not quite as mentally capable as you make out.' He held up a palm to silence her and gave her a smile. 'I don't intend that to be construed in any cruel or derogatory way. Heaven knows you've made enormous strides and come back from a very dark place, and I applaud you for that. I should also explain at this juncture, that's also one of the reasons I've denied your requests to lead your old team. I'm sure you've felt frustrated by my decision and I want to make it clear, it was down to genuine concern for your health. I don't think you are quite ready yet. Maybe this investigation will give me a good reason to change my mind about you.'

She held her anger in check. He was not going to goad her into saying something she'd later regret. He didn't care about her. This was no more than a false act to justify him keeping her shut away in the back office, unable to further her career, or even get back to where she was before Chris was murdered. Dickson's lips were moving. She'd shut him out, mind on her own thoughts. She tuned back in.

'Even though the investigation has, due to Heather's death, become high profile, you will continue to act as lead officer.' He looked away for a moment, pinched his nostrils between finger and thumb until his nose turned white then released a lengthy sigh. 'My neck is on the line as much as yours. The chief superintendent wants results and I expect you and your team to be exemplary in every way. Make sure you don't let me down. That will be all.'

They rose at the same time, face to face, the atmosphere tense. He held her gaze for the briefest of moments, but it was long enough for her to interpret it. John Dickson hated her.

'We've got an address for Christian Laurent,' said Morgan as soon as Kate stormed back into the office. Kate snatched up her car keys.

'Come on. We're going to talk to him.'

Jamie looked up. 'Everything okay, guv? You look majorly pissed off.'

'I just want to get on top of this as quickly as possible, so make sure you find out every minute detail about this Christian Laurent and gather every bit of information possible on Heather. Send it to our email address.' She turned on her heel and marched out.

◆ ◆ ◆

The journey to Hints, a small affluent village between Lichfield and Tamworth, was mostly quiet. Morgan spent the majority of the time checking his mobile for emails and reading out any useful information regarding Christian Laurent.

'He was born in Lichfield in 1981. Married his partner, Sophie, eight years ago. They have a ten-year-old boy. Worked for a solicitor's firm in Lichfield until 2019, then took up a position at Tomkins Solicitors in Stafford, and moved to Hints in the same year.'

Her mobile interrupted his monologue. Emma's name flashed up on the car display. She hit the speakerphone button on her steering wheel.

'Go ahead, Emma.'

'Heather's mobile provider has finally stumped up the information we requested. I've not had long to go through the list of numbers called, but a pay-as-you-go phone rang her, the morning before she died. I flagged it because there were a few calls between the two phones during August and it was also the last number Heather rang, about an hour before she left Trentham House. I'll message the number across to you. I'm about to chase up Laura

Dean's phone provider again. They're dragging their heels. Some crap about being short-staffed.'

'Okay. Thanks for the update.'

They pulled onto a large roundabout.

'Not far now. You need to get into that lane,' said Morgan, pointing out the road markings.

'You know your way around here?'

'Not really, but there's a Michelin-starred restaurant at Hints.'

Kate snickered and apologised. 'Sorry, it's the idea of you eating in a Michelin-starred restaurant.'

'Yeah, I know. Not my usual pint and a curry night out. I went under protest. An ex-girlfriend's parents invited us both there to celebrate her birthday. I made a total dick of myself, didn't eat with the correct knife, swigged the red wine like it was lemonade. In my defence, I *was* nervous as hell. Anyway, we split up a few weeks afterwards. Not because of the meal,' he added.

'Her loss.' The comment earned her a smile.

Hints initially appeared to be a one-street village, with properties set back from what had been the main A5 route until a dual carriageway bypassed the place. The other side of the road consisted of nothing but vast fields, used for cultivating strawberries. Turning onto School Lane, they found themselves travelling alongside stone walls, steeped banks and tall, thin trees lining the narrow thoroughfare, their shadows darkening the way. The route twisted past farms and grand properties with stable blocks, paddocks and lengthy approaches. They crossed over an ancient hump-back bridge and descended into the heart of the village. Morgan let out a low whistle.

'Look at that house. Tasty! These places must cost at least a couple of million each.'

'Uh-huh. I guess so.' Wealth didn't impress Kate. She'd come from humble beginnings. Hers was a modern, two-bedroomed

127

detached property, simple in design, but homely. It couldn't compare to the grand designs along this road but she'd never hankered after bigger or swankier. All she'd ever wanted was somewhere for her and Chris: a house that would one day become a family home.

'This is it! Oh my freaking days, look at this pad!'

An architect-designed, bold, two-storey structure came into view. Although it was in the shape of a traditional house, that was where all similarity ended. It was as if the entire building had been chopped in two, with one half pushed back a metre before being reattached to its twin, so it didn't realign correctly. The roofs were offset and the entire frontage, top to bottom glass, was interspersed with metal panels. An attached, single-storey wing, which appeared to also serve as the entrance, was set at an adjacent angle in between each half.

'Is this some sort of squashed gravel?' asked Morgan. The minuscule, pale grey stones, the length of the driveway, resembled polished marble.

'No idea. But whatever it is, there isn't a weed in sight,' she replied with little interest. Morgan might be blown away by the weird, glassy drive and the identical squares of lawn, interspersed with more squares, alternately filled with late-flowering red and white roses, yet there was something lacking in this picture-perfect set-up.

'I'd love a gaff like this. It'll have cost a fortune.'

'He's a lawyer. Probably pulls in a decent salary each year.'

'It's like the glass pyramid outside the Louvre, except not a pyramid, only glass: stylish, tasteful. Really *out there*. You know what I mean?'

'I get the idea. You like it. A lot.'

He gave her a sheepish grin. 'My bad. I don't normally get carried away. This is kind of my dream house. Modern. Different. Okay. I'll stop. I'm over it now. So over it.'

'You sure?'

'Sure.' He flicked her a smile again. 'Might need to check out the bathroom though and go for a wander around while we're here . . . you know? To gather inspiration for my own future-build.'

'I really hope you're kidding me.'

'Course I am.'

He got out and Kate quickly checked her phone, saw Emma had sent the phone number as promised, then jumped out to join him at the front door.

'There's no doorbell,' he said.

'Knock. Gently. In case you smash the glass.'

'As if.' All the same he curled his mitt before tapping it against the door.

A figure appeared, a mobile pressed to his ear. He frowned at the visitors then opened up, speaking to the person on the other end of the phone. 'I have to go. Something's cropped up. Catch you later.' He ended the call and looked from Morgan to Kate. 'Can I help you?'

They raised IDs in unison. 'Mr Laurent?'

'Yes.'

'I'm DS Morgan Meredith and this is DI Kate Young. We're from Stoke-on-Trent Constabulary. Would it be possible for us to come inside?'

'Not until you tell me what this is about.' His eyes narrowed, lips compressing slightly.

'Laura Dean.'

'Why?'

'I'm sorry to tell you she's dead, sir.'

'Oh. Oh, my Lord! That's terrible news.'

'Would you mind if we came in and asked you a few questions?'

'What about?'

'We'll discuss that inside,' said Kate.

'Erm. Okay. I guess so, but I don't know how much help I can be. I haven't seen her in a long time.'

They followed him into what seemed to be a cross between a conservatory/living room and a botanical garden with wide-leafed cheese plants and potted exotic palms in huge grey pots, and an ornate cage where two yellow parakeets fluttered from perch to perch.

Christian offered them seats on a curved rattan sofa with duck-egg blue cushions and chose a matching hanging chair for himself. He dropped into it with practised ease. 'I'm truly sorry to hear about Laura. What happened? An accident?'

Morgan replied, 'She was attacked on Friday evening.'

He rested his hand against his throat. Kate, trained in body language, noted the automatic and involuntary gesture of vulnerability. Christian was anxious about saying the right thing. 'That's truly dreadful. And how can I be of assistance to you?'

Morgan continued with the questions, allowing Kate to observe mannerisms. 'Firstly, can you describe your relationship with Laura, sir?'

'As you probably know, she was a legal assistant at the practice where I work.'

'Would you say you had a purely professional relationship with her, then?'

'Yes. Yes, I would say that.'

'Purely professional,' Morgan repeated.

Christian rubbed his chin, backwards and forwards a couple of times before dropping his hand to his lap. With his large presence and stony gaze, Morgan was the right person to press him on the matter.

'Sir, we need you to be open with us. If you were involved in more than a working relationship, we really need to know: to eliminate you from our enquiries. Do you understand?'

He nodded once, then twice more. 'Yes, I understand. We might have met up a couple of times outside work.'

'As work colleagues?'

'We were most certainly colleagues. Nothing more.'

Morgan stared in silence at the man.

'I haven't seen Laura since the day she handed in her notice, or been in contact with her.'

Morgan handed across the photo booth picture. 'Could you explain this, then?'

He gave a weary smile. 'It was taken at a party, last summer. All the guests were invited to have their pictures taken.'

'And you chose to go into the booth with Laura. Why her in particular?'

'I went in with loads of people, not only her. My wife and I were hosting the party. I reckon I had my picture taken with almost every guest.'

'The thing is, Laura kept this picture in a book of love poems. It obviously meant something to her.'

When Christian didn't respond, Morgan pressed on with 'Were you in a relationship with her?'

'No.'

'Yet she hung on to this photo for some reason.'

He levelled his gaze at Morgan. 'Probably because of my sister, Ilsa. That's her in the picture.'

'Are you saying they were in a relationship?'

Christian looked away. 'I don't see what business it is of yours.'

'Let me remind you, we're conducting a murder enquiry. Everything we ask is relevant, so I suggest you assist us.'

'I've told you what you need to know.'

'Would you please confirm that Ilsa and Laura were in a relationship, sir?' asked Morgan.

Christian sighed. 'What Ilsa gets up to is her business, not mine.'

Kate interrupted. 'Do you get along with your sister?'

'Again, I fail to see the significance of your question and I have nothing further to say on the matter. I know nothing about the attack on Laura. So, if you have no further questions, would you mind leaving. I'm rather busy.'

'Do you know why they broke up?' Morgan opened his notebook, scribbled a note then looked up, waiting for a response. Christian watched the parakeets bouncing from branch to branch.

'Sir.'

He dragged his gaze away from the birds. 'Ilsa's always breaking some poor cow's heart. She sets her sights on someone, charms them and then dumps them. For what it's worth, I don't approve of her methods and Laura didn't deserve to be treated so badly. She was far more sensitive than some of my sister's other flings. That's all I'm prepared to say about the matter. If you want all the details, you'll have to talk to Ilsa. As usual, I kept out of it. I find that's often the best way to behave as far as she is concerned.'

Morgan lifted his pencil in readiness and requested contact details for Ilsa Laurent. Once written down, he glanced at Kate, a signal for her to ask anything she had on her mind.

'Mr Laurent, did Laura contact you after she left Tomkins Solicitors?'

'No.'

'Did she talk to you about Ilsa at work, during the time they were together, or after the break-up?'

'Never.' Although his response sounded assertive, he glanced down as he spoke.

'Even though Ilsa is your sister? Surely, you must have at least exchanged pleasantries from time to time, or even met them both at social events, other than the party where you had your photo taken with them both.' Kate gave a half-smile, enough to cause his hand to raise again to his throat. He was anxious about this line of questioning. 'Well?'

'No. I've already explained that I didn't want to get involved in my sister's love life.'

'So, there weren't any moments when the two of you were alone in the office and chatted about Ilsa?'

A frostiness crept into his voice. 'We didn't hang out around the water cooler, shooting the breeze, or discussing her love life, if that is what you wanted to know. She was an efficient legal secretary and pleasant to work with.'

'You liked her?'

'Yes. I liked her, but not in any romantic sense. She was . . . fragile and I felt slightly responsible for her dismay.'

'Why?'

'If I hadn't been stuck in a meeting when Ilsa came to visit me, she wouldn't have had time to get so friendly with Laura and chat her up.'

The way he spoke gave rise to a fresh notion and Kate hesitated a moment before speaking again. 'Sir, can I ask you, were you jealous of your sister's relationship with Laura?'

He spluttered loudly, an exaggerated, guttural explosion that gave Kate the answer. 'What a preposterous suggestion. Why on earth would I be jealous?'

Kate allowed the smile to remain on her face. 'Very good, sir.'

Morgan made a show of writing something down in his notebook and snapping it shut before saying, 'We will need to establish your whereabouts on Friday evening. If you wouldn't mind providing us with that information, purely for elimination purposes.'

'Oh, for crying out loud! You can't imagine I was responsible for the attack.'

'As I said, sir, it's for elimination purposes.'

He threw his head back and spoke in a monotone to the ceiling. 'I was working late and left the office sometime between eight thirty and nine o'clock. On my way home, I stopped off at the Red Lion at Hopwas, to attend the celebrations for Geoffrey Tomkins' birthday. Several of my colleagues who were already there at the time will vouch for me. My wife will be able to verify that I returned around eleven.'

'Can anyone confirm you were in the office at that time you say you were there?'

'No. Everyone else went to the pub. I was held up, working on a difficult brief.'

'I see,' said Morgan. 'If you don't mind, we'd like to take a quick DNA sample from you.'

'Whatever for?'

'Again, it's for elimination purposes.'

'No. Absolutely not. Now, if you'll excuse me, I have to get on.'

'I've one more question,' said Morgan.

'Make it snappy.'

He flicked through some images on his phone, stopping at one of Heather, before handing the device to Christian. 'Do you know this woman?'

He glanced at it and shook his head. 'No.'

'Take a good look, sir. Her name is Heather Gault.'

He stared for a moment longer before passing it back. 'I don't recall ever seeing her.' He jumped to his feet, sending the parakeets fluttering again. Kate placed a business card on the table.

'This is my number in case anything comes to mind. Tell me, sir, are you a member of any clubs or gyms?'

'No. I have a personal trainer who visits here twice a week. He puts me through my paces.'

'Resistance training and running?'

He shook his head. 'Mostly circuit training and sparring.'

'Boxing?'

'Yes. I find it helps relieve stress.'

'Have you ever practised any martial arts?'

'I did a bit of kick-boxing a few years ago. I really don't see the relevance of—'

Kate didn't let him finish. 'And, do you recognise this phone number?'

She showed him the pay-as-you-go number Heather had been calling.

He shook his head.

'And what about last night? Where were you?'

'Last night? I was at the office.'

'Again?'

'Yes. *Again*. I have a demanding job.'

'What time did you leave?'

'Why?'

'Could you answer the question, please?'

He sighed. 'About a quarter past eight. My wife was expecting me home at eight and I was a little late.'

'Was anyone else working at the office at the time?'

'No.'

'And do you usually work on a Saturday?'

'Yes, if I have a lot of work to catch up with, and yesterday was one of those days.'

'Thank you.'

'Right.' He stared at Morgan, who took his time in rising from the sofa and stood in front of him, towering over the man.

'Thank you for your time, Mr Laurent. We might need to talk to you again.'

'I'd appreciate it if you rang me first to arrange a time.'

'We'll try to remember that, sir.'

CHAPTER THIRTEEN

Ilsa's studio flat was capacious and well designed. She'd maximised the space by leaving it uncluttered. The hob over which hung a steel hood looked like it had barely been used and all kitchen equipment was out of sight, hidden away in cupboards, so not even a canister of coffee or a mug were on display.

Kate perched on the edge of a round swivel chair with a half-moon back and thick cushioned arms. It was more a sofa than a chair and easily capable of accommodating two people, as long as one of those people wasn't Morgan, who'd opted for a bright green plastic chair that matched the bed throw and cushions that jazzed up the grey furniture. Ilsa Laurent sat cross-legged on her bed, a box of tissues in front of her. Devoid of make-up, her skin was blotchy and her eyes sparkled with tears. Sitting in a vest and wide-legged lounge pants, she displayed lean, muscular arms bearing various yoga-inspired tattoos: a moon, lotus flower, the OM symbol and the chakras. She lifted her chin. 'I'm actually lost for words. Poor Laura.'

She reached for the tissues once more and blew her nose. 'Sorry. This has been quite a shock.'

'I understand and I'm sorry to give you such bad news. Do you feel able to answer a few questions about Laura, now?'

'Sure. Whatever I can do to help.'

'I'd like to start with your relationship. Why did it come to end?'

Ilsa's voice was light and gentle. 'It was on me. I'm not very good at long-term relationships. They always seem to go the same way. I start off thinking "This is the one", and then I realise it isn't. Laura wasn't what I was looking for. I thought she was, but she wasn't.' She glanced at the copy of *Shakespeare's Sonnets* resting on Kate's lap. She'd already admitted having gifted it to Laura. 'It's so sad that she kept that book and the photo. I thought she'd get over me, just like I did her, yet all the time, she was hanging on to a reminder of the past and us. Terribly sad.'

'We were told that you split up over some misunderstanding on Facebook. There was an ex-schoolfriend who kept liking Laura's posts.'

'Oh, yes. I remember. Kevin. He was a pest. A bit of a Facebook stalker. I don't know why she couldn't see him for what he was. Then, I happened to be passing a café and spotted them sitting together and saw how he looked at her. I waited until she came home and explained that he was interested in her. *Properly* interested in her. I told her she ought to stop pandering to him and we argued. She thought I was being unreasonable when I was only concerned about her. She couldn't see that and things got out of hand. Next thing, she was in tears because she was reminded of her parents who would argue and then she became highly emotional, crying and blurting out all sorts of stupid shit about how much she loved me, that she couldn't live without me and couldn't bear it when we argued. She was so . . . needy, it turned my stomach and in that moment, I had an epiphany – she wasn't the one for me. She begged me to tell her I loved her and I'm sorry to say I did exactly the opposite. I was so pissed off by her attitude, I said some things I'm now ashamed of. Once spoken, you can't take back the things you say, can you? I hurt her and, at the time, I didn't care.

I just wanted to get out of the relationship before it suffocated me and so I left.'

'Did you see her again?'

'A few times, but each time we met up it was a disaster. She acted bizarrely: crazy, desperate, to the point when I knew I couldn't face even seeing her. I told her it was definitely over, and that it was my fault that we'd rushed into a relationship. She persisted in ringing me until I blocked her number and she finally got the message. I didn't hear from her again.'

'When was the last time you had any contact with her?'

'Late November, last year.'

'You didn't know she'd left the law firm in February?'

'As it happens, I did. My brother mentioned she'd quit. He wasn't happy with me. He thought it was my fault she'd gone.'

'Did he get on with Laura?'

'Oh, yes. Thought the sun shone out of her arse. He certainly wasn't pleased when I started seeing her. He warned me off, but I never listen to him.'

'Why did he warn you off?'

'He knows what I'm like about relationships . . . and thoroughly disapproves of my behaviour.' She scowled for an instant. 'It's not as if I deliberately set about sabotaging them. I simply seem to have no luck in them.'

'Did he warn you off other women?'

'No, only Laura.'

'Have you any thoughts as to why?'

'Why do you think? He had a thing for her.'

'You're saying he fancied her?'

Ilsa gave a knowing smile. 'Yes. I would say he fancied her. She was exactly his type – quiet, submissive and innocent. Nevertheless, Laura was *my* girlfriend, not his, and his interest in her wasn't reciprocated.'

'Are you sure?'

'Completely. Laura wasn't able to form relationships with men. She found them . . . too challenging.'

'Yet she was friends with Kevin Shire.'

'He was an exception. Have you met him? He's . . . unthreatening and, quite frankly, completely wet.'

'Apart from Kevin, she wasn't friends with any other men?'

'No. She didn't have many friends, male or female. There was her old schoolfriend, the nurse. I've forgotten her name.'

'Alicia?'

'That's her. Laura used to meet up with her, once or twice a week.'

'But you never tagged along?'

Ilsa let out a low laugh. 'No. Laura was too embarrassed to let on about our relationship. She'd never come out about being a lesbian, and the prospect of doing so terrified her. That was one of the reasons I knew it couldn't work between us. I don't believe in hiding my sexuality. It's nothing to be ashamed of.'

'What about work colleagues? Was she friends with any of them?'

Ilsa shook her head. 'She got along with them, but didn't socialise.'

'Can you think of anybody who'd wish her any harm?'

'Nobody at all.'

'What about her father and his partner? Did she speak about either of them?'

'Rarely. I suggested we visited them together, but she wouldn't hear of it. She was convinced Steve hated her. It was mutual, by the way. She convinced herself Steve had been having a relationship with her father all the while he was married to her mother, and that Steve even helped kill her. It was ludicrous, of course. Her mum was really unlucky and got cancer. The trouble was, Laura couldn't come to terms with the fact that shit like that happens. And she simply couldn't accept her dad had, and that he'd moved on.'

She stared at the tissue, twisted it between her fingers and tiny fragments, like minuscule snowflakes, sprinkled onto her lap and she let out a shuddering sigh. 'I should have been kinder. If I'd let her down more gently, then maybe she wouldn't have moved away and this wouldn't have happened.'

◆ ◆ ◆

A further fifteen minutes with Ilsa produced nothing new to assist them with their investigation. She was completely in the dark about Laura's shoplifting episode and depression and, like Christian and other work colleagues, was unaware she'd moved to Abbots Bromley. Laura had been erased from all their lives, leaving Kate wondering how many people the woman had really been able to count upon as friends. Other than Alicia, she'd made little impact on any of them, and Kate found that saddening. Morgan was still processing what they'd heard, his face set. 'What do you make of them both?' asked Kate.

'Christian was twitchy and not because I was death-staring him. He's a lawyer, he should be used to pressure, yet he definitely seemed nervous to me.'

'I picked up on a couple of gestures: rubbing his neck, not fully focusing on you when you asked certain questions. Of course, he might have felt intimidated, so we shouldn't read too much into it. In light of what his sister just told us, I'd guess he had a crush on Laura, which might also explain his nervousness.'

'I think there's more to it.'

'I'm not sure. He didn't know Heather, and so what if he liked Laura? Ilsa said it wasn't reciprocated.'

'Exactly! Maybe he was incredibly frustrated that she wasn't into him. What if his feelings ran deeper than just fancying her? And if he was jealous enough, he might have attacked her.'

Kate wrinkled her nose and considered his theory. It wasn't too far-fetched. Morgan was talking eagerly now.

'It takes, what, around thirty minutes to travel from Abbots Bromley to the Red Lion at Hopwas? He has no solid alibi to confirm he was actually at the office, so it'd be possible to place him in Abbots Bromley around the time of Laura's murder instead. It would give him ample time to commit the crime and still reach the pub to meet his colleagues after nine o'clock. Same for Saturday evening. His office is within walking distance of Trentham House.'

'But that still doesn't explain Heather.'

Morgan gave a shrug. 'Who's to say he didn't fancy her too?'

'We're still looking into Kevin. We've already got grounds to suspect . . .' She shook her head. 'No, you're right. We should check out Christian's movements. Get the tech team to pull any CCTV or surveillance footage in the vicinity of his office. See if you can spot either him or his car, around the times he claimed he left work.'

Morgan gave a low grunt of acceptance then added, 'I got the impression he recognised Heather from the photo. He was too quick to dismiss it. I'm going to do some more digging on him.'

'That's what I like to hear – dedication.' She glanced at her watch. It was coming up to four o'clock.

'Don't forget you have to talk to Cooper's daughter too. Time's ticking, Kate.' She was startled by the voice in her head. In the last few hours, she'd barely given Chris a thought.

She turned to Morgan. 'There's a petrol station up the road. Would you stick fifty pounds of fuel in the car for me, while I grab us coffee and snacks?' While she was inside, she'd ring to see how the girl was doing, maybe even arrange to visit her later today. Losing Cooper was a blow, especially as there was no one else she could ask about the murder at the club. Farai wouldn't talk to her again. Sierra really was her last hope.

'No probs. Could you get me a cappuccino?'

'Sure. And do you want a chocolate leaf or a heart motif on top, or maybe a unicorn?'

His shoulders rocked with silent mirth. 'A frothy white with sugar will do nicely. No design.'

They drew up beside a petrol pump and Kate leapt out, leaving Morgan to fumble with the disposable pump gloves and filler cap. She headed across to the coffee machine and selected a white coffee and as the machine whirred and spluttered into life, she rang Sierra.

'Hello?'

'Sierra, it's Kate.'

'You heard about Dad?'

'I'm so sorry. How are you? Have you got somebody with you?'

'A friend. I'm . . . numb. I don't believe for one second he killed himself. He was prepared to serve his sentence. I only saw him the other day and he wasn't depressed. If he'd even been thinking about . . . I'd have known. And . . . what about me? He wouldn't do something like this without leaving me a note or saying goodbye.' A note of hysteria had crept into her voice.

'I'd like to come and see you. We can talk things through.'

'You don't believe it either, do you? Can you find out what really happened to him?'

'I don't know—'

'But he wouldn't take his own life. He wouldn't!'

'We can discuss this later.'

'Yeah. Okay. When?'

'I can't say exactly what time. As soon as I can get away.'

'Fine. I'll be here.'

'See you later.'

There was a hiss of steam from the coffee machine and foam erupted over the sides of the paper cup; spume like bubbling lava oozed down the sides. She cursed, snatched up the cup and wiped down the sides with a thin serviette before ramming on a lid. She placed another cup in position, pressed the espresso button and, while it filled, grabbed a selection of chocolate bars off the shelves by the window. From there, she observed Morgan shaking the last drops of petrol from the nozzle before returning the dispenser to its position. She beetled back to the coffee machine to collect the coffees and settled the bill. For the time being, she set aside thoughts of Sierra and Cooper and hastened back to join Morgan.

CHAPTER FOURTEEN

Kate drained the cup of cold coffee she'd purchased at the petrol station, and cast about the office.

'Right, folks, what have we got?'

Emma was quick to respond. 'Deepa Singh rang us. She's given some thought about what happened yesterday and not only did Heather check her mobile several times prior to leaving, as if expecting a message, she also headed to the washroom before she left and reapplied lipstick. Deepa didn't think much of it at the time, but now wonders if Heather had arranged a meeting with somebody.'

'Boyfriend?'

'If so, Heather didn't mention him.'

Kate nodded. It deserved looking into. Emma continued.

'As far as she knew, Heather had no dealings with Tomkins Solicitors or Christian and there were no open cases that might indicate any connection between the two victims. At the time of Laura's shoplifting incident, Heather was working on a different case. She didn't recognise the pay-as-you-go number, but she did give me a possible lead. In July, Heather was assigned a case involving a local man who'd been threatening his ex-boss. She found evidence on CCTV he'd been on the premises around the time of an arson attack. I think she had some trouble with him and was going to look into it.'

'Okay. Good work. Any idea when we'll be able to get our hands on Heather's computer?'

'It's being sent to the techies. The big cheese wouldn't let it come directly to us.' The big cheese, in this case, was Dickson.

'Were you given any reason as to why it had to go to the lab?'

'Something about not wanting crossover of information.'

Kate didn't understand the logic. She wasn't interested in every case Heather had been investigating, only if she'd contacted either Laura, Kevin or even Christian. The fact that Dickson appeared to be making life as difficult as possible for her, even though he'd demanded results, only served to make her further suspect his motives. Was he deliberately setting her up for a fall so he could have her demoted or transferred, out of his life? She'd tackle him face to face about it at the earliest opportunity.

Bloody Dickson.

She tried not to let her irritation show. 'Any fresh thoughts or information?'

Jamie slumped in his seat, stared at the half-eaten bar of fruit and nut chocolate in his hand. 'I can't get hold of any of Christian's workmates. No idea where the hell they all are, but none of them are answering their phones.'

'Maybe they turn them off on Sundays to spend quality time with their families,' said Emma.

Jamie made a harrumphing sound. 'Quality time with families. That would be nice.'

Kate let him gripe. He'd been expecting to spend the day with his pregnant wife and kid. That was the problem with the job – it ate into weekends and encroached on family life. At least she and Chris had been able to work around their anti-social work hours and snatch some time together. 'Try them again tomorrow when they're back behind their desks. Emma, have you uncovered anything that might give us a clue as to who owns that pay-as-you-go phone used to contact Heather?'

Emma shook her head. 'She used WhatsApp messaging so we're stuffed for the time being until the tech team can help us out.'

'There must be some other way of finding out what was going on. Heather was clearly involved with somebody – lipstick, meeting and a pay-as-you-go phone,' said Morgan.

'I think the phone belongs to a married bloke,' said Jamie. 'That would explain why he's using a burner. Doesn't want his missus to find out. It could even be Christian.'

'She needn't have been seeing a man,' said Emma. 'Laura was involved with Ilsa.'

Jamie's brows drew together. 'You think Heather was seeing Ilsa too?'

'No, I didn't mean that,' Emma said. 'Simply saying it's possible Heather wasn't necessarily seeing a man.'

Kate didn't add to the speculation. The only way to establish the truth was through facts and evidence. She broke in with 'Whoever it is, we still need to identify them. Jamie, what about CCTV footage?'

'I came across the same problem as Emma. Couldn't get anyone to look into it yet. The tech team is always short-staffed on a Sunday.'

'Okay. What about the gyms and clubs? Did you check to see if either of them had joined one?'

'I did, and the answer is no. Heather didn't have any memberships to any local gyms in Stafford or Longdon, where she lives, but she was into horse riding. She has a horse stabled nearby at Blackfields.'

'Right. Thanks, Jamie. What about Laura's phone records? Did they reveal any contact with Christian?'

Emma answered. 'There were only a couple of brief calls and a message to do with a meet-up with them all, sent late August. Nothing afterwards.'

'Was there no other unusual activity on her phone?'

'Nothing I could spot. I emailed a copy to Felicity and asked if she could spare a few minutes to check it over.'

Felicity Jolly was head of the technical department, a fifty-seven-year-old gamer with a wicked sense of humour and a passion for technology. Kate always felt comfortable around Felicity, but the technician rarely socialised, other than with her partner, Bev, so Kate only saw her at work. She fumbled with her cup, picking at the cardboard edges, ripping it away. They had so little to go on and so much to prove. She was clutching at straws with an idea that had begun percolating after leaving the petrol station. 'How much do we know about Richard Dean's partner, Steve Rushmore? Have we done any background checks on him?'

Morgan grunted. 'No, but I suppose we should. There was some animosity between him and Laura.'

'Shall I leave that with you?'

'Yep. On it.'

An email alert sounded on Emma's computer and she glanced at the subject title. 'The pathologist's report for Laura is in.'

'At last. I'll take a look at it,' said Kate. She abandoned her frayed cup and shifted into position behind her own monitor. 'It's a bastard we haven't a damn thing to link Laura and Heather to either Christian or Kevin.'

'Or to *Ilsa*,' said Jamie. He pointed his chocolate bar at Kate. 'We haven't seriously considered that possibility either. Want me to dive in and check it out?'

'Go ahead.' She opened the attachment and read the report, heart sinking as she did so. The attack had been more brutal than they'd imagined with Laura sustaining serious internal injuries. The vagus strike hadn't killed her, merely knocked her out, and she'd regained consciousness during the rape and the ordeal of having letters cut into her flesh, before being strangled to death. Harvey hadn't been able to identify what had been used to cut her, only that it appeared to be a thin sharp blade, possibly belonging to a knife or even a thin-headed screwdriver. Kate closed her eyes. The poor girl must have been terrified. Tilly's face danced before her shut lids. At least her stepsister's life had been spared. Laura's fate had been sealed from the start.

◆ ◆ ◆

By five thirty, Kate decided to leave them to it. She needed to speak to Sierra, and the team could manage without her. With instructions to ring her should they unearth anything significant, she headed to Uttoxeter.

Driving the familiar route to a town where she'd once lived conjured up further memories of Tilly and Daniel. It was late, but she wanted to visit her stepsister after her meeting with Sierra. Tilly had offered an olive branch and they needed some time together, even if it was only a snatched hour. Kate couldn't let Tilly go back without making an effort to rekindle what they'd once had. She dialled Tilly's number and was greeted with a cheerful 'Kate! I didn't expect to hear from you. How's the investigation?'

'Not going brilliantly.'

'That's a shame. I expect that means we won't make the theme park for a few days.'

She could hear Daniel asking if it was Auntie Kate on the phone. Her heart melted. 'I'll try to juggle my schedule so we manage a couple of hours or even half a day together.'

'That would be wonderful.'

'I can drop by for a quick drink in an hour or so, if you like.'

'I'd love that. Have you eaten?'

'Not yet.'

'I'll order takeaway pizzas.'

'Won't it be too late?'

'Not at all. Daniel, would you like pizza for supper?'

She heard a cheer in the background. 'I've got to interview somebody in Uttoxeter before I can come to you. I'll give you a quick call when I set off.'

'Super. See you in a while.'

The market town of Uttoxeter, rich in history and famed for its racecourse, had always felt a little too sleepy to Kate. In spite of all the redevelopment that had taken place since she'd left, it still maintained a uniqueness, a hint of a bygone era, evident in the proliferation of buildings, domestic architecture and layout. Streets and alleyways led to the historic Market Place, site of a war memorial and a monument to Samuel Johnson, who'd paid penance by standing bare-headed in the pouring rain here for refusing to man his sick father's book stall.

Kate wasn't interested in the past. Her father, however, had been and, whenever he'd accompanied his daughter out and about, had insisted on providing an interesting fact about the place. This was the only one she could recall.

She circumnavigated the pedestrianised centre of town, passing a supermarket that stood on land which had, when she'd lived there, belonged to the weekly livestock market, drawing in farmers from all over the county. Sierra's home was one of the numerous houses built on this vast area. Kate found a vacant spot on the roadside, parked up and headed on foot to number 112, a very different abode to the one Sierra had shared with her father, prior to his prison sentence. This was a simple plain-fronted terrace house with a tiny front garden and blinds at the windows. It had nothing to make it stand out from the others, which, Kate mused, was probably why Sierra had chosen it.

Although she'd spoken to Sierra on the phone, she hadn't seen her in several months and was shocked to see the pinch-cheeked twenty-year-old with dark trenches under her eyes who opened the door. Her voice was a mere whisper. 'Thanks for coming.'

Kate followed her into a kitchen where a cat was curled asleep on one of the two blue wooden chairs under the table, furniture that hadn't come out of their old house. This place was ultra-modern with the new construction smell, a combination of the entire mixture of chemicals, volatile organic compounds, evaporating from new paints, sealants, flooring, wood and the other building materials used in the construction of the place. There was nothing here Kate recalled seeing in their home in Abbots Bromley; even the mugs on a rack appeared to have been recently purchased. She assumed everything had been left behind, along with the bad memories associated with the place.

Sierra offered Kate a drink. 'No, thanks, I've already overdosed on caffeine today. I wanted to see how you were doing?'

'Pretty shit, really. I'd accepted Dad was going to be away for a while, but for this to happen!' Cooper being sent to prison had taken its toll on his daughter. Yet Kate saw the same fierceness in Sierra's face she had seen in Cooper's own. 'He didn't kill himself, Kate. He got on fine with the other inmates, even helped some of them to get fitter, taught them some self-defence. And he was certain he'd be released early for good behaviour. He had no reason to top himself. Dad wouldn't do that.'

'For what it's worth, I don't think he did, either.'

Sierra slapped her mug down onto the top. 'Then prove it. Do something about it. Make whoever did this to him pay!'

'It's not as simple as that. My hands are tied. The prison will handle everything and I don't have anyone on the inside I can turn to for help.'

'Somebody wanted him dead and I want to know who and why.'

'I'll figure out a way. But first, have you any idea what he wanted to speak to me about?'

'No.'

'Okay. Tell me, word for word, what he told you to say to me?'

Sierra half-shut her eyes then spoke. '"Get hold of DI Young. Tell her I must speak to her alone. It's urgent. She needs to know."'

'Needs to know what?'

'That's all he said.'

'What had you been talking about beforehand?'

'This house and how he was looking forward to seeing it, and how proud he was of me for sorting everything out back home for him.' Her eyes leaked tears as she spoke.

'Did he hint at or mention anyone or anything he was anxious about?'

'No.'

'Are you sure he didn't say anything else? Take your time and think about it. You see, somebody might have overheard you both, and whatever your dad knew might have cost him his life.'

The tears continued unchecked down the girl's cheeks. The cat slowly unfurled with a small yawn, a tiny pink tongue and sharp white teeth on display. It regarded Kate with wary eyes. 'Maybe. I can't be sure.'

'Go on, Sierra. It could be important.'

'It was as I was leaving. I might be wrong though.'

'What was it?'

'I think he said something about you, or maybe it was me, being careful and mentioned a train. At the time, everyone was getting ready to leave and there was a lot of noise so I might have misheard him. Or, it could have been somebody else speaking and not him at all.'

Kate met the cat's eyes, heart thudding. Sierra *had* heard her father speaking. He'd been wanting to talk about the gun attack on the train. Kate would have to uncover the truth behind Cooper's death because it would lead to answers that might implicate Dickson.

Sierra put down the mug, folded her arms. 'What should I do?'

The only option was for Sierra to have her father's body examined by another pathologist and to lobby for it to be sent to the morgue at Stoke-on-Trent, where someone not linked to the prison would examine it. Maybe Kate could even involve Harvey Fuller.

'The best way to go about it is for you to contact the prison and demand a second, independent autopsy.'

'What happens if they refuse?'

'You need support, somebody who might know a lawyer or something about the law, or people in high places.' An idea popped into her head. 'What about your father's friend, Bradley Chapman?' Kate had met and interviewed Bradley several times during the investigation into his son-in-law's death. He'd served with Cooper in the SAS, and they'd remained friends after leaving the armed forces.

A spark appeared in Sierra's eyes. She nodded slowly. 'Yes. He knows loads of important people.'

'Ring him. Tell him what you suspect, and ask for his help. He most likely has his own suspicions about your father's death; after all, they were best friends.'

Sierra picked up her mobile straight away, made the call and spoke to Bradley's wife before shaking her head. 'He's out. Should be back in half an hour.'

Kate looked at her watch. She couldn't wait around here. Tilly was expecting her. 'Okay, call me after you've spoken to him and we'll take it from there.' She hesitated for a moment. Bradley might not take kindly to her involvement; after all, she'd put a great deal of pressure on him during the investigation into his son-in-law's death. He might refuse to help if he found out she was involved. 'Don't mention me. It's better if we keep that between ourselves for the time being.'

Sierra gripped the mobile tightly and nodded. 'I'm sure he'll help. He has to.'

Kate mentally crossed her fingers that Bradley would have the clout needed to ensure a second autopsy took place. It would be the only chance they'd get to determine what really happened to Cooper.

Tilly flung her arms around Kate as if she hadn't seen her in years.

'Kate!' Daniel was equally pleased and waved a triangular slice at her in delight. 'Mummy got pizza.'

'He couldn't wait. Sorry.'

'That's fine. It's quite late to eat, isn't it? I bet he was starving.'

'Yes. He wasn't hungry earlier. Our body clocks are still all over the place. I was trying to keep him up later than usual, in the hope he'll sleep through the night and we can have a fairly normal day tomorrow.'

'So, is it a good pizza, mate?'

'Brilliant!' He revealed perfect white teeth and his enthusiasm was heart-warming. She couldn't help but smile at his dimpled cheeks and red-stained lips from enthusiastic chomping.

'What did you do today?'

'Skiing,' he said, through a mouthful of food.

'I took him to the SnowDome at Tamworth and we both had lessons, didn't we, champ?' He nodded, eyes sparkling. 'He took to it straight away. Way better than me.'

'Mummy fell over.'

'Three times!' Tilly stroked his hair with her free hand, letting it rest on his head. Claws raked across Kate's heart. In that moment, she'd have traded places with Tilly. Motherhood had brought out a good side to her stepsister and she couldn't ignore the first tendrils of envy wrapping around her heart like ivy covering an aged tree trunk. She had to suppress it.

'I don't suppose you've got any wine to go with it, have you?'

'I certainly have. Here, take this.' She handed Kate the pizza box, warm to the touch. Kate flung open the lid, and breathed in the aroma of herbs and cheese before tearing away a piece and biting into it.

'Mmm!' She kept her gaze on Daniel, who emulated her, and together they filled the room with appreciative noises, each louder than the preceding one. Tilly laughed.

'Okay, that'll do, you two. Here you go, Kate.'

Kate reached for the glass and winked at Daniel. It was nice to have a modicum of normality in her life.

CHAPTER FIFTEEN

Kate rested her forearms on Chris's desk and stared at the corkboard on his wall, fingers wrapped around a smiley-faced stress ball – a joke present for Chris that she'd found in his top drawer. There were several notes pinned to the board, each containing names and dates, and green string stretched between push pins. What she had in front of her was an ever-growing spider diagram that would eventually lead to one name written in red – Dickson.

'If a second post-mortem shows Cooper didn't commit suicide, I'll know I'm getting closer. It'll prove he was silenced and the only reason for that would be to stop him talking to me,' she said.

Although Chris didn't reply, she guessed his answer would have been along the same lines as her own thoughts. Not only would the coroner have to okay the request, but there were also strict guidelines concerning such matters. On top of which was the question of corruption within the force. How far had the rot set in and did Dickson's reach extend far enough to prevent a second autopsy from taking place?

'If you have any better ideas, now would be a good time to share, because I'm fresh out.'

Kate hurled the rubber stress ball at the board. It hit the side of the desk and landed on the carpet, grinning face upwards. She knew her plan was flawed, yet what else could she suggest? It wasn't as if she had any criminal contacts or snitches inside Thamesbury Prison who could throw any light on the matter. The names on the board were connected: Farai, Cooper, Dickson and Chris. She stooped and reached for the ball, curled her fingers around it and squeezed it tightly. 'Well?' She chucked the ball into the drawer, slamming it shut. There was still no answer.

'I'm going to ring Bradley. Hopefully, he'll be more amenable after speaking to Sierra. I'd better have played this right because if I haven't, he'll tell me exactly where to get off and I'll have nobody else left to ask.'

Bradley had been a suspect during the murder investigation and she hadn't gone lightly on him. She wasn't sure he'd open up to her.

'Trust your gut, Kate.' She heaved a sigh of relief at hearing the whispered words.

Bradley was a driving instructor, so it was easy enough to uncover his contact details with a quick Google search. She ambled through to the kitchen and stared out onto the garden. Crimson leaves had blown from next door's acer and were heaped on her patio and on the garden furniture. It ought to be covered in preparation for winter or it would turn mossy. An empty bird feeder, hanging from the branch of an ornamental cherry tree in the corner of their plot, swung in the breeze. Chris had kept it replenished, but since January it had remained empty. She locked onto it.

'You should top it up,' Chris's voice said. 'No point in it being there if you don't keep it filled. There's some seed under the kitchen sink.'

'I shall.' She dialled the number and waited for a response.

'Hello?' Bradley sounded half asleep.

'Morning, Mr Chapman. It's DI Kate Young. I'm sorry to ring you so early. I wondered if we could meet for a quick chat about a mutual acquaintance.' She hoped she was being sufficiently cryptic for him to work out she didn't wish to mention Cooper's name over the phone. She'd played it right. His tone became instantly alert.

'I think I can arrange that.'

'Would it be possible in, say, thirty-five minutes?' She needed to speak to him before she was due to start work. She couldn't afford to be missing during the investigation. She held her breath and willed him to agree.

'Where?'

'The reservoir car park.'

'Okay. I'll see you there.'

The phone went dead and Kate gave a small nod of satisfaction. He neither refused her request nor questioned her phone call. It was a positive. She glanced at her watch. Time was tight but there was sufficient for a quick shower before the meeting. She had to keep up appearances and not give away any signs that she was working two cases: one unofficial. She was breaking rules and, if caught out, would most certainly lose her job.

◆ ◆ ◆

The water was as dark as coal. A figure in a black leather jacket, jeans and boots was leaning on the wall, staring over the reservoir. Bradley Chapman turned as she drew into the car park and immediately strode in her direction. She unlocked the doors and he dropped into the passenger seat, bringing cold air with him. Bradley hadn't changed one bit since she'd last seen him. He wore his experience on his strong face and carried himself with a confidence that only came with the most assured of people.

'DI Young. I can't say I'm surprised to hear from you. I spoke to Sierra last night.'

'I asked her not to mention my involvement.'

'She didn't, but after you rang this morning, I put two and two together. I won't waste your time. Firstly, I don't think you stand a hope in hell of getting a second autopsy, which is what I also told Sierra; however, I've agreed to support her request. She needs to know what really happened to her father and, for what it's worth, so do I. Cooper would never have taken his own life. I know that. Secondly, let's say it transpires Cooper was murdered; how would you go about finding his killer?'

'I couldn't. There would have to be an internal investigation.'

His nostrils flared slightly. 'Then why are we having this conversation? I thought you wanted to seek justice for Cooper.'

'You're right and I do. Unfortunately, I can't go about it the way I'd like to. Did you know Cooper asked to see me?'

'No.'

'Then you don't know what he wanted to speak to me about?'

His brow furrowed. 'I've no idea.'

It was disappointing news. 'But you've visited him since he was imprisoned?'

'Yes.'

'And did he, at any time, tell you anything more about the train attack in January? The one in which my husband was murdered.'

'Is that what this is about?'

She gave an imperceptible nod. 'I suspect Cooper was killed because of information he wanted to pass on about that attack. He asked Sierra to contact me, saying it was urgent he speak to me, and yet, the very morning we were due to meet, he died. That's surely no coincidence. The two things are connected, and if we can establish he was murdered, my suspicions will be confirmed.'

'And then what will you do about it?'

'I haven't got that far yet. I only know I *need* to follow this up. Cooper was mentally fit and healthy, with a daughter he adored. If he'd harboured any dark thoughts, Sierra, or you, would have picked up on them. His death was made to look like suicide and somebody is covering it up.'

'I see.' He pursed his lips, then said, 'One thing I learned is if you want to get inside information, you need somebody on the inside.' He continued to look ahead at the tiny waves sailing across the surface of the water. 'I might be able to help you.'

'How?'

'My brother, Jack, is serving time for GBH. It so happens, two months ago, he was transferred from Winson Green to Thamesbury. I haven't had a great deal to do with him since he was convicted, but I could speak to him to find out what he knows. He liked Cooper. Cooper had a soft spot for my wayward brother back in the day. They used to go clay pigeon shooting together.'

'I'd appreciate that, Mr Chapman.'

'Can I make one thing clear? I'm doing this for Cooper and Sierra. Not you. I don't think there's any need for either of us to pretend we like each other. I'll help you because I want to get to the bottom of this, find the answers Sierra needs, and I want my best friend to be remembered for the good he did in his life, not for his mistakes. I don't want him falsely accused of being a coward who took his own life because, DI Young, he was not. He had more courage in his little finger than most people have in their entire bodies.' He flung the door open, allowing a blast of air to enter, and he was gone in a flash. Ignoring the wind tugging at his scarf, he marched towards a Range Rover and clambered inside without a backward glance.

She watched the red tail lights disappear to the right before she fired up the engine. 'Chris, do you think I can trust him?'

His voice seemed distant, as if he were outside the vehicle. Was she losing him? She repeated the question, trying hard to conjure up his face as he answered, 'Yes. *He'll* make sure he gets answers.' She detected the little note of rebuke in his voice, adding to her fears about whether she was really pursuing all of this as much as she could.

'I hope you're right.' She checked her reflection in her rear-view mirror. Her hair was pinned back, her lipstick nude and her cheekbones subtly rouged. She looked the part, a DI in control of a murder investigation. What she needed though was evidence and suspects because no matter how tidy she looked, ultimately only results mattered.

CHAPTER SIXTEEN

Twenty-one-year-old Olivia Sandman bustled down the path, fumbling in her overlarge bag for her car key. She had to be at the residential care home in twenty minutes and she was running late. All she needed now was to get held up in traffic and she'd be completely screwed. She'd already had two warnings about her punctuality.

If she hadn't stayed up late binge-watching *Queer Eye*, she might have remembered to set the alarm on her phone and not had to fly about the house in a state of panic. She hadn't made her bed or tidied her room either, meaning she'd be in for another lecture from her mum later on when she got home, which was something else she could do without. Mum was certainly behaving like a right cow these days, accusing Olivia of treating the place like a hotel. Yeah, right. A one-star hotel. The property was a new-build but cramped and characterless: a far cry from the four-bedroomed, detached farmhouse they'd moved from. The divorce had taken its toll on her mother. Losing what had been her home for twenty-five years was only part of it. What had truly hurt her had been the betrayal. Olivia's father had left her mother for a far younger woman, emptying her mother's heart and draining her spirit. It was because she'd sided with her mother that Olivia now found herself living in Weston, meaning she had to drive every time she wanted to go out and see her old friends or go to work.

The house in Salt Lane hadn't provided a fresh start for her mother, who, from the day they'd moved in, had sunk into an even greater depression, and seemed unable to do anything except knock back gin most nights and complain about her lot in life. Still, Olivia had no intention of living here for much longer. Now she had a steady income, she was saving every penny of her salary for a place of her own, even if it meant renting it. She didn't want to spend the rest of her life shacked up in Weston with a sad sack of a mother.

She swallowed to lubricate her dry throat. In the mad rush to get ready, she hadn't even had time for her usual cup of tea and slice of toast. There'd be no chance of grabbing anything later at the care home. She had a busy schedule ahead. On top of her other duties, she was responsible for two residents in particular: assisting them with washing, dressing, personal hygiene and day-to-day stuff, like helping them to pay bills, or simply sitting and chatting to them. No two days were the same and today, she was also supposed to take one of them into town to help her choose a present for her daughter who was coming to visit this week. Maybe she'd be able to buy a sandwich while she was out shopping. Where on earth was the car key? She was sure it was in the bag. She remembered dropping it in there when she came in the night before. Her groping fingers couldn't locate it. It'd got buried under the other paraphernalia in there. She really should give the bag a good sort-out. She tried shaking it, but no keys surfaced. Bloody hell! The day was going from bad to worse. She walked onto the empty street and towards her Kia, parked behind her mum's car. Their house was one of several terraced properties, many still unoccupied, opposite a building site. When the next phase of housing was complete, they'd overlook houses identical to these; however, by then, Olivia would be long gone. It was eerily silent down this road, but in the distance the morning traffic was already humming along the main road to Stafford. Shit! Where was the damn key?

She crouched beside her car, tipped the bag's contents onto the ground, eyes scanning over the packet of cigarettes, lip gloss, mirror, chewing gum, old receipts, pencil and notebook until she spied it. She grabbed it and, at the same time, a noise glued her to the spot. What was it? A cough. No, it wasn't a cough. It was bird noise: a duck or some other wildfowl on the canal at the far end of the road. She unfroze and hurriedly swept her belongings back into the bag and jumped to her feet. As long as she didn't get stuck in any hold-ups en route, she still could reach work in time.

The man appeared from nowhere and the blow came out of the blue, extinguishing all thoughts as she crashed to the ground.

CHAPTER SEVENTEEN

Emma was already ensconced in front of her office computer when Kate arrived at seven thirty on the dot.

'You alone?' asked Kate.

'Uh-huh. I couldn't sleep. Went for a workout at five then sparred with Greg. Bugger put me through my paces.' Greg was Emma's oldest brother, who owned the training academy where she regularly worked out. 'Has Tilly rung you?'

'No.'

'She dropped by with Daniel. By the way, he's adorable. Greg took him off to the office and plied him with fizzy drinks and played games with him on his laptop while I gave her a quick run-through of some basic self-defence moves. She's a fast learner.'

Kate was pleased her stepsister had taken up the challenge so readily. 'Oh, that's great. Thanks again.'

'Yeah. It was nice to meet her. We're going to have another session tomorrow. I actually enjoyed teaching her. She's fun.'

Kate smiled. 'Yes. She was always a laugh.' *Until the attack.* Kate was not only pleased that Tilly would be armed with some skills to defend herself, but that she'd made an impression on Emma. Maybe, when she settled more permanently, she'd become even more interested in Taekwondo and join Emma in future sessions. Before the attack, Tilly had been hugely popular – a girl who knew no fear and who attracted boys like a magnet. The combination of her frail looks with her devil-may-care attitude had been an intoxicating combination for teenagers and Tilly had never been short of admirers or boyfriends. She would find love again. Of that, Kate was certain.

Emma cleared her throat. 'Right. I spoke to the DS in charge of the investigation Heather was working on, regarding the local man and the threats she had afterwards. She uncovered CCTV footage that incriminated him, but it transpired he was simply in the wrong place at the wrong time and wasn't guilty. I got a name – Ollie Rankin. I ran some checks and his ex-wife has an injunction against him. I thought I'd follow it up. Might be worth a go.'

'I don't suppose you've established any link between this man and Laura Dean as well, have you?'

'Nah. Maybe he'll let something slip if I talk to him.'

The door flung open and Jamie sauntered in. 'Morning!'

Emma replied with 'You're very bright and breezy. You been at the caffeinated drinks already?'

'That's very funny, Sarge. No, the missus stayed over at her sister's last night with Zach, so I got a good night's sleep. Guv, can I ask if we'll be working overtime tonight?'

'It's a murder enquiry. There's every chance we'll be working late. Is that a problem?'

'No. I really could do with the money. Especially with another mouth to feed. It's just that the missus asked if I'd be around to look after the lad. She's been offered some cleaning work at a block of offices. Every penny, and all that.' He maintained a cheery voice. 'I'll tell her to expect me when she sees me and to ask the mother-in-law to babysit Zach. What do you want me to tackle first?'

'Christian's whereabouts for Friday night.'

'Sure thing.' Within moments he was at his desk, notebook open. Kate picked up a file from her desk. Morgan had left information on Richard Dean's partner, Steve, a jeweller by trade who owned Lichfield Jewellers. Morgan had also added an addendum:

Note: Christian Laurent was born in Lichfield and worked there for Bennett and Spillane Solicitors until 2019.

'Anyone know where Morgan is?' There were only headshakes. 'Jamie, remind me where Heather lived?'

'Longdon.'

Kate pulled up Google Maps. Lichfield was less than five miles away from Heather's house. Her work records showed she'd moved to Longdon with her ex-husband in 2015, and following their divorce three years later, in 2018, she'd remained in the marital home.

Jamie ended a call and waved his mobile. 'Geoffrey Tomkins can't be sure of the exact time but confirmed Christian turned up at the Red Lion in Hopwas around nine thirty and stayed until they all left. About ten forty-five. Want me to check with his other colleagues?'

'Yes. I think Morgan has requested CCTV to back up Christian's story about working in the office both Friday and Saturday night, but double-check that's happening,' said Kate. 'For the time being, I'm keeping Christian in the frame. From what his sister told us, we can assume he liked Laura far more than he admitted, and his whereabouts are still hazy. I can't pin any definite connection between him and Heather, but if he worked in Lichfield until 2019, and Heather lived in Longdon, which isn't far from the city, there's a chance she bumped into him. But we also need to establish a link between Heather and Kevin.'

'He lives close to Heather. Maybe he drank in her local pub. There are a couple in Longdon. I'll look into it,' said Emma.

Kate tapped the note Morgan had written. 'And now there's Steve Rushmore, Laura's father's partner. He's been trading in

Lichfield for the past twenty years. If we're searching for possible connections between the victims, then the fact they both lived close to Lichfield might be significant.'

'Let's see what we can find out,' said Emma, typing details into the search engine. She scanned the information on her screen. 'Lichfield's a popular city. Given where both women lived, it's almost certain they'd have shopped there. It's only about a ten-minute drive from Heather's house and double that from Laura's.' She clicked onto a link. 'According to this site, there are only two jewellers there. Lichfield Jewellers seems to be much larger.'

Kate got to her feet and looked over Emma's shoulder at the stylish website, which offered designer jewellery and luxury accessories. Emma scrolled down the page. Steve's face beamed out at them. 'His shop also offers a repair service. Who knows, both women could even have been his customers.'

'You read the notes on Steve, then?' said Morgan, who'd appeared in the doorway. 'I thought you'd be interested.'

'I agree it's worth looking into.' Kate paused, eyebrows drawn together. 'I'd prefer to delve further into possible connections between Kevin, Christian and our two victims. Both suspects lived near the two women and although it's only a gut feeling, I'm sure both are keeping something from us. You felt that way about Christian too, when we spoke to him.'

'I did and I've been looking into him some more. I haven't found anything yet to arouse any further suspicions. I don't think we should ignore this though. Steve and Laura didn't get along.'

'But Heather?'

'He might not have needed a reason. He could have selected her for some arbitrary reason: had an argument with her or . . . maybe she reminded him of Laura. After all, they look very similar.'

Kate pondered the possibility. Morgan had a point.

'I'll check out Kevin,' said Emma. 'The same reason applies. He might have attacked Heather because she reminded him of Laura. And for what it's worth, I think Morgan's right. We should look into Steve.'

Kate glanced at Steve's friendly face. People often wore masks to disguise their real emotions. It was conceivable that Steve was an expert at wearing one. 'Okay. I'll leave you and Jamie to dig further. Morgan, we'll pay Steve a visit,' she said.

'The shop won't be open yet.'

'Then we'll tackle him at home.'

◆ ◆ ◆

Richard Dean, in pyjama bottoms and sweatshirt, sat slumped in an armchair. He had refused to leave Steve alone with Morgan and Kate. 'This is nonsense. Steve had nothing to do with Laura's death.'

Steve slotted a cufflink into position and tugged the shirt into place over his wrist. 'It's fine, Richard. Calm down. I'm sure the officers wouldn't be here without good reason. Now, how can I help?'

Morgan, standing in the centre of the room, spoke. 'We understand you own Lichfield Jewellers.'

'Indeed, I do.'

'Have you seen this woman before? Either at your shop, or around Lichfield?' Morgan passed over the photograph of Heather.

Steve gave the photograph his full attention before returning it with a shake of his head. 'Her face looks vaguely familiar, but I couldn't say with any certainty if she's been in the shop or not. You could try asking my staff. They might have served her. I tend to work in the back office on repairs, rather than deal with the customers.'

'You don't recall serving her, at all?'

'No.'

'Does the name Heather Gault mean anything to you?'

'I'm afraid not.'

'You didn't do any work for her?'

'No. Sorry I can't be of any further help. I take it that's everything?' His round face became broader as he attempted a smile.

'As a matter of fact, it isn't,' said Kate. 'We'd like to know your whereabouts on Friday and Saturday evening.'

'This is preposterous!' Richard leapt to his feet, his face inches from Morgan's.

Morgan didn't budge. 'Please sit down, Mr Dean. It's perfectly normal procedure for us to question the whereabouts of everyone who knew your daughter. As a crime writer, you'd know that.'

Richard didn't obey, instead jabbing his finger at Morgan's chest. 'What I do know is that it's lunacy to ask if my partner has anything to do with my daughter's murder! He was here with me on Friday evening *and* Saturday. Take a note of that, DS Meredith, and then find whoever killed her instead of wasting time here.'

'I understand you're very upset about your daughter, but please don't prod me.'

Richard registered the act, dropped his head and mumbled an apology. Kate turned towards Steve. The wide-eyed look he'd briefly thrown in Richard's direction when he vouched for his whereabouts hadn't escaped her attention. 'Is that true? Were you here all evening?'

'Yes.'

'Mr Rushmore, you understand we can request CCTV footage, or indeed your sat nav to check your vehicle's movements. Then there are phone records—'

He tugged at both cuffs, head lowered, then said, 'I might have popped out for a while.'

'Steve!' Richard hissed.

'I've nothing to hide.' Steve's face had lost some of its ruddy colour.

'Where did you go, sir?' asked Morgan.

'I dropped off a pearl necklace with a client. She needed it the following day, for her daughter's wedding. It had been in the shop for repair and was trickier to fix than I'd first thought. It wasn't ready when she called in late Friday afternoon to collect it. Given it was a family heirloom, and imperative the bride had it for the wedding, I promised I'd personally drop it off at her house that evening.'

'Can you give me a name and address of the person you delivered to?'

Richard jumped in again. 'No need. You could ring them. Steve has the phone number.'

'Yes, yes. I can give you her number. She'll confirm exactly what I've told you. As I said, I've nothing to hide.'

The evasion tactics weren't working on Kate. 'Where did the client live, Mr Rushmore?'

Another look passed between the men then Steve shut his eyes for a pinch of time before saying, 'Uttoxeter.'

Kate gave an exaggerated sigh. There were three main routes from Lichfield to Uttoxeter; one passed through Abbots Bromley. 'And what time did you deliver this necklace?'

'About seven thirty.'

'And you left your shop in Lichfield and drove directly to Uttoxeter?'

'Yes.'

'Which road did you take?'

'Steve!'

Richard's hiss was urgent but Steve ran a finger under his collar and answered, 'The shortest, through Armitage and Abbots Bromley.'

'And did you come back the same way?'

He nodded.

'What time did you pass through Abbots Bromley on your return trip?'

'Around eight thirty.'

'I see.'

'I have nothing to hide,' Steve repeated. 'If I was guilty, I'd have let Richard cover for me. I'd rather you knew the truth.'

'You realise it places you at the crime scene at around the time the attack occurred?' Kate said.

'I didn't attack Laura and I didn't see anything unusual as I drove through the village. I'd had a long day. I only wanted to get home.'

Morgan spoke again, attracting Steve's attention. 'It's true you and Laura didn't get along, isn't it?'

'We've made no secret of the fact, have we, Richard?'

'No, we haven't. Many families don't get on. None of this makes him a murderer.'

'When did you last see Laura, Mr Rushmore?' asked Morgan.

'Ages ago. I haven't seen her in months.'

'And how long have you known Mr Dean?'

Steve shrugged. 'Years.'

'How many years exactly?'

'Twenty or so?'

'Then you knew Mr Dean while he was married?'

'Yes.' He stroked his beard. 'We knew each other.'

'Can I ask, did you begin your relationship while Mr Dean's wife was alive?'

Richard shook his head. 'Stop right there. Steve, don't answer them! DS Morgan, our private life is none of your concern, nor does it bear any relevance to your enquiry. Steve told you where he was, and I can confirm we were at home last night. Check our

171

phone records or whatever you need to do, but we were both *here*. Now, if you want to caution us and continue this interview at the station, then do so, otherwise, I'd respectfully ask you to leave us alone. I have a lot to deal with and arrangements to make for my daughter's funeral.'

Morgan remained poker-faced. 'I had to ask you, sir, because Laura told her friends she believed you and Steve were involved in a relationship before her mother died, and that you were responsible for her mother's death.' Richard's mouth flapped open but Morgan continued smoothly. 'If Laura voiced her suspicions to her friends, she might have spoken to relatives or your friends and I'm sure those accusations would have had an impact on you both.'

The writer's eyes narrowed into slits. 'She was a mixed-up teen-ager and grief twisted her thoughts. She lashed out, searching for somebody to blame for her mother's death – a death brought on by natural causes and not by others' actions.'

Steve pleaded with a look that was ignored and Kate quickly read the situation. 'Then, you *were* involved before your wife passed away.'

Richard gave a loose shrug. The truth was out. 'I can assure you Megan never knew about our relationship. Laura only found out about us a few days before her mother passed away, and Steve and I put our relationship on hold immediately afterwards. Laura needed me. I sacrificed my relationship with Steve to give my daughter the time she needed to grieve and only when I felt she was sufficiently recovered did we began seeing each other clandestinely again, until I decided she could cope with the revelation. Unfortunately, she didn't take the news as well as we'd hoped. Regardless of how difficult or rude she was to him, Steve took it all in his stride and has *never* had a bad word to say about her.' He looked across at Steve, gave him a half-smile. 'I don't how he managed to put up with her, but he did. He's been patient and understanding and he would never, ever harm her.' His shoulders sagged and Steve scurried forward, put an arm around his partner. He met Kate's eyes.

'I think it might be time for you to leave. You can see he's terribly upset. He's lost his only daughter and you've been speaking to him like he's a criminal.'

'That was never our intention, sir,' said Kate. 'We are dutybound to follow all lines of enquiry.'

'I know you are,' said Steve. 'It's just that, in the early days, she caused a great deal of trouble with her repeated accusations, and it took quite a long while for the rumour mill to die down. It was an upsetting time for us all, especially for Richard, and for you to bring it all back up again, especially in light of what's happened to poor Laura, well . . . you understand.'

'Yes, sir. I'm afraid we'll still need to take DNA samples from you both before we leave. Purely to eliminate you. We have to ask everyone who might have had contact with her.'

'What!'

Steve shushed him gently. 'It's okay. We must let the police do their job. They have to find out who killed Laura.'

Richard nodded his consent. Steve looked at Morgan. 'Do it.'

CHAPTER EIGHTEEN

The car park outside HQ had filled up and they'd found the last space, sandwiched closely to a police van and a four-by-four.

'We'll see if anything comes back from the DNA results,' Kate said as she squeezed out of the vehicle. Since leaving the two men, she and Morgan had been discussing the likelihood of Steve being their killer. Although a phone call to the owner of the pearl necklace had confirmed the timings, Kate was still on the fence regarding the overly helpful Steve.

'He didn't seem that upset by Laura's behaviour. After all, she did try to sabotage their relationship.'

Steve didn't strike her as thick-skinned and would surely have been hurt by Laura's attitude. Nevertheless, she wasn't as keen as Morgan to place Steve in the frame. Especially as they'd nothing concrete to support his suspicions. They'd stopped off at the jeweller's on their way back to the station, shown Heather's photo to the staff and drawn another blank. Nobody remembered seeing her in the shop. Morgan slammed the car door shut. Understanding his frustration, Kate said, 'Delve further into Heather's background. See if you can make a connection between her and Steve.' It was sufficient to appease him.

'Guv!' Jamie was barrelling towards them. 'I've spoken to Christian's work colleagues who all confirm he was at the Red Lion on Friday night, though none could confirm what time he arrived, so I'm headed over to technical support to check through CCTV.'

'Okay. Anything else I should know?'

'The super was looking for you. I told him you were interviewing potential suspects. He asked if you could drop by his office as soon as you returned.'

'Right.'

'I'll get off.' Jamie spun on his heel and hastened away.

Kate paced towards the entrance, head held high. Dickson would undoubtedly pile on the pressure. She headed first to the ladies' washroom, checked her appearance, tucked her blouse in where it had lifted from the loose waistband on her skirt, then climbed the stairs.

'Come in.'

'Sir, you wanted to see me?'

His head was lowered over a report. He glanced in her direction. 'It was to let you know that ITV intend on broadcasting a televised reconstruction of the attack on Heather as part of *Real Crime* that airs tonight. Before you say anything, the order's come from upstairs. I know it causes extra work for you all, but something useful might come from it. Also, I want you and your team to attend the filming.'

'May I ask why? This isn't normal procedure.'

'I want eyes on the crowd observing the filming, in case the murderer is among them.'

'That's not likely. Not unless he knows about it.'

'The programme makers have been granted permission to publicise this reconstruction. They've been shouting about it on social media.'

'And I wasn't informed? You're planning on baiting the killer, draw him back to the scene of the crime and flush him out of a crowd of – I don't know how many people – and yet I wasn't consulted?' she hissed.

'You had other priorities at the time and I'm informing you now. Look, it's a long shot, I know, but it has to be tried. He's an arrogant son of a bitch, and that sort of cockiness often results in mistakes. Sometimes perpetrators will attend the crime scene, savour the moment of hiding in plain sight among other onlookers when the emergency services arrive. We're testing out the same theory by giving him the opportunity to attend a reconstruction – relive the thrill of the moment – and we need eyes there to establish if anyone is displaying any unusual behaviour. We don't want to frighten him off so I want your team on it, not uniforms.'

'And what if a huge number of people turn up and we can't spot any one individual?'

'As I said, the decision came from above and I expect you to carry out instructions. If there are lots of people there, then you'll have to deal with that situation.'

She opened her mouth to speak again, but was cut off with a stony look.

'That will be all, Kate. Make sure you and your team are there by half past five, before the filming begins.'

'Yes, sir.'

Back in the office, she told Morgan about the new plan. He scratched his scalp, brows knitted together. 'Let me get this straight. All of us are going to mingle with a crowd of onlookers at a crime reconstruction, in the hope the killer attends the filming?'

'In a nutshell,' Kate replied. 'So, make sure everyone is at Newbury Avenue by five thirty, and in the meantime, let's get on with trying to track him down.'

'If it's one of the guys we've been looking into, he'll spot us and scarper,' said Morgan.

'We'll have to keep our eyes peeled then and hope we spy him first,' she said. Regardless of how she felt about it, they had to obey orders.

'Okay, let's get to work. I want to find out more about that bracelet Heather wore, so ring her ex-husband and see what he can tell you. I'll start on her friends to find out if she was seeing anybody.'

The first on her list, Zoe Farrington, kept a horse at the same stables in Blackfields as Heather. She could see Morgan's jaw working as he spoke, but she concentrated on her own call and the melodic voice at the other end of her phone. She introduced herself and broke the news about Heather. Zoe's voice thickened with emotion.

'Yes. Poor Heather. Everyone at the stables is in total shock. I can't get my head around it.'

'Did you know her well?'

'Yes, pretty well. We've been friends for ages.'

'We're doing everything we can to find out who was behind the attack. I was hoping you might be able to tell me a little about her private life. She didn't divulge a great deal to her fellow work colleagues and we only have a few scant details. We believe she arranged to meet somebody Saturday evening, and we'd like to talk to whoever it was. I don't suppose you have any idea who that might have been, do you?'

'It might have been Paul. She met him on Tinder and went out with him a few times. He works at Uttoxeter Racecourse.'

'Doing what?'

'Marketing.'

'Do you know his surname?'

'Sorry, no.'

'Have you met him?'

'No, but Heather was keen on him. She showed me photos of him. You don't think he attacked her, do you?'

'The investigation is at a very early stage. We're trying to establish if she was supposed to be meeting him that night.'

'If she planned on it, she didn't mention it to me when we were riding that morning, before she went to work.'

'Did you often ride together?'

'At least once a week and most weekends.'

'And you chatted while you were out?'

'Of course.'

'Did Heather ever discuss her job?'

There were sniffs and a pause as Zoe blew her nose, then, 'Not very often.'

'She didn't mention anyone called Ollie Rankin?'

'Yes. I remember him. He menaced her for a while. Nothing awful happened, but she stayed with me for a couple of nights because she was worried about being at home alone. It all got sorted out.'

'I don't suppose she said anything about a shoplifting case?' asked Kate. 'It happened in February last year.'

'Erm. Actually, yes, but Heather passed the case on to somebody else.'

'Did she tell you why she handed it over?'

'I didn't need telling. I knew why. It dragged up some bad memories.'

'What sort of memories?'

There was a brief silence before Zoe answered. 'Personal ones.' There was another pause and then, 'After Greg left her, she was in a really shit state. She couldn't even face riding or coming to the stables. I took her shopping – a girls' day out in Solihull to cheer her up. It didn't really work out. She was downhearted the whole time. On the way back to the car we stopped at a department store so I could buy some face cream. While I was at the make-up counter, I happened to look up in time to see her put a perfume gift set into her bag and walk off. She obviously wasn't going to pay for it. I headed straight for her, grabbed hold of her arm and asked her what the hell she was playing at. She became upset and confused. She claimed she had no idea why she'd taken the set; it wasn't even a perfume she used or liked, and she had enough money to pay for it. I made her put it back before she got caught. She'd have lost her job if anyone else had seen her. Anyway, the case reminded her of that day. Heather said the woman was going through exactly the same sort of hell she'd gone through, following a break-up. She didn't feel she was impartial enough to deal with it.'

Kate wrote Heather's name on her notepad, along with Laura's, and drew a circle around both names. She had another link.

Morgan finished his call soon after Kate had ended hers. 'Greg bought Heather a bracelet from Lichfield Jewellers. From the way he described it, it might have been the same silver one she was wearing when we found her body. I'm going to email him a picture of it.'

'Was Heather with him when he bought it?'

'I don't think so, but if it is the same bracelet, she took it back a couple of times to get the clasp fixed. Which means Steve could have been lying to us all along and knew her after all.'

She gave a thoughtful nod. 'Worth looking into, although when did Greg purchase the bracelet?'

'June 2015. It was for her birthday.'

'Okay. If Greg confirms it's the same bracelet, talk to Steve.'

'Will do.'

'I've spoken to one of Heather's friends and it appears our victims might have known each other after all. Heather knew enough

179

details about Laura to turn down working on her shoplifting case. And, we might have another lead. I need a surname, but Heather had been seeing a guy called Paul.'

'And you think he might have been the person she was meeting after work?'

'Worth looking into. I'll head to Uttoxeter and have a word with him.'

Loud clomping in the corridor announced the arrival of Emma. She chucked her bag onto her seat with the practised aim of a basketball player. 'We can forget Ollie Rankin. He spent the weekend in Southend with his girlfriend and her kids. Only got back home late last night. At 8.23 p.m., he stopped off at the Welcome Break services at Warwick North and bought fuel and four Burger King meals. According to his partner, he's never raised a hand to her or the kids.'

'He admitted to intimidating Heather, though?' said Kate.

'He did. Claimed he was worked up at being falsely accused and let rip with empty threats, for which he later apologised. He's not heard of Laura Dean.'

'Morgan and I have a couple of other avenues to pursue.'

'Fine. I've got loads more stuff I want to go through here.'

'Actually, I want you to head over to the technicians, smooth-talk Felicity and find out what they discovered on Heather's laptop and I mean *everything*. Be subtle about it.'

Emma grinned. 'Charm offence?'

'If necessary.'

'Shouldn't be a problem. Felicity likes me.'

'Oh, and you need to be at Newbury Avenue by five thirty. Morgan will explain.'

Kate collected her belongings and made for the door, aware the clock was ticking on this and they had still covered insufficient ground. Dickson was waiting for the moment to pounce. The thought spurred her on and with quick steps she hastened from the building into her car and away. She didn't glance up at his office window but some sixth sense assured her he was watching from it. 'I'm gunning for you too,' she said, through gritted teeth.

◆ ◆ ◆

Uttoxeter Racecourse hosted year-round chase and hurdle meetings, along with other events such as concerts, family-days out, exhibitions and private functions. The sign to the entrance indicated eleven were to be held this month, including a doggy day, a quilt and stitch village and two outdoor cinema experiences. Nothing, however, was programmed for today and groundsmen on green tractors, or wielding heavy-duty strimmers, were tending to the vast, oval-shaped course. In spite of living close to one of the UK's leading hunt tracks, Kate had never attended a race day. She wasn't a mingler or a party animal. Many would call her dull, but Chris had understood her reluctance to mix with others in large gatherings where she often felt isolated within a crowd. She felt more relaxed at small occasions, friends' parties or evenings out with one or two other couples.

She'd googled the name of the manager and one of the grounds staff directed her to Paul Avery's office where she found him hunched over a table filled with photographs. He stood up to greet her.

'Good morning. What can I do for you?' The voice was gentle, his face youthful and earnest, with sandy hair and cornflower-blue eyes. His outfit of jeans, shirt and jacket created the right balance of professional and relaxed, and Kate couldn't help but notice the gleam from his light-brown leather boots. Chris had always believed in good-quality footwear and even when abroad on assignments, he'd taken a travel-set of brushes and polish to keep them shining.

The sudden recollection of her husband pulled her up short. She hadn't spoken to him in a while. Palpitations accompanied the thought. He was slipping away from her, little by little.

The man in front of her was waiting for a response. She dragged herself back into the moment, lifted her card and introduced herself. His sparse eyebrows pulled into a light frown.

'I'm here about Heather Gault.'

'Heather? Why?'

'You definitely know her, then?'

'Yes, we've been seeing each other for a couple of months.'

'When was the last time you saw her?'

'Friday evening, after work. She came around to my house and we shared a bottle of wine and a takeaway. What's this about?'

'I'm afraid I have some bad news. I'm sorry to tell you that she's dead.'

He rested his palms on the table, covering the pictures of horses thundering towards the finish lines with cheering masses in stands urging them on, and released a long breath before saying, 'Okay . . . Okay. When did this happen?'

'Saturday night. She was attacked on Newbury Avenue.'

'Attacked and killed?'

'Yes, sir. I'm very sorry. Do you feel up to answering a few questions for me?'

He flopped onto the chair like a puppet whose strings had been cut. 'I can try.'

'Firstly, can I ask your whereabouts for Saturday evening and night?'

'I was here. There was a large private event and I had to be here to ensure it all went well.'

'Can anyone confirm you were here?'

'Many people. It was a drinks event, and I was on hand all evening.'

'You didn't arrange to meet Heather that evening?'

'I invited her along to the do but she was working and unsure what time she'd be finished, so she declined.' He ran his hands up and down his cheeks as if rubbing life back into them. 'Oh, God, this can't be true.'

'How did you and Heather stay in contact? Was it mostly phone calls or messaging?'

'Invariably WhatsApp. Messaging was more convenient for us both.'

'And was it normal not to hear from her for a few days?'

'Absolutely. We're both independent people with demanding jobs and lives outside work.'

'How often did you see each other?'

'A couple of times a week. Much depended on work commitments.'

'And you got along well?'

'We were getting on really well.'

'Do you recognise this phone number?' Kate slid across the pay-as-you-go number. Paul looked at it and shook his head.

'It's not mine.'

'Did she ever discuss work with you?'

'Neither of us did. When we met up it was purely to have fun, forget about work and enjoy ourselves.'

'Mr Avery, do you know anyone called Laura Dean?'

'No. The name isn't familiar.'

Emma's name flashed up on her mobile. 'Would you excuse me? I have to take this.'

'Go ahead.' He stared at the photos on the desk and rested his head in his hands. Kate went outside the office and took the call.

'Kate, there's been another victim. A young woman was found on a building site in Weston.'

'Same MO as the others?'

'One difference. She's still alive. Critical but alive. They've taken her to County Hospital.'

'I'm on my way.' Kate pocketed the mobile and made her excuses to Paul Avery before running for her car.

CHAPTER NINETEEN

Kate remained bolt upright on the high-backed, fabric seat, as she had done for the last hour. She breathed in the mixture of chemicals, none of them identifiable, but combined gave a sense of cleanliness, a smell she found strangely comforting. The private room, used for giving individuals bad news about their loved ones, was bare apart from four wooden-framed blue chairs. She shifted in the one she'd chosen. The cushion pad had flattened and was beginning to become uncomfortable. She concentrated on the window affording her a view of the busy corridor, where she observed the by-now familiar faces of nurses who bustled up and down, pausing every time they passed the anti-bacterial machine to disinfect their hands. She stood up, took three paces across the room then back again. She needed to talk to the victim, now identified as Olivia Sandman, but the senior consultant had refused her permission to visit the girl.

She wasn't going to leave, not until she'd spoken to Mrs Sandman, who was apparently with her daughter, and not before one of her own team had come to replace her. She also needed assurances she'd be notified as soon as Olivia became conscious. She paced yet again to the far wall, three long strides, and back, and was relieved when her mobile buzzed.

'Go ahead, Emma.'

'Okay. Well, first off, Christian's alibi checks out. There was surveillance coverage of the street where he parked, showing his car didn't move until five to nine. We also have clear footage of him actually getting in and out of the car at the relevant times. Likewise, it was there on Saturday evening, parked in almost the same spot. We can't say with 100 per cent certainty he didn't leave his office that night, but given he hasn't shown up on any of the cameras in the vicinity, it's looking highly unlikely he headed to Trentham House to attack Heather.'

'What about Heather's bracelet? Any joy there?'

'Morgan's spoken to Steve again. He can't remember if he repaired the bracelet or not. Apparently, he sees hundreds of pieces of jewellery, so he can't be certain. He definitely doesn't remember selling it to her husband, and Greg didn't recognise the photo of Steve we messaged him. Steve insists he's employed several salespeople since 2015, so any one of them might have dealt with Heather.'

'No news on his DNA sample yet?'

'I'm afraid not. There's a backlog of work at the lab and both his sample and Richard's are waiting to be processed. I asked if they could push them along for us.'

'Thanks. You don't happen to know how long Morgan will be, do you?'

'When I spoke to him a few minutes ago, he was already on his way to the hospital, so he should turn up in a quarter of an hour or so.'

Fifteen minutes wasn't too long to wait, although she'd rather be back in the office. Emma spoke again.

'Which leads me on to Heather's computer. Felicity wasn't keen to let me see what was on it, but I convinced her. In the end, she ran through it with me but it was all pretty much work-related.'

'So why the reluctance to tell us?'

'She was instructed to contact us only if she found anything relevant to our investigation, and the computer was for her eyes only.'

Kate was puzzled. This wasn't usual procedure. The investigating team was always granted access to information on any device.

'Anyway, I explained Olivia was in hospital, fighting for her life, and asked if I could check to see if there was any connection between her and Heather, and she caved in.'

'You find anything at all?'

'I'm afraid not. Felicity ran her name through all the documents and emails but turned up nothing.'

'She wasn't working on any cases involving Sunny Bank Residential Care Home, where she might have bumped into Olivia?' They'd established Olivia was an assistant care worker at the home in Stafford.

'No, but there was one investigation I've not heard of: Operation Agouti. It took place last month.'

'Who was in charge of that?'

'Superintendent Dickson.'

Dickson! 'Any clue as to what the investigation was into?'

'No. The emails were only regarding meeting times, nothing to indicate what the case was about.'

All police operations were given names chosen from a pre-approved list of random names. Agouti was one Kate wasn't familiar with. What was also puzzling was his decision to choose a CIO over one of many police officers under his command. Dickson hadn't mentioned working with Heather, and that rang alarm bells. It also went some way to explaining why Dickson had instructed the computer be taken directly to the technical department to be examined, rather than giving her team access to it. He hadn't wanted Kate to find out.

'Any sign of Olivia's mother yet?' asked Emma.

Kate made out the hesitant steps of a diminutive woman, being guided by a nurse, heading in her direction. 'I think she might be here now. I'll talk to you later.' She jammed the mobile into her pocket and stood back. Mrs Sandman entered first, a robotic shuffle that came to a quick halt.

The nurse spoke in a soft voice. 'If you need anything, Rebecca, I won't be far away.'

Kate edged forward slightly. 'Mrs Sandman, thank you for seeing me. I appreciate it. I'm DI Kate Young. I'm heading the investigation into the attack on your daughter. Would you like to sit down?'

The woman obeyed and the nurse backed away, shutting the door behind her. Kate pulled her chair forward to be nearer to Olivia's mother. 'I'm very sorry about your daughter. How is she?'

Her red-rimmed eyes were sunken in her hollow face. 'She's not come around yet. I was told I should talk to you. I ought to be with her.' She clawed at the strap on a worn leather bag as she spoke.

'I won't take up much of your time.'

She didn't seem to hear Kate. 'I keep thinking, what if she screamed for help? I didn't hear her. What if she was screaming for me and—?' The words turned to snuffles and she rooted in the bag for a tissue and blew into it noisily.

'None of us know what happened. You can't punish yourself like this.'

'But if I'd woken up and got up earlier, seen her car was still there and rung the police, they might have found her before this happened to her. She looks—' Her face screwed up and she fanned a hand in front of it. 'Sorry. It's so awful. She was found at the building site opposite. So close to home.'

'None of this was your fault. You did what you could. She's alive. That's what's important. She needs you now.'

Olivia's mother blinked away the heavy tears.

'Do you feel up to answering a few questions?'

A clattering outside made the woman jump in her seat. She squirmed around in her chair, spotted the porter pushing an empty trolley and turned back with a sigh.

'I'll try,' she said.

'Listen, if it gets too much for you, say and we'll stop.'

'Okay.'

'What time did you notice Olivia's car was still parked outside?'

'Not until I got up, at ten. I'm on a late shift today, so I had a lie-in. I thought maybe it hadn't started and she'd taken a taxi to work, or got a lift and forgotten to tell me she was going with somebody. Her mobile was switched off, so I rang the residential home where she works, and they said she hadn't turned up. Then I began to worry. I didn't know what to do next. I tried all her friends and got the same answer – nobody knew where she was. I got a bad feeling about it, so I rang the police. They told me not to worry, and even suggested she was maybe playing hooky and would turn up later. I knew that couldn't be the case. I explained how much she loved her job and how she was caring for three elderly people in particular, and wouldn't let them down. An officer came out to take details and then about half an hour after he left, I got a phone call to say a young woman had been found on the building site opposite our house and rushed to hospital. She had no identification and they didn't know who she was, so I drove here as fast as I could. I prayed it wasn't her. I prayed so hard.' She ran a finger under her eye and wiped away sooty smears. 'That makes me a bad person, doesn't it, because I wanted some *other* mother to go through this torture and not me?'

Kate shook her head. 'It's a natural reaction.'

'I should have done more.'

'There was nothing more you could have done.'

Her bottom lip trembled. 'Maybe. Maybe not.'

'Has Olivia got a boyfriend?'

'No.'

'But she has had relationships in the past?'

'Yes. None were very serious. The longest one lasted about three months and she's been single for over a year.'

'So, she wasn't getting any unwanted attention from anybody, text messages, phone calls?'

'Not that I know about.'

'Do you mind me asking if you're in a relationship?'

'Me!' She spluttered. 'I haven't dated anyone since my ex-husband and I split up, last year.'

'Have you had any men friends around to the house?'

'No. Only my brother when we first moved in. He lives in Ireland.'

'I see.'

'He wouldn't have hurt her. He adores her.'

'I'm sure he's not involved. He's in Ireland at the moment, isn't he?'

'Yes. He's a headmaster at a school in Limerick.' She rolled her bag strap around her hand. 'Can I go now?'

'Very soon. Just a few more minutes. Did you notice if Olivia was troubled in any way? Has she been tense recently?'

'Not in the least.'

'The houses on Salt Lane haven't been up long, have they?'

'No.'

'When did you move there?'

'Two months ago.'

'And where did you live before that?'

'Stafford. Olivia wasn't happy about the move, but we had to sell the old house and this one was brand new – a fresh start.'

'Was there any reason she didn't like living there?'

190

'She preferred being in town. She missed her friends and the nightlife.'

'Have you by chance noticed anyone hanging around your street in the last few days, or has Olivia mentioned any strangers in the area?'

She stared vacantly at Kate. 'No. It's quiet there. There are only two houses occupied. The others are still up for sale.'

'You weren't aware of any prospective buyers looking around them? Maybe cars parked that you don't usually see in the street?'

'No. Nothing.'

'What about any comings and goings – vans, delivery men, builders?'

'They don't use our street. The site entrance is on another road that runs parallel to ours.'

'That's helpful. Thank you.' Kate gave her an encouraging smile and then asked, 'Did Olivia express concern about any of her work colleagues?'

'She loves her job and gets along with all the staff and residents. There's nobody I can think of at all.' She made to leave. 'I don't know anything. I need to see her. What if she's . . . what if she dies while I'm here with you? I have to go.'

'I'll find a nurse to escort you back to her. If you can think of anything at all, please give me a ring, no matter what time of day or night. This is my personal card.' She handed it across. Rebecca took it without looking at it. 'Mrs Sandman, I need your permission to speak to Olivia as soon as she comes to. Would you please tell the consultant you are happy for me to talk to her?'

'Yes. I'll do that.' She chewed at her lip for a moment. 'I haven't told her father. I came straight here.'

'If you'd rather, we can arrange for somebody to contact him.'

'Please. Now, I must go.'

Kate gestured to the nurse, waiting on the other side of the glass window, who came forward immediately.

'She's all I have,' Rebecca said. 'I don't know what I'll do if—'

The door eased open. 'Rebecca, are you ready?'

She jumped to her feet and scuttled away without a goodbye.

Kate watched them disappear, her heart heavy for the woman. Even if Olivia were to recover, she, like Tilly, would be haunted by the memory of what had happened to her. She watched as another member of staff pumped gel onto their hands and wondered how much longer she needed to wait. Olivia could be unconscious for hours or longer. Morgan would soon replace her, ensuring an officer was on site should the girl come to. It left her a man short; however, until William arranged extra officers to cover this duty, they'd have to suck it up.

Olivia's attacker had known her movements, been waiting for her to leave for work. He must have hidden somewhere nearby to observe her routine. Laura, Heather and Olivia. He'd been familiar with all their comings and goings. Who was this man who got close enough to his victims to build up an idea of their every move without drawing suspicion to himself?

She sighed and thumbed through speed dial for the number for HQ where she requested an officer inform Olivia's father of the current situation, then went back to pacing the room. Her mind returned to the conversation she'd had with Emma, before Rebecca Sandman's appearance. It bugged her that Heather's computer had bypassed her team and been sent directly to the technicians. She couldn't let go of the idea that pertinent information was being withheld. Dickson's cool attitude towards her only served to fuel her suspicion. He had to be behind the instruction to send the computer to the lab, yet pursuing it would only make matters worse, especially if Dickson found out.

She halted by the window, stared at her mobile screen for a minute, then made the decision to place her faith in Felicity. Felicity wasn't into office politics and got along with only a handful of people who she liked. Kate was one of those. The phone call was answered immediately.

'Hi, Kate. How's the latest victim?'

'She's hanging on at the moment, but I haven't been able to talk to her yet. By all accounts it's touch-and-go.'

'Poor girl. Emma was here earlier and told me about it.'

'Yes, I wanted to talk to you about that.'

Her voice dropped. 'I shouldn't have let her have access to the computer, so I hope you understand I went out on a limb, only because I like you both.'

'I know and I really appreciate it.'

'As I explained to Emma, there really wasn't anything on it that would have been of any use to you. Heather used it largely for work and a little online shopping. There was nothing that raised any red flags.'

'I'm sure if there'd been anything encrypted or deleted, you'd have found it.'

'You know me so well.' She followed the statement with a suspicious 'And I know you, so tell me what is this phone call really about?'

'Can we keep this conversation between us?'

'It'll be as if it never took place. You can trust me. Guide's honour and all that.'

'Were you a Girl Guide?'

'I have several hard-earned badges to prove it.'

Kate felt her lips pull into a smile. She found it hard to equate the self-acclaimed, anti-social Felicity as part of any such organisation.

'Spit it out,' said Felicity.

'Who instructed you to keep the contents to yourself?'

There was a soft intake of breath. 'I really shouldn't tell you.'

'Felicity, I'm up against it here. We have two dead women and another whose life is in the balance. The perpetrator is on a killing spree and if I can't get my act together, heaven knows how many more women will die. Imagine if Bev were to become one of his victims!'

'Don't say that.'

She'd struck a nerve. Felicity doted on her partner.

'We can't let this man strike again. I'm concerned I'm being kept in the dark. I can't have that. Nothing should get in the way of this investigation. Tell me who it was and I won't pester you again.'

She thought the line had gone dead but Felicity spoke at last. 'It was Superintendent Dickson.'

'Did he explain why?'

'There was some sensitive information on it, regarding an operation he was overseeing. I was instructed to download all files pertinent to the case, email them to him, then delete them from the computer.'

'You didn't happen to see what the case was about, did you?'

'It didn't involve your victims, not unless they were underage sex workers.'

Kate stopped breathing for a few seconds as she processed this news. *Underage sex workers. Like Rosa and Stanka, those girls that Farai told me had been booked for guests at the Maddox Club?* She was about to press the technician further on the matter, but Felicity spoke first.

'Let me make it clear, I didn't read through any of the files. I didn't need to know what it was about. Nor do you. Look, Kate, "Operation Agouti" wasn't relevant, so no matter how vexed you are that you weren't given primary access to the computer, it wasn't some deliberate ploy to scupper your investigation. I can assure you there was nothing else.'

'Thank you. I'm . . . getting frustrated. I hoped the computer would hold some vital key.'

'I understand. You're facing a tough challenge and this year hasn't been kind to you. I've been straight with you, so although it's probably not the answer you hoped for, you have one nevertheless and . . . we didn't have this conversation.'

'Thanks again.' She hung up and tapped the phone against her chin. Felicity had referred to the operation by its name and probably knew more than she was willing to say on the phone. So, Agouti involved underage sex workers, girls and boys like those Dickson and his friends had slept with. She still couldn't fathom out why a civilian officer had been brought on board to assist. This was a valid puzzle piece but she was unsure where it fitted within her own personal Dickson jigsaw. 'Chris, I've not given up on uncovering the truth about you. You understand that, don't you?'

There was no reply. She searched for the mental connection she required to respond in his voice, but this time she couldn't. A lump rose in her throat. He was drifting away and it was because she wasn't dedicating enough time to his cause. 'I shall. I'll find time. Don't go, Chris.'

A movement caught her eye and she recognised the large figure at the reception desk. Morgan had arrived to replace her. She shouldered her bag and exited the waiting room.

CHAPTER TWENTY

'For crying out loud, what the fuck *do* we have to go on?' Kate patrolled the small space between her desk and the whiteboard with all the ferocity of a guard dog. 'Well?'

Emma showed her palms. 'We're struggling, Kate. We've interviewed all the builders who were working on the site where Olivia was found. Their alibis all check out. None of the neighbours heard or noticed anything suspicious. Nobody at the retirement home has a clue as to what might have happened and are all devastated. It's dead end after dead end.'

Kate thumped the whiteboard hard. 'No! No, it isn't. There must be connections. The killer knew his victims. How? How the hell did he know these women? Look at them all again. There is something that connects them. We need to look harder! Time is ticking. And we don't know when or where he will strike next.'

Jamie cleared his throat. 'Guv, we've spoken to everybody.'

'We haven't. There are many more people we could talk to. Get a list of every delivery driver that dropped off at the building site in Salt Lane and check them out. What about Kevin Shire? Where was he this morning?'

'According to him, he was in bed until eight,' said Emma.

'Anyone able to confirm that?'

'No. And Saturday night, he claims he was at home, watching television. Again, no witnesses. We can't prove if he was or wasn't where he said. I've put in a request to the mobile provider, to see if his phone can be placed at either Stafford on Saturday, or Weston this morning. Oh, and he claims to never have heard of either Heather or Olivia. I hit a brick wall with pubs he visits. It seems neither Heather nor Laura were pub-goers. It would have been unlikely he met them there. I have had one more thought. Kevin did some part-time work last year for a local courier service. I'll ring the company. Find out if he ever delivered anything to any of the victims' places of work or home addresses.'

'Good. Do it.' Kate turned away, prodded the board. 'Why did our perpetrator choose *these* women to be his victims?'

'Their looks,' said Jamie.

'Yes, he's definitely drawn to a type – small-framed, youthful, dark-haired and brown-eyed.' *Like Tilly*. She tried to dismiss the thought. 'I don't believe he chanced upon his victims, plucked them out from a crowd and then stalked them until he knew enough about them to act out whatever warped fantasy he has. It would have taken time to gather information on their habits and routines. He must have raised suspicions.' She was speaking more to herself than her colleagues, frustration engraving lines on her forehead. 'He knew the exact times they went to and from work, where and when they exercised, and he knew where to lie in wait for them.' She paused to study the photos, giving herself an opportunity to order her tangled thoughts.

'He attacked them all in areas close to industrial bins, skips or large refuse containers and I think that's important to him. But why?' She tapped either side of her temples lightly then clicked her tongue. 'He disposes of his victims as he would any rubbish. I'd even go as far as to say he hates women, which is why he dumps their bodies in this fashion.'

Jamie made to interrupt, but Kate was on a roll, articulated theories now streaming from her lips. 'He chooses locations that fulfil this purpose, cases them out, ensures they have no CCTV and then, at the given moment, lies in wait, hidden from view. All of this preparation takes time: weeks, even months. And he follows the same pattern each time. I think he's been planning this rampage for a long while and if he knew his victims this well, they undoubtedly knew him. The question is how?'

Jamie hesitated then said, 'He's a friend.'

'We've cross-checked all their online friends and actual friends. We haven't found anyone that all three knew.' She shut her eyes. *Think, Kate, think.* She had nothing other than the knowledge she should see beyond the pictures on the board: Laura dumped in an industrial waste bin on a car park; Heather left in a skip by a car park—

Emma gave a defeated sigh. 'We've looked at work colleagues and until Olivia became our latest victim, we'd made some connections between Heather and Laura. Shouldn't we go back to those as well? See if we can make some of them fit Olivia as well?'

Olivia left by a dumper truck on a building site, alive. Kate opened her eyes. 'The third attack differs to the first two in that it didn't happen at night, and the victim survived. He wasn't as methodical.'

'Two different killers?' suggested Jamie.

'That's plausible, but I'm sure it's the same perpetrator and he's getting careless. He stalked these women for ages to learn about them, which indicates he was meticulous in his planning yet now, he's raping and murdering them, day after day. The two behaviours don't correlate.'

'Unless his initial intentions were to find out about these women, a sort of hunting game, but something triggered him into actually carrying out the attacks,' said Emma.

Jamie pursed his lips. 'Do you think he has a list of women he fantasises about raping and killing and now he's going through it?'

Kate swivelled around. 'That's possible. I'd go as far as to say he's motivated by the high each attack brings him and that, in turn, spurs him into attacking again, to feed the high. Yes. That makes sense. However, the speed and intensity with which he's carrying out the attacks is making him careless. Olivia is still alive.'

'You think she'll recover?'

'Hard to say. She's in a bad way. My request to place a uniformed officer outside her room has been approved, so Morgan will be back here soon. Right, who are we looking for? Who would be able to find out information about these three different women without arousing suspicions? That's what we need to establish. Once we've done that, we might be on the right path to identifying our killer.'

'I take it you're making progress, then?' DCI William Chase had arrived unheard and threw them a half-smile.

'Not really,' said Kate, dismissively. 'We're bandying ideas.'

The smile evaporated. 'Ideas? That's not good enough. We need leads and a suspect.'

'And I need a larger team to work this investigation, but we don't always get what we want, do we?'

He silenced her with his palm. 'Not here, Kate.'

She followed him into the corridor and lowered her voice. 'Look, William, it's no good piling pressure on us. We're busting our guts as it is. You can't expect instant results when all I have are three officers, all of whom have to attend a bloody crime reconstruction on the back of a half-baked idea the killer will show up to watch it.'

'That'll do, Kate. Don't make a scene here. We'll continue this in my office.' He marched towards the staircase, leaving her dumbfounded. She hadn't been making a scene, merely expressing her viewpoint as she often did with William. He had a bee in his bonnet over something and it wasn't because she had stood up for her team and their lack of progress. Nevertheless, she did as she was bidden and climbed to the next floor where she joined him in the office, shutting the door behind her. They'd had many a friendly discussion in this room but there was no camaraderie in his cold eyes today.

'What's going on, William? You haven't dragged me upstairs to haul me over the coals over my flare-up. I was justified and you know it.'

'Did you send Emma to the lab to uncover what was on Heather's computer?'

'Yes. We needed to know what was on it.'

'You were told the computer was with the technical team and that you'd be informed if they found anything relevant to the investigation, but instead, you instructed an officer to find out, first-hand, what was on it.'

'Sorry, you've lost me here. Why is that a problem?'

'The computer contained highly sensitive information that appertained to other investigations and wasn't for your or your officer's eyes.'

She couldn't believe her ears. 'That's crazy. I take full responsibility for tasking Emma with it, but she only requested information relevant to the investigation. There was a third victim in hospital and it was imperative we checked to see if there was a connection between her and Heather.'

'I don't think reading through Heather's emails was *relevant*.'

'Well, I do. There might have been clues in them. She might have struck up a friendship online via email with her killer.'

William thawed slightly. 'And were there any clues?'

Now was the moment to say something about Dickson, but Chris had included William's name on the list of potentially corrupt police officers, and until she worked out why it was there, she couldn't trust her boss. 'None that we know of.'

He sighed. 'So, on the one hand you berate me for not giving you extra manpower and yet you wasted one of your team's time checking up on something that could have been dealt with over the phone.'

She was at a loss for words. She lifted her hands in submission. 'Okay. I accept that might not have been the best use of Emma's time, but when I sent her to the lab, I had no way of knowing it would lead nowhere, and we were scratching around for leads, any leads.'

His expression didn't change but his voice softened. 'Well, now we understand each other, maybe you should get back to the task in hand and try not to fire off at me again.'

'Understood.'

She left the office, irked by William's behaviour. They'd worked together for many years and he'd never chastised her before when she'd followed her instincts and gone out on a limb. The only logical explanation was that Dickson had found out about Emma's visit from Felicity and ordered William to admonish Kate. *Shit!* It seemed Felicity hadn't been able to keep quiet about it, after all.

She had no time to dwell on the matter; there were other more pressing ones. She stormed into the office and picked up her car keys. She caught the look Emma gave her. 'I've got something to sort out. You can reach me on my mobile. You know what you're doing here?'

'No problems.'

Kate paused. 'I've not come across a pattern of acceleration like this before and it makes me wonder if the killer already has form for stalking, raping or GBH against women. Go back over any cold cases where there were similarities to these attacks and dig through unresolved rape cases. I have a feeling our man has a history of violence towards women.' She took off, her jaw set. She wanted to talk to Deepa Singh – alone.

CHAPTER TWENTY-ONE

Deepa shifted in the wide chair and shuffled her bare feet on the blue matching footstool, until she was more comfortable. She stared out of the French windows onto the small grassed area. A large bouquet of yellow roses, arranged in a blue vase, perfumed the room and Kate inhaled their delicate perfume while Deepa gathered her thoughts.

'I liked working with Heather. Not everyone did. She could be . . . intense, but I understood why. After she split up from her husband, the job became even more important to her and she poured herself into it to the point where it was all-consuming and almost her only topic of conversation.'

'You shared an office, didn't you?'

'That's right.'

'Were you good friends?'

She hesitated then shook her head. 'Good? We got along well. Heather was . . . a closed book. Personally, I think it was a front; others might disagree.'

'Did this happen after she and Greg split up?'

'No. She was always stand-offish. She rarely let slip what was going on in her personal life. It was always job first with her, and if she wound people up, she'd shrug it off and say she wasn't there to make friends.'

'Did she wind many up?'

'A few. She was a doer. She wouldn't suffer fools so if an investigation was stalling, she'd voice her opinion or concern.'

'Had she annoyed anyone in particular over the last few weeks?'

Deepa gave a small splutter of mirthless laughter. 'Probably everyone at Trentham House. They called her Hot Sauce.'

'Hot Sauce?'

'On account of the fact what you saw wasn't what you got with Heather. She could be very hard-going at times. That was the way she got results. Not everyone liked her approach.'

'Can you think of anyone in particular who she fell out with?'

'No. Sorry.' She shifted position again. 'Are you sure I can't get you a cup of tea or anything?'

Kate offered her a smile. 'No, thank you. I'll be upfront with you. We're struggling to find out who might have attacked her, and I could do with your help.'

'I've told your officers everything I know.'

'I know you have and you've been helpful, but maybe there was something she spoke about in confidence, or you overheard, or something that took place in the office that felt wrong at the time.'

'I can't think of anything.'

'Were there no instances when she voiced any concerns or seemed worried about anything?'

Deepa's dark eyes glistened. 'Over the last couple of days, I've thought about her a great deal and I've raked my memory for any clues to help work out why this happened to her. And all I established was, I actually knew next to nothing about her other than bland, insignificant details. Yes, we'd chat about television shows, clothes, even food, or moan about a case we might both be working on, and I'd talk endlessly about my family. She only had one passion outside of work – horse riding. She owned a horse, Tobias the Third, and took him eventing in her free time or simply around country lanes, or would spend hours grooming him and clearing out his stable. The only time I ever saw her animated was when she talked about her horse or riding.' She gave a sad smile.

Kate made a mental note to talk to the hands at Blackfields where Tobias the Third was stabled. They might have seen a different side to Heather. 'She didn't fall out with anyone you can think of?'

'No.' She scratched the top of her head and then said, 'Apart from Superintendent Dickson. She was working on a case with him last month – all hush-hush, and went to a meeting with him. When she came back, I could immediately tell that it had gone badly. She wouldn't tell me what had transpired, but the upshot was she'd been removed from the operation.'

A tingle raced over Kate's scalp, but she kept her questioning casual. 'She didn't mention what the case was about?'

'She was too professional for that.' Kate spotted the sudden flush to her cheeks.

'Do you know what the investigation was about?'

Her cheeks reddened further. 'I might have overheard the odd conversation. It wasn't intentional. We did share an office, after all.'

'I understand. It might help me, if you told me what you heard.'

'She spoke to somebody about an illegal, underage prostitute. Might that be relevant to your investigation?'

'I'm not ruling anything out at this stage. You didn't overhear a name, by any chance?'

She shook her head very slowly. 'No . . . Erm . . . Maybe . . . Somebody called Fadhi, Fahad . . .'

'Farai?' asked Kate.

Deepa's eyebrows lifted. 'Yes. You're right. I think it was Farai. Do you know him?'

'I've come across the name in connection with drug-dealing.'

Deepa pushed herself upright with a soft groan.

'Are you all right?'

'Fine. The baby kicked me, that's all. My husband is convinced it's a boy and that he'll be a professional boxer or kick-boxer.'

Using the interruption to her advantage, Kate moved on, away from the focus on Farai and Dickson. 'I understand it's difficult to think of anything that might be relevant, but if you cast your mind back over the last couple of weeks or even longer, can you recall any strangers hanging about outside the building, or maybe waiting in the car park?'

She shrugged both shoulders. 'I didn't notice anyone acting suspiciously.'

'No unusual activity . . . a car that appeared regularly for a while and then disappeared?'

Deepa rested her hands against her belly again. 'Sorry.'

'Whoever did this knew Heather was working at Trentham House on Saturday evening. Looking back, can you think of anything at all that might be relevant – a sighting of a car you didn't recognise, a delivery person, a telephone engineer, working outside?'

'We spent all day in the office, and you can't see the street from our window. We didn't even leave for a lunch break.' She gave a sad shake of her head.

A robin landed on the garden fence and stared at the women, its head turning this way and that as if weighing them up. Kate watched it drop to the lawn and peck at an insect before flying away again. She had what she'd really come for – information about Dickson. It was time to depart so, with thanks, she got to her feet and found her way back out to her car.

Heather had been working on a case involving an illegal prostitute and Farai. The pieces were slotting into place: Dickson, Farai and underage prostitutes. If she could only uncover Dickson's reasons for removing Heather from Operation Agouti, she might even be able to link him to her death. *No.* She wasn't acting like a proper detective, allowing fantasy to replace clear logical thinking and facts. Dickson wouldn't be so audacious as to have a CIO killed and her death made to look like the work of the rapist. Yes, he would. Look at what had happened to Chris.

A shimmering, ghost-like vision of Chris watched her from the garden: a strangely comforting sight. He had not yet deserted her. She would probe deeper because Dickson was up to no good – a dirty copper who hid behind his badge of seniority.

The alarm on her mobile buzzed to remind her of the time. The families of three women were counting on her, and as much as she wanted to pursue this new line of enquiry into Dickson, she had to attend the crime scene reconstruction at Trentham House. Chris vanished, leaving a vacuum in her chest. She sighed sadly and rang Morgan to ensure the team was on their way too. If the killer was going to show his face, they'd need to be ready to pounce.

◆　◆　◆

She parked fifty metres from the car park where Heather's body had been found and, half-hidden by television crew vans, she walked briskly towards a group of dark-clothed individuals, relieved to see a crowd of only about thirty interested citizens gathered on the pavement opposite, held at bay by a man holding a megaphone. A young woman in a blouse, skirt and jacket similar to Heather's was in conversation with a short, bespectacled man. Snippets of conversation lifted on the breeze and Kate caught the odd comment, 'we'll start there', 'Trentham House', 'walk at the agreed pace', 'one take'. Catching sight of William in plain clothes, elbows on the roof of his car, she slowed her pace and joined him.

'Not many here,' she said, taking up position next to him. From here she had a clear view of the onlookers.

'There's time for more to arrive.' He turned around, back to the crowd. 'You've got a clear view of the onlookers from here and we'll arouse less suspicion if it appears we're chatting.'

She scanned the faces. Morgan was standing behind everyone, back against a wall, a bored look on his handsome face. Emma was further up the street, phone pressed to her ear as if having a conversation with someone. She couldn't see Jamie at first then spotted him talking to a middle-aged woman in a blue Puffa jacket, blending in perfectly.

'We had no choice but to pursue this angle, Kate.'

'I know.'

'This isn't a reflection on you or your team, but we have to do whatever we can.' He paused before saying, 'Laura's father is making an appeal tonight.'

'Is that wise? Won't the public get jittery?'

'He insisted on doing it.'

'I thought the media office was supposed to be drip-feeding information to the press. Now we've got reconstructions and appeals and it will only lead to one thing – panic.'

'Things changed.'

'An appeal and a reconstruction in the same night! As soon as the media starts shouting out about a serial rapist and murderer—'

'Look, this wasn't my call to make.'

'Whose call was it? The superintendent's?'

'It came from even higher up. We only heard about it an hour ago. Richard Dean contacted the press, not us. These are two separate events. I'm as unhappy as you are about it, but we knew we couldn't keep a lid on this forever.'

She let the silence that fell between them swell. It carried greater gravitas than words. Heather's stand-in and the man parted company. Her bobbed hair framed her small features and she stepped away with the grace of an accomplished actress or dancer. Kate was again reminded of how similar the victims had looked. Although different ages, they'd exuded a youthfulness, enhanced by slim hips, narrow waists and shoulder-length glossy hair. Maybe their attacker had chosen them because they seemed easy targets, rather than because of their fragile beauty. There was a pattern, a reasoning to his choice and it frightened Kate because somewhere, another woman who was similar in looks was probably being stalked at this very moment and might well be attacked tonight. Standing here was squandering the valuable time she needed to track down this bastard.

Another couple joined the other curious bystanders. The camera crew were in position, cameras hoisted onto shoulders and a booming voice instructed everyone to remain silent during filming. The megaphone was lowered and mobile phones lifted to film as if celebrity spotting. Kate couldn't understand it. What attracted people to something as morbid as this?

She allowed her gaze to bounce over the eager spectators on the opposite side of the road, hunting for somebody whose face or posturing gave him away. Heather's double was walking purposefully along the pavement, head lowered, handbag over her shoulder. Kate searched the faces: two women in their twenties, glued to the spot; a man next to them, head down, texting; a couple of twenty-something-year-old men, one with a long-lensed Nikon camera pointed at Trentham House, the other observing in silence – reporters for the local rag, mused Kate. She caught Emma's eye and made no sign of acknowledgement. Emma slipped next to a trio of young women, with arms interlinked. Kate studied the couple in their late forties, the only pair not videoing the proceedings, and mumbled,

'None of these people look like a potential murderer.' William grunted.

She picked out two guys in dark clothing and hoodies, leaning against the wall, hands in pockets. Morgan had clocked them too and was keeping an eye on them. Jamie was still talking to the woman in the blue coat; his gaze, however, was falling over her shoulder to the people behind her. Some late arrivals meandered along the pavement. Kate kept her eyes trained on the group opposite. William kept his focus on the woman and said, 'She's almost reached the point where Heather was attacked.'

Nobody displayed any signs of excitement or anticipation. Kate glimpsed a late arrival, a middle-aged man in a duffel coat, carrying a plastic bag. Did he seem out of place here? She honed in on his unshaven face. The killer would recognise the spot where he'd struck Heather and dragged her into the garden. Maybe there'd be a widening of eyes, a licking of lips or an intensity to their gaze, but she spotted none of those giveaways. The man watched with the interest of somebody watching a dreary television drama. The scene played out, the woman was felled with a blow and dragged away from sight.

'Nothing,' she said. 'I can't see anyone who strikes me as odd.'

William shifted position, glanced in the same direction as her. 'The guy in the red beanie?'

She latched onto the young man, head lowered over his mobile. 'No, he's been more focused on texting than on what's going on. The killer would want to watch every move.'

'The two hooded lads?'

'Their stance is all wrong. They're jokers, attention-seekers. They're not really interested in what's happening. They most likely want to get on camera and pull faces.'

'What about the man with that plastic bag?'

'It's a local supermarket bag. I have a feeling he's on his way home from there and got caught up in this.' She watched as a few individuals drifted away. The camera crew were moving down the road towards the car park, further away from the dwindling crowd.

William sighed.

'What time is Richard doing his appeal?'

'It'll be the lead story on the local news.' The station broadcast the news at seven and the reconstruction would go out at eight o'clock.

'Action!' She lifted her head. The woman walked down the road again, the light bounce to her step reminding Kate for a brief moment of Tilly. She wondered how her stepsister was getting on and hoped she and Daniel were doing something interesting and fun that would encourage them to settle here for good. She'd give her a call as soon as she could. More people broke away. The hooded youths shuffled past Morgan. Jamie had left the woman in blue and joined Emma, who was shaking her head.

'William, this is hopeless. The killer isn't here. I'm calling off the team,' she said.

William gave her a nod and she signalled to Morgan to meet by her car. They arrived one after the other to join her. The film crew stood about, waiting for confirmation that they had enough footage, ignoring the few stragglers still waiting for more filming. Kate took another look at those who'd remained. There was nothing to indicate they were anything other than curious bystanders.

'Fucking pointless,' grumbled Morgan. 'We've got stacks to wade through and this was a waste of time.'

Kate was in full agreement. No matter what television police dramas might portray, or how much her superiors wanted results, the fact remained: policework took time.

'We carried out orders. It didn't work out, but we've all been in that situation before. We might get a witness out of this.'

211

'And a shitload of timewasters,' said Morgan.

'Lighten up,' said Emma. 'You're getting cranky.'

'I hate wasting fucking time and—'

'None of us like wasting time,' Kate interrupted. 'And you're not going to like what I'm about to tell you – Richard Dean has decided to do a television appeal on the evening news.'

'Oh, for fuck's sake!' This time it was an outburst from Emma.

Kate left it unchecked. 'It goes out at seven, so if you want to grab some food or take a break, I suggest you do it now because in about an hour, the phones will be red hot.'

Jamie ran a hand over his stubbled chin and cleared his throat.

'Problem?' said Kate.

He pulled out his mobile from his pocket. 'Just that I'd better warn the wife. She planned a girls' night out tonight and I promised I'd look after Zach. She isn't going to be happy.'

'For real?' said Morgan with a sneer. 'She's got you under her thumb.'

'No, she hasn't.'

'Sounds like it to me. Look at you, racing off to apologise.'

'It's not like that.'

'Then why are you so worked up?'

'I'm not—'

'Off you trot. Go and grovel to your missus.' He waved Jamie away with both hands.

'Aw, fuck off, Sarge.'

Kate caught sight of the sudden cloud of fury that stretched across Jamie's features before he stomped off, phone pressed to his ear, and disappeared out of sight. This was a side to him she hadn't seen before. Jamie always seemed easy-going. The strain of the case was beginning to take its toll on them all.

'Happy now?' said Emma to Morgan. 'You can be such a shit at times.'

'He's a wet arse. Look at the way he's stormed off to make the call so we can't overhear him grovelling.'

'He cares about his family, that's all. Come on, there's a drive-through McDonald's down the road. We'll pick up something.'

'That tosser can buy his own.' Morgan took off.

Emma shrugged at Kate. 'He'll get over it. I think he finds Jamie a bit much at times. One minute he's desperate for overtime and the next, he's fretting that he isn't around enough for his family. Morgan doesn't get it because he doesn't have the same sort of responsibility.'

'Do you find him a bit much too?'

'No. He's friendly and hard-working and I'm far more easy-going than Morgan,' she replied, a twinkle in her eyes. 'Shall we see you back at the station?'

'Yes. Did Jamie come with you two?'

'No, he was out somewhere, checking on a witness statement, and used his own transport. Probably just as well given Morgan's mood. And just so you know, I spoke to the courier company Kevin worked for. They have no record of deliveries to any of the victims, or to their places of work. And, on my way here, I heard from his mobile phone provider. According to them, he sent and received several texts from his mobile on Saturday evening, all from his house. I think we'll have to take him out of the frame.'

'Another suspect out of the picture and nobody else to fill the space,' said Kate. 'Damn!'

'I know. We'll have to hope this turns up something. See you in a bit.' She hastened after Morgan. Kate looked back at what was now an almost empty pavement. Why had she and her team been sent on such a wild goose errand? Surely nobody had truly believed they could entice a killer back to the scene of his crime to observe a reconstruction. William was now sitting in his vehicle. Waiting for what? She couldn't see if he was taking a phone call and couldn't think why else he'd still be here.

Chris's voice was faint and she strained to hear him. 'Haven't you twigged yet? He's keeping an eye on you. This is a set-up to make you look inefficient. It's part of Dickson's plan to get you out of his station and life. Although, if you don't follow up the Agouti angle, he won't need to. Every minute you spend distracted by this case is allowing him more time to cover his tracks. At this rate, he'll get away with it, you won't have any leads left to follow and this investigation into my death will become a cold case. Is that what you want? For it to disappear? For me to go?'

'No!' Heat flooded her veins. She couldn't bear being without Chris, even if she was going to be seeing more of Tilly and Daniel. She lifted her warm face to capture the cool breeze and observed row after row of cirrocumulus clouds displaying an undulating, rippling pattern like fish scales – a mackerel sky, heralding a change in the weather.

'Then you have to topple Dickson before he destroys you.' The last words petered into the distance, as though carried by the wind.

'I know.' She dropped her head and unlocked her car. As she pulled away, she took one last look back at William's car. It hadn't moved.

He tries not to smile at the banality of the situation. Did they really think he would fall into such an obvious trap? Since when did this crime show broadcast the fact they'd be filming a reconstruction and give out the location? It was demeaning to insult his intelligence in this manner. On the plus side, he was clearly unnerving his hunters if they had to resort to such low tactics.

He's going along with it, of course. Not because he hopes it will help him relive the delicious moments he attacked Heather, but because this is a game he can win, hands down.

He's puzzled though. Heather had definitely been alive when he'd dumped her in the skip. She'd smashed her nose trying to escape and bled a fair bit, but he'd been in control that time. He hadn't lost concentration and throttled her to death like he had Laura. He'd checked her over and felt a pulse. Perplexed as he is, he isn't going to panic about it; after all, he's not going to get caught.

DI Kate Young is in position on the street opposite him, trying to look casual, but actively scanning the crowd. Talk about obvious! She might as well have I'm a police officer illuminated above her head. Her scrawny frame and hollow-eyed stare betray many sleepless nights. He hopes the more recent ones are on account of his actions. If she had any idea of how much he knows about her and her sister, she'd be even more troubled. He keeps his head lowered, fully aware she is shooting looks at them all, hoping to spot a facial expression or giveaway gesture and here he is, right under her nose and she is none the wiser. This almost makes up for killing Heather. It doesn't give him the same high as attacking his stand-ins, but it's bolstered his ego. If she were his type, he'd make her his next victim. His hunter turned prey. Although the thought excites him, he knows he'd find it impossible to become aroused by her, even with his hands around her throat.

The trick is to look disinterested in the filming, or only mildly curious about the reconstruction. And although the stand-in resembles Heather, he isn't going to allow himself trips of fantasy. Besides, he has another victim already lined up: an entrée before the main dish. He is ever closer to his ultimate goal. He's been messaging his first love and she is ready to invite him back into her life. He is dizzy at the prospect, his excitement reaching new highs. Nobody is going to stop him getting to her, especially DI Kate Young.

CHAPTER
TWENTY-TWO

The scent of freshly picked lemons infused the kitchen. Kate plunged the sponge mop into hot water and slapped it onto the kitchen tiles, grunting as she mopped, backwards and forwards. All the while, she could hear Chris's voice and maintained a steady stream of conversation as if he were right there beside her. She hadn't heard him so strongly in days. His voice was loud, bordering on bossy and concerned her slightly. Was she becoming too obsessive?

'You have to try Farai again. Drag it out of him, find out what Dickson was up to and convince him to let you speak to the sex worker who slept with Dickson. I don't think you can do it without raising suspicions so, like it or not, you need somebody to work with you and I think I have the very person to help you out – Dan Corrance. We worked together, investigating a paedophile ring, and he helped me compile the list in my journal.'

Dan had found the journal taped underneath a drawer in Chris's old desk and given it to her, in the hope she'd be able to bring charges against some of the people and institutions named in it. The Maddox Club had been one of them and the information in the journal had helped her solve that investigation; however, she'd done no more with it, other than keep it hidden. She maintained the momentum, arms moving tirelessly while she replied. 'You're telling me to put my faith in a journalist I don't know. Great idea, Chris.'

'You know you can trust him, because, instead of keeping my journal for himself, he chose to hand it over to you. He'll be a good ally.'

'He wanted me to handle it in my capacity as a detective and for the people named in that book to be convicted for their crimes. All I've done is sit on it, wondering how best to use the information to drag Dickson down. I ought to have done something about them before now. He won't approve of that.'

'You're wrong. He didn't give you the information because you're a detective. He gave you the journal because you're my wife! Listen to me, Dan is your best shot. You're not able to touch Dickson, but if you let Dan in on what you're doing, he'll be able to rattle cages and, at the very least, print something.'

'For fuck's sake, he'll probably get sued for libel or, even worse, murdered like you were!' The words burst out from her lips and she kicked out at the plastic bucket, sliding it across the sparkling, tiled floor. Water slopped over the sides, leaving large tear-shaped puddles.

She ran the sponge over the water, sucked it up then carried the bucket to the sink, where she tipped it out. The almost clean water gurgled down the plughole noisily. It was three o'clock in the morning and she was still wide awake. Richard Dean had made his appeal on the local news and begged anyone who'd been in Abbots Bromley on Friday evening to come forward. The team had gathered in front of a computer screen in the office as he spoke without the use of prepared notes. His voice had cracked when he held up the photograph of his daughter and told those watching that she was a beautiful, gentle human being who'd been robbed of any life and future happiness, and at that point tears had fallen. There had been no sign of Steve. The phones had begun ringing before the broadcast was over, every detail and claim noted by her officers. They were still handling calls regarding Laura's death when, following the broadcast of the crime reconstruction outside Trentham House, the second wave began. At midnight she'd drawn an end to it. They'd pick up where they left off the following day – probably more bloody dead ends. They were so busy chasing up all the possible sightings of individuals in the area, they had no time to go back over what they'd already uncovered.

'Try Dan. Give him the journal and let him do what he sees fit to do. Give him the extra ammunition we have on Dickson, as well. He'll be able to use it.'

'You're not listening to me, are you? It's too dangerous for him to get involved. I can't risk his life. This is *my* problem and I'll resolve it.'

'But how?'

She ignored the question, opened a drawer and removed a clean cloth, then, using an anti-bacterial spray, began puffing another citrus aroma into the air, this time clementine. She wiped the surfaces, lifting jars and cleaning under them, over and over. *How?* She could go ahead and press charges against Dickson for sleeping with underage sex workers, but what she truly desired was proof he was somehow involved in her husband's or Cooper's death. That would carry a heavier penalty and, combined with the other offences, would ensure he was locked up for a very long time. She began rubbing the cupboard doors: intense, frenzied motions that didn't seem to tire her. Only after she'd cleaned every single one of them, along with the fridge and kettle, did she stop, cloth still in her hand.

'I'll wait to see what Bradley comes up with first,' she said. 'His brother might have information about what really happened to Cooper.'

'And if he doesn't?'

'I'll consider involving Dan.' She picked up the spray and made for the bathroom. There was plenty of cleaning upstairs to keep her occupied until she felt drowsy.

◆ ◆ ◆

By six, she still hadn't slept. She'd spent the last hour in Chris's den, going back over the journal that contained the names and dates of men who he suspected of being paedophiles. The way she saw it, she had two choices: hand the book over to the Paedophile Investigation Unit so they could begin looking into the names, or, as Chris had suggested, give it to Dan Corrance. If she passed it over to the police, Dickson would hear about it and extricate himself. It would also put him further on guard and she'd find it harder still to connect him to the train massacre that saw her husband murdered, and Cooper's apparent suicide. With a heavy sigh, she acquiesced. Chris's reasoning made sense and as reluctant as she was to part with her husband's journal, she would. He'd left her the file of suspected corrupt officers on his computer, and that was what she was mostly concerned with.

She got to her feet and stretched. It would soon be time to return to the investigation and leave this to one side. She picked up the book, caressed the leather, feeling for any residue of her husband, any leftover energy that might have been transmitted onto it.

'There's nothing, Kate. It's only a work journal.'

'Not any journal. It was yours.'

'You have other objects to remind you of me. You don't need another one.'

A decision had been reached. 'Okay.'

She headed to the kitchen where her phone lit up. Tilly had sent a message to say she was up early and had gone training with Emma again. She rang her back.

'Morning, early bird.' Tilly sounded on form.

'You can talk.'

'Daniel was up at five so I thought I'd take him along to play computer games with Greg and do a quick workout.'

'Hi, Daniel!'

She could make out a cheerful but muffled hello.

'We're going to the Sea Life Centre in Birmingham later today. Thought we'd catch the train there.'

'Sounds great fun. Wish I was going with you.'

'Well, maybe you could come next time. I was thinking of inviting Ryan along for some adult company but decided it would be better without him. This is Daniel's treat.'

'Ryan?'

'Yeah. Apparently, *Happy Feet* is one of his all-time favourite films.' She sniggered. 'I thought he might like to see the penguins. Anyhow, I changed my mind. I'll sort out something else with Ryan.'

Kate tried to sound upbeat. She didn't want to come across as a killjoy. 'Fair enough. Anyway, have a good workout and I'll try and visit you later.'

'We'll bring you back something from the gift shop at the Sea Life Centre,' said Tilly.

'Make sure it isn't a shark.' She heard Daniel laughing merrily before Tilly hung up.

There was no queue at Jeanette's snack van, nor was anyone sitting at the brightly painted tables, scattered on the square beside it. Jeanette was visible behind the serving hatch, preparing sandwiches. The takeaway van was a familiar sight to anyone visiting Stoke, together with its snaking line of customers, eager to purchase one of the famous, home-made savoury pastries, and a hot drink. Chris had adored one of her specialities, sausage rolls made with herbs and onion relish. They'd fuelled him on many a long day at the office that overlooked the van. In the better weather, he'd often hold meetings at one of the tables, and Kate found it easy to picture him there, sipping a foaming cappuccino. *The Gazette* staff worked on the fourth floor but she wouldn't have to go upstairs in search of Dan. He, like most of those who worked at the newspaper, would stop at Jeanette's first. It was a ritual all the journalists seemed to follow.

'Hi, I don't suppose Dan Corrance has been by, has he?' she asked Jeanette.

The woman turned a bright smile on her. 'Not yet, love.' She hadn't imagined this comely, middle-aged woman when Chris had spoken about her. 'Want to wait for him? He usually turns up around this time. Early bird and all that.'

'Thanks. I'll have a coffee too, please. White. No sugar.'

Jeanette busied herself with the machine, which hissed into life, spluttering hot water into a paper cup.

'Anything to eat with this?'

'I'm fine, thanks.' She paid up and chose a seat that afforded her a view of the front door to the block, in case Dan decided to bypass the van today. Within seconds of sitting down, her mobile rang. It was Bradley although he made no preamble when she answered.

'I have an appointment this morning.'

She interpreted his cryptic message immediately.

'That's good and you'll let me know the outcome.'

'Most definitely.'

It meant Bradley had arranged a visit to Thamesbury Prison to speak to his brother, Jack. She pressed end call and caught sight of the journalist she'd last seen on her doorstep in May. He didn't notice her at first, not until he was almost at the van. She signalled to him. He said something to Jeanette and meandered across.

'Hey. How are you doing?'

'Better. Thanks.'

'Good.'

'The last time we met, you gave me something.'

'Uh-huh.'

'Well, I think you should have it. Chris would have wanted you to follow it up.'

'I thought you'd want to nail the people named in it. That's why I gave it to you,' he said, then glanced around. 'Those bastards should pay for what they did.'

'In truth, it's out of my jurisdiction. I wouldn't be allowed to follow it up, only pass it on to the appropriate unit. If you're determined to go down that route, then take it to them yourself, tell them what you and Chris found out.'

She hunted in her bag for the journal and pushed it across the table towards him. 'I think you and Chris spent a great deal of time amassing this information and I'm sure it could be very useful to you.'

A small crease appeared between his brows. 'Really?'

'Really.'

'You're happy for me to delve further, even write about this if my editor agrees?'

'Yes, although there is one caveat.'

'What's that?'

'Be careful about how much and what you divulge. Some of the people named in here have a great deal of influence.'

He waved his hand airily. 'Like I care about that.'

'You should. Look at what happened to Chris.'

The eager, hungry look on his face vanished in an instant. 'Shit! Sorry. I didn't mean—'

She shook off his apology. 'It's fine. You must be cautious. When cornered, powerful people can be extremely dangerous.'

'I'll make sure I cover my back.' He slipped the journal into a canvas satchel.

Jeanette called out, 'Dan, your bacon sandwich is ready.'

He shouted back his thanks and got up. 'Should I contact you about anything relating to this?'

'No, do whatever you feel fit with it. Do what Chris would have done. I have to get off too. Good luck, Dan.'

'You too.' He raced off to collect his breakfast and Kate left him deep in conversation with the van owner.

Jamie was working, with a cling-filmed sandwich and an open can of Coke on his desk. 'Morning, guv.'

'Morning.'

He shifted position to face her. 'About yesterday evening and that business with Morgan. I was a bit stressed, what with a few money issues and the new baby due in a few months and Zach—'

'You don't need to apologise to me.'

'I was out of order. It won't happen again.'

She brushed it away with a wave of her hand.

'Sophie's found the move to Stoke harder than we expected and lately, Zach's been playing her up.'

She waited in case he wanted to unburden himself further, but footsteps sounded in the corridor and Jamie turned away. Within seconds, Morgan bowled through the door.

'Morning, Kate. Okay, Jamie? Let's take a look at you then.' When Jamie faced him, Morgan made a show of studying him then chuckled. 'No black eyes. You got off with a tongue-wagging, did you?'

'That's actually not funny,' said Jamie.

'Only trying to lighten the mood, mate,' Morgan replied.

Kate winced. He'd done the opposite. Any apology Jamie might have offered would not materialise now. She was about to intervene and dissipate any feelings of animosity, when Emma arrived.

'Hi. I've brought us a treat. Greg's girlfriend's been making cakes and she's a wicked baker. These are melt-in-the-mouth, to-die-for brownies. She's baked enough for an entire army so, here you go, Morgan. Try and leave a couple for us.' She handed him the plastic box, accompanied by a grin. The mood shifted.

Kate used the moment to bring everyone back on track. 'Thanks, Emma. Right, we still have loads of follow-up calls from last night's broadcasts to get through.'

Morgan popped the lid on the box. 'These look delicious. Here, grumpy guts.' He passed the box to Jamie, who took one without comment. 'I thought we'd handled all the calls from Richard Dean's appeal.' He picked up a cake and took a bite.

'There are still a couple of people to follow up. One of them saw a motorbike pass through the village on Friday evening,' said Emma. She searched through her notes and stabbed at a name. 'Mr Procter. He's dropping by first thing this morning.'

'And do we have many calls left to chase up from the crime reconstruction?' asked Kate.

'At least a dozen,' said Jamie.

Morgan emptied his mouth. 'I still don't see why we had to attend that. I didn't spot anyone in the crowd.'

Kate wasn't going to cover the same old ground again. 'We'll divide the names on the list among us and that way, we'll get through them more quickly.' She crossed the room to Jamie's desk to collect the details, each on separate notes. 'I maintain our killer isn't a novice. These aren't frenzied attacks. The victims are deliberately chosen, their routines observed. How else would the killer know where and when to lie in wait for them? I'm sure whoever committed these crimes has assaulted or raped before Friday. He might even have previous form.'

'I go along with that theory. Serial killers often start small and build up. They maim animals or have offended in their youth. Same goes for rapists. They're likely to be stalkers or flashers before they begin raping,' said Morgan.

Emma nodded in agreement.

Kate's eyes rested on the board containing the photographs of the victims. It was a speculative long shot, but what other options were left open to her at present? 'Morgan, can you look back at old cases in Staffordshire, involving rape or assault on women, especially those where the victim received a blow to the neck or was threatened or attacked with a weapon? Anything that resembles this perpetrator's MO.'

Jamie placed his uneaten brownie on a notepad. 'Guv, I understand the logic of your arguments, but what if this perpetrator has never been caught before? Many rapes don't get reported and Laura could be his first actual murder victim. He might even not be from this area or even from this country, making it impossible to work out who he is.'

Morgan snapped, 'If you've got any better suggestions, we're all ears.'

'No, I haven't. I was voicing an opinion. I thought that's what went on in this team, or is anyone under the rank of DS expected to hold their tongue?'

Morgan puffed out his chest, the alpha male displaying his prowess, then checked himself before locking horns with Jamie. 'Fair point. I concede.'

'Jamie, I've already considered those very thoughts; however, unless we get a lead, we're scratching around and I have to pursue every avenue I can come up with. It's imperative we get leverage on this investigation, so if we can turn up something by looking through old cases, it'd be worth it,' said Kate. 'Emma, are there many martial arts clubs, centres and gyms in the area? This guy must keep up his training somewhere.'

'Loads. I'm still looking into them.'

Kate wrinkled her nose. She'd hoped there would only be a few. It would be a huge help if they could get a description of the perpetrator. 'Okay. Stick at it. And for the time being, carry on following up the calls. Any more questions or concerns?'

'I'm cool with it all,' said Morgan. 'Jamie?'

'Nah. Fine.'

'To work, then,' said Kate. She glanced at the first name on her list and dialled the number. The man at the end of the phone was vague and unsure of what he'd seen. As was often the case, people were often well intentioned but not very observant. His description of the two young men sounded like the youths they'd already interviewed. She thanked him for his time. The second call was time-consuming and fruitless. By the time she'd ended it she was already experiencing defeat at such a fruitless task, until she noticed Jamie had spun round to face her and she spotted the fresh sparkle in his eyes.

'I've come off a call to a woman who is certain she saw a motorcyclist smoking in Newbury Avenue car park, on Saturday at around five o'clock.'

'Any description?'

'Black helmet, black bike.'

'But if he was smoking, surely he'd have removed his helmet?'

'The visor was lifted and she couldn't see his face, because he turned away from her when she drove past.'

'Tall?'

'Medium height.'

'That's it?'

'Uh-huh.'

'If he was smoking, there might be a cigarette butt around. I'll check with Ervin. Emma, what time is your witness coming in?'

'Mr Procter? He said it would be first thing, so any time soon.'

'Well, that's two separate sightings of a motorbike. Let me know when Mr Procter arrives and we'll see if he can give us a clearer description.' She rang the next name on the list, a jogger who thought he'd seen a woman matching Heather's description with a man in a local pub, late on Saturday night. It would have to be checked out, although Kate was sure that by the time this witness spotted the couple, Heather was already dead.

'Kate. He's here,' said Emma. Kate passed the task of looking into the possible pub sighting to Jamie and joined Emma to meet Mr Procter.

CHAPTER
TWENTY-THREE

Brian Procter was straight-talking with clear indigo eyes, a chiselled jaw and cropped silver hair. He added intensity to his words by pausing and cocking his head at the end of every meaningful sentence. The science teacher was sure about what he'd seen, and Kate felt he was a trustworthy witness.

'Would you mind repeating what you told DS Donaldson over the phone, please?'

He shuffled into position, hands relaxed in his lap. 'I left my house in Doveridge at seven o'clock on Friday evening, to visit my parents, who live in Blithbury. The most direct and quickest route is via Abbots Bromley and traffic was light in both directions. I was listening to an audiobook, possibly a little too intensely, and was surprised when a motorcyclist appeared from nowhere and overtook me at speed. I didn't think anything of it at the time or when I saw it again in Abbots Bromley. The rider had stopped on the roadside, beside the restaurant car park. I wondered if the bike had broken down, but the rider didn't dismount and I had to swing out into the road to pass by. I glanced at the biker but he or she looked away as I overtook them. I didn't see the bike again.'

'Where did the bike overtake you?'

'Soon after the Willslock crossroads.'

'Did it come from the same direction as you – Uttoxeter?'

'I can't be certain. It might have joined at the crossroads.'

The junction he was referring to was only five minutes out of Uttoxeter, but if he was correct, the bike could have travelled along country lanes from almost any direction to reach the road in question.

'Are you able to give us a description of the person or their bike?'

'I know nothing about motorbikes. It was black and shiny.'

'And the person riding it?'

'Tricky to say because they were sitting down. Quite tall because their feet were flat on the ground and the bike was large. I'd guess about my height – six foot. They were dressed in a black leather jacket, grey jeans, black boots and a full helmet, so I didn't see their face. I can't be sure of their gender.'

'What about build?'

'Medium, although it was hard to tell because the jacket was shapeless.'

'What about the bike's registration? Did you notice it or any stickers on it that might help identify it?'

'Nothing.'

'The bike didn't have a registration plate?'

'No, and that's why I contacted you. My initial thought was that it might have fallen off, but after seeing the programme last night, I wondered if it had been deliberately removed.'

'Was there anything else you thought strange?'

'I can't think of anything else.'

'And you're sure that the bike that overtook you was the same one you passed in Abbots Bromley?'

'Unless there were two identical black bikes, both without number plates. I came here because I thought if you had some pictures of motorbikes, I might be able to pick out the one I saw.'

'We can certainly try that.'

'I have a photographic memory.' He gave a small smile. 'It can be useful at times.'

Emma agreed to go through images of motorbikes with Brian, so Kate left them to it. He'd provided them with a potential lead. If they could get an idea of the make and model of the bike and run checks through CCTV footage, this could be promising. Kate was almost at the office when her mobile rang and she got the news she'd been waiting for. She immediately set aside all thoughts of the black bike and poked her head around the door. 'Jamie, I need you to take over from Emma in interview room A. She'll fill you in. Ask her to meet me in the car park. Olivia Sandman has regained consciousness and we've been granted permission to talk to her.'

◆ ◆ ◆

The sign on the door was written in large bold type. Nobody was to pass through to the ward without first putting on clean gowns and PPE equipment from the trolley outside. Kate told the police officer assigned to watching over Olivia to take a short break. Once they'd put on the PPE, she and Emma entered and waited by the nurses' station. Nobody was behind the glass windows and a few minutes passed before a nurse came to their assistance. Kate explained the purpose of their visit and was met with expressive emerald eyes and a soft Irish lilt.

'We were expecting you. Although Olivia keeps slipping in and out of consciousness, you are allowed to talk to her. However, I'll have to remain there with you, to make sure she's okay.'

'Has she said anything yet?' asked Kate.

'Only confused mumbles. She's still in a very poorly state.' Her gown rustled with efficiency as she led the way to a private room.

Kate crossed the threshold and halted. The *beep, beep, beep* of the heart monitor brought back memories of her father's last days. Such beeping seemed to be a permanent audio-wallpaper for most wards. Kate had discovered not every alarm indicated a serious problem, as seemed to be the case here. The IV medication bag was almost empty and the nurse set about replacing it. Kate let her gaze fall on the dark-haired girl, lost under the white sheets. Her hair was scraped back from her pale forehead, the only part of her face not covered in a myriad of dark colours. Kate couldn't see her lips, hidden by the oxygen mask, undoubtedly swollen from the brutal attack. A new bag was attached and the nurse beckoned Kate and Emma closer before saying, 'Olivia, you have visitors. Can you hear me, Olivia?'

Her eyelids fluttered.

'Olivia, the police are here. They want to ask you a few questions.' She stood to one side.

Kate took a step closer. 'Olivia, I'm Kate and this is Emma. We're police officers.'

The eyelids opened then shut again. For the briefest of moments, Kate had spied bloodshot eyes. She tried again. 'Olivia, you're in hospital. You were attacked. We want to find out who did this to you.'

The girl managed to open her eyes once more, this time a little longer. Kate moved closer to her bedside. 'Hi. I'm DI Kate Young.'

This time the girl blinked and her head moved slightly from side to side. She let out a low groan.

'You're okay. You're safe now. You're in hospital.'

The monitor indicated an increase in the girl's heart rate.

'Can you tell us anything about the man who hurt you?' Kate asked.

Olivia released another moan and the electronic noise amplified in conjunction with her accelerated heart rate. The nurse rushed forwards. 'Sorry, but I'll have to ask you to leave. This is too distressing for her.' Olivia mumbled something.

'One second,' pleaded Kate, leaning in to hear the girl. 'Say that again, Olivia.'

'You're . . . mine . . . forever.' The alarm increased in volume and the nurse made rapid hand signals for them to leave. Kate stepped away from the young woman, whose eyes were once again tightly shut. Emma was already at the door and they left the nurse standing by the bedside, watching the numbers on the screen descend to an acceptable level.

'What did she say?' asked Emma.

'"You're mine, forever." You know, I think she was repeating what he said. I think those were the words he used. It would explain the word cut into her back too.'

'*MINE*. It sounds as if he wants to own all these women.'

'Yes. I think he has a sort of weird infatuation with his victims. He's been branding them.'

Emma's brow furrowed deeply as she spoke. 'Mutilating them, more likely. What he's doing is revolting, degrading and downright cruel. Do you think she'll make a full recovery?'

Kate shrugged. 'I hope so. Much will depend on the extent of any internal injuries. We don't know what other damage he inflicted on her yet.'

'What an evil bastard. She looks such a mess.'

The bruising on Olivia's face bore testament to the ferocity of the attack. 'He's harbouring a lot of rage. We have to track him down before he strikes again. I doubt his next victim will be fortunate enough to survive.'

CHAPTER
TWENTY-FOUR

Jamie stuck the photograph of a Honda CB 125 F motorbike, as identified by Brian Procter, on the whiteboard.

'Is he certain that's the one?' asked Morgan.

'As sure as he can be. We narrowed it down to a naked bike.'

Morgan scowled. 'What the fuck is a naked bike?'

'A standard bike or roadster. They're usually recognised by their upright riding position. It's partway between the reclining rider posture of a cruiser and forward leaning position of a sports bike.'

'Whoa! You've already lost me. Cruisers?'

Jamie held up another picture, of a Harley Davidson. 'This is a cruiser.'

'Oh, okay. You know about bikes?'

'Before we had Zach, I owned a couple of Triumphs and a Ducati. Mr Procter could be right. They're very popular city bikes.'

'He can't be sure. He only saw it fleetingly,' said Morgan.

'He has a photographic memory. He came to the station specially to identify the bike.'

The bickering between Morgan and Jamie was getting on Kate's nerves and judging by the look on Emma's face, she felt the same way. She halted this latest disagreement. 'Will you two please give it a rest? It's in the hands of the technical team.' On her say-so, the technical division were currently searching CCTV footage along the road from Uttoxeter to Abbots Bromley for any black motorcycles. 'We'll soon get confirmation if it is a Honda whatever-it-is, naked-or-otherwise, or not. They're also examining footage around Newbury Avenue for Saturday evening, around the time of the attack on Heather, and also on the main road to Weston, on Monday morning. If the bike is significant, it could well show up on a camera.'

'Motorbikes are noisy. Surely, the killer would have wanted a more discreet mode of transport? An engine roaring away from a scene of a crime would attract attention,' said Morgan.

Kate groaned. He was like a dog with a bone, but Jamie twisted around to face him. 'No, mate. It's down to the size of the muffler. All bikes can be kept quiet, especially larger models, and the larger the engine, the deeper the tone. You'd hear no more than a quiet rumble. They're also easier to hide out of sight than a car.'

Morgan grunted and returned to his work.

The two independent sightings of a black motorbike were certainly promising. If the biker had been smoking, as one witness had claimed, there was a chance he'd left behind a cigarette stub. Kate had rung Forensics only to discover Ervin was out. Rather than leave a message about it, she was in the process of sending him an email.

'You busy?' asked Emma.

'Not any more,' said Kate, pressing the send key.

Emma placed a printout on Kate's desk.

'What's this?'

'A list of thirty-eight martial arts studios, academies, clubs and training centres in Staffordshire.'

'How did you find time to come up with this?'

'I didn't. My brother has been helping me out and he sent the list across. He knows every place in the area and besides, he's friends with many of the owners.' It made sense. Greg would want to know about any local competition.

'Great.' She glanced down at the names.

'I've already checked those with a cross beside them. That still leaves twenty-six.'

'Okay. Do what you can. Maybe Olivia will be able to give us a description of her attacker.'

'That would certainly make my life easier. I'll plough on. By the way, Tilly's doing really well. I think she could handle herself in a difficult situation. Thought you'd like to know.'

Kate smiled. 'It's a weight off my mind.'

Time passed at speed, yet by five o'clock, the team had made no further progress. Morgan stood up and bashed the side of the flickering strip light.

'When *is* somebody going to fix this fucking thing?'

'When hell freezes over,' said Emma.

'I'm going to put in a complaint to maintenance,' he replied.

Emma placed her hands behind her head and yawned noisily. 'This is fucking hopeless. I've no idea how many old cases I've trawled through so far.'

Kate considered she might have to admit defeat on the matter, yet the possibility that another victim would be attacked and killed today spurred her onwards. However hopeless a task it might seem, there was a chance it would lead them closer to identifying the perpetrator.

'At the risk of repeating myself, we have to exhaust every avenue.' It was beginning to sound like a tired refrain, even to Kate's own ears. 'Can we not trace that pay-as-you-go phone that was in contact with Heather's?'

Morgan answered. 'It's no longer operational.'

'I tried one of my techie contacts in Manchester,' said Emma. 'Ours are too busy to deal with any more requests. He's trying to track historical activity on the number, which could lead us to the owner.'

Kate stuck a large map of the county she'd been examining on the board. 'I'm sure the perpetrator lives somewhere on our patch, not outside it. He'd need to live close enough to monitor his victims' movements. I've circled each of their homes and drawn connecting lines between them.' The result was a scalene triangle of almost equal lengths that she proceeded to shade lightly with a red pen. 'I wonder if this area is where he lives and operates.'

'If not within the triangle, close to it,' said Jamie.

'Have there been any rape cases reported in this area over the last few years?' she asked Emma.

'Let me check.'

Kate rolled her shoulders to ease the tension caused by the knowledge she was clutching at straws. At the same time, her mind butterfly-hopped. 'Who spoke to the staff at the retirement home?'

'Me,' said Jamie.

'How long had Olivia worked there?'

'Only nine months.'

'Okay.' An idea bubbled in her brain but wouldn't surface. Emma came back with an answer.

'No cases reported from anywhere within that triangle.'

'What about stalkers? Have there been any incidents reported of stalking?'

'How far back do I go? Ten years?'

'Yes. Go back further if you don't find anything.' Kate returned to her desk where she stared at an identical regional map, and began searching for locations: clubs, pubs, petrol stations, anywhere the killer might have first set eyes on his victims. The list soon became exhaustive and her neck sore from bending over it.

She sat back and clicked her ballpoint repeatedly, stopping only when a text message caught her eye. Bradley wanted her to ring him immediately. She gathered up her phone and hot-footed it out of the building to her car. The digital dashboard display lit up, reminding her it would soon be evening. There was every chance the killer would strike again and another woman would be attacked. The thought was unbearable and anxiety gnawed at her innards as she remonstrated with herself. Unless she got her shit together quickly, there would be another death. And it would be on her.

She ought not to be breaking off to deal with what was a personal matter and an illegal investigation. At the same time, she couldn't ignore Bradley's message. To do so might mean losing Chris completely. His voice would only remain strong if she continued to pursue this avenue. Bradley wouldn't have asked her to ring him if he didn't have vital information concerning Cooper's death. She cast a glance at Dickson's office window. There was no sign of anyone standing there so she made the call.

A gruff voice answered almost immediately. 'We need to meet.'

'Can't you tell me now, over the phone?'

'No.'

She let out a lengthy sigh. She shouldn't go, not with a killer on the loose. However, if she was quick and kept her mobile switched on, it would take no longer than stepping out for something to eat. 'Same place as last time?'

'Yes.'

'When?'

'Tonight. At seven.'

'I'll be there.'

He'd rung off before she could say any more.

'Chris?'

No reply was forthcoming and she dropped her head into her hands. How much longer could she keep this investigation into Dickson a secret? If he had managed to have Cooper killed, then he might also have eyes on her. She was getting out of her depth. Running an illegal investigation into her superior, at best, would result in suspension, and, if she was right about Dickson, at worst – death. She let out a groan. She had no choice other than to continue her one-woman crusade. To drop it now would mean to lose Chris. Squaring her shoulders, she sat up. She had a team to lead.

Things had shifted a gear in the short time she'd been outside. There was speculation upstairs over a new picture on the whiteboard, of a thick-set man in his thirties, with a shaven head and neck tattoos.

'Who do we have here?' she asked.

Morgan answered. 'Alan Smallwood. In 2017, he was sentenced for six months and a level 5 fine for stalking one of his work colleagues. He reportedly put his hands around her throat and threatened to strangle her. He's a roadside technician for White Knight Road Recovery, which is like the AA or RAC, but more local, covering Staffordshire and Derbyshire. We couldn't find out if any of our victims were signed up members, so Jamie and I are heading to Brocton to interview him. Emma's gone to check out gyms and clubs again.'

Although it might come to nothing she was willing to let them follow it up. 'Keep me in the loop.'

With the office to herself, Kate rested her hands behind her head and urged the universe to send them a lucky break. Her eyes alighted on the wall clock. She couldn't ignore the nagging voice in her head, reminding her another victim would be taken, and with sudden urgency sat up straight to take over reading through the list of alleged stalking offences. Her gut was telling her their killer had offended before. Leaning closer to the screen, she began the laborious process of checking through the details, acutely aware of the moving clock hands, reminding her that time was running out.

◆ ◆ ◆

Kate didn't converse with Chris on her journey to meet Bradley. Her mind was occupied with concerns that no new leads had been uncovered. The man found guilty of stalking had been working both nights of the murders and, in spite of her efforts, Kate had not found any other potential suspects.

Her husband's voice was temporarily muted, unable to offer any suggestions or advice, that was until she began the descent to the reservoir and was drawn to its shimmering surface. A pair of swans glided alongside each other, heads bowed in unison.

'They only have one partner and bond for life, you know?' he said. 'If one of them dies, the other one can die of a broken heart.'

She jumped slightly at the sound of his voice. Last time she'd tried to speak to him, he'd not answered. A lump in her throat rendered her unable to respond. Some days she felt she couldn't continue existing without Chris. These make-believe conversations made life easier because, for a while, she could convince herself he was still by her side, even though she was fully aware she was playing with fire. Every conversation she had with him strengthened the belief he was somehow alive and in spite of all the reasoning, she couldn't break the habit.

Since Tilly had arrived, there'd been fewer chats. She understood full well why that was the case; Tilly was filling the void. While this was a positive, it also frightened Kate. If Tilly were to move back as she intended, it would probably mean Chris would fade away for good. Soon she would have to accept that reality and she wasn't sure she could.

She turned into the gravelled car park and followed the dirt track alongside the reservoir to a secluded spot where her car was not visible from the road. There were no other vehicles in sight and she waited, eyes anchored on the fields the other side of the water, rather than seek out the swans. This spot afforded her a sense of serenity and a chance to order her thoughts. Bradley must have news for her. What news, would dictate her actions.

'What's more important, the investigation or trapping Dickson?' said Chris.

'They're both as important as each other.'

'Nah. You know that isn't the case.'

She dropped the conversation. It was only serving to create self-doubt. She would handle both. A Range Rover appeared, crawled past her car and came to a halt even further down the track. She stepped outside to meet the driver, who wandered directly across to the water, a camera slung around his neck.

'Didn't have you down as a twitcher,' she said.

'The art of deflection. A man with a camera dressed in a drab outfit doesn't attract attention. Here. Aim those over there.'

He passed her a pair of binoculars, and she pointed them at a group of fine-looking Holstein cows, peacefully meandering down the hillside close to Blithfield Hall. 'What do you have for me?'

'Jack says they were ordered to return to their cells five minutes after they'd been let out. The official line was that staff were following sudden information about hidden drugs and wanted to conduct cell checks, but he thinks that was bullshit. There were no drugs.'

'It's only hearsay though, isn't it? Not enough for me to use.'

'Ah, well, that's where you're wrong because Jack had a name for me – Warren Gates, one of the kitchen hands who'd been let out of his cell early to prepare breakfast. He saw Cooper head towards the shower followed by a guard, Tom Champion.'

'Could Jack get Warren to talk to me?'

He sucked his teeth. 'I don't know. Warren's only nineteen and too frightened to speak out. He's due for release in four months and wants to keep his head down until then. Besides, Champion has a reputation of being an utter bastard. If he got wind Warren blabbed, heaven knows what he'd do to the kid.'

'What did Cooper use to slit his throat?' she asked.

'Razor blade.'

'They'd be locked away, wouldn't they?'

'Rumour is, he either stole it or bought it from a fellow inmate. According to Jack, that's more bullshit. No one is admitting to selling him a blade.' Bradley glanced over at a car crossing the causeway. 'And, supposing Cooper *had* been determined to commit suicide, he'd have done it in his cell while his cellmate was asleep. He wouldn't have run the risk of being stopped in the act. None of this adds up.'

'I take it the authorities haven't held an internal investigation into how this happened?'

'No, they haven't. The governor is sticking to the suicide line. As far as they're concerned, it's an open-and-shut case.'

'Any luck getting a second post-mortem?'

His face looked like he'd sucked on a lemon. 'They're stalling us. All the same, we're pushing for a second report and I'm not going to let it drop. I've got Sierra's back on this. What do you think you'll do next?'

'Honestly, I don't know. I'm not going to be able to get a confession from Tom Champion or interview Warren Gates, not without rousing suspicions.'

'You might not be able to get Champion to speak, but I could.'

Although in his early sixties, Bradley was muscular and fit. His regular training had kept him lithe, and darkness glittered in his eyes.

'No doubt your methods would be illegal?'

'Illegal but effective. You have a problem with that?'

The swans had glided across the water and were almost directly in front of Kate, their pristine white feathers shining in the evening light. One lowered its head and the other copied its movements, their beaks touching for a second as if kissing. *Bonded forever.* 'Do it,' she said.

◆ ◆ ◆

Kate hunted in the fridge for something edible, settled on a piece of cheddar and an overripe tomato, and sat at the table, glass of wine in her hand. 'Soldier's Poem' by Muse played loudly on the sound system, mournful notes drifting throughout the kitchen. The lyrics, about there being no justice in the world, echoed in her head, and once the song was finished she aimed the control unit at the speaker and pressed replay. She raised her glass to her lips, let the liquid warm her throat, and then waited for it to blur the edges of her day. There'd been little justice for Chris and, as things stood, none for Cooper. How many others had she failed in her career, all the while believing she was doing good, yet at the same time officers like Dickson were playing by different rules? The thought soured the wine and she pushed the glass to one side. It made a farce of her vocation, the one thing she'd believed in. The music was replaced by 'Exogenesis: Symphony, Part 1: Overture', the tempo rising and crashing like her beating heart imprisoned in her chest. Farcical. She was little more than a puppet, her strings pulled by Dickson and others like him. Chris's file had startled her. It had contained faces she'd known for years: faces of people she'd trusted.

She nibbled at the cheese with no appetite and got to her feet once more. She should ring Tilly. She hadn't intended to neglect her all day but one thing had led to another and there'd been little time to chat to her stepsister. The food in the bird feeder had been eaten and it swung in the breeze. She crossed to the cupboard and grabbed the bag of bird seed and headed outside. It was imperative it remained full.

When she returned, it was to a missed call. She redialled Tilly's number. Her stepsister sounded cheerful.

'Hey. Hope I didn't catch you at a bad time,' Tilly said.

'No. I was actually about to ring you.'

'Then you've got time for a quick chat?'

'Sure.'

'I went on a date this evening.' She followed it with a small giggle, reminding Kate of the teenaged Tilly.

'With Ryan?'

'No! I wouldn't *date* Ryan. If we went out together, it'd only be as friends. We've both been quite clear about that. He suggested meeting tonight, but I'd already arranged to meet Henry. Henry's the guy who came to fix my telly.'

'Did you have a good time?'

'Uh-huh. We went to an Italian restaurant. Very posh.'

'Are you going to see him again?'

'No. He's not into kids. He didn't realise I had a little boy.'

'How could he have missed Daniel?'

'I guess he was too dazzled by me.' She sniggered again. 'Daniel was playing with the boy next door when he came around to mend the television, so I didn't actually tell him until after the meal. I suppose it was a bit mean of me.'

243

Kate shook her head in mock dismay at the phone. This was exactly like the old Tilly, the girl who'd go out with and drop boys on a whim.

'I don't want anything serious – the odd night out. Light-hearted conversation. You understand, don't you? I feel I deserve it.'

'Yeah. I get it. Take care though, Tilly.'

'I'm not fourteen any more, Kate.'

'You know what I mean. You're vulnerable. You're still coming to terms with what happened with Jordan and you're in a country you're not over-familiar with. Things have changed since you left and there are bad people out there.'

The voice was softer now. 'Yes. I know. I deserve some me-time and fun, though.'

'I know.'

'I'm meeting a guy from the gym tomorrow, for a lunchtime drink. Emma knows him.'

'What about Daniel? Have you got a sitter for him, or do you need me to look after him?'

'All taken care of. He's popping next door again. He's getting on really well with their little lad. I've not seen him this content for ages.'

'Well, if you're sorted—'

'I am and don't worry. I'll keep my hand on my ha'penny.'

Kate laughed at the old-fashioned phrase used by Tilly's grand-mother, to warn both girls to keep their virtue safe from boys while going out on a date.

Tilly's voice grew serious. 'I've been lonely for a long time, Kate. I only want to let my hair down.'

'Of course you do. Let me know how you get on tomorrow with . . . What's his name?'

'Chevy. It's a French name meaning horseman or knight, so he might be my knight in shining armour.' Laughter tinkled down the line.

Kate smiled. 'Enjoy yourselves.'

'Will do. And Kate . . .'

'Yes.'

'I love you.'

She put down the phone before Kate could answer.

CHAPTER
TWENTY-FIVE

Kate had spent much of the night wondering if she was being over-cautious about Tilly. She blamed the investigation for her reaction and vowed to be more positive the next time they spoke. It wouldn't hurt for her stepsister to meet new men and if it meant she gained confidence, then that could only be an added bonus. However, it didn't prevent Kate from checking out Tilly's dates. Although she'd have to ask Emma about Chevy, a quick look on the police general database for information on Ryan Holder confirmed he had no previous convictions, not even a parking ticket to his name. Checking through her old school website, she uncovered a photo of a fresh-faced Ryan, captain of the football team. She had a vague recollection of applauding a lanky individual during a school assembly as he collected a trophy from the headteacher, but nothing more than that.

Having decided she was being an interfering busybody, Kate flicked through the files appertaining to the investigation.

Jamie was once again the first team member to appear, a child's rucksack over one shoulder. He cleared his throat and cast about before saying, 'Erm, guv, would it be okay if I nipped off at about two thirty to pick my lad up from school and drop him off at his nan's again? I'll come back once I'm done. Sophie's got a hospital appointment.'

'Sure.' She took in his haggard appearance. He looked as if he hadn't slept all night. 'Everything okay?'

'Yeah, fine.'

She kept one eye on him as he tucked the bag under his seat, then fired up the computer. Satisfied he didn't wish to discuss the matter further with her, she resumed her own musings. The fact the killer had knocked out his victims with a vagus strike, yet not killed them, and then chosen to strangle them rather than inflict a second, deadlier blow, still bothered her. The former would have been a quicker way to dispatch his victims and would have reduced the risk of him being caught. She could only conclude that the killer wanted them to be conscious throughout the rape attacks, the cruel carving of the word *MINE* into their shoulders, and for them to be fully aware of their intended fate. She wondered if it was worth asking a profiler to give them a clearer picture of who they were searching for. Her ruminations were interrupted by Emma and Morgan, who arrived together, both in a far sprightlier mood than Jamie.

'I've been thinking,' said Morgan, pausing to thump the overhead light. 'We didn't double-check Steve's whereabouts for Monday morning. We ought to do that.'

'Have we not got his DNA results back yet?'

'No. We haven't had any DNA results back.'

'That's crazy. Don't they know we're up against it here? Chase them up. It would save us a lot of legwork.'

She clicked onto her emails. The voices around her faded into a jumble of noise, merging with the buzzing overhead light. Ervin had replied to her message about the motorcyclist's cigarette end. He had several of them to examine and would get back to her. He still hadn't identified the weapon used to cut the women.

She ran both hands under her long hair, leaving cool fingers resting on the nape of her neck as she stared at the screen, then, reaching for her car keys, she said, 'I'll be with Ervin if anyone wants me. And we haven't received Heather's pathology report either. Emma, will you talk to Harvey and see where he is with it?'

'No probs.'

With one last glance at her team, she strode off.

Ervin was wearing a yellow cravat with green polka dots, the top of it peeping over his lab coat. Kate couldn't begin to imagine what he'd teamed it with, although it would surely be flamboyant. Ervin didn't do ordinary.

'I know. I know. Your investigation is stalling and the forensic department is being of no help whatsoever,' he said as soon as she walked into his office. 'What can I say? We simply haven't found any evidence to help push it along.'

'I've come to clear my head, not to bully or complain.'

'Good because I've had enough of both already,' he replied.

'I'm sorry to hear that,' said Kate and meant it. Ervin always went above and beyond expectations.

'Bloody Dickson,' he said in a conspiratorial whisper. 'I got it in the neck for slacking! As if? I don't care how frustrating it is for senior officers in murder enquiries, we can only work at one speed and that's invariably flat out.'

'He gave me grief too. He wants answers and somebody charged.'

Ervin pursed his lips. 'Don't we all?'

The office overlooked the main laboratory and Kate glanced out at the trio of scientists occupied at various stations: one using an array of optical instruments, another by stainless steel ovens and the third seated at a bench, dropping liquid from an electronic pipette into a container. She knew little about forensic science and admired her colleagues in this department, especially Ervin, whose knowledge on the subject was encyclopaedic. Ervin, however, wasn't in the mood to discuss the lack of findings or bandy any suppositions as was his usual wont. He was fixated on Dickson.

'It's not as if I need pressing on the matter. We've examined every scrap of evidence retrieved from Abbots Bromley and believe me, there was plenty of non-crime-related material there. It's ten times more difficult to lift relevant evidence when a crime is committed outside in a public area.' He dropped onto the edge of his desk and gave her a serious look. 'I'll tell you here and now, I don't think we'll find anything related to the attack on Heather.'

'Other than DNA and fingerprints?'

'There are no fingerprints on either body. I highly suspect the perpetrator wore gloves. Given we've been unable to retrieve mobile devices, handbags or any personal items he might have touched, we haven't been able to lift any prints, although we got plenty from the industrial waste containers – too many!'

'I get it. It doesn't matter how quickly we want things to proceed, the fact is, all of this requires time.'

'Exactly! Which is why I'm somewhat irked by the superintendent's attitude. Still, enough of that.'

'What about the sweet wrapper you found at Abbots Bromley? Did you get anything from it?'

He shook his head. 'It had been there several days.'

'Any new thoughts on the weapon used to cut the women?'

'I'm afraid not. As you know, trying to work out the dimensions of a weapon can be inaccurate due to the effect of elasticity and skin shrinkage on withdrawal of the weapon. At this stage, we've only really determined the tip of a blade was used and on each occasion the perpetrator kept his lettering to a similar size and position. Always below the right shoulder.'

'Given he strangled his victims soon afterwards, I'm guessing he never intended them to see this word. It seems as if he only wanted them to know he'd carved it into them and possibly feel the pain as he did it. Why would he do that if he didn't want them to live with it, be reminded of what had happened?' She answered her own question. 'It's his signature, his moniker.'

'He's branding them, like cowboys with cattle, or pimps branding sex workers.'

She glanced out again, digesting Ervin's words. The oven doors were now open and the scientist wearing padded gloves lifted out a container. She'd thought the same earlier in the investigation. Maybe branding was the answer. Ervin was now talking about clothing. 'We collected various threads and fibres, again all to be cross-matched with those lifted from the second crime scene. Nothing so far from Salt Lane though. That scene is relatively clean.'

'What about DNA on the victims?'

'The killer used a condom; therefore no bodily fluids were left behind, but we lifted enough DNA from items of clothing to provide a match should you come up with a suspect.' He waved his hands in front of his face. 'Sorry. That was rude of me. I know you'll find whoever is responsible. Ignore me. I got out of the wrong side of bed. Well, I didn't actually get to bed so technically, I didn't get up. You know what I mean.'

'You didn't spend all night here, did you?'

He dropped onto a stool, trousers rising to display yellow socks and boots. 'Most of it, then I went out for a late-night takeaway with Terry and we ended up at his place, drinking and putting the world to rights until the wee hours. There was little point in snatching an hour's sleep after that, so I went home to shower and change and came back in. I'm on my fifth cup of coffee already and grateful there isn't another crime scene to attend. I'm short-staffed and out of sorts.'

'Where is everyone?'

'Most of them are still at Weston, checking out the building site where Olivia was dumped.'

'I'm under the impression this killer is very well organised. He knows exactly when and where to strike.'

'He's definitely controlled,' said Ervin. 'I imagine he's disciplined. People who perform martial arts usually are.'

Another thought rose like a bubble. Martial arts clubs. They still had that avenue to explore. Ervin muttered, 'Bloody man.'

'The killer?'

'Him too. I was referring to the super.' Ervin really had a bee in his bonnet today, thanks to Dickson. It was most unlike him to bitch about anyone and she became more than a little curious when he said, 'And I'm not the only person he's wound up recently.'

She faltered momentarily. Was he referring to her? She'd deliberately kept her feelings about the man to herself, unless she'd accidentally let something slip. 'Who else has he cheesed off?'

'Heather, for one. Last month, he dropped her from an investigation.'

'How do you know about that?'

'Do you remember I told you she sent me a thank-you gift?'

'A bottle of brandy.'

'That's correct. A bottle of Hennessy X.O cognac, to be precise. A dark, complex cognac that retails at around £125 per bottle.' He studied her with bright eyes, waiting for her to make the correct assumption.

'Whatever you did must have been valuable to her.'

'Exactly. It seemed excessive given all I did was test a bottle of liquid for her.'

'And what was this liquid?'

251

'Turned out to be ketamine.'

Ketamine was a dissociative drug that made the consumer feel detached from reality. With nicknames including Special K, vitamin K and cat Valium, it was used by doctors and veterinarians as anaesthesia, but was popular on the underground scene as a date rape drug. 'Did she tell you anything about it?'

'Uh-huh. Insisted it had to be kept hush-hush until I identified the bottle's contents.'

'Ervin, I've known you for years and whenever I've made similar requests, you've always wanted to know the reasoning behind it.'

A flicker of a smile tugged at his lips.

'You're a professional, through and through, and you wouldn't work on something unless you were sure of both its origin and why you were being asked for help. You *must* have wormed it out of her.'

'You know me too well.' The friendly smile had finally appeared. 'To be honest, I had no intention of helping her out and told her to go through the proper channels. Then she swayed me. She was certain that somebody else, assigned to the same investigation, was deliberately doing away with evidence and she didn't want that vial lost or destroyed.'

'Did she tell you who she suspected?'

'No. And her reason for not telling me was that she didn't want to put my job at risk. I thought she was overstressing until she rang to say she'd been dropped from the investigation, and that I should definitely keep quiet about the ketamine if I valued my job. Naturally, I followed her advice. After all, there was no need to rock the boat and I do have a hefty mortgage to pay off. I didn't give it any further thought until Sunday morning. Since then, it's played on my mind and I've been getting crazy notions that she was murdered because of that vial. Bonkers, isn't it? A product of an over-active and over-worked mind. After all, the MO is the same for all three women.' He continued rambling at speed.

A buzzing began in Kate's ears . . . evidence . . . Operation Agouti . . . Dickson. She almost missed Ervin's next comment.

'It felt a little cloak-and-dagger to me and yet, Heather wasn't somebody prone to flights of fancy, was she? Naturally, I wanted to return the brandy. She wouldn't have any of it.'

'Did she tell you what she did with the ketamine?'

'I assumed she'd presented it along with her suspicions to the superintendent.'

'And did she tell you why she was taken off the investigation?'

'No. There could be any number of reasons, including not following procedure. And after my ear-bashing this morning, I've been wondering if the superintendent hasn't guessed at my involvement. There was something in his tone today when he spoke to me . . . hostility. Either that, or I was simply over-reacting thanks to supreme fatigue.' He gave a loose shrug.

Tiredness had not affected his perspicacity. They were both used to working ridiculous hours and Ervin had the ability to remain astute and focused, regardless of how little sleep he got. He was confiding in her not only as a friend, but because he believed there to be some truth in the matter and also had doubts about her superior.

'Did she give you any idea as to what the investigation was about or who she was working with?'

'Nothing more than I've already divulged.'

'And she didn't reveal where the liquid came from?'

He shook his head. 'I don't suppose it's relevant to your investigation.'

'It's unlikely to be, but you've helped me form a better picture of who she was. Seemed a highly dedicated individual.'

'Which might also account for why Dickson is in such a tizzy to find somebody to hold accountable for her death. He feels guilty at dropping her.'

It was Kate's turn to shrug. 'I think he's under pressure from above.'

Ervin gave a non-committal response and got to his feet. The yellow socks vanished under dark grey, pin-striped trouser legs that looked as if they'd come straight from a Corby press. 'Talking of which, I'd better resume my duties. I shouldn't have sounded off at you. You have enough on your plate without listening to my woeful meanderings. I can be a fearful grump, particularly when I'm sleep-deprived.'

Nothing could be further from the truth. Ervin was well adjusted and, in spite of the difficulties of the job, rarely down-hearted. He must have been upset to have spoken about Dickson. 'We all get grumpy in this line of business. It goes hand in hand with the hefty responsibility we cart about.'

He put a hand on her shoulder and gave a light squeeze – an unspoken thank you.

'Let me know if anything comes back from those cigarette ends. I'm desperate for a breakthrough,' she said.

'I'll be sure to ring you personally.'

◆ ◆ ◆

Back in her car, she recapped on what she'd uncovered. The fact that Heather had been onto somebody in the team was of importance, probably not to the actual murder investigation, but certainly to Kate's personal one. She really needed to talk this over with some-body and yet, there was no one she dared confide in, so she did what she always did when she wanted to draw on his strength and guidance: she spoke aloud to her husband.

'Could Dickson be behind your death, Cooper's and Heather's? All of you had information that linked back to him.'

'Let's look at this logically.' Chris always approached everything with journalistic thoroughness. 'Firstly, you still have no proof he was involved in my death. Secondly, you actually don't know why Cooper wanted to see you. And lastly, if Heather had suspected Dickson of disposing of evidence, she'd be unlikely to have confronted him. She'd have approached somebody higher up the chain of command.'

'You're right. As usual.' She tapped her hands against her cheeks and blew out noisily through her lips. She was so desperate to pin things on Dickson she wasn't thinking clearly. 'Would I be stupid to consider the possibility he might have hired somebody to kill her and make it look as if it was the work of Laura's attacker?'

Two lab assistants emerged from the building and crossed the car park towards a pickup truck. Chris's response came a few minutes after they'd driven away.

'What about the motorcyclist spotted at the car park in Newbury Avenue? The same person seen in Abbots Bromley, by the restaurant. Where does he fit in? Unless you think Dickson hired that person to kill both women, you can't pin Heather's death on him.'

CHAPTER
TWENTY-SIX

When Kate got back, only Emma was in the office. She was quick to report on her findings. 'I spoke to Harvey and he sent over the pathology report on Heather. As with Laura, there was significant damage to throat and neck structures, broken hyoid bone and a definite blow to the vagus nerve, with damage to the tissues surrounding it. There was bruising to the inner thighs associated with this type of attack.' Kate had seen similar marks before, large haematomas caused by the victims' resistance to their attacker's demands. Emma passed her the photographs of the mottled abrasions on Heather's legs where she'd tried desperately to hold them together and resist her attacker. Kate looked through each picture, noting the patterning of the dark markings against the alabaster skin.

'And of course, we have that sinister message cut into her back.'

'I'm more convinced than ever that he brands his victims.' Kate explained her thoughts and received a nod of agreement.

'The cause of death was asphyxiation, same as Laura. He strangled them both.'

Kate was still going through the photographs, looking at Heather's scraped hands. 'Nothing under her fingernails?'

'Earth, grass and a black cotton thread.'

'No skin cells?'

'None. Harvey believes the assailant kept a tight hold of her wrists and the thread might have come from a glove or a face covering. It's been sent to the lab to be examined.'

Kate shuffled the photographs back into a pile and returned them to Emma before reading the pathology report, on the off-chance there was some clue they'd overlooked. She faced the whiteboard and the photos of the three victims. It could soon be four women, and a feeling of helplessness washed over her. Evil was out there, lurking and waiting to pounce again and still she had no fresh leads to follow or suspects to question. 'Where are Morgan and Jamie exactly?'

'Interviewing another ex-rapist. He was released two months ago.'

'Does he own a black Honda motorbike?'

Emma's nose wrinkled as if a bad smell had permeated it. 'Erm, not exactly. He's got a red and black Kawasaki.' Before Kate could interrupt she rushed on with 'We thought it might be possible he borrowed a Honda from a mate. He's a member of a Stafford bike club. We decided it was worth looking into. The guy used to wrap his hand around his victims' throats and threaten to kill them if they made any noise.'

Kate let it go. There were sufficient grounds to question him. If she'd been in the office when his name came up, she'd have sent somebody to interview him. They couldn't afford to let anyone slip under the radar.

'Still no CCTV footage of this motorbike?'

'Nothing so far.'

'I'll see how far they've got.' She punched Felicity's name on the screen and got an immediate pickup.

'Your ears must have been burning,' said Felicity. 'I was talking to Rachid and he's spotted your suspect's bike on the Stafford to Weston road, Monday morning at five thirty. We're running the footage back to make sure, but there doesn't seem to be any registration plate on the vehicle and the driver is dressed as your witness described. I'll email you some captures in a jiffy.'

'What about the cameras in Stafford or on the road to Abbots Bromley?'

'We've been fixated on Stafford Road, so we haven't got around to those yet. Rachid will email you anything as soon as he comes across it.' Kate could picture the calm, smooth-faced young man who worked on all the technical data, alongside two other colleagues. In his late twenties, he was recognised as one of the department's best technicians.

'I'd appreciate that.' She held on to the mobile. A man on a bike. It was all they had.

It only took the length of time for her to examine the faces on the whiteboard and consider why the assailant had shown such violence to the three women, before her inbox pinged. The image was grainy and slightly distorted but she could make out the back of a rider in a black leather jacket, dark trousers and boots on what appeared to be a black bike. There was no registration number plate. She stuck it on the board and wrote *Stafford Road, Weston, 5.30 a.m.* Emma looked up.

'Our killer?'

'Looks that way.'

'Clever son of a bitch, isn't he? Nobody would give him a second glance. Plain bike, black clothing and no number plate. Anonymous.'

'He's becoming careless. Olivia is still alive.'

She rested her hands on her desk. Serial killers were not the roaming homicidal individuals portrayed in horror films and were far more likely to kill on their home turf. Like Jack the Ripper, who in 1888 stalked and killed in London's Whitechapel district, today's killers had a comfort zone, an area in which they'd operate, anchored by a point – their home or place of work – and crime statistics revealed serial killers were most likely to commit their first murder close to where they lived.

Their perpetrator was a local. There had to be some way of flushing him out.

'This pay-as-you-go phone,' Emma said. 'We weren't having any luck with it, so I asked a friend who used to work for Intelligence for help and he's come up with some information.'

Kate's head snapped up. 'And?'

'Heather was the only person who both made calls to and received calls from this number. Other incoming calls came from other pay-as-you-go numbers.'

Kate felt her eyelids flutter. Burner phones. Drug dealers invariably used disposable phones, throwing them away after one use so they couldn't be traced. What had Heather got involved in?

'She rang it a total of fifteen times, had four conversations, each lasting less than a minute and received only two calls from it, one on August the second, at ten o'clock in the evening, lasting five minutes; the other was made at five past nine on Friday morning, lasting only a few seconds.' Emma pressed her lips together and looked at Kate, who shook her head from side to side slowly. It made little sense.

'She made a call to that number immediately before she left Trentham House. How long did that call last?'

'There was no pickup. My contact reckons by then the phone was no longer operational.'

'Could it be connected to a case she was working on?' Kate asked.

Emma's thick eyebrows lifted. 'I reckon it could.'

Kate scratched at a sudden itch on her neck. *Operation Agouti?*

Emma continued, 'Anyway, my friend did some digging, discovered its IMEI number and found out it's a Nokia 105 2G mobile handset that was first activated on July the thirtieth. It's one of the cheapest pre-paid mobiles around, doesn't have any web browser, no social network support and no camera, making it ideal as a burner phone.'

The itch was bothering Kate. She clawed at it again. She couldn't understand why Heather would be in contact with the owner of the burner phone. Possibilities trampolined in her mind.

'He thinks he knows where the phone came from.'

Kate held her breath.

'Manchester Mobiles in Cheetham. It was one of forty handsets that were stolen on July the twenty-fourth. I contacted the lead officer on that case and he believes the phones found their way into the hands of local drug dealers and gangs.'

'Another dead end, then,' said Kate.

'Erm, well, it would have been if my friend wasn't an expert hacker.' A smile twitched the corners of her mouth. 'He reckons the first call made to Heather's phone came from one of the red-light districts in Manchester – Strangeways – and the last was made at Stoke-on-Trent station. I checked with the tech team and they confirmed the tracker on Heather's car shows she went to Stoke station soon after she received that call.'

Red-light district, Manchester, underage sex workers and Dickson. Pieces of what had been a complex puzzle shifted and interlocked to present a breathtaking possibility. Dickson had formed a small unit to track down underage sex workers, more spe-cifically Farai's girls, Rosa and Stanka. Why? He wanted to ensure they didn't spill the beans about him sleeping with one of them at the Maddox Club. He hadn't banked on Heather being so thor-ough at her job. Even after being dismissed from the investigation, she'd continued searching, found the girls and contacted them, determined to keep the information from the team she believed was untrustworthy. Why else would he have asked Felicity to delete information appertaining to the case from Heather's laptop after first sending a copy to him? He'd wanted Operation Agouti to remain secret. That left one question unanswered. Who, on the team, had been tampering with evidence? It could have been one of the officers, or even Dickson himself. Chris would say she was making this fit what she wanted to believe and she needed facts. Her gut said this wasn't make-believe; she felt this was right.

'There's CCTV at Stoke station, so I suggest we run through it to see if we can find Heather and whoever she was meeting.'

Emma's words became muffled and distant. If Farai had been truthful, Rosa and Stanka were in danger. She couldn't let the girls be questioned at the station or allow Dickson to get wind of what the team had discovered. She'd have to confront the girls on the streets, keep them away from Dickson. The itch was worse than ever. She rubbed furiously at it. 'Leave that with me,' she said. She could feel rather than see the look Emma was giving her. 'Until we can prove this meeting was nothing to do with one of Heather's investigations, we need to keep this quiet. I've already been warned not to delve into territory that isn't ours, so I'd appreciate it if you kept this between us for the moment.' Emma bought it.

'Sure. I understand.'

'Good work, by the way.'

She didn't like deceiving any of her team, but she couldn't risk Emma, or anyone for that matter, finding out who Heather met at Stoke station. Her investigation into Dickson depended on secrecy. She had no idea how far up the ladder the corruption went.

CHAPTER
TWENTY-SEVEN

Kate inhaled deeply in an attempt to steady the chaotic beating of her heart. She should never have come here, not in person. She still wasn't ready for this. It wasn't the cool wind that was causing the uncontrollable shaking in her hands, which she forced into her coat pockets, but the elaborate Jacobethan building with gables, finials and chimneys and a portico of eight arches, now filled in with arched windows and entrances, stonework and red bricks, the colour of dried blood. She could turn around, walk away and request the CCTV footage be sent to her email, yet the doors to the booking office slid open and her feet propelled her forwards, past the ticket machines and around travellers meandering around the foyer to the platform, as if they had a will of their own.

There were only a handful of travellers on the southbound platform and as an announcement sounded that the three-thirty train from Euston was now approaching, she stared up at the classic roof that spanned the platforms and half-expected a steam engine to chuff through, black smoke billowing from its stack like smoke from an angry dragon's nostrils. The distraction was deliberate. This place held bad memories, for it was at this very station, from this very platform, that she'd climbed onto the outbound Euston train that fateful day in January, only to find carnage and, among the dead, her husband.

Some internal compass had sent her here, as if coming back would reverse time and Chris would dismount from the incoming train and throw his arms around her with a 'Did you miss me?' She dropped her gaze and spied the snout of the train, snaking its way into the station. Her palms became damp as it drew up to the platform, the driver passing her with barely a glance in her direction, and the first-class carriage drew level with her. There was no blood splatter on the windows, no faces with sightless eyes resting against the glass, only passengers wearing headphones, eyes closed or reaching for luggage in the overhead racks. A high-pitched alert indicated the doors were opening and, rooted to the spot, she waited, like a huge boulder in a fast-moving river, as travellers streamed past her. Chris did not disembark and she felt a tsunami of loss wash over her as the last passengers raced away. A whistle sounded and the train pulled away again. It was an ordinary journey on the Euston train.

The train rounded the bend and disappeared from view. The trembling in her limbs ceased as quickly as it had begun. Dr Franklin would undoubtedly have an explanation for it and she didn't need a shrink to tell her what she already knew. She felt Chris's lips brush her neck and heard a whispered, 'You survived the experience. That's my girl.' She shook herself from her reverie and turned her attention to the platform opposite, reached either by a lift or the passenger subway, where only two men waited, one crouched on the floor, a can of lager in his hand, and the other with a satchel slung across his chest, eyes on his mobile. Anyone heading to or from Manchester would disembark at that platform, where there were no coffee shops, newsagents or first-class lounge, only a waiting room, toilets and a couple of benches. An online timetable had given her the information she needed. It took thirty-eight minutes to travel from Manchester to Stoke and a train had arrived at exactly five past nine on Friday morning.

She looked for surveillance equipment and, having decided the cameras were exactly where she'd hoped they would be, she continued along the platform to the British Transport Police offices where her arrival was expected.

The footage was grainy but good enough to make out the girl in a pale pink dress who got off the train, phone to her ear. The other passengers made a beeline for the subway with bags, briefcases and bikes, all jostling for space as they scurried towards the exit, but she did not, choosing instead to stand at the far end of the platform, overlooking the car park, where she stood motionless as if she was well accustomed to waiting.

She was petite with long dark hair held in a ponytail by a pink ribbon. At a distance, in the shapeless shift dress, with flat pumps, she looked exactly like a teenager to Kate, a girl out for the day, hoping to meet up with friends. How had she fallen into this industry at such a tender age? She didn't have long to dwell on the matter as she instructed the officer to fast forward the footage until Heather came into shot, half an hour later. The two gravitated towards each other and, choosing one of the benches, sat down and talked. With heads lowered, there was no way Kate could make out what was said, but when they parted at ten past ten, Heather gave the girl a hug.

'Can you do me a few captures of the girl's face, please?' she asked. 'And send me the entire footage.'

Only one person would be able to identify the girl and confirm she had been sent to the Maddox Club that night in January. But he would be reluctant to speak to Kate again. Nevertheless, she had to flush Farai out and if it took all night to do so, then that's what it would take.

◆ ◆ ◆

It was gone six o'clock before Kate managed to find a striking youth, answering to the name Benji, who exited the Lounge Bar in a dingy street in Stoke, with a middle-aged man. They climbed into an estate car, parked on the far side of the road, and after the interior light extinguished, Kate approached the passenger side of the vehicle and tapped on the window. Benji's head jerked up from the man's lap.

Kate pressed her ID against the glass. Benji was shoved away and a trouser zipper ratcheted back into place. The driver door opened.

'Look, Officer, I wasn't—'

'It's perfectly obvious what was going on, but you could be in luck. I want a quick word with your friend. That's all. Out you come, Benji.'

She opened the passenger door, holding on to it while he unfolded into the evening, lips drooping and arms folded in defiance.

'I need to find Farai,' said Kate.

'He left.'

'I know he's in Manchester. I need to know where he might be tonight. It's important.'

'Can't help you.'

'Okay. You don't know where he is, which is a shame, because it means, instead of looking for him, I now have time to take you down the station and charge you for soliciting. And you too, sir.'

'Wait a minute. I wasn't doing anything wrong. We were only chatting.' The bloke straightened his spectacles and tried to affect an offended tone.

'There was clearly no talking going on.' Kate stared pointedly at his ring finger. 'You married, sir?'

'Yes.'

'Maybe you'd like to give your other half a call to explain you're going to be detained at the station for a while.'

He called across to Benji. 'Tell her where this person is!'

'I'd listen to your client, if I were you. You don't want to spend a whole night at the station,' said Kate. 'Not when all you have to do is tell me where I can find Farai.'

Benji's amber eyes seemed to glow as he turned towards Kate. 'The Hangout Café near Strangeways. He's there almost every evening.'

'That wasn't so difficult, was it?' said Kate. Benji's face remained expressionless. She raised her voice a little so it drifted across to the man, now shifting from one foot to the other.

'I suggest you return home, sir.'

'Wait a minute. I paid him.'

'I ain't giving no refunds,' said Benji.

'That's robbery,' the man blustered.

Kate cocked an eyebrow at Benji. 'He has a point. After all, it isn't his fault I interrupted proceedings. The gentleman paid for services he didn't receive. Cough up.'

'He got half a job so he can have half of it back.' Benji pulled out a screwed-up ten-pound note and tossed it through the open door, onto the passenger seat.

'Go home, sir,' said Kate and shut the passenger door with a determined bang.

The man climbed back into his car, scowled at them both and pulled away.

'You lost me good money,' grumbled Benji.

'But you got to keep your freedom and made ten pounds for doing very little. Now scarper before I take you in.'

He sloped off, back towards the bar no doubt to pick up another punter.

◆ ◆ ◆

It took her a fraction under an hour to reach the Hangout Café, one of five run-down premises in an area undergoing a vast amount of development. Decades of exhaust fumes and traffic had transformed once white facades into grimy frontages streaked with soot. Little attempt had been made in recent years to jazz up the décor other than the obligatory graffiti that seemed to appear on boarded windows and doors in every city: names and words that meant nothing to Kate. The café, sandwiched between the graffitied building and MoMo's barber, with a facade like deceased skin peeling away from its host, looked semi-presentable in the dimly lit street. As she pulled up opposite it, Kate made out three figures, huddled around a circular table in the window, one with a long, drawn, skull-like face. She'd struck lucky.

The men were having a heated conversation, with large gestures. One of them, bald-headed and narrow-shouldered, jumped to his feet and thumped the table before leaving, phone clasped to his ear. The third occupant moved behind the counter, leaving Farai alone at the table. Kate unbuckled her seatbelt then slipped out of the car, heart thudding.

A dog barked in the distance, a deep angry bark that ended in a lengthy howl. There were lights on in one of the flats above the shops and a small window ajar, releasing loud, frenzied music, a drumbeat that rat-a-tatted in her chest, faster than her own frantic heartbeat. Five strides saw her across the road and onto the pavement outside the café. Nobody had noticed her approach. Now she had vision on another table inside, with two men at it. She steeled herself and pushed the door open quietly.

All eyes turned in her direction. The man behind the counter, squat, square-shouldered with dark eyes and a heavy five o'clock shadow, tutted loudly.

'This one of your *girls*?' he asked Farai.

The men in the corner guffawed, sitting back lazily to watch the show. The place was heavy with the aroma of recent cocaine usage.

'That's very funny,' said Kate, lifting her ID card and peering over the counter at the filthy fridge and wash basin. A bluebottle buzzed angrily behind a Perspex screen of leftover food before settling on an open container of something unappetising, the colour of cow dung. 'I think the hygiene boys would love to come and pay you a visit and listen to your jokes. Maybe we could even invite some of the vice squad and make a proper stand-up comedy evening of it.'

His lip curled. 'What do you want?'

'A word with him,' she said, pointing at Farai. 'Alone.'

She gestured for the men at the other table to depart. They didn't move and continued to stare her down.

'Looks like you'll have to hold your conversation in public,' said the man behind the counter. He lifted a small espresso-sized cup to his lips and slurped noisily.

'Fair enough. I'll take Farai to the station and chat to him there.' She swivelled in the pimp's direction and he lifted up disproportionately large hands, the size of his head.

'No need for that, Officer. Besides, I got some business to attend to here.'

'I don't want to discuss what I have to say in front of anyone,' Kate insisted.

Farai's sunken cheeks seemed to implode further. 'I thought I told you not to bother me again?'

'I didn't want to, but this concerns a murder investigation and unless we can talk one-to-one now, you'll have to accompany me back to Stoke.'

He sat back in his seat, one leg over the other and casually swung his foot. 'I can't help you.'

'Then you leave me no option.'

A smile pulled his lips into a thin line. 'You scratch my back, and I'll scratch yours.'

'What's that supposed to mean?'

'I'll keep quiet about our last meeting if you talk to me here. Or, I can come with you to Stoke where I might let something slip about you handing me a significant amount of money. Somebody might be very interested in why you did that.'

She curled her fist and stepped towards him. He thought he had her over a barrel and he thought wrong. She lowered her voice.

'You leak one word and I won't be able to guarantee your safety. I won't be able to protect you from the person who will send you to prison, nor from those who will ensure you don't come out.'

He stopped swinging his foot then guffawed. 'Tough talk always wins out. Okay, gentlemen. You heard the officer. Best if you leave us alone. Nando, why don't you go upstairs for five minutes and watch some of that shit you love on telly?' Farai's deep voice carried weight and the men rose. With hostile stares in her direction, they walked out.

The café owner, Nando, hesitated for a moment and only when the door was shut did he speak. 'Five minutes. No longer.'

Kate pulled out a plastic chair from under Farai's table and dropped onto it. It was time to play hardball. 'I'll come straight to the point. I need to know who this is.' She passed over the stills taken from the CCTV footage at Stoke station. Farai's face grew serious.

'Why've you got this picture?'

'You can't answer a question with a question.'

'Why?'

'Which one is she? Rosa or Stanka?'

He glared at her.

'She was in contact with a CIO called Heather Gault.'

'Never heard of her.'

'I think you have. Heather was in communication with a number belonging to a pre-paid mobile phone. It was one of a batch stolen from Manchester Mobiles, and belonged to this girl.'

His hands tensed but he wouldn't reply.

'This isn't how I wanted to do this, but we haven't got time to faff about. You're out of your depth, Farai. We both are if we aren't open with each other, so in order to gain your trust, I'm going to tell you something important, in exchange for an honest answer. Okay?'

'I'm listening.'

'Heather was part of an investigation team looking into something to do with you. She was taken off the case, but managed to track down this girl and talked to her last Friday morning. The following night, Heather was murdered.'

'I have an alibi for Saturday night. I was in the back room of the Wild Cat nightclub. I can call upon several witnesses to confirm that fact, and there'll be CCTV.'

He leant back and draped his arm over the back of his chair. The casual stance was betrayed by glittering eyes. Kate continued. 'I don't know much about the investigation, only that it involved underage sex workers, but I know who was heading it, and it doesn't look good for you.'

'I didn't kill no woman called Heather.'

'Who is this girl?' She wasn't leaving until she found out. 'Is she one of the girls you sent to the Maddox Club in January?'

A small ring in his left eyebrow glinted as car headlights swept by outside. The vehicle drew to a halt and a door banged shut. A shadow fell across the door. She hadn't got long left with Farai before more customers came in and he refused to speak to her.

'Farai, she could be in danger.'

There was shuffling from above them. Nando was on the move. She'd run out of time.

She'd have to take Farai to the station and drag it out of him and then he said, 'Rosa. That's Rosa.'

'Where is she now?'

'I don't know. Nobody has seen her since Friday morning. She isn't answering her phone.'

The door opened and four men entered. Farai shook his head, a gesture Kate interpreted to mean the conversation was over. Rosa's disappearance was another blow.

◆ ◆ ◆

She glanced at the dashboard in dismay. It was a quarter to eight and she'd nothing to show for her venture. The clock was ticking. Their killer could have another victim in his sights or even struck again and she'd wasted time chasing after the CCTV footage because, ultimately, the pay-as-you-go phone had nothing to do with their investigation, and nor did Rosa. She'd been so determined to implicate Dickson and even link him to Heather's murder, she'd lost sight of the facts. Now, once again focused on the investigation, Kate acknowledged that Heather had been killed by the same person who murdered Laura and attacked Olivia, and that she had wasted valuable hours chasing up an unrelated incident. Worse still, another day had passed and the killer was still on the loose and they hadn't really narrowed down their suspects.

Her phone rang and Tilly's cheerful voice, over the hands-free, lifted Kate's anxious mood.

'Hi, how's it going?'

'So-so. I'm on the M6 heading home.'

'I don't suppose you fancy dropping by, do you? Daniel's got a playmate staying over and they're both as high as kites, charging around the place. I could do with some adult company.'

She could be at her stepsister's place by eight thirty. 'Okay. I'll be half an hour.'

'Thank you. This is one of those moments when I really appreciate having a sister.'

CHAPTER TWENTY-EIGHT

Tilly opened the door and flung her arms around Kate, before dragging her into the sitting room and plonking a glass of wine in her hand.

'Daniel!' she shouted.

The boy came rushing into the room, his face pink with enthusiasm. 'Hi, Kate. I've got a new friend. He's called Toby.'

'And what have you both been doing?' asked Tilly.

'Playing dinosaurs.' He gave a realistic roar and bared his teeth.

Tilly rolled her eyes. 'See what I mean? They've been chasing each other around the house for the last hour and aren't the teeniest bit tired.'

'Do you want to come and see our dinosaur park?' he asked.

'Poor Auntie Kate has been at work all day and she's going to have a drink with Mummy first. Haven't you got something you want to give her though?'

He sprinted over to a white-painted, oak cupboard and retrieved a bag from inside before returning to Kate with his arm outstretched. 'I chose it.'

The bag bore a Sea Life Centre logo.

She placed her glass on a small table and crouched to meet his gaze, taking the bag from him. 'Thank you very much. What did you see at the Sea Life Centre?'

He didn't need to think. 'Sharks. Lots and lots of sharks and stingrays and clown fish and penguins.'

'Wow! What was your favourite?'

'The big sharks. You can walk under a tunnel and see them swimming above you.' He shifted from one stockinged foot to the other. Upstairs, another small voice shouted out his name.

He waited while she opened the bag and peered inside before pulling out a soft, red, toy starfish. It had a smile as wide as Daniel's. 'Oh, it's lovely!'

'It's a starfish,' he said.

'Also called a sea star, and one of the most beautiful animals in the ocean,' said Tilly. 'And what did we learn about starfish, Daniel?'

'If they lose an arm, it can grow another,' he said, his eyes widening at the thought.

'And what else?'

'They bring good luck.'

Toby called out again and Tilly said, 'You'd better go see what he wants.'

'Thank you, Daniel. It's the best present I've ever had.' Kate gave him a hug, relished the warm embrace while it lasted, then smiled as he scampered away.

Tilly looked after him with fondness. 'Where do they find their energy? They've been on the go since six. It's nice to see him so happy.'

'You have spoken to him about what's going on, haven't you?'

'He's too young to understand. He's enjoying the big adventure. And he doesn't seem to be missing Jordan. He never saw much of him anyway.' Jordan was a long-haul truck driver who

274

spent most of his time on the road. 'We could live anywhere in the world and Daniel would be happy as long as he has me and could see Jordan now and again.' She took a quick sip of her wine. 'Daniel's the best thing to come out of our marriage. I love him more than . . . anything.'

The pride was there, in her voice, in the way she held her head and in the light that crept into her eyes as she thought about him.

'So, how did it go with Chevy?'

'He was okay. Bit too much into his fitness regime though. Takes it all too seriously. Didn't drink alcohol and avoided all carbs, which is pretty much the exact opposite of me. He did have a super six-pack though.' She winked.

'Not seeing him again?'

'Nah. I messaged Ryan earlier. I'll probably fix up something with him.'

'I don't remember much about him from school,' Kate said. 'You never told me you went out with him.'

'I guess I was a little embarrassed to mention it. After all, he wasn't my usual type. We had a laugh, found out we liked quite a few of the same things – films, music, bands. We snogged and made out on the green a couple of times, but I wasn't really into him in that way.' The green had been the nickname given to an area on the school playing fields, frequented by couples or smokers.

'It only lasted a couple of weeks. I broke up with him and started seeing one of his friends, Ashar. And Ashar dumped me soon afterwards. Looking back, I guess I was always searching for love, or at least some sort of affection.'

A memory rushed to the forefront, bringing with it the envious emotions Kate had experienced at the time, and for a split second, she saw herself passing the school lockers in the corridor where Tilly stood, surrounded by good-looking boys, vying for her attention. While Kate was ignored, Tilly enjoyed popularity with the opposite sex, making it all the more difficult for her to accept Tilly into her life. She blinked back the memory, turning her full attention to the conversation.

'That was before I was attacked.' As she lifted her glass to take another swig, her hand began to tremble. The trembling intensified, slopping the wine and she swore. She put the glass down firmly and clamped her hands between her thighs, chewing at her bottom lip.

'Hey, it's okay. It's in the past.' The sudden realisation that Tilly was still deeply affected by what had happened to her frustrated Kate. That her stepsister was still suffering all these years later was wrong. Had Tilly received better support and/or more counselling immediately afterwards, she wouldn't be in this state. Her annoyance was directed at her father and Ellen, who ought to have done more.

Tilly's sad tone yanked her from her reflections. 'It happened in the past but I haven't left it there. It's haunted me all my life. Not only the memory of what happened, but the horrendous, sinking feeling that I deserved it, that it was repayment for how I behaved and how I treated boys back then, flirting with them, teasing them and encouraging them, knowing I was desired.' Her eyes filled. 'You know, there were days, weeks even, when I wouldn't let Jordan near me? I'd push him away or scream at him, I wouldn't even let him hold me, all because I felt so disgusted with myself, never him . . . me. He said he understood, but as time went by, he understood less and less. He treated it as if it were an illness and believed I'd eventually be cured. He was wrong. I can be fine for ages, then something will trigger a memory and my body is flooded with fear and loathing and I retreat into myself. I can't control it. It's little wonder he found another woman.'

'Oh, Tilly! I had no idea this had gone on for so long.'

'How could you? Anyway, apparently, it's normal to have a psychological reaction brought on by returning to where the attack took place. Hence the shaking hands. I spoke to my therapist about it and she warned me I'd probably get overwhelmed from time to time while I was here.'

'You have a therapist?'

Tilly brushed an invisible speck of dust from her blue top. 'Yes, I've been seeing her on and off for years. I'm pretty mixed up, Kate. Not just because of what happened at Bramshall Park, either. I was carrying a shitload of guilt about stealing Jordan away from you. I had all sorts of . . . issues, which took a lot of figuring out. More recently, there've been the problems with Jordan . . . yadda. It was her idea for me to revisit all the old haunts, exorcise the demons and learn to forgive myself. I have to go through this process if I want to remain here and, Kate, I do. Australia was somewhere I escaped to, and running away wasn't the long-term answer. My real home is here in the UK where I can start afresh. I want Daniel to grow up here too and get to know you.'

She shifted her light weight and sat cross-legged. Painted toe-nails, like shimmering shells, caught the light of the free-standing lamp behind the settee.

'You could settle anywhere in the country. You don't have to return to this particular region.'

Tilly stared over her stepsister's shoulder at the drawn curtains covered in gold and silver circles. 'I do. Facing up to it is the only way I'll be able to heal and, besides, I want to be near you.'

'Why didn't you mention any of this before to me?'

'You were dealing with losing Chris. I couldn't add to your burden. You rescued me once before. I thought you'd worry that if I dragged up these memories, I'd return to that dark place.'

'No, Tilly. I'd have backed you up every step of the way. You only had to tell me.'

Tilly hung her head. 'This is something I have to handle myself.'

'You don't. I can come to the park with you, talk things through, help you see it wasn't your fault.'

'Thank you, but no. I'll get through this – alone.'

Tilly lifted the wine glass again and shook her head before drinking. Kate was glued to her pale face, the shining eyes. Her stepsister looked so frail and doll-like, small hands cupping the glass, and the urge to hold her and protect her burned in Kate's chest.

'You've got this, Tilly. I believe you're strong enough to get through it. And, I'm here for you.'

'You have no idea how happy that makes me.' Her face became serious again. 'And, just for the record, although I've been out with a couple of guys, I've no intentions of getting serious with any of them. It's a morale-boost. Part of my therapy, if you like. I told both of them I was married. There was no point in stringing them along. It was nice to have some male attention and feel no pressure.'

'I'm not concerned about you getting involved with anyone. The case we're investigating has highlighted the need for us all to be vigilant. A couple of women were attacked and murdered, and a third is in hospital. I only wanted to remind you to take care when you're out and about. Not only when you're seeing somebody you don't really know; when you're going about your business, walking to and from the shops, using public transport. Try not to be alone. Stick to crowds. I don't mean to scare you, but I do want you to exercise extra caution.'

'Well, thanks to Emma, I could put up a good fight and probably manage to drop kick an assailant.' The smile accentuated tiny creases around her eyes, but the sparkle was back in them. Kate didn't want to lecture further. She'd made her point.

Sudden, thudding footsteps above them accompanied by loud giggling stopped them from talking. Tilly cocked her head. 'I'd better go and see what that pair are up to. He really did choose the toy starfish himself. He thought the smile on its face would make you feel happier on days when you were sad, chasing criminals.'

Kate lifted it up and beamed at the smiling face. Tilly paused by the door.

'And, we both think you're a star. A unique, wonderful star.'

CHAPTER
TWENTY-NINE

The engine vibrates between his thighs and gives a final satisfying low growl as he turns it off. He shouldn't have long to wait. Daisy works three evenings a week at the popular White Horse pub and is invariably dropped off at the same place by a co-worker. She walks through the park before emerging close to the estate where she lives.

He props the bike up on its stand. The driveway he's using is empty. The house has been unoccupied for over a month and stands on a corner plot so it's unlikely anybody will take much notice of the dark bike parked outside the garage. To be sure it isn't picked up on any cameras, he's removed the number plates as usual. He'll screw them back on when he gets home.

He tugs off his gloves, finger by finger, so he can undo his helmet and places it in the box. The last thing he wants is somebody stealing it. There are only a few houses along this one-way street, overlooking Festival Gardens, one of the smaller parks in Lichfield, with footpaths that allow pedestrians to pass from one side of the Western Bypass to the other without having to cross the busy main road.

He slides the balaclava over his face, puts his gloves back on and makes his way into the park. Daisy always gets out of the car at the clock tower roundabout and takes one of the footpath links towards the silvery brook and turns left towards the underpass, emerging from the short tunnel into neatly tended gardens, where she climbs the path up a steep slope and crosses the road towards Friary Gardens where she lives. Although not tonight. She'll get no further than the underpass. The tunnel doesn't contain graffiti or smell badly and isn't occupied by youths or druggies. Lichfield is a proud city and the park is one of many acres maintained by the local council.

He likes the anonymity of the city, which is really only a large town with a cathedral. There are so many visitors, he can easily mingle and draw no attention to himself and yet it isn't too far from where he lives.

Although the paths are well lit, the shrubbery affords plenty of hiding places, so he finds a suitable dark patch where he can see the ancient clock tower and where he has a view of the path Daisy will follow, and waits in the cool dampness.

A green car draws up to the pavement. The door opens and Daisy steps out. She's wearing a belted coat and boots. Underneath she'll be in the uniform she wears behind the bar, a white T-shirt and black skirt.

'Night, Michelle.'

He can't make out the muffled reply but he clearly hears the door slam and watches Daisy pick her way down towards him. She pops earbuds in and begins searching for a suitable track to listen to, her head lowered over the mobile device. She doesn't see him step out until he is in front of her and before she fully lifts her head, his hand sweeps towards her neck.

◆ ◆ ◆

Kate rested her palms on the padded leather armrests of Chris's office chair. Gentle light fell from the desk lamp and spotlighted the few personal objects he'd kept there: a photograph of the two of them taken at picturesque Robin Hood's Bay in North Yorkshire, a bronze, rotating, kinetic gyroscope and a Mont Blanc fountain pen, a reward to himself for getting his first job as a journalist – his lucky talisman.

The house was silent apart from the odd familiar creak as it seemed to stretch and yawn around her. She'd never felt alone or frightened here, or had to switch on a television set, or play music for company. She preferred the comfortable silence that settled around her, the familiarity of her home. It was a content house and when she closed her eyes at night it would whisper happy echoes of the past. Of all the rooms that brought back vivid memories of Chris, the study was the one place where she felt his presence most strongly. She'd occasionally spray his favourite aftershave into the room, allowing the tiny droplets to infuse the chair and cushion where he'd always sat.

She'd enjoyed the evening with Tilly but sitting here, she felt a sense of loss. Normally, she would converse with Chris as if he were present, yet try as she might to conjure him up, she could not. Her head was too full of Tilly's laughter as she and Kate had chased after Daniel and his friend Toby, all pretending to be dinosaurs. It was as if so much life had eradicated the ghost of Chris, a notion that chilled her.

She switched off the light, found her way out of the room and into the hallway, lit only by moonlight coming in from the small pane of glass in the front door.

'Did you fill up the bird feeder?' Chris called.

On hearing his voice, a wave of relief washed over her. 'Yes, of course I did. Where have you been? I wanted to speak to you.'

'You didn't want it enough, Kate.'

The room plunged once again into silence.

CHAPTER THIRTY

The strip light vibrated noisily. Kate, who'd been working alone in the office since seven o'clock, no longer registered the sound. Her takeaway coffee had gone cold and a half-eaten pot of yogurt lay neglected on her desk. She'd been going over past rape cases and been working for well over an hour by the time Emma came in.

'Morning. You been here all night?'

'Feels like it. Is it half eight already?'

'On the dot.'

'I'm guessing Tilly didn't join you this morning. She had her hands full with Daniel and his new friend when I last saw her.'

'No, you're wrong there. She's taking her training seriously. She dropped off both boys with the neighbour and came in for a quick half-hour session.'

'Hey!' Morgan's greeting was subdued and his eyes baggy. 'Anything new?'

'Not yet.'

'At least there don't seem to be any new victims,' said Emma.

'Let's hope it stays that way too,' Morgan replied. 'Three are three too many.'

Computers were switched on and heads lowered. Minutes passed in silence before Kate asked, 'Any idea where Jamie is?'

'He was outside, talking to the super when I came in. Either brown-nosing or begging for more overtime.'

'Don't be mean,' said Emma.

Morgan grunted. 'He gets on my wick.'

'Because he's keen and enthusiastic?' said Emma.

'No, because he borrowed twenty quid off me and still hasn't paid me back.'

Kate zoned out. She wanted news on Olivia. The sooner they could hear what she had to say, the better. She dialled the hospital and waited to be put through to Olivia's ward. Jamie appeared while she was on the phone. She noticed Morgan pointedly ignored his greeting.

The information from the hospital wasn't what she hoped for. Nevertheless, she relayed it to the others. 'Olivia had a poor night and her recovery has taken a setback. The doctors are hopeful she'll improve, so we'll have to continue to be patient. She might still provide us with vital evidence.'

Morgan groaned. 'Now what? We're getting nowhere.'

'No, we are making progress, admittedly, slower than any of us would like, but I have complete confidence in this team. For one thing, we're sure the killer has been using a black Honda motorbike without registration plates. I've asked for this information to be released to the press and for them to circulate it. A member of the public might well have spotted the bike and we might get lucky. We *shall* get to the bottom of this.' She searched for any questioning looks, saw flickers of hope in her officers' eyes and returned to her desk, pep talk over.

Her screen came to life again and she picked up where she'd left off, looking at a past rape case. The unsolved assault had taken place the year before, in Rocester, only a ten-minute drive north of Uttoxeter. When Kate had been part of a running group, they'd often trained around the landscaped grounds of the JCB factory that took pride of place opposite the village.

She clicked onto the victim's photograph and took in the limpid, coffee-coloured eyes that seemed to gaze trustfully at her, and the elfin face framed by dark hair, with espresso hues and golden-brown tone, cut in a long bob. This young woman bore a strong resemblance to the other victims and Kate's pulse quickened as she scrolled through the information. Bianca Moore was a twenty-one-year-old shop assistant, who lived with her parents in the village. One Saturday evening, last October, she'd been jumped on her way home and dragged to scrubland behind a car showroom building which stood close to the shop. Her heart rate intensified as she read the girl's statement. She wasn't rendered unconscious by her assailant. He'd attacked from behind and clamped a hand over her mouth and forced her, using threats, to the place where he raped her. He'd worn a balaclava and had been abusive throughout the rape, swearing and defiling her verbally as well as physically. The itching was back. Kate scratched at her scalp, her eyes glued to the screen. The man had wrapped his hands around her throat, threatened to kill her but instead released her with a hard laugh and the words 'You're mine'.

Kate reread the last line and wiped moisture from her palms on her skirt. There was now little doubt in her mind that they were searching for this assailant. His modus operandi had evolved; he'd introduced the vagus strike to render his victims helpless, and now, after raping them, strangled them.

'Our priority must be to interview Bianca Moore,' she said, after she'd summed up her finding. Faces were once more alight and Emma had already picked up her car keys in anticipation of joining Kate. 'I know Emma's been looking into it, but we need to up the ante and be making earnest enquiries at local martial arts schools and centres to see if anyone started classes or training more intensely during the last year, or if anyone expressed interest in performing or practising vagus strikes. He'd have required tuition to learn to aim his blow accurately, wouldn't he, Emma?'

'For sure. It's not something you can pick up from YouTube, not if you want to perform the manoeuvre perfectly.'

'Pursue that angle while Emma and I interview Bianca.'

There was a soft rapping and a low cough. A man in blue overalls, holding a toolbox, in the open doorway spoke up. 'Maintenance. I've been sent to fix the strip light.'

'About bloody time,' said Morgan. 'It's doing my head in.'

Kate got to her feet. She hadn't registered the incessant hum for a while. She might even find the place too quiet once it was silenced. At least the repair would help pacify her team.

◆ ◆ ◆

Bianca no longer worked at the local shop in the centre of Rocester and had moved out of the village to Ashbourne, a market town in the foothills of Derbyshire. Kate let her mind digest the facts, while Emma was at the wheel. Dua Lipa sang as they whistled past the impressive JCB World Headquarters where mirrored frontage reflected the silver shimmering of one of the three lakes and fountains shooting spray into the sky.

'That thing always freaks me out,' said Emma, referring to the metallic, spider-like structure made up of mechanical diggers and resembling an earth-invading creature from a 1950s science fiction film.

'The Fosser?' said Kate, absent-mindedly.

'Is that what it's called? What's a fosser?'

'It's Latin for digger,' said Kate.

'You speak Latin?'

A flicker of a memory: her father enthusiastically pointing out an article in the paper along with the promise of a day trip to explore the park area and lakes and view the sculpture created by a famous Polish artist. The trip had never happened. By then his illness had already taken hold of him and the promise simply slipped his memory. 'No, my dad told me. He was into local history.' *That's enough.* She clamped her lips shut. She rarely spoke about her father. A blue and silver helicopter hovered over the helipad and took off in the same direction as they were travelling, the *chop, chop, chop* of the blades reverberating through Kate's body as it flew over the car then climbed up and away. The lakes disappeared and the scenery changed, a never-ending patchwork of green and beige fields, dark hedgerows and aged trees with sweeping branches that passed her in a blur of colours.

Soon they were turning towards Ashbourne at the foothills of the Peak District National Park, a town of slopes and cobbled streets and architecturally pleasing buildings, given over, in the main, to tourism. The town centre was built around a one-way street lined with tea rooms and quaint shops. The pavement outside the florist shop, situated at the foot of a cobbled street, was awash with colourful dahlias, asters, delphiniums and chrysanthemums. Walkers in sturdy boots and sensible jackets marched behind each other along the narrow street. The traffic had slowed, snarled up behind a lorry trundling up the steep, narrow road towards the Peaks.

'One of my friends took their first driving test here,' said Emma.

'Here?' It had some of the steepest inclines Kate had come across.

'Yes. Big mistake. He failed on the hill start. I can understand why,' she said, shoving the vehicle into first gear and waiting for the lorry to pick up enough speed so the rest of the traffic could move forward.

'It's not much further. We can park and walk to her place.'

Within minutes they were stationed on the large, triangular market square.

Emma jammed the key into her back pocket and said, 'You know, back in medieval times, they used to sell pigs here, horses at the bottom of the square and sheep further down in King Street, which was called Mutton Lane.'

'I had no idea,' Kate replied.

'Neither did I until we found out Bianca lived here and I googled the place,' said Emma with a quick grin.

Kate's calf muscles strained, threatening to rip as they paced up the steep slope to where Bianca now lived. Vehicle after vehicle belched out fumes in a never-ending procession beside them, and it was with some relief when they turned off the main drag and into a side street, even steeper than the one they'd already ascended, in the direction of a black-and-white cottage, where she rang the doorbell.

Bianca looked older than the photograph on file. The lustre had gone from her hair, which was now styled in a pixie cut that suited her face but made it look more angular. Emma made the introductions and they soon found themselves in a kitchen diner. They refused the offer of a drink and instead got down to business.

'We'd like to talk about what happened to you last October.'

Bianca stood stock-still, kettle in hand. 'Okay. But why are you asking me after all this time? Are you reopening the case?'

Emma nodded. 'After a fashion. We're investigating a similar case and noticed there were similarities between what happened to you and another victim.'

'And you think it might be the same man?'

'It's a possibility we're looking into.'

'Is she okay? This other girl?'

'She's stable but unconscious at the moment. That's why we really need your help,' said Emma.

A cat flap opened with a clatter and a small panther-like animal bounded in, made for Bianca and brushed its tail up her legs. Bianca replaced the kettle and knelt by the cupboard under the sink. 'What do you want to know? Everything I told the police should be in a report.' She stood up again, a tin in her hand and hunted through a drawer until she found an opener.

'We've read your statement about what happened, but we'd appreciate it if you could go through what happened that evening, so we can see if there are any other comparisons.'

Kate had once again taken up the role of observer, watching the hand tremors as Bianca opened the can, and her eyes, as they darted around the room when she recalled the events of that evening. The young woman remembered it with clarity.

'I finished work at the usual time, six thirty, and headed home. My parents' house was only a five-minute walk away from the shop and I knew the area really well. I'd lived there all my life. Rocester was a sleepy village. I never imagined that could happen, not there, not right near my house. I'd almost crossed the car showroom forecourt that was next door to the shop, when I was yanked backwards and a hand covered my mouth and nose. I couldn't breathe so I struggled and my attacker said, "The more you fight me, the worse it will be for you." I knew I couldn't get away from him. He was gripping me so tightly, I'd never have wriggled free, and I was terrified I'd suffocate so . . . I stopped moving and . . . it all happened very quickly . . . He forced me to the far side of the building, to the grassland behind it. It was pitch black, but I could see my house from there and the upstairs light was on, behind the curtains in my parents' bedroom, and I knew they'd have no idea what was happening to me. I was . . . terrified.'

'It must have been dreadful,' said Emma gently.

The cat was ignoring everyone and delicately picking through the food Bianca had put down for it.

She hung on to the empty can. 'He asked me to nod if I promised not to scream and I did. I wanted to live. He took his hand away and I gulped in some air and then . . . he shoved me so hard with both hands, I fell onto my knees. And . . . he violated me. I didn't scream. I didn't make any sound. I kept looking at the bedroom window and thinking soon I would be home. I don't have to tell you exactly what he did, do I?'

'Not if you don't want to. We've read through your statement and the report so there's no need. There's only one thing we want to clarify with you. He spoke to you afterwards.'

'Yes. He told me to keep my head down and count to a hundred before I left.'

'Did he say anything else to you, Bianca?'

She put down the empty can at last and clamped her hands under her arms. 'There was something else. He said, "You're mine".'

'Those exact words? Nothing else?'

'Nothing else.'

'Did he harm or threaten you with a blade?'

'No.'

'Did you get any sense of how tall or large he was?' asked Emma.

'He was taller than me and he had big hands. They covered all my nose and mouth.'

'Were they rough or smooth?'

'Smooth-ish.'

'Did you happen to notice if the backs of his hands were hairy at all?'

'No. I couldn't see them.'

'Do you remember any particular smell, maybe aftershave or deodorant? Every detail, no matter how minor, could help us.'

'Sorry, no. I was struggling to breathe. I don't remember any smell.'

Kate spoke up at last. 'Did you hear any car engines or noise soon after he left?'

'There were cars in the background but the noise was probably coming from the main road.'

'Did you hear an engine fire up nearby?'

She rubbed her lips together and stared into the distance. There was no noise other than a barely audible ticking from a peach-faced clock on the wall. The second hand jerked through thirty degrees before Bianca finally answered. 'I can't remember for certain, but I think I heard what sounded like a motorbike start up.'

Tilly rang as they were on their way back. She sounded flustered. 'I've left my purse with my credit cards and money in the locker at Greg's. The place is shut up and I can't get hold of him on his mobile. I've been trying to get hold of Emma. I think she has a key for the place.'

'Emma's here with me. She can hear you.'

'Hi, Tilly. Greg's at a martial arts event in London. He'll have his mobile switched off.'

'Oh, bugger. Can anyone else let me in?'

'Only me. He went with Chevy, who's the only other person with a key.'

'I know it's a total pain in the bum, but is there any way you could meet me there? I haven't any cash on me and I've just had to abandon an entire trolley of shopping in the supermarket.'

'Sure. I've got a key on me. We can scoot by on our way back to the station.' She glanced at Kate as she spoke and received a nod of consent. 'We'll meet you there in about half an hour. Is that okay?'

'You're an absolute life saver. Thank you so much. I'll see if I can get the supermarket to hang on to the goods for me until I can get back and pay for them. See you there.'

The phone went dead and Emma asked, 'Did you two always get on so well?'

'Not at first. We grew to like each other and then, yes, we got along really well.' Kate didn't wish to divulge too much about her past life.

'I'd have loved a sister. Living with seven brothers was heavy going. They tended to either ignore me or torment me. I suppose it was good training for standing on my own two feet. Couldn't stand it in the end and went to live with Gran. I get on best with Greg. He was always the kindest to me.'

'You see much of the others?'

She shook her head. 'They've pretty much gone their separate ways. Now and again, we meet up to celebrate some event, but generally we keep out of each other's way. I often wonder what it would have been like to have had a sister.'

'They steal your make-up and clothes and try to get out of housework when it's their turn to do it.'

'Bit like my brothers then,' said Emma, with a chuckle.

◆ ◆ ◆

The martial arts academy was a non-descript unit, housed in the corner of a business park. A blue board, bearing the name *Greg's*, didn't give away what might be inside the building. There was no sign of Tilly so Emma unlocked the door and beckoned Kate inside, snapping on the main light to illuminate the space, far bigger than Kate had imagined from outside. Fans whirred, swirling the aroma of pine disinfectant into the atmosphere.

'You've never been here, have you?' said Emma. 'Let me give you a quick tour. Obviously, this is where we have fights or practice fights,' she said, as they passed the boxing ring.

'What about training kit? Where do you keep that?' asked Kate.

Emma pointed to the line of mirrors that ran the length of the room. 'The mirrors slide open and all the equipment is stored in the cupboards behind them. It keeps the place free of clutter and helps avoid accidents: somebody tripping over a skipping rope or slipping on a pad.'

She moved through an open archway into another room, far lighter than the first, illuminated by light coming in from the half-dozen skylights. 'This is where I tend to do most of my training.' The floor was clear with floormats rolled and stacked in a large open box. Six punchbags hung from hooks and in the corner were three dummies.

'This is where I've been training with Tilly, although she's been using the resistance equipment in the next room, as well. There's also a studio for classes, changing rooms and Greg's office.'

It was a professional set-up and Kate was impressed at how far back the unit extended, belying its unprepossessing frontage. 'Those the dummies you use to practise strikes on?'

'That's right.' She blinked a few times. 'I've had a sudden thought. I wonder if our killer has a dummy of his own to practise on. He might not even train at a gym at all.'

'I hope not. I'm banking on him using a gym.'

'Me too. He'd have had to learn it from somewhere professional and if we assume he's only started using the manoeuvre on his victims in recent months, we still might be able to track him down.'

Kate blew out her cheeks. 'You have no idea how much I want to find him. I'm worried sick he'll attack again. Every hour that goes by, I wonder if he isn't stalking his next victim or assaulting her.'

'At least we know we're searching for the same man who attacked Bianca. It was almost the same MO, holding her down, raping her, and it can't be a coincidence he spoke the very same words, "You're mine".'

There was a small gasp from behind them. Tilly's hand was pressed against her lips.

'Tilly?' Kate moved towards her stepsister. The colour had drained from her face. 'Tilly, what did you hear?'

Tilly shook her head. 'Not much. You were talking about a rapist.'

Emma looked sheepish. 'I didn't hear you come in.'

'It's okay. I should have coughed or something,' said Tilly, regaining her composure. 'Thanks for meeting me here. I've managed to convince the supermarket to look after my trolley. I didn't fancy going around again and selecting everything.'

'I'll fetch your purse for you,' said Emma.

'Oh, thanks.' Tilly watched as Emma disappeared then faced Kate, her voice an urgent whisper. 'I heard everything about the man who rapes and kills, Kate. "You're mine." Kate, the man who raped me said exactly the same words.'

Something exploded in Kate's head. 'What?' she whispered.

'That's what he said when he'd finished with me. "You're mine."'

Two decades had passed since Tilly was raped. What was the likelihood of this attacker being the same person?

'I . . . Shit, Tilly! What do I do?'

'You can't tell anyone. Not Emma, not anyone. Please. I don't want to be dragged back into it.'

'But I have to. It's vital information.'

Tilly reached for her hands, held them in her cool ones. 'No. I beg you. No.' Hearing footsteps, she broke away, feigned a casual stance.

'Here you go,' said Emma, holding out the purse.

'You are an angel. Thanks so much. I have to rush off. Daniel's waiting in the car.'

'See you in the morning?'

'Hope so. I won't bring this though. In case I forget it again.' She waved it in the air. 'Bye. See you soon, Kate.'

She half-jogged, back through the archway.

'I hope I didn't scare her, talking about the investigation,' said Emma.

'No. I spoke to her while you were in the changing room. She's fine. She was just taken by surprise.' Although she knew full well she should tell Emma everything, the horrified, pleading expression on Tilly's face was engraved on her retinas. She couldn't allow Tilly to become part of the investigation. She was doing her utmost to put the past behind her. This was one angle she would have to investigate alone.

Even though the bath water's gone cold, he doesn't move. His feet are propped up by the taps, his yellowing toenails on display. The empty bottle of bath and shower gel is beside him, its top floating in the water, and the scent of ginger and lemon is on his flesh. Water drips from the tap, but still he lies there. Something has gone wrong. The excitement, the adrenaline, the euphoria, have all vanished.

Daisy had been an ideal substitute. Exactly like his first love. And yet, once he'd knocked her out and dragged her to nearby bushes to molest her, he'd had no arousal. He'd abandoned her limp body in the undergrowth and, before she fully regained consciousness, raced away. The desire had vanished.

He stares unblinking at the cream ceiling and the light where a spider twists and turns and dangles on its gossamer thread before climbing back up it, industrious in creating a new web. He has no problem with spiders. They're only hunting prey much as he does. He employs the same techniques: captures his prey, paralyses it and, when finished, dispatches it. Disappointment fills his chest cavity, swelling like an ever-inflating balloon until he thinks he might explode.

The spider has swung across to the extractor fan and is descending rapidly on a fresh invisible thread, like a soldier abseiling from a dizzy height. It comes to a rapid halt above his head and begins its patient swaying. He watches it gather momentum, swinging backwards and forwards, the hypnotic motion bringing clarity to his thoughts. His failure to follow through was down to one person – her. She's wormed her way back into his fantasies and it is her face he sees every time instead of his victim's.

He messaged Tilly earlier and a meeting is definitely on the cards. It is now down to her. He can't wait much longer. His victims no longer arouse him. He only wants what he should never have let escape. He's had Tilly once and he is going to have her again.

And this time he won't let her escape.

He will end it once and for all.

CHAPTER THIRTY-ONE

Kate's decision not to drag Tilly into the investigation was playing on her mind. She'd crossed another line by keeping the personal connection secret. The only way to justify her actions was to use what she knew about her stepsister to her advantage, and locate the killer.

Tilly had been attacked in Uttoxeter, so if Kate added that location and Rocester to the map they already had triangulated in the office, it suggested the killer lived somewhere within a fifteen-mile square radius. Who had Tilly known who still lived in the area? With the question came a lightbulb moment – Ryan Holder, the man she'd been messaging and was planning on meeting. She dialled Tilly's number immediately.

'Tilly, I've been thinking about who might have attacked you. You said they knew you. Could it have been Ryan?'

There was a pause and a little chuckle. 'No, Kate. Ryan was one of the shyest and most courteous boys I went out with – a proper little gentleman! He even asked if he could kiss me the first time we snogged, and apologised afterwards in case he wasn't any good. I was more forward, but he wouldn't follow my lead, if you get my meaning, so we spent most of our time together simply holding hands and chatting. Ashar, his friend, was more mature, more grown up and experienced, even though they were the same age. I guess that's why Ryan and I get on so well now. We didn't ruin things back then.'

'What about Ashar?'

'No. He's married to a gorgeous woman, has three kids and lives in Hertfordshire. I friended and messaged him on Facebook too, but his response was lukewarm. I don't think he even remembered me. Not heard from him since.'

'Have you connected with anyone else from school on social media?'

'Quite a few girls, but only those two boys, well, men now.'

'Can you think of anyone else, Tilly? One of our parents' friends who might have said something suggestive to you, a neighbour?'

'No. Although I bumped into somebody in Uttoxeter, the local butcher. Do you remember Wayne Grimshaw?'

Wayne left school the year after Tilly joined. For a while, he'd shown a great deal of interest in her stepsister, walking her home from school and hanging out with her. He'd been a thuggish-looking boy, with a shaven head and an earring he refused to remove. He'd hated school, backchatted the teachers and was frequently seen outside the headteacher's office. Tilly had been attracted to the rebellious Wayne, who suited her own non-conformist attitude. They'd shared cigarettes and alcohol and probably drugs, although Kate couldn't be sure about the latter. When Wayne got expelled for hitting a teacher, he and Tilly drifted apart.

'I remember him. Why have you brought up his name?'

It went quiet at Tilly's end.

'Tilly?'

'I was walking down Uttoxeter High Street with Daniel, and he came out of nowhere, shouting my name and when he caught up with me, he swept me up in a bearhug. It was . . . embarrassing. I couldn't wait to get away from him.'

'Oh.'

'Yeah. He reeled off a load of things we'd got up to, none of which I could remember, including skipping off school to go to town, so he whipped out his wallet to show me a photograph of the two of us, taken in a photo booth in the Post Office. On the day of the attack. He remembered almost everything we'd done together. The whole thing was surreal. Freaky even. I'd completely forgotten all about him. He was all for ditching work and coming bowling with Daniel and me until I told him I was meeting my husband at the CineBowl. Luckily Daniel didn't say anything.'

'And how did Wayne react to that news?'

'Best word for it would be crestfallen, I suppose. He patted Daniel on the head and sloped off. I didn't think much of it at the time. I was too keen to get away.'

Surely Tilly would have recognised his voice if it had been Wayne who'd attacked her, although she'd said his voice had been muffled by a balaclava and he'd spoken in a low growl. It was still possible he'd been her rapist.

'I'll pay him a visit.'

'You haven't told anyone at the station about what happened to me, have you?'

'No, but you know I ought to. I'm running a massive risk keeping this to myself.'

'But if you tell them, you'll be removed from the case, won't you? Isn't that how it works? If there's a conflict of interest and you can't be objective, you'll have to hand over to somebody else.'

'That's not why I'm keeping your name out of it. I would happily pass it across if it meant this perpetrator was found. I'm doing this because you asked me to and I don't want you to regress. You're trying to put it behind you.'

There was soft sigh and a relieved 'Thank you. You understand, and that means so much to me.'

Was she really doing it purely for Tilly's sake or was part of her desperate not to give Dickson recourse to remove her from the investigation?

'Hang on a sec, Daniel is shouting for me. He's going on a sleepover next door tonight. You'd think he was moving in with them. Oh, and I messaged Ryan to suggest we meet up tonight.'

'In a busy place?'

'Of course. The Queen Anne pub. I'll text or ring you if there are any problems. I'll even make up that I need to visit the washroom and send you a text while I'm there, to let you know how it's going and to put your mind at ease.'

'You don't have to go that far. Well, I suppose you could fill me in on how much he's changed.' She couldn't wrap her sister up in cotton wool.

'He's certainly better-looking than he used to be, but still seems sweet-natured. I'm looking forward to seeing him. Oh, there's Daniel shouting again. He probably wants to pack all his dinosaurs.'

'You get off. If you think of anyone else I should speak to, message me.'

'Love you, Kate. Thank you for being there for me.'

'Always.'

As with many high streets, the shops' identities had altered over time, but the only thing different about the butcher's shop was the name. *Grimshaw the Butcher* was written in thirty-centimetre-high letters across the front window. The pink flesh of the cuts of meat, expertly displayed in the cabinet, made Kate's stomach flip:

pork chops facing all in the same direction, garnished with blobs of parsley to make them more appealing, next to trays of diced meat. The sight of so much raw flesh made her feel slightly nauseous. She fumbled for a mint to suck, all the while watching the square-shouldered man behind the counter. His meat cleaver rose and fell with precision as he portioned a side of beef, before tossing steaks onto a piece of greaseproof paper laid out on the scales. She opened the door, and a mournful *bee-beep* announced her arrival.

'Won't be a sec,' said Wayne. The customer had completed his order, so Wayne folded the paper into a neat parcel and passed it across the counter.

Kate took the opportunity to study his features. The deep-set eyes and shaven head were the same, but he'd muscled up over the years and his turned-up overall sleeves strained over thick forearms covered in tattoos. The man paid up and left the shop. Wayne wiped his hands on a towel.

'Right, what can I get you? We've got a great deal on brisket today.'

She placed her ID card on the counter. 'I'm here on police business. Would it be possible to have a quick word with you?'

'What about?' The door opened as he spoke and another customer entered. 'Okay. Come around the back. We can talk outside. Gavin, can you take over here, mate?' He motioned for her to follow him.

Weeds poked up between cobbles in the enclosed yard. Two wooden gates were closed to the road beyond. Judging by the dark oil stain spread in the centre of the courtyard, this was where they parked the delivery van. Wayne lit a cigarette, dragged on it and lifted his face to the sky, releasing the smoke between pursed lips. 'What do you want to talk to me about?'

'Firstly, I'd like to ask you where you were on Friday evening between eight and nine o'clock.'

'For real? What am I supposed to have done?'

'If you could simply answer the question, it would be helpful.'

'Home.'

'Where's home?'

'Above the shop.'

'Can anyone confirm that?'

'I was alone.'

'What about Saturday evening?'

He pointed up to the flat again.

'Did you go out?'

'Didn't feel like it.'

'How about Monday morning, around five o'clock?'

'In bed. Asleep. Alone.' He sucked on the cigarette and cocked his head. 'Does that help you?'

'I guess you own a delivery van?'

'I do. It's out at the moment.'

'Is it being repaired?'

'No. Why would you think that?' he said. 'Oh, the oil stains. They're not from the van. They're from a motorbike. Bloody thing made a right mess.'

'Your bike?'

'No. It belongs to one of the blokes who works here – Henry Oldham.'

'Is he around?'

'He's on holiday. Nipped off to Tenerife with some mates on Monday. He'll be back in a week.'

'Do you happen to know what make of bike it is?'

He shrugged. 'Honda, Suzuki. I don't know. I'm not into bikes. You'll have to ask Henry.'

'Where does he live?'

'Doveridge.' The village in question was about two kilometres away, east of Uttoxeter, almost on the Staffordshire/Derbyshire border.

'Any idea where in Doveridge?'

'I'm afraid not.'

He held the cigarette in between his thumb and finger and took another puff. 'Is that it, then?'

'Not quite. You look like you work out.'

He guffawed. 'Are you hitting on me? Want to feel my muscles?'

'I'll pass, thanks. Just wondered if you worked out locally?'

'As it happens, I do. The leisure centre. They've got great classes and a decent gym. I go most weeks.'

'You ever done any martial arts?'

'I've done a bit of kick-boxing, yeah.' He dropped the cigarette end. Smoke continued to spiral from it. 'I've got customers to serve and it's closing time soon, so I'd like to clean up the shop. Are we going to be much longer?'

'I've one more question. Tilly Nugent. Have you seen her recently?'

Tilly's maiden name had the desired effect. His neck flushed scarlet. 'I might have seen her a couple of days ago.'

'Did you, or didn't you?'

'Yeah, I did,' he said. He ran broad fingers over his head. 'Why are you asking me about Tilly?'

'You and she were an item at one point, weren't you?'

This time his cheeks flamed. 'Sort of.'

'What did you talk about?'

'Not much, actually. I caught sight of her walking past the shop and I nipped outside to chat to her. She couldn't stop for long though. She was meeting her husband.'

'You recognised her immediately?'

'Erm, yes. She hadn't changed much.'

Kate didn't believe him. Twenty years had passed since he'd last seen Tilly and although she hadn't changed hugely, it was unlikely he'd catch a glimpse of her in the street and immediately know who she was. After all, he clearly didn't recognise Kate. A sheen of sweat had appeared on his brow. 'Okay. Well, thank you for your time.'

'That it?'

'For now.' Until she had good reason to request a warrant to search his flat, there was little point in pressing him further.

He marched across to the gates, unlatched one and held it open. 'It'd be better if you didn't go back through the shop. I don't want the customers to think I'm in any sort of bother. Gossip spreads quickly and I have a reputation to uphold.'

◆ ◆ ◆

Kate followed her nose back to where she'd parked her car. The streets and buildings in this part of town hadn't transformed a huge amount, maybe there were different-coloured front doors or new window frames, but history was welded to each: the stuccoed White Hart Hotel with its rusticated quoins, a projecting porch and grand columns, which reminded Kate of a Greek temple; Lathropps Almshouses, in red brick with stone-framed windows and a four-centred arched doorway, above which was an inscribed plaque; timber-framed cottages and renovated dwellings still bearing stained glass etched with the original pub name, George & Dragon. The sense of familiarity was so strong she felt dragged back in time and understood why Tilly had experienced a similar effect when she'd visited. Kate moved aside to allow a woman with a double buggy to pass and dialled Tilly's number. A noisy bus trundled past, the acrid fumes wrinkling her nose as she pressed the mobile to her ear to hear better.

'Hi, Kate. Have you spoken to Wayne?'

'Yes.'

'Did he act as strangely with you?'

'He didn't recognise me and I didn't tell him I'm your stepsister. I need to do more digging and, obviously, I shouldn't discuss the details of the investigation with you.'

'That's understandable. I've tried but I can't think of anybody else you should talk to.'

'Okay. I'll see if I can get my hands on your old casefile, although I don't want to arouse any suspicions. Leave it with me.'

'Oh, I got a response from Ryan. The meet-up is on. I'm just sorting out what to wear.'

'Tilly, can't you wait a few days?'

'Why?'

'The investigation—'

'Oh, come on! This is Ryan, I know him.'

'You only know him from Facebook. There are dangerous people out there, pretending to be somebody they aren't.'

Tilly laughed. 'It's Ryan for certain. There's no way a stranger would be able to chat about the stuff we've discussed. I'll be careful. I don't intend walking down any deserted streets or meeting up in remote locations. I avoid places like that. Besides, we're meeting in a popular pub, so there'll be plenty of people around.'

'We're hunting for a man who rapes and murders his victims. I'd rather you held off until we've got more information.'

'And that could take months.'

Kate sighed. She was fast losing this argument and had to question whether or not she'd be urging caution if the friend Tilly wanted to meet was a woman. She decided she wouldn't.

'Okay. I give up. Just promise me you'll take extra care.'

'Promise.'

'And by the way, you'll look great in anything.'

She halted again by railings that ran the length of the pavement. A young cyclist was approaching and she beckoned them towards her. The teenager nodded thanks.

'Sorry, Kate. The doorbell's ringing. It'll be Toby and his mum, coming to collect Daniel. I have to dash.'

'What time are you seeing Ryan?'

'At six thirty. I'd better get a wriggle on if I'm going to be on time.'

'Have fun.'

'I intend to.'

'And Tilly . . . Please take care.'

'I always do.'

The line went dead. Kate reached her car. A high-pitched siren wailed loudly, the signal that the level-crossing gates behind her would soon be closing. She was headed in the opposite direction, so she climbed in and pulled away. Wayne was a concern. He had no firm alibis for the times of the attacks and possibly had access to a motorbike. On top of everything, he knew and still had feelings for Tilly.

◆ ◆ ◆

The office was warm and smelt strongly of coffee. Emma was on her own, feet up on the desk. 'Morgan and Jamie aren't back yet, but the strip light is fixed. You got a minute?'

'Give me two seconds. I need some info on a motorbike.'

Felicity answered on the first ring. 'I hope whatever you're going to ask me for isn't going to take all night. I just rang Bev to say I was on my way home.'

Kate explained she needed to find out what type of bike Henry Oldham owned.

'Doveridge, you say? Right-ho. Leave it with me. I'll put Rachid on it.'

'Thanks, Felicity. I owe you – again.'

'Don't worry, I'm keeping a tally,' Felicity replied, with a deep chuckle.

Kate turned to Emma. 'Okay, what's the problem?'

'It's not a problem, more a question. This came in earlier. A young woman, Daisy Weatherford, reported being attacked on her way home last night. She said a man struck her on the neck. She lost consciousness and came to a few metres away from where she was attacked, in some undergrowth. Apart from being hit, she doesn't appear to have been injured or molested and nothing was stolen.'

'That's odd. Was it a vagus nerve strike?'

'That's why I'm flagging it up. I think it might have been.'

Kate pressed her fingertips against her temples in thought. 'It's probably worth us talking to her. It might be the same assailant,' she said, reaching for her ringing mobile. 'DI Young. Is she? Okay, we're on our way.'

'Not another victim?' asked Emma.

'No. Olivia. The doctor says she can talk to us.'

◆ ◆ ◆

It was calmer at the hospital than the last time Kate had visited. There were no gurneys, or porters shunting patients in wheelchairs, or queues waiting to check in, only the occasional visitor and member of staff, heading in the opposite direction to them. A police officer sat on a plastic chair outside Olivia's ward, and leapt to her feet when she saw Kate and Emma approaching.

'Ma'am. I was instructed to wait for you and leave once I'd checked in with you. Olivia is still conscious and able to converse.'

'Yes, that's fine,' said Kate. 'Off you go.' She didn't think Olivia was in any danger from her attacker, who should, in theory, believe she was dead. The media office had deliberately kept news of this attack out of the press, so he had no way of knowing she had survived. Security was stringent enough, and entry not permitted unless it had been okayed by a member of the medical staff. She rustled into the protective clothing and, after pressing the entry buzzer, squirted fresh-smelling sanitiser onto her skin, rubbing it between her fingers and around her nails. Inside the ward, the lights had been dimmed and inside the nurses' station to the left, voices murmured. The life support machines beeped as one.

Olivia's room was also softly lit. She was still attached to monitoring equipment, but her eyes were open. Her mother sat beside the bed, her hand covering her daughter's.

'Mrs Sandman,' said Kate.

'Call me Rebecca,' she replied.

'Rebecca, this is DS Emma Donaldson. Thank you for arranging for us to talk to Olivia.'

'If it will help find whoever did this to her—' She faltered.

'Thank you,' Kate repeated. She moved to the opposite side of the bed.

'Hi, Olivia. It's good to see you looking better than the last time we spoke,' said Kate. 'How are you feeling?'

'Not too bad. They gave me painkillers.'

'Are you up to answering a few questions?'

Rebecca interrupted with 'The doctors said she wasn't to get stressed.'

'We won't let that happen. We'll stop whenever you want us to,' Kate replied. 'Olivia, are you able to remember anything at all about the man who attacked you?'

'It's quite hazy. I remember flashes but not everything.'

Shock could well have forced her mind to shut out what happened. 'That's completely normal. Tell us what bits you can remember.'

'He was strong,' she began. 'He had large hands. That's all.'

It was disappointingly little to go on. Kate continued. 'Did you see his face?'

'No.'

'Was he wearing a mask?'

'I don't . . . I don't know. I don't remember his face. He was behind me. He put his hand over my face.'

'Olivia, take your time. Anything you can tell us might help us. Anything.'

She squeezed her eyes shut and a tiny tear leaked from the side. 'His hands.'

'What about his hands?'

'A tattoo.'

'Can you describe it?'

'A black heart with a red blood drop leaking from it.'

'Which hand, Olivia?'

There was a pause and her eyes opened again. 'Right. The right hand.' Her lips trembled.

'Can you point out where on the hand?'

She ran a finger between her thumb and index finger, traced an outline to her wrist. A sob escaped her lips.

'You're doing really well,' said Kate. 'Really well. Last time, you told me something important. You said, "You're mine, forever". Why did you tell me that?'

'I heard him say it to me. He told me to lie still while he left me a message I'd never forget. At first, I thought he was writing on me or scratching me, then it stung and I could feel it bleeding and I realised he was cutting me with a blade. I begged him to stop and he warned me if I opened my mouth again or moved, he'd stab me in the heart. When he'd finished, he said, "You're mine. Forever." I've seen what he did to me—' Her voice cracked and her eyes grew misty.

'Hush, sweetheart. The doctors will fix that.' Her mother's face, drawn and long, exuded pain. Kate had seen a similar look on Ellen's face when Tilly had told her about the attack on her.

'Olivia, did he say anything else to you?'

Two silvery tears trickled down her cheeks. 'I . . . can't remember.'

'It's okay. We'll stop there. You've been really helpful. Thank you. We'll talk again when you next feel up to it.' Rebecca got to her feet and stroked her daughter's hair all the while, making more soothing sounds. Kate and Emma edged out of the room, into the corridor. They had something else to go on.

'A black heart tattoo,' said Emma, jerking the protective cap from her head, and raking a hand over her hair. It settled into its usual functional and tidy position.

Kate was only half-listening. Her mind had immediately turned to Wayne Grimshaw, the butcher with tattooed arms. She'd pay him another personal visit. She pulled off the protective shoe covers and added them to the clothing in the waste basket and hot-footed down the white corridor, footsteps thudding gently in time with Emma's. Rachid from the technical department rang before they'd left the building.

'Hi, Kate. I've got a make and model on Henry Oldham's motorbike. It's a Honda CB 125 F.' The same bike that had been identified. 'I hope that's good news.'

'It could be, Rachid. Thanks for getting onto it so quickly.'

'Any time.'

Her pace increased. She had to speak to Wayne immediately and test out her theory that he used Henry's bike as transport to and from the crime scenes, although there was now a better way of identifying him as the killer – a tattoo. She couldn't tell Emma what she planned. To do so would bring Tilly into the investigation. As if she'd sensed Kate was thinking about her, a message alert pinged and she read Tilly's message.

All going well.

Ryan's really sweet.

I won't do anything stupid.

☺

XX

The doors swished open and they tumbled out into the night. Kate inhaled to remove the smell of the hospital. At least she didn't have to worry about Tilly.

CHAPTER THIRTY-TWO

The church clock struck the half-hour. It was gone chucking-out time at the pubs and a few people were strolling home. A trio of young men stood outside the kebab shop, eating from cardboard cartons. The heavy beat of a sound system grew as a customised Audi A4 came into view. It revved its engine close to the group and the driver gave a short blast on his horn.

'Fuck off, Dizzy!' shouted one of the group, hurling a chip at the vehicle. The others jeered good-naturedly, and the driver made obscene gestures with his wrist before the car growled away. Laughter followed the departing vehicle and the men began walking away from Kate.

It was a friendly town with a strong farming community, and many of the inhabitants had known each other all their lives. Friendships formed at local schools had lasted into and throughout adulthood, although those outsiders like Kate were kept at arm's length, not ignored but never accepted in the same way. Tilly had been the exception, made welcome by almost everyone.

She reached the end of the street and walked in the direction of the butcher's shop, craning her neck to see if the lights were on in the flat above, indicating Wayne was still awake and up, a task made impossible thanks to the blinds at his windows. She rang the bell at the side entrance and waited.

The Audi was back, circling the area with its music on full blast. By the time the *boom, boom, boom* of the beat had faded, Wayne was at the door. His face pushed through the gap, and he scowled.

'I need to ask you a couple of questions about Henry Oldham's bike.'

'What about it?'

'Can you confirm it's a Honda CB 125 F?'

'I have literally no idea what that is. It's simply a black motorbike to me.'

'Never owned one?'

'Me? No way!' He lifted a cigarette to his mouth and sucked on it.

'That's an interesting tattoo,' she said, inching forward.

Smoke curled from his nostrils as he spoke. 'Which one?'

'The one on your hand.'

He held out his right hand and examined the scorpion with its lifted tail. 'Yeah. It's okay. I've got better ones on my back and chest.'

'Got any hearts?'

He extracted a microscopic piece of tobacco from between his lips with his other hand and laughed. She honed in on the movement. The tattoo on his left hand was a spider. 'Hearts? You're joking. I'm into skulls, lions, guns, macho stuff.'

She'd discovered what she needed to. As disappointing as it seemed, Wayne wasn't the perpetrator. 'Has Henry got any tattoos?'

'Tats? Henry? That's not his thing at all. Besides, his girlfriend would probably make him get any removed.'

'Okay. If I need to I'll talk to him in person when he gets back from his holiday,' she said.

Wayne's eyebrows drew together. 'That it?'

'That's everything. Thank you.'

He shut the door with an exasperated huff.

It had begun to rain lightly, and she jogged back to her car. If Wayne wasn't responsible for the attacks, she was back to square one. She rested her head momentarily on the steering wheel and groaned. They were running around in never-ending circles.

Chris sounded like he was in the back seat, his words quiet. 'Pull yourself together, Kate. It's no more than a setback.'

'I haven't got the energy or fight for all of this: the investigation into these attacks, Dickson, Tilly, you, all of it.'

This was getting out of hand. All this talking to herself. She shut her gritty eyes for a moment. She was pushing too hard, so hard she didn't have any clarity on the investigation, which was her priority, especially now it involved Tilly. If she wasn't careful, it would destroy her. She ought to go home and recuperate and, for the time being, concentrate on what mattered most – finding whoever was responsible for these heinous acts. As much as it pained her, Chris would have to wait.

CHAPTER THIRTY-THREE

In spite of her intentions to focus solely on the investigation, the 5 a.m. phone call forced her to change her mind. Bradley Chapman wanted to meet her by the reservoir. She rubbed at the sticky substance bonding her eyelids together. An extra hour's sleep would have been welcome; nevertheless she showered, dressed and even forced herself to eat cereal and glug milky tea before jumping back in her car.

The sun was beginning to rise over the reservoir, casting rose light across the shimmering expanse of water. A flock of seemingly pastel pink sheep were clustered on the hillside towards the water's edge and before them, the swans were feeding, dipping their graceful necks in tandem.

The leaves on the trees in the woods behind the lake were changing colour but in the morning light those colours took on a fresh intensity. If Kate had been an artist, or photographer, she'd have stopped there and then to capture the hues before traffic spoilt the scene.

Bradley had parked his Range Rover in the same spot as the last time, far enough away from the road to be out of sight from any passers-by who might be out and about at this early hour. She did likewise. No sooner had she switched off the engine than he was by the passenger door. She let him in, bringing with him a masculine woody scent with a hint of spice. He filled the seat, legs bunched up, knees against the dashboard yet he seemed unperturbed by the discomfort and held out his phone.

The man on the video screamed.

'What the hell?' she said.

'Just watch it.'

The blindfolded, pale-faced man with soaking wet, straw-coloured hair begged to be released. He twisted under his bonds until a person wearing military fatigues appeared on the screen, the upper body out of camera shot, and poured water over his face. He spluttered and coughed, mouth opening and closing like a fish's, as he struggled for breath. He gulped lungfuls of air.

'Tell us,' said a disguised, robotic voice.

'No . . . I can't . . . No.'

The same person moved again, more quickly this time. Water was poured over the man's eyes, then his nose and finally his mouth. He retched and hacked.

'We can keep this up for hours. You can't,' said the robotic voice.

'Okay. Okay. I admit it. I killed Cooper Monroe and made it look like suicide.'

'Tell us exactly what happened.'

'He was in the shower. He didn't hear me. I crept up behind him, surprised him and slit his throat with a razor blade before he could react.'

'And then?'

'I got cleaned up, changed into a spare uniform I'd already left in the changing area, and called for assistance.'

'Why did you kill him?'

316

He shook his head. 'Please don't make me tell you. I'll lose my job, everything.'

'You don't tell us and you'll die. Which is it to be?'

The man didn't answer and was waterboarded yet again. He gasped for air and made terrible choking noises, so bad that, for a moment, Kate thought he was going to stop breathing altogether.

'I was paid to make it look like suicide. I needed the money. My dad's got advanced dementia and needs medical care—'

'How much?'

'Thirty grand.'

'A poxy thirty grand for a man's life?'

'He was a criminal!'

His legs and lower body bucked under the leather restraints as more water was poured into his mouth. He blew and gasped and blew again. The water stopped.

'Who paid you?'

'An officer.'

'A police officer or a prison officer?'

'Police.'

'Who was this police officer?'

'No. I can't tell you.' He was tortured again. This time he pleaded for his life.

'Give us the name of the officer who paid you.'

The man gave it up at last. 'Superintendent John Dickson.'

Bradley paused the video. 'I'll email you an encrypted copy.'

Kate could hardly breathe. This was compelling evidence, proving exactly what they'd suspected all along: that Cooper had been murdered and Dickson was every bit as corrupt as she'd believed. Her heart drummed a resounding beat in her ears. This was a huge piece of information and proof of Dickson's guilt, yet how could she use it to bring him down? She forced herself to remain calm. 'Was that the guard we talked about last time we met?'

'That's him. Tom Champion. It took a while to extract the confession from him. He's a tough bastard.'

'Where is he now?'

'Taking a holiday with his family. I've got somebody keeping an eye on him. We've warned him if he tries to contact Dickson, we'll return to finish the job. He's too scared to do anything stupid.'

Although she had no reason to doubt Bradley, a court would take a different view, suggest Tom had been forced to confess to the murder and to implicating Dickson. That aside, it was also completely unprofessional and immoral to accept this video. She wasn't a lawbreaker, although she'd already broken rules by investigating Dickson and by keeping Tilly out of a hugely important investigation, but this . . . this was one step too far. It went against everything she'd stood for. She'd spent her whole life with her head held high, abiding by the rulebook and following procedure. She'd never once strayed and yet, in the space of a few months, she'd found herself moving ever further away from the right path. 'I don't think I can condone this, Bradley. Besides, this evidence will be inadmissible in any court. You *tortured* a man to get it. A judge will throw it out in a heartbeat.'

'I'm aware of that, but how else would you have found out the truth? You asked for my help, remember?'

'But not to beat up a man until he confessed to whatever allegations you threw at him.'

'As I recall, you weren't against me using unlawful methods when we talked about it the other day. You can't have it both ways, DI Young. Either you want the truth and the bad guys caught, or you want to polish your cap badge and do exactly as you're told.' His voice dripped scorn. 'I had you pinned for a bit of a maverick, somebody with gumption, who would be prepared to cross the line if they had to, yet when it comes to it, you're nothing more than a yes-man.'

'I'm neither a maverick nor a yes-man. I *want* to bring Dickson down.'

'Then you need to be braver. You have to be prepared to take risks, because if you don't, that bastard is going to get away with this, the death of your husband and heaven knows what else, and he'll grow into an even bigger monster than he is already.'

'He's right.' Chris's voice was so faint she could hardly hear it.

'I'm going to push for Cooper's body to be sent to Stoke for a second post-mortem. That might set the ball in motion for a proper enquiry into his death and get Champion put away. However, Dickson is another matter. I'll email the entire recording to you, whether you want it or not, and then you'll have to decide how best to proceed. I hope I've been right about you, DI Young. And that you are strong enough to handle this.'

She answered with a nod. She owed it to Chris to use this information.

'I've hired Sierra a top lawyer to fight her corner, so we expect the green light any day.' Bradley's face was gravely serious. 'Champion might go down for killing Cooper and if he does, my money is on him keeping quiet about Dickson, so it's up to you to nail the fucker. If you can't, then I'll be forced to do something about him. *I'm* not afraid to cross the line if I have to.'

She cleared her throat. 'Okay. I understand. Let me know when Cooper's body is released to be re-examined. Make sure it's sent to Harvey Fuller.'

'Uh-huh. Where shall I send this recording?'

She gave him Chris's email address. He slipped out of the car, leaving Kate numb. She was out of options. Bradley had made her see sense. A dirty copper had to be caught using dirty methods. She'd made her decision and would breach the rules and do whatever was necessary to punish Dickson, even though it meant she'd be abandoning the moral code she'd followed all her career. The weird thing was, part of her didn't care. If it got results, then it was the only option left.

◆ ◆ ◆

When Kate arrived at the office, Morgan, Emma and Jamie were discussing the gyms and martial arts centres they'd visited.

'What have you got for me?' she asked.

Emma held up a piece of paper, one of several on the desk. 'An extremely long list of people who perform martial arts that involve practising strike manoeuvres. We're trying to find out if any of the guys on these lists own a black Honda motorbike.'

'And the light's fixed,' said Morgan.

'So I heard.'

'Yeah, Graham did it in a jiffy. Spent more time chatting than working.'

'You know him?'

'I do now. He gave me a potted history of his life and all about his family.' He rolled his eyes. 'His daughter's at Oxford University. He even showed me photos of her. At one stage, I thought he was trying to matchmake us. I told him I had to get off.'

Another fat bubble rose in Kate's mind, and this time it didn't burst or disappear. Who better than a workman to enter a place of work, observe people and even get to know them? A friendly workman could have found out enough information about his victims to decide to stalk them. She'd not given Graham, the maintenance man, a second glance. How many others would do the same? The familiar rush of blood pulsing in her ears indicated she was on the right lines. Jamie bowled up at that moment and Kate tested her theory on the team. Jamie waved his pen enthusiastically at her.

'I think you could be onto something, guv.'

'Right, let's find out if any workmen, phone engineers, window cleaners, or anyone you can think of, visited Trentham House, Sunny Bank Residential Care Home and the solicitors in Stafford, in recent months.'

'Laura left Tomkins Solicitors in February and then moved house. The killer couldn't have known she'd moved to Abbots Bromley. Even her colleagues didn't know where she'd gone,' said Morgan.

Kate pulled a face at the obvious flaw in her argument, then after further thought, said, 'Try Abbots Bromley village hall. Maybe he knew about the yoga classes. Check with the caretaker you interviewed.'

'Peter Grantham,' said Emma.

'Yes. Him.'

'What about these lists?' asked Morgan.

'Jamie, you stick with those.'

'Sure thing.'

'Morgan, try Sunny Bank. I'll take Trentham House.'

The next hour rushed past in a blur of activity: pens jotted down notes, phone calls were made and the atmosphere was electric as, one by one, they came up with results. There was one common denominator – all three had approached green energy companies to quote on how to make the places more energy efficient.

'We've got three different companies who sent along salesmen and engineers,' said Kate. 'We now need to find out who they sent and interview those people. Also run cross-checks to see if any of them appear on that martial arts list and own a motorbike.'

'Kate?' DCI Chase wandered in.

'We're onto something,' she said and explained what they were doing.

William's face brightened. 'Good work. I'll leave you to get on with it.'

The team hit the phones, contacting the energy companies to determine who might have been sent out to all the destinations. Kate wandered across to Jamie's desk. 'Mind if I take a look?' she said, picking up the list he'd been working on.

'Go ahead,' he mouthed.

Her phone rang at the same time and she hastened back to take the call. It was a subdued Tilly. She moved out into the corridor.

'Hey, is everything okay?'

'No. Kate, I'm a complete screw-up.'

'No, you're not. What's happened?'

'Everything. I've spent all night awake and I've realised something important. All this running away and hoping to find a future back in the UK. I've been fooling myself. I couldn't see what was under my nose. I was convinced I wanted one thing, but what I really wanted was something else altogether – for Jordan to notice me again and for us to have a proper, meaningful relationship, like we used to have. It took going out with Ryan for me to finally comprehend what I should have known all along.

'I rang Jordan earlier. He misses us like mad and, after a long talk, we've decided we're going to make another go of things. He's going to change jobs so he isn't away as often.'

A leaden lump formed in Kate's stomach. She'd only just got used to the idea of having Tilly and Daniel in her life, and now that would change.

'We've only got three weeks left then?' she said.

'I'm so, so sorry, Kate. I don't want to hurt you. Jordan's been in bits since I walked out and after spending time here, I think I'll be able to move forward with him and repair the damage I helped to cause.'

Kate swallowed the disappointment. Tilly's happiness was paramount. 'It's far more important you and Jordan sort yourselves out. Daniel needs you both, in spite of what you might think. We were both brought up by one parent and understand the heartache involved in never seeing or knowing the other.'

'I feel absolutely terrible about letting you down.'

Although the stabbing in her chest suggested otherwise, she replied, 'Me? You haven't. Anyway, we've got time before you leave. What brought on the phone call to Jordan? Last night you seemed to be getting on well with Ryan.'

The silence made her heart jump. 'Tilly?'

'He was a total shit.'

'What happened? Things were going great when I heard from you, earlier.'

'It changed pretty fast. He went from charming to creepy. When he told me that he'd been waiting for me for a lifetime and asked if I ever thought back to those *special days*, I couldn't think of what to say. Obviously, that was the wrong response, and he started kicking off. He accused me of leading him on when we were at school and said I was doing exactly the same thing again. I reminded him that he friended me on Facebook, not the other way around. I'd been transparent during our messages, told him I was married with a son and we were only friends, catching up. He pushed his drink away, called me a prick tease and stormed off. I gave it ten minutes before I left, but the fucker was waiting outside for me. He grabbed hold of my wrist and told me I was a bitch when I was at school and that I was still a bitch, and that I deserved to be taught a lesson.'

'Fuck, Tilly! Why didn't you ring me when he left the pub or arrange for somebody to accompany you to your car?'

'I didn't need to. After you warned me about walking the streets alone, and with everything that's been happening, I wasn't going out without taking precautions. I'd already made a home-made pepper spray and had it in my hand, on the off-chance the attacker was hanging around. When he surprised me, I was ready for him. First, I gave him a good squirt in his eyes and then kicked him really hard in the nuts. Emma's training paid off big time. He crumpled. I raced for my car and drove off before he had a chance to recover.'

'Has he any idea of where you're staying?'

'No. He definitely didn't follow me and I didn't tell him where I lived, only that I was renting a place in Stafford.'

Kate lifted her head to the ceiling and blew out her cheeks. Tilly had had a lucky escape. The list was still in her hand and as she listened to Tilly saying how much the experience had made her realise she needed Jordan, she read the four names on Jamie's list. Her eyes rested on one in particular.

'And he has a tattoo of a bleeding black heart. He kept rubbing it while he spoke. It was one of the creepy things about him.'

'Lock your door and don't answer it until I come around. I'll explain when I do.'

'But . . .'

'Just do it, Tilly.'

The paper in her hand flapped as she rushed into the office. 'Ryan Holder. He's on Jamie's list. Has his name come up?'

Emma looked up from her phone, eyes wide. 'The manager at Green-Go Energy is on the line. He sent Ryan to all three places.'

'Everything you've got on him and an address, now!' Kate was off again, pounding the stairs to William's office. They'd got him at last.

CHAPTER THIRTY-FOUR

He hurls the hand grip exerciser against the wall. Fucking bitch! She'd finally accepted his friend request on Facebook and he'd hooked her with his messages of sincerity and surprise she was back in the country. He'd suggested they meet up for a drink when she had a moment, been nice to her. He'd been patient, played it cool and at last, she'd taken the bait.

There'd been little possibility of planning a surprise, and although he wasn't comfortable with the last-minute decision to meet up, he'd had to play it by ear. Tilly had disrupted everything, rattled him and now, instead of satiating his appetite as he had been doing for years, he'd lost control. It was down to her that a sense of urgency and anger had crept into his carnal acts. The recent decision to use one of his thinnest screwdrivers to cut the word MINE into his victims' shoulders had come out of the blue, and while it accentuated the thrill of the attack, he was aware that in straying from the chosen plan, he was endangering himself. If only she hadn't returned, bringing with her such overwhelming feelings of inadequacy and desire. He still wanted her as much as he had when he was seventeen.

The new plan had been to strike after she invited him home. It was clearly what she intended – a drink or two to loosen up, then back to her place. She was still the same old Tilly, a long way from her husband, and clearly in search of male company.

*Although the evening had started promisingly, something changed
after the first drink and, spying the same look she'd given him that day
in the school canteen, an anger brewed and simmered, threatening to
destabilise him. There was a brief exchange, during which he called her
a prick tease and walked off. Stupid! He should have held his emotions
in check, kept up a front and then followed her car home and attacked
her there. What the fuck happened to him? Instead, overwhelmed by
a fury that clouded all rational thoughts, he waited outside for her to
emerge then, instead of attacking her, he lurched for her and grabbed
her wrist.*

*The bitch was prepared, sprayed him in the eyes, temporarily blind-
ing him and then rendered him helpless with an almighty kick to his
balls that knocked all sense out of him and left him screaming in pain.
He's screwed up royally and now he can think clearly once more, he will
find out where the hell she lives and carve his initials in her fucking
heart.*

◆　◆　◆

The two unmarked squad cars darted through Uttoxeter, one
directly behind the other. Green-Go Energy confirmed Ryan had
taken a sick day. His phone was switched off, its last location his
house at eleven thirty, the night before.

Kate was in the lead car with Morgan. She was unfamiliar with
the road beyond the racecourse that led to Draycott in the Clay. As
she'd suspected, Ryan had targeted women on his patch – not close
to where he lived, but the area he covered in his job as an engineer
for the company, which spanned most of Staffordshire and some
of Derbyshire.

Kate fitted her receiver in her ear, and checked her connection
to Emma was working. 'Emma, can you hear me?'

'Loud and clear.'

The plan was for Kate and Morgan to enter via the front door while Jamie and Emma covered the rear. The housing began to thin out and within seconds, they turned into the crumbling driveway and drew up behind a van, blocking the garage door. Jamie and Emma parked on the roadside and made directly for the back garden, gaining access by climbing over a gate. Kate strode to the arched porch and rang the doorbell. The house remained silent. Morgan peered through the bay window. 'Empty,' he said.

'We're in position.' Emma's voice had dropped. 'No sign of suspect.'

Kate rang the doorbell again. When nobody appeared she nodded at Morgan, a signal to use the enforcer he was holding, the small battering ram that would gain them entry to the property. The door broke open and she took the lead, stepping over the threshold, into the gloomy hallway.

'Ryan Holder. It's the police. Show yourself.'

A musty aroma clung to her nostrils. A pair of work boots stood next to the door. A padded jacket, bearing the Green-Go logo, hung on the banister. Morgan moved to her left into the sitting room, pulling back almost immediately with a shake of his head. By her calculations, the door to the right led into the garage. She tried the handle and came almost nose-to-nose with a mud-splattered Go-Green van. There were only a couple of inches of space between its roof and the ceiling, but edging around it, she discovered a corner dedicated to fitness, with a free-standing punchball, a workout bench and a stack of dumbbells. Other than various DIY tools, there was nothing else in the garage. She sidestepped back past the vehicle into the hallway and almost bumped into Morgan.

'Sitting room and kitchen are both empty,' he said.

'There's no motorbike in there, and no number plates either. I reckon he could be out on it.'

She spoke to Emma. 'Place seems to be empty. We're checking upstairs.'

'Shit. Shall we stay here?'

'For the moment.'

Although the stairs creaked noisily under the threadbare carpet, giving away their location, nobody rushed out to challenge them. Morgan threw open the door to a bathroom and peered inside. Kate caught a glimpse of an opaque, plastic shower curtain.

'Clear.'

Kate took the next room and faced an unmade bed with rumpled sheets and a white duvet sunken in a heap like a melted snowman. Shoes, socks and jeans were heaped in a pile on a rug and a black polo shirt was thrown over the back of a chair, next to a desk. A recent copy of *Motor Sport* magazine and a hand grip exerciser were on the bedside locker. If he'd packed up and gone, he hadn't taken the blue sports bag on the wardrobe floor, or the suitcase perched on the top shelf. She opened the desk drawer and rifled through the bills and paperwork there. His passport was among them.

'Kate.' Morgan's voice was wary.

She joined him in the bedroom at the far end of the landing. The fitted wardrobes were the only reminder of its intended use. Morgan stood behind a large wooden table, but the pens, packs of sticky notelets, blobs of Blu-Tack putty, sheets of paper or scissors weren't why he'd called her into the room. Every wall was covered with photographs of women, grouped pictures of each individual: close-ups of their faces, pictures of them going into their houses, by their windows, jogging, walking, sitting in cafés. Beside each collection were coloured sticky notes, detailing where the women lived, worked and their daily routines, along with printed maps of routes they used regularly. There were at least thirty women, all of slight build, with brown eyes and dark hair. Morgan pointed out one particular collage – Laura Dean outside Abbots Bromley village hall. Others were of her out and about in the village, leaving her house or offloading shopping from her car.

'Stalker pics,' said Morgan. 'Printed out on that, no doubt.' The printer was in the corner of the room, still connected to the socket.

Kate spoke to Emma. 'He's not here. Do a sweep outside then leave Jamie to look out for his return. Come in. You need to see this.'

'There's Heather.' Morgan pointed at the CIO, dressed in horse riding gear. 'Bastard followed them everywhere. I'm amazed he got away without being spotted.'

'He might have used a long-lens camera. The pictures are grainy as if they've been enlarged.' She scoured each face, hunting for her stepsister among the many here. She couldn't spot her.

Morgan opened the wardrobe door and pulled out a box. 'No camera here. There is this bag though.' He held up a canvas bag with *I heart YOGA* written on it.

'Laura's?' said Kate.

'Could be. No sign of her phone or house keys in it.' He put it down and turned his attention back to the wardrobe, pulling out a pastel chequered patterned jumper, a mixture of reds, blues and pinks, each section a floral design: roses, daisies or small blue flowers. 'What's this?'

An ice-cold hand gripped Kate's heart and squeezed. Although she hadn't seen the jumper in years, she instantly recognised it. It had been Tilly's, bought from Next with her pocket money and cherished. She'd worn it the night she was attacked and had left it in the park. The police had considered both the possibility her attacker had taken it, or a passer-by had stumbled across it and kept it. It hadn't been recovered. Until today.

'I don't think he's twigged we're onto him yet. And there's every chance he'll return. Make sure the front door is fixed, so as not to immediately alert him to our presence and leave Jamie here, for the time being, until I can arrange a surveillance operation. I'll get an alert issued in case he's actually gone walkabout.' The alert would inform other regions of the absconding suspect and ensure the network of cameras, known as the automatic number plate recognition system, would track his motorbike and movements.

She had to check on Tilly. Ryan had taken the day off work for some reason and it was no coincidence it was after Tilly had fought him off. Judging by the photo gallery in the bedroom, Ryan was a meticulous planner and even though Tilly was sure he didn't know where she lived, Kate feared he might. The man was rebuffed, angry and dangerous, and she needed to know Tilly was safely at home.

Emma bounded up the stairs. 'In there,' Kate said, as they passed on the landing. She held up the mobile. 'I have to make a call.' She'd dialled Tilly's number before she'd reached the hallway. Tilly didn't pick up. Panic set in. Why wasn't she answering the phone? Had Ryan already tracked her down? She raced outside where she gulped in air and attempted to steady her heart rate. Jamie looked over, eyebrows knitted together.

'Everything okay?'

'Give me your car keys.'

He dangled the key above her outstretched hand. 'What's going on, guv?'

'Sorry, I haven't got time to explain now. I have to be somewhere urgently. Morgan will fill you in when he comes out. Keep a lookout for Ryan.'

'Okay.' He let the cold metal fall into her palm.

She made the call to William as she drove, her flashing lights clearing traffic in front of her. She gave him a brief rundown of what they'd uncovered and put in her request for an alert to be out on Ryan's Honda.

'Have you any ideas as to where he might have gone?' asked William.

'We only know he told his employer he was taking a day off due to illness. Even though he's switched off his mobile, I don't think he's done a runner yet. He could be anywhere, simply going about his business. I'd like immediate backup assistance to ensure his house is watched, and we'll conduct enquiries, talk to his family and acquaintances to see if we can track him down.'

She was ten minutes away from Tilly's house. She couldn't allow herself to consider the possibility that Ryan had Tilly in his sights.

'I'll sort out your extra officers and when you get back, we'll need to consider using the press to help us track him,' said William. 'Good work.'

'Praise is a little premature, William. We haven't caught him yet.'

She ended the conversation and tried Tilly. The phone went to voicemail again. She accelerated around a BMW and powered on. If anything happened to her stepsister, she'd never forgive herself and what about Daniel? Would Ryan harm him too? She rubbed her dry lips together. She couldn't let that happen. She rang Morgan, instructed him and Emma to contact Ryan's family and friends to try to locate the man.

She turned on the siren, clearing a path at junctions and roundabouts, and was soon on Tilly's road. She pulled up outside the house and raced out of the car, hurtling towards the door and banging on it with both fists. 'Tilly!' There was no answer. She shouted again. She ran over the patch of grass and peered through the window. A large plastic dinosaur stared back, its teeth on display. There was no sign of her stepsister or nephew. Her car had caught the attention of the next-door neighbour, who came outside.

'Are you looking for Tilly?' asked the woman.

'Yes. I'm her sister. Have you seen her recently?'

The tension left the woman's face. 'Her sister! I saw the car with the flashing lights and assumed she was in some sort of trouble.' She gave a nervous half-laugh. 'She dropped Daniel off about half an hour ago.'

'Daniel's with you?'

'Yes, playing with Toby.'

'Did she say how long she'd be?'

'No. I told her to take as long as she needed. Toby's been very happy to have a new friend around.'

'How did she seem, when you spoke to her?'

'Fine,' she said. 'Well, maybe a little flat . . . subdued.'

'Did she mention where she was going?'

'Something to do with unfinished business before she left the UK.'

'You don't happen to know if she left with anyone?'

'I saw her car drive off, but not who was in it. Is everything all right?'

'I think so,' said Kate. 'If she returns, or rings you, will you get her to call me immediately?'

'Sure.'

Kate sprinted back to the car wondering what business Tilly might have been referring to. It wouldn't be Ryan. She'd already dealt with him and wasn't aware he was the man who'd raped her. Not unless she'd gauged anything from Kate's urgent demand to stay at home and lock the doors. She surely wouldn't be stupid enough to hunt him down alone, would she? She wrestled with the idea of Tilly, confident in her newly acquired martial arts skills, challenging Ryan. Then it hit her. *Unfinished business.* She had a good idea where Tilly had gone.

◆ ◆ ◆

Kate spied Tilly's hire car and parked behind it, opposite the gates to the park, with their familiar black railing and gold finials. Tilly had spoken about visiting the spot where the attack had taken place to exorcise the demons. If she wanted to return to Jordan and start afresh, she'd feel compelled to face this challenge. It would be the final step to freedom.

She pushed through the gate to Bramshall Park, which opened with a tired squeak. This was the town's principal park, retaining much of its 1920s layout. She and Tilly had often wandered around the footpaths together. It was a place to escape the house and chat without being overheard, and they'd spent hours sitting beside Picknall Brook, where once they'd spotted a kingfisher darting across the water. After the attack, Tilly had refused to go near the place and Kate had also boycotted it.

There was no sign of life, apart from a pair of crows, investigating the contents of a bin, that hopped away when she approached. A few metres in and the footpath split into two, one way leading up towards the town, the lower path heading deeper into the park. She took the latter, which bordered a grassy bank to the brook, and marched quickly along it. Not a sound reached her ears: no excited dogs chasing balls, no children's voices from the playground. She wondered where Tilly might be and considered calling her name out, then a movement caught her eye and a figure shot out from behind a tree and made its way down the bank, oblivious to Kate's presence.

She sped up and, as she reached the highest point, could make out Tilly, her back to her, sitting by the water's edge. She hadn't caught wind of the man snaking down the slope towards her.

'Tilly! Run!'

Tilly's head jerked up and, catching sight of the man, bounded to her feet and sprinted away. A fast game of chase ensued with Tilly zigzagging in all directions, the man fast in pursuit. Kate lost ground and began to fear the man would catch her stepsister before she could reach them both. She powered on, spotted Tilly racing up a steep grassy bank, where she suddenly turned to face her assailant and, adopting a martial arts attack position, let out an angry roar. The man came to a shuddering halt. Kate pounded forwards, arms and legs pumping. Tilly seemed to be holding her own and the man backed away, two and then three steps, only to spin around and race away from both Tilly and Kate.

Kate tore after him, down to the brook then back up the grassy slope, towards the trees. She was concentrating all her efforts on decreasing the gap and didn't notice he had stopped, stooped and picked up something, until the branch swung in her direction. Everything went black as she fell to the ground.

◆ ◆ ◆

Her vision gradually returned. Tilly was by her side and Ryan was nowhere in sight.

'Kate, are you okay?'

Her shoulder was on fire. 'I'm fine. Where is he?'

'Gone. He came for me again, but I screamed really loudly and then yelled that I'd rip his fucking balls off if he touched me. He headed towards the leisure centre.'

'Ryan's the prime suspect. I have to call it in.' She tried to sit up. The world spun for a moment. 'Go home. Lock your door. If he appears, put in a call to emergency services.' She fumbled for her phone. Tilly placed her hand on hers. The look on her face tore at Kate's heart.

'Please, Kate, no. You promised to keep me out of it, especially now I've finally made peace with myself.'

She forced herself onto her feet and swayed unsteadily before stumbling forwards. Every minute spent talking meant Ryan was getting further away, yet Tilly's intense gaze held her in its spell and prevented her from ringing for backup. The police officer inside her battled on until she replied, 'I can't see how we can keep a lid on it. He's sure to bring up your name during interview.' She made for the park entrance. If she hurried she might still spot Ryan. In spite of her strong will, her legs wouldn't cooperate. Tilly was still pleading.

'What if I message him and beg him not to. Promise not to press charges against him.'

'No way.'

All the same, Tilly pulled out her mobile and tried turning it on. 'Oh, shit. It must have run out of battery. Probably because I spent so long on it, talking to Jordan.'

That would account for why Kate had been unable to contact her and had been forced to come in search. The flat battery had probably saved her life. They were now at the fork in the footpath. 'No. *Don't* message him. Don't have anything else to do with him. Charge your phone and send me a text to say you're safely back home. We'll deal with the fallout if and when we have to. Now, go.'

'If you're sure.' With one last look at her stepsister, Tilly bounded away and slipped through the entrance gates towards her car. Kate's finger hovered over the button. If they'd lost Ryan because of this, she'd resign. Once it came to light about Tilly, she'd probably resign anyway. She drew a breath in preparation, then paused as a motorbike engine roared into life. She turned towards the sound, in time to see a black motorbike, pulling out of the leisure centre car park. The muzziness evaporated and, fuelled by an adrenaline surge, she sprinted to her car. There might still be a chance to turn this around.

CHAPTER THIRTY-FIVE

Kate yelled into her radio. 'Suspect on the move, headed along Hockley Road towards the centre of town. I'm in pursuit.'

Jamie responded, 'I'm in position at suspect's house.'

'Maintain your position.'

Emma was next to answer. 'Currently en route to Stafford. Returning to Uttoxeter immediately. ETA ten minutes.'

Kate pressed on. She'd chosen to follow without the siren. Alone, she could not head Ryan off if he chose one of the numerous routes leading out of Uttoxeter. Much hinged on how quickly she could reach the junction at the end of the road, where he could turn either left or right.

Emma's voice filled the car. 'Backup requested and on its way.'

Fortune was on Kate's side. Temporary traffic lights had held up the motorbike, which was in front of a van. She used the wider vehicle to conceal her presence and waited for the lights to change, then watched as the bike sped away. 'Suspect turning onto Market Place.'

She maintained a steady distance behind the van, one eye on Ryan, who was adhering to the speed limit and apparently unaware he was being tailed. As soon as he followed the bypass to the racecourse roundabout, she had a hunch where he was headed. 'Suspect appears to be headed towards Wood Lane. I think he might be going home.'

'Still in position, guv.'

'Stay out of sight.'

The van took a different exit at the roundabout, affording her a clear vision of Ryan. She didn't have long to formulate a plan. 'Remain hidden until he pulls up on the drive. Then block the driveway with your vehicle. I'll be right behind him.'

It was a difficult balance trying to stay back far enough so as not to draw suspicion to herself and ensuring she was close enough to help capture him. Why was he going home? He'd surely guess Kate would send officers to his house. Maybe he thought there was sufficient time to grab possessions, passport and money, or maybe he wanted to hide the evidence that would point to his guilt. Either way, it was a big mistake on his part.

The bike accelerated away and she lost sight as it rounded a bend. Had he spotted her? She held her nerve and willed him to stop at his house. She was rewarded when she came out of the bend to see an unmarked police car coming to a rapid halt on the driveway. She floored the pedal and screeched to a halt, bumper to bumper with the other car, and sprang out. Jamie and a fellow officer were already racing towards Ryan, who was undoing his helmet. The uniformed officer raced up the driveway. Ryan was quicker. He leapt from the bike and took off like a rocket, darting to the side of the house and scrambling over the locked gate. The officer hauled his bulkier frame to the top of the gate and then yelled as he was struck by something and fell backwards onto the ground. Blood spurted from his nose as he wriggled and swore. Jamie ignored the man's distress, leapt at the gate and catapulted himself over it as deftly as an accomplished gymnast. Kate, less flexible, followed suit. Catching Ryan was their priority. The officer would recover.

A discarded helmet, no doubt the weapon used to floor the officer, lay in the damp grass. Her feet slipped as she pounded behind Jamie, slowing progress, but allowing her time to weigh up the situation and scout for possible escape routes. The hedges were too tall to vault and too thick to squeeze through. Even as she thought it, she knew Ryan had a plan. He was heading towards a point in the hedge with purpose, but it was only when he dived onto the ground by a lichen-covered plastic seat, and wriggled forwards, did she spot the gap under the leylandii. The soles of his boots vanished before Jamie could grip them. He emulated the movements and by the time he was through, Kate was also on the ground, elbowing her way through the gap.

She emerged into a field of allotments, tended patches of autumn-ripening bounty: pale-orange butternut squashes, green-leaved kale and fat marrows. The light was fading but she caught sight of Ryan speeding willy-nilly through crops, knocking over canes of late-producing tomatoes, beans and raspberries, trampling across lettuces and kicking over protective coverings. He darted from one area to the other, searching for a path out. Jamie's arms and legs were pumping furiously. He shouted for Ryan to stop several times. Kate tried to gauge the best direction to take to head off the suspect, and with silent apologies to the allotment owners, raced over sticky earth and onion crops, and bashed fruit with her elbows as she surged forward. She was a runner, used to marathons rather than sprints. The men ahead were flagging, whereas she was still in the zone.

A streetlight spluttered into life, silver light falling across a hedgerow, wooden gate and narrow pathway, and she made for it. Ryan must have spied it at the same time for he was now running in the same direction. Jamie had fallen back and was several metres behind their quarry. Kate jumped over beds of marrows, fern-like carrot tops and small lettuces, ran and leapt again. Ryan slipped on some plastic sheeting, his arms propelling until he regained his balance and sped off again, this time less quickly. Kate and Ryan were converging, both aiming for the exit point. Kate's legs felt heavy yet she dug deep, treated this like the final sprint in a race, lowered her head and charged at him. She hadn't anticipated how solid he would be. The sickening impact caused them both to stagger and fall. Her already injured shoulder screamed in pain and stars detonated in front of her eyes. The scene became a blur and before she could recover, Ryan was back on his feet. She rolled onto her side, reached out fingers in a weak attempt to grab his ankles. She was too slow. Ryan was off again. Pain paralysed her momentarily, then she heard a mighty roar and felt air whoosh over her. The thud as the bodies hit the earth reverberated through her bones. She staggered to her feet. Jamie was on Ryan's back, blinking at sweat trickling into his eyes and breathing heavily.

'You have the right to remain silent,' he gasped.

Kate bent over, shut her eyes and listened to Jamie caution the man. This was a result, not only for the families of the murdered victims and for Olivia, but for Bianca and Tilly. They had him at last.

CHAPTER THIRTY-SIX

Morgan and Emma were in the small, windowless room with Ryan. Both Kate and William sat in the adjacent room, watching the interview unfold on the monitor. The strong painkillers prescribed by the hospital doctor had numbed the shoulder pain but made her too woozy to conduct the interview herself. In spite of the discomfort and light-headedness, she considered herself lucky she'd only sustained severe bruising and ripped ligaments.

Ryan's lawyer, a bald man in his late forties, remained silent as Morgan continued his questioning. The screwdriver used to cut the word *MINE* into the women's flesh had been uncovered, along with minute traces of blood, undoubtedly belonging to one or more of the victims. Ryan had been charged for the murders of Laura Dean and Heather Gault, the rape of Olivia Sandman and Bianca Moore, and the attack on Daisy Weatherford. The question was, how many more women from the collage of potential victims, posted on his bedroom wall, had he attacked? It would take time to find and talk to them all; however, another team had been tasked with that. Kate was certain more victims would come forward and Ryan would face additional charges. A forensic team had already begun searching through his house and as well as the evidence on his bedroom wall, his laptop had revealed searches to some very disturbing websites to do with rape. They'd also uncovered Heather's handbag. Ryan had admitted to destroying and disposing of its contents, along with Laura's personal possessions in a nearby recycling centre.

He hung his head, his spirit crushed.

'Tell me about the tattoo on your hand,' said Morgan. 'The black, bleeding heart. Is it to remind you of your victims?'

He shook his head.

'Don't you want to tell me about it?'

'Not really.'

'I'd have thought a bloke like you would want more macho tats.' Morgan gave a slight sneer, part of the act to rile Ryan.

'Fuck off.'

'I suggest you watch your mouth.'

'I suggest you stop asking stupid questions. It's a fucking heart, all right? It means something to me. I don't give a shit what you think about it.'

Too late, his lawyer issued a warning. Morgan was using the man's temper to his advantage.

'Sensitive, are we? You a bit concerned about your macho image?'

Ryan leant forward. 'I don't have any trouble with my image.'

'That surprises me; after all, you're nothing but a sicko who knocks out defenceless young women to have sex with them. I bet you've never had a normal relationship with a willing partner. Can't you get it up unless they're unconscious?'

'Fuck you.'

'Turns you on, does it, to have them submissive? You know what I think. I think you're actually scared of women. You're frightened they'll tell you to take a running jump if you try anything on with them. They'd make you feel this big?' said Morgan, holding his finger and thumb apart an inch.

Hostility blazed in Ryan's eyes.

'I guess a bloke like you can't get a girlfriend . . . or a boyfriend.'

Ryan jumped up with a snarl, grabbed Morgan's shirt and gripped it tightly with both fists. Morgan smiled. Ryan released him instantly and sank to his chair. His anger fizzled out as quickly as it had flared. 'It's a reminder.'

Emma cleared her throat. 'I think it's sort of romantic. Is it?'

The bad cop, good cop approach worked. 'It reminds me of someone.'

Kate's heart began to thud so loudly she was sure William would hear it. This line of questioning could result in her dismissal. If Ryan mentioned Tilly, she'd be hauled in front of her superiors with no comeback.

'A girl I once had strong feelings for,' he said.

'What was her name?'

'It's unimportant. It happened a very long time ago. She's married now. Even got a kid. She doesn't feel the same way about me.'

Kate held her breath, willing Ryan to shut up and for Emma to stop pursuing this line of questioning. Her prayers were answered. Morgan took over as lead, elbows now resting on the table.

'There were a lot of photographs on your bedroom wall. Have you attacked any of those women?'

He shrugged.

'If you confess now, it will be better for you.'

'Better how?'

His lawyer stepped in. 'I think we can agree my client is not going to be pressured or cajoled into confessing to any additional attacks.' He closed his notebook and looked pointedly at Morgan.

Emma, meanwhile, kept her eyes trained on Ryan. 'Okay, Ryan, let's get down to real business. Why the sudden spate in attacks? You attacked four women in a week.'

'I don't know what happened. It wasn't part of the plan.'

◆ ◆ ◆

Thunder rumbles in the distance and a lightning flash casts a brilliance over the car park. He spots her descending the path from the village hall, takes in her pale face, the sexy mouth, the shining hair. It is Tilly. The desire to punish her inflames him and he makes his move, slips out of the darkness and knocks her out cold with one swift, practised movement. She weighs next to nothing and he carries her body away from the road and car park, onto a grassy bank. As soon as he forces himself on her, she comes to and struggles hard, fighting to escape, but she is no match for him and he pushes her face into the grass, and keeps his full weight on her, spitting cruel words at her, calling her every name he can think of as he thrusts harder into her.

When he is spent, he rests his forearm on her neck and warns her to remain still if she values her life. He takes out the thinnest of his electrician's screwdrivers from a jacket pocket and carves into the bitch – MINE. Like the scratches Tilly left on him years ago, now hidden under a black, bleeding heart, he's branded her for life. He pants with exertion and the woman on the floor sobs quietly. Rage rises once more and he rains blows on her already bruised body. He then hauls her to her feet, slides his hands around her throat and squeezes. This is the final part of the act before he will release her with these new, life-changing memories that can never fade. He relaxes his grasp and stares at her, expecting resignation, but realises something has changed. She's no longer afraid of him. Her features have altered into defiance and hatred sparks in her dark eyes – Tilly's eyes. Tilly sneers at him before hawking phlegm directly into his eye. How dare she! His hand tightens its grip again and he squeezes tighter. 'Apologise, bitch!' There is no apology or remorse. Her eyes grow dull and her head lolls to one side. He releases her, at the same time coming back to his senses. This isn't Tilly, only one of the many women he's chosen as her substitute.

343

He traces the heart tattoo inked in memory of the one woman he can never forget and acknowledges that Laura Dean is now dead because of his rekindled obsession with Tilly and the fact he is once again in contact with her. Thanks to Ashar's revelation that Tilly had friended him on Facebook and was back in Staffordshire, he'd found her and sent her a friend request, which she'd accepted. They've already exchanged messages, vague, catch-up chats, and it has taken every ounce of control to keep them light-hearted. He has to see her soon. This woman lying on the ground is a lousy replacement. He lifts her lifeless body and carries it to the industrial waste bins. He wants the real thing. And now that Tilly is in the area once more, he will get what he truly desires – his first true love under his control.

◆　◆　◆

'There must be some reason you attacked one woman after the other,' said Emma.

He hung his head. Naturally, there was a reason, one he was unwilling to share with these people. They would never comprehend the effect she'd had on him. 'There was no reason,' Ryan said eventually. 'I just had to do it. Something made me and I couldn't stop.'

Kate knew he was lying either to them or to himself. Cluster attacks like these were often caused by a trigger, in this case, Tilly's return to the UK. She'd unwittingly set off a deep-seated desire to attack again – this time more urgently and frequently than before.

Ryan leant forward and spoke earnestly to Emma. 'Believe me, I never intended on killing any of them. Laura's death was an accident.'

'And what about Heather? Was that another accident?'

'I didn't kill her.'

'There are marks on her throat and damage to her neck structures to suggest otherwise,' said Emma.

He shook his head. 'No, you don't understand. I admit I grabbed Heather around her throat, but not hard enough to choke her to death. I swear she was alive.' He looked at his lawyer, who opened his pad again and made a note.

Morgan wasn't going easy on him. 'If you didn't intend on strangling them, why did you wrap your hands around their throats?'

'It was part of the game.'

'Wow! You play some seriously warped games,' Morgan replied.

'After this *game*, you checked to see if she was still breathing then, did you?' asked Emma.

'Yes, and she was.'

'And then you carried her up the road and abandoned her in a skip in the car park?'

'Yes.'

'Why the skip?'

He shrugged a reply. 'I noticed it in the car park and decided to leave her there.'

Emma gave him a cold stare. 'Like she was discarded rubbish?'

'I hadn't thought of that.'

Kate doubted he was telling the truth. It was no coincidence he'd chosen similar places to dump his victims.

'After you flung her into the skip, did you check again to see if Heather was still alive?'

Ryan stared at Emma, mouth moving but no words forthcoming.

'Did you check her pulse again?' she repeated.

He turned to his lawyer. 'She was alive. I'm sure of it.'

'You left a woman with facial injuries, who you'd beaten, raped, mutilated and half-strangled, in a skip without checking to see if she was still breathing at that point,' said Emma.

The lawyer gave a small shake of his head. 'My client wishes to make no comment.'

'Tell us why you attacked these women, Ryan.'

Ryan wiped a hand over his face. 'I had to.'

'Had to?'

'It's an urge. A sort of sickness. I can't control it.'

Morgan's voice was thick with disgust. 'You can't blame this on an imaginary sickness. That's a cop-out. You enjoyed torturing them. You didn't want to stop.'

A knotted vein pulsed in Ryan's neck. He thumped the desk. 'You don't know what goes on in my head. You have no idea how much I tried to fight this.'

Emma butted in. 'Do you like women, Ryan?'

A sneer tugged at his lips. 'No. You're all bitches.'

His lawyer intervened. 'I think we're done here for the time being. I'd appreciate some time alone with my client.'

'Very well. We'll call an end to this interview.'

William shifted position with a light groan.

'You all right?' asked Kate.

'Yes, yes. Touch of old age. My back stiffened up. Good thing I'm thinking of retirement. I'll be able to put my feet up, not spend hours in cramped rooms, staring at monitors or computers.' He got to his feet and stretched. 'You did a good job, especially bringing down Holder. Jamie told me about your rugby-tackle.'

'It would have been more effective if it had been Morgan, rather than me, who'd floored him. If it hadn't been for Jamie, we'd have lost him.'

He smiled and held her gaze. 'Mitch would have been proud of you, you know? Very proud indeed. Some days, I really wish he was around to see who you've grown into.'

'And other days?'

'He'd have reminded me that he was also a pain in the arse at times and you take after him in many ways. Seriously, Kate, well done. You turned this around and you showed them all.'

A lump rose in her throat. William was the only person, other than Chris, to have stood by her in recent years. 'Thanks, William. That means a lot.'

He gave her a salute and headed for the door. 'I miss Mitch a great deal. He was one of the best.'

Chris gave a low chuckle. 'Don't be fooled. William is corrupt.'

She tried to guess what her journalist husband might have uncovered about her mentor then abandoned the thought. She'd seen the look on William's face as he spoke about her father, and heard the crack in his voice. Chasing after Dickson was one matter, but not William. She cared about him too much. She got to her feet and left the room. There were some things she was unable to accept.

CHAPTER THIRTY-SEVEN

Emma dropped a weary Kate off outside her house. Her shoulder was throbbing and her sole thought was to go to bed and sleep for a fortnight. She waved goodbye to Emma with her good arm, then faced her silent house. She ought to download an app to turn on the lights and heating before she came in, so it felt as if somebody was there for her. And buy a cat, or a dog, or a parrot. She could do with the company.

The intruder light illuminated and she fumbled for her key, had to drop her bag on the doorstep to fish it out, then opened the door. She could immediately sense something wasn't right. The tiredness evaporated and her keen eyes swept the entrance and the stairs directly in front of her. She spotted the evidence somebody had been in, or was still in, her home. The large wooden capital letters that spelled out the word HOME and ran along the wall beside the white staircase were out of alignment. The letter 'M' had been knocked.

She didn't move, straining her ears for any sound, her nose twitching to pick up any strange scents. She crept first to the lounge, then the kitchen, and finding them both empty made for

Chris's study. The smiley stress ball lay on the floor and the top desk drawer was slightly ajar.

'It was to be expected,' said Chris. 'You know who's behind this. You solved the investigation and didn't screw up as Dickson hoped you would. He's got no reason to discredit you, so now he wants to find out exactly how much you know about him. Whoever broke in was careful, but not careful enough. My keyboard's been moved. I expect somebody has tried to access my computer.'

She sighed. This was becoming a dangerous situation. Fortunately, she'd taken down her makeshift board of suspects. However, if the intruder had got their hands on the interview with Farai and the video Bradley sent her, heaven knew what might happen to her.

'You'd better make sure the USB is safe,' Chris said.

'First, I'm going to make sure nobody is still here,' she replied and tiptoed up the stairs. There was no sign of any intruder. Whoever had broken in had left.

'Check it,' Chris urged again.

She made for the kitchen and padded to the cupboards where she pulled out the bird seed from under the sink before unlocking the door into the garden. She lifted the empty, swaying bird feeder from the hook and undid it, checking as she poured in the seed. The USB was still taped to the underside of the lid. Nobody had uncovered it.

Back indoors, and wrapped in her duvet, she knew she couldn't say anything about the break-in. It was best to pretend she wasn't aware it had happened. She was glad she'd downloaded Bradley's video onto the stick and deleted the email, and got rid of Chris's journal. At the moment, she was one step ahead of Dickson and she intended to keep it that way.

CHAPTER THIRTY-EIGHT

There was a huge roaring of engines, causing Tilly to shout, 'Look, Daniel, there's one taking off now.'

First a nose cone appeared as if rising out of the terminal building, then the blue and yellow fuselage of the airplane as it left the runway behind the airport, climbing rapidly as it flew over the car park, until it was the size of a large bird.

Daniel watched it disappear into the clouds while Tilly wiped her eyes. 'Don't come inside. I'll be in bits if you do. Say goodbye here.'

Kate embraced her, fiercely. The last couple of weeks had reset the clock and she felt even closer to Tilly than when they'd been younger. The pain in her chest was real. She was going to miss her and Daniel, who now stood to one side, clutching the handle of his suitcase in one hand and the toy dinosaur Kate had bought him at Drayton Manor Theme Park. She released Tilly, who gulped noisily, her eyes moist and shining with unshed tears.

'I need to blow my nose. I can't check in like this, blubbing like a kid.' She gave a brave smile. Kate dropped to her knees to embrace the child, inhaling the fruity scent from his freshly shampooed hair. She rubbed his back then planted a kiss on his head. Her heart splintered.

'You promise you'll visit us?' said Tilly.

'I promise. I'll book some leave when I can – at least a month.'

'And you'll Skype us as we arranged, once a week?'

'Definitely.'

'And you'll look after yourself and not get too serious about work?'

'I'll try.'

Tilly looked at her through still damp eyes. 'Stay in touch.'

'I promise.'

'Thank you. Thanks for . . . you know.'

'Say hi to Jordan for me.'

'For sure. Okay, champ, you ready for the long journey back home to Daddy?'

He grinned and nodded.

'Bye, Kate,' said Tilly.

'Bye. Love you.'

Tilly made the shape of a heart with her hands, then took the handle of her suitcase. 'I won't look back. I hate goodbyes.'

Kate couldn't leave the car park, not until she'd watched the automatic doors swish open and the terminal interior engulf the two people she loved. Tilly hadn't turned around but Daniel had, waving the toy dinosaur at her and grinning. She would keep her promise and go to Australia. They were the only family she had, and Chris would have wanted her to visit them.

Back home, she kicked off her shoes and headed straight for Chris's office where she'd already laid out photocopies of documents from the Ryan Holder investigation. Although Ryan was going to be charged with Heather's death, he'd been adamant she was alive when he left her in the skip. The more she thought about it, the more she believed his version of events; after all, he'd admitted to accidentally murdering Laura, and killing his victims went against what he wanted most – for them to remember him.

She'd downloaded the video of Heather talking to Rosa at Stoke-on-Trent station onto Chris's computer and although she'd watched it a few times, she couldn't guess what they were discussing.

Rosa had disappeared soon after the meeting and Heather had died the following day. There was no way she could shake off the ever-growing, nagging feeling that Dickson was behind her death.

She glanced at the time. Tilly would still be in the airport departure lounge, waiting for her flight to board. She texted her to wish her a safe journey and got an immediate reply. Their flight had been called and they were on their way to the boarding gate. Kate sent an emoji heart then meandered into the kitchen, poured a glass of wine and watched a robin peck at the feeder. 'Best hiding place ever, Chris,' she mumbled.

Taking the glass with her, she returned to the computer and pressed fast forward on the video, speeding up the process. A few travellers arrived on the platform, standing some distance from the two women. None of them looked like Dickson. She drained the glass, considered having another drink, then hit the pause button. She'd glimpsed a face she recognised. She rewound the footage and watched again as her officer, Jamie, emerged from the subway and lounged against a wall, his head turned in the women's direction. Heather stood up, hugged the girl and headed off down the same subway, followed by Jamie. The timeclock showed it was ten past ten. His explanation for being late when he was unable to reach Abbots Bromley on Friday morning had been little more than a pack of lies. Jamie must be working for Dickson, feeding him back information about Heather and Rosa. Jamie was probably also keeping Dickson informed about her every move, which would explain how Dickson had found out about Emma's visit to Felicity. Only the team members knew Emma had been to see her and got information from Heather's computer.

'Fuck. Looks like I've got a spy on my team. The cunning bastard's put somebody inside to keep an eye on me.'

She rested her head in her hands. What the hell was she supposed to do about this? Dickson didn't trust her one inch, and who on earth was she supposed to trust?

She downloaded the video onto a fresh USB stick before deleting the original and the email it came attached to. She'd hide this information in a second bird feeder. Sitting back in Chris's chair, a tsunami of fatigue washed over her. She suddenly didn't have the energy to fight whatever it was she was battling against. Corruption was rife. Chris's file was testament to that fact.

Heading upstairs, she dropped onto the bed, hugged the toy starfish she'd propped against Chris's pillow and stared at her reflection in the long mirror. The harder she looked, the better she could picture Chris beside her, until the mirage seemed so realistic, she felt sure she could reach out to him and interlink fingers with him. She blinked to dispel the image. All of this wasn't helping her: imagining he was talking to her, lying beside her. She was losing her grip on reality and was close to mania. She knew it and yet she smiled at the mirror. Chris became brighter again.

'Stay with me. Please. I can't seek vengeance for your death or the wrongdoings against my father – I simply can't do this alone. I'm not up to it.'

Her face transformed, her voice grew gruff and she answered, 'Don't worry, Kate. I'll never leave you.'

ACKNOWLEDGMENTS

I can't convey how much I've enjoyed writing *A Cut for a Cut* and it's largely down to the dynamic and enthusiastic team at Thomas & Mercer, who held my hand throughout the process.

Biggest thanks go to Jack Butler, who took on Kate and helped me develop a one-book idea into an entire series. His enthusiasm for the project has matched my own and together we have conjured up ideas for future Kate Young books.

I also have Jack to thank for teaming me up with Russel McLean, an author in his own right and a top editor, whose sense of humour has me in stitches. He has, once again, worked his magic on my manuscript, transforming it into one I can be truly proud of. Russel, thank you for the laughs along the way.

Many thanks to everyone at Jane Rotrosen Agency, especially my agent, Amy Tannenbaum. I am so grateful for all your support.

Other thanks go to my amazing street team, who keep me going on days when I struggle, and who always offer generous amounts of their time to promote my books. I love you guys.

To all the book bloggers, readers and reviewers who champion my work. A simple thank you never seems to be reward enough for the amount of effort you put into supporting us authors. It is enormously appreciated.

Massive thanks to technical guru Xavier Hugonet, who constantly astounds me with his knowledge about all things technical and who has been a great help to Kate and her team.

To Alicia McCarty for lending her name to one of the characters in the book.

It isn't really a proper acknowledgement, but I'd like to mention here that Abbots Bromley is a truly lovely village. The village hall is not as described in the book, nor have any murders taken place in the village or region. (At least, none that I am aware of!) The place and the surrounding area, especially Blithfield Reservoir, have provided me with endless inspiration and I count myself incredibly fortunate to live in such a wonderful part of the country.

To you for purchasing *A Cut for a Cut*. Thank you for your kind emails and messages, telling me how much you've enjoyed reading my books. They mean the world to me.

And last but not least to the man who manages to survive months of neglect while I work on the books and never complains about it – Mr Grumpy. You are the best!

ABOUT THE AUTHOR

USA Today bestselling author and winner of The People's Book Prize Award, Carol Wyer's crime novels have sold over 800,000 copies and been translated into nine languages. A move from humour to the 'dark side' in 2017 saw the introduction of popular DI Robyn Carter in *Little Girl Lost*, and proved that Carol had found her true niche. Carol has been interviewed on numerous radio shows discussing 'Irritable Male Syndrome' and 'Ageing Disgracefully', and on *BBC Breakfast* television. She has written for *Woman's Weekly, Take A Break, Choice, Yours, Woman's Own* and *HuffPost*. She currently lives on a windy hill in rural Staffordshire with her husband, Mr Grumpy . . . who is very, very grumpy. When she is not plotting devious murders, she can be found performing her comedy routine, *Smile While You Still Have Teeth*.

To learn more about Carol, go to www.carolwyer.co.uk or follow Carol on Twitter: @carolewyer. Carol also blogs at www.carolwyer.com.

Did you enjoy this book and would like to get informed when Carol Wyer publishes her next work? Just follow the author on Amazon!

1) Search for the book you were just reading on Amazon or in the Amazon App.
2) Go to the Author Page by clicking on the Author's name.
3) Click the "Follow" button.

If you enjoyed this book on a Kindle eReader or in the Kindle App, you will be automatically offered to follow the author when arriving at the last page.